D1384284

The Lapone Sisters

Barry Wilker

This is a work of fiction. All of the characters, names, incidents, organizations, and dialogue in this novel are either the products of the author's imagination or are used fictitiously.

Archway Publishing books may be ordered through booksellers or by contacting:

Archway Publishing
1663 Liberty Drive
Bloomington, IN 47403
www.archwaypublishing.com
844-669-3957

Because of the dynamic nature of the Internet, any web addresses or links contained in this book may have changed since publication and may no longer be valid. The views expressed in this work are solely those of the author and do not necessarily reflect the views of the publisher, and the publisher hereby disclaims any responsibility for them.

Any people depicted in stock imagery provided by Getty Images are models, and such images are being used for illustrative purposes only.

ISBN: 978-1-6657-2345-9 (sc)
ISBN: 978-1-6657-2343-5 (hc)
ISBN: 978-1-6657-2344-2 (e)

Library of Congress Control Number: 2022908452

Print information available on the last page.

Archway Publishing rev. date: 06/24/2022

For David, Lucy, and Nicholas

And the day came when the risk to remain tight in a bud
was more painful than the risk it took to blossom.
— Anais Nin

Chances are rare, change is valuable.
— Barry Wilker

A Family's History

My name is Schmellda. My name bothered me for the longest time. I was almost five years old the first time I asked my mother, Yvonna, why I had such an odd first name. At that point, I had been hurt by my playmates' teasing of my name. Over and over, my mother would tell me the stories of her childhood. I was too young and naive to comprehend the full scope of what had happened to her family and that my name was part of my mother's family history. I was almost eight when I truly began to understand the complete scope and nature of the tales she was telling me. I think back and remember a faraway, somewhat melancholy look in Mother's eyes as she told me what her life had been like as a child growing up in Romania — of being young and hopeful, and suddenly not. The war changed everything. It is the reason my sisters and I are named after my mother's sisters.

Let me take you back to April 1944, to the city of my mother's birth, Bucharest, Romania. Yvonna was twenty years old. She and her family resided in a lovely, large four-bedroom apartment in Bucharest's city center, an affluent neighborhood known as Old Town. She, her parents, and her four siblings lived comfortably. They considered themselves happy and urbane. In that same year, her brother Ivan was a hardy and healthy eighteen-year-old. Her sisters were younger and all still doing their studies. The "baby" sister, Esmerelda Una, was seven; Sorina Luna, twelve; her favorite, Schmellda Radmilla, fourteen. My mother and her sister Schmellda shared one large bedroom, and her other two sisters, Sorina and Esmerelda, shared another. My grandparents, Grandmother Lulu and Grandfather Marion, quite naturally had the largest bedroom. Ivan slept alone in his own room, which was extremely small by current standards. My mother always compared it to the size of a modern walk-in closet. She remembers that the building where they lived was five stories, and each floor had two or three units. Her family's apartment was on the fifth floor. It was light and airy with a beautiful view of Old Town and a large park across the avenue. She even remembers the name of their street, Strada Coltei. Their building was known as The Sonesta. It was one of the newer structures in central Bucharest. From almost any window in the apartment, one could view the sweeping landscape and sights of the city. All the building's windows were full-length French-style and opened inward. Each window was adorned with waist-high heavy black iron Art Nouveau window guards, designed to offer both safety and decoration. The building itself was gray stucco and had a stunning steel-gray slate-tiled mansard roof. Judging from the only photograph she still has of The Sonesta, it was significantly influenced by French design.

As we know, Europe was a treacherous place to live during World War II. In Romania during that time, the king had abdicated, and the country was in alliance with Nazi Germany. The dictatorship that had taken power was merciless. Russian troops were advancing toward the country as the tide began to turn against the Axis. Life had become perilous. The daily routines of lives changed from one week to the next. At one point in January 1941, my mother's entire family had attempted an escape from the country. They had left Bucharest on foot to travel to the eastern port city of Constanta, where they planned to pay, bribe, or barter their way onto any ship that was headed to Turkey or any other safer ports. After much planning, that first attempt failed. Only about ten miles outside of the city, they were stopped at a security point and directed back to their apartment. It was my grandfather who helped save the family. He was a prominent family physician. The arresting officer knew of him, and with much coercion from my grandfather, and no doubt a substantial bribe, the officer let them return home.

My mother remembers that as days passed, fear, boredom, and paranoia crept into their lives. Then came April 4, 1944. My mother has never been able to let go of the memory of that horrific day. I cannot even fathom the gravity of the sadness that followed. My mother and grandmother were out shopping. On this particular day, the sky was sunny and blue, and the air was cool, clear, and breezy. Neighbors and townspeople were going about their daily business. No one had an inkling of what was about to happen.

As my mother tells the story, she and Grandmother were having coffee at a sidewalk café when suddenly the day was interrupted by the sound of air-raid sirens. The possibility existed that this was just another test of the emergency alert system, so they continued to enjoy their day. The mood quickly turned to fright, helplessness, and chaos when fighter planes became visible in the far sky. They were most assuredly heading toward Bucharest. Lines and groups scattered as everyone began to scramble for safety, shelter, and their lives. My mother and grandmother ran toward a massive government building nearby, hunkering in against grand marble steps leading to the building's ornate entrance. Moments later, black dots began falling through the air, black dots that exploded as they hit the city. The bombs descending across the sky resembled pepper being scattered from a shaker. The ground shook as the bombs landed and exploded. The thunderous explosions and terrified screams of people penetrated the once peaceful morning. The city was under attack. People were running in the streets, madly seeking shelter anywhere possible. My mother still trembles when she tells this story. She and her mother were completely devastated by disbelief and shock; their beautiful city was being destroyed.

Originally, the city of Bucharest had been spared destruction due to the Romanian government's early concessions to Nazi

Germany, to whom it supplied oil, equipment, and troops. The Allies and Russia intended for those supplies to stop. When what had seemed like hours of bombardment and destruction quieted, all watched as the planes disappeared, floating away across the smoke-filled sky as quickly as they had arrived. The longest minutes of their lives slowly passed until the all-clear siren sounded. People began to emerge from their safe places. Many had been injured and were bleeding from flying debris, and sadly, many buildings had been leveled. The real horror began to reveal itself. Death and injury were the painfully obvious result of the sixty-minute torrential raid. Heaps of stones, shattered glass, and twisted iron were everywhere. Areas of Old Town were in shambles. All was chaos.

My mother and grandmother, as quickly as they could climb through the rubble, made their way the two blocks back to their apartment building to discover The Sonesta was gone — completely destroyed. It had collapsed under one of the bombs; it was as if it had never existed. My grandmother began sobbing and wailing as she collapsed on the street by the two limestone steps that were all that remained of the once graceful entrance to the building. Everything else was gone, flattened. The silence of the spot where the building had once stood was almost as loud as the explosions. In my mother's memory, the debris mound was almost twenty feet high. There were shards of glass, parts of sinks and bathtubs, crumpled pieces of furniture, and photographs — but no signs of life. She knew that her family all had been at home that morning, and now they were nowhere to be found. A complete sense of helplessness, bewilderment, and uncertainty prevailed. Then the shock set in, along with an uneasy feeling of desperation and wonder. Had they somehow survived? It took weeks to confirm that their sadness was a permanent reality. One by one and all too slowly, unrecognizable bodies were discovered, forty-eight from that one site. They would learn that thousands had lost their lives that day.

Traumatic and unforgettable to this day, my mother, at twenty years of age, had lost her sisters, brother, and father all in a moment. Only she and her mother had survived the bombing, merely by chance. During their time of uncertainty, they stayed at my great-aunt Ida's home. Ida was my grandmother's older sister. She and her family lived on the eastern edge of Bucharest in an area completely untouched by the bombing raid. During that time, Mother and Grandmother made the decision that they would leave Romania. They would find safety elsewhere. Their time had come to be out of the city, out of Europe, and away from war. Once Grandmother Lulu set her sights on something, that something might just as well have been set in cement. In the following weeks, all Lulu could do was plan their journey to freedom, and with the help of her sister and her sister's family, she soon realized their route.

Leaving my great-aunt Ida and her family behind, they set out on foot to make their way to the small port town of Constanta on the Black Sea. Train travel had been destroyed by the bombings; roads were perilous. Twice they were able to ride on a farmer's wagon as he made his way to market. Their countrymen came to their aid more often than they would have thought possible. Ida had sent them off with food to sustain them for a few days. Along the way, they were fed by strangers on farms and in villages. Water came from village spigots or streams they passed. Twelve days and 126 miles later, they reached Constanta, on feet blistered and bruised. They found shelter in the darkness of a warehouse near the port. It was in this hiding place that they met two brothers, Anton and Dorin Klepsa, who were embarking on a journey similar to their own. The older brother, Anton, was eighteen, tall and broad, with dark hair and fair skin. Dorin, at fourteen, shared his brother's fair skin, but was slight and still growing. The boys had lost their family in a bombing as well. The future in Romania seemed hopeless and bleak to the boys. America was their destination. The four decided to travel together.

The warehouse where they hid was a loading facility for shipping containers. A ship already laden with iron ore and machine parts was bound for Turkey and presented them all with a chance to flee. Anton and his brother miraculously, through luck and happenstance, procured seamen's clothes for the four. On a moonless

May night, in the wee hours of the morning, four seafaring mates made their way onto the ship. Each carried a small duffel of necessities and the remaining tidbits of their pasts. Grandmother had sewn her important jewelry into the lining of a heavy coat before leaving Bucharest; it lay folded and stuffed in the bottom of her duffel. Both Mother and Grandmother carried money concealed on their persons and in the inner pockets of their bags.

The ship they had boarded was time-tabled to depart at eight the next morning. It left port as scheduled. Their good luck prevailed. The ship, destined for Turkey, would indeed dock there to unload present cargo and take on a new load. Then it was to cross the Mediterranean Sea, sail through the Strait of Gibraltar, skirt the western coast of Europe, and finally berth in Galway, Ireland. Once safe in Ireland, they would be assured the opportunity to immigrate to the United States.

A seaman working in the engine room discovered the four hiding in a recess behind a giant cluster of the ship's machinery. The discovery was made before they had reached their first port, as my mother remembers. What were the chances? It was, most assuredly, their worst nightmare. Lulu had never been shy. She immediately, directly, and sternly spoke to the man. She explained their situation and introduced them all. The seaman's shock became empathy in a heartbeat. Truth came to light when he confessed he was a naval officer from and on his way home to the United States. The ship they had snuck onto was an American freighter disguised as a Turkish shipping vessel. The ship and its crew had delivered goods and weapons to the Romanian resistance. Sympathetic to their situation, he allowed them their hiding spot and told nary a soul on board about the stowaways. He showed them the only toilet in the dank area, assuring them it was rarely used. Out of pure kindness, he snuck food and water to them under cover of night. The ship docked on June 10, 1944, at the port of Galway, which, to their surprise, was not their point of disembarkation. From Galway, Grandmother, Dorin, Anton, and my mother, Yvonna, remained in hiding all the way to the shores of the United States.

Schmellda Radmilla Lapone

June 16, 1976

I finally graduated from Middle Tennessee State University with my bachelor's degree in home economics. It was quite an ordeal living in my parents' home in Nashville and commuting to school down the road in Murfreesboro for four years. Drive time was only about forty-five minutes, but there were days when those forty-five minutes felt like forever. Daydreaming was a lifesaver while tootling along the interstate at sixty-five miles per hour. I finished school three weeks ago and will be starting a new job at a real estate firm in Green Hills. I have passions I discovered while working toward my degree, and they're on hold for the moment. Right now, I need to focus on making some money to cover rent on my new apartment and living expenses. This job is simply a practicality. Eventually, I want to pursue a career in the floral business.

I had a brief exposure to the business one semester during my junior year. My department offered a wonderful elective in floral arranging. I was lucky to enroll in the small seminar course that was limited to fourteen students. The professor was passionately committed to his subject. He began with a cram course in botany. We learned a lot of the basics needed for professional floral arranging.

We had lab for actual floral construction. Projects were assigned to construct arrangements for various occasions. A nominal lab fee covered everything we needed so far as supplies were concerned. We worked with floral foam and wires, and there were buckets and buckets of flowers, albeit plastic or silk. I loved every minute of the class. To be honest, it was probably the most fun I had in any class during my entire college career.

Nashville, Tennessee, has always been and will always be my permanent home. I'm moving into a lovely upscale area called Green Hills. The apartment is awesome. I rented the top floor of a duplex, with two bedrooms and a small kitchen with a rust-colored linoleum floor in a brick pattern. The apartment has a good-sized living room/dining room combination. The only bathroom has a step-over tub with a shower. The floor of the bathroom has this classic, small black-and-white hexagonal tile, and the tub, sink, and toilet are an aged white. The other flooring is hardwood in a golden oak color. I think the distinctive flooring throughout the unit was the final touch I needed to decide to lease the apartment. The entrance to my new home is accessed from an outside iron stairwell that traverses the side of the building. The front door is protected by a half-round metal awning overhead. Also in this apartment's favor is that it's only about a mile from the main shopping area in the center of Green Hills. On pretty days, I will be able to walk to the grocery. If it isn't obvious, I am simply over the moon about this, my very first apartment. I cannot wait to begin decorating. At the moment, I only have some of my clothes, a queen-sized bed, and a bunch of weird odds and ends moved in. My college stuff is still at my parents' house. Mother has offered me some dishes and pots and pans she doesn't use anymore. I told her anything she wants to give me is welcome.

An older gentleman lives in the downstairs unit. His name is Mr. Wallace Walloppe, and he seems very nice. He told me he is retired and used to work at the FDA in Nashville as a meat inspector. In speaking with him I discovered he has a really cool hobby. He makes furniture from salvaged tree limbs and twigs right in the living room of his apartment. We were introduced by Tom Frazier, the owner of the duplex, who is a lifelong friend of my parents. Tom explained that Mr. Walloppe's wife passed away five years ago from brain cancer. After selling their home, Mr. Walloppe moved in here and has been a tenant for a little over four years now.

Today will be my first day working at Hill and Garden Realtors. I met the manager, Mr. Pangle, a couple of weeks ago when I applied for the job. He surprised me when he hired me on the spot. As a beginner with the firm, I will be starting out as a receptionist. Mr. Pangle insists the position will give me exposure to the business. Along with receptionist duties, I'll be shadowing several of the agents and helping them however I can. I am sure it will be fun. Still, I am nervous about learning the telephone system and meeting all the agents. Mr. Pangle said the agency employs about thirty full-time agents and fifteen or so part-timers.

This morning, after a quick shower and a little makeup and hair fluffing, I got in my car and drove the short distance to Flanda Castle's Café to meet my two sisters for an 8:00 a.m. breakfast date we set up days ago. When I arrived, the clock on the dashboard of my 1972 blue Pontiac Le Mans displayed 7:50 a.m. I was early, of course, because I am always early. I can't help being ten minutes early anywhere I go. This quirky habit is definitely a result of my trek to and from school in Murfreesboro every day of the week for the last four years. I suffer self-induced anxiety from not wanting to be late to anything, which in turn of course makes me arrive early for everything. The extra ten minutes this morning means that I can tell you quickly a little bit about my new home, Green Hills.

Green Hills got its name from seven hills surrounding the suburb. It's a well-to-do area with the best shopping center in the city. Green Hills Village is a long strip center with two department stores, Cain-Sloan and Castner-Knott, at opposite ends of the strip; in between are thirty smaller shops. Green Hills has pretty much everything you might be looking for: restaurants, banks, gas stations, doctors, and all the other professional services you would expect.

For whatever reason, a popular hangout for high school boys is Yates Pharmacy. The other drugstore, Wilson-Quick, has the local soda fountain. They serve a great burger and their french fries are the best around! The local music store specializes in old musical instruments and antique sheet music. Green Hills is also home to one of Nashville's premier florists, The Dancing Flower, owned and operated by Eddy Francis. I love to go in there and just look at everything. The ice-cold flower cases are always filled with tall buckets brimming with loose stems and small arrangements for quick purchase. I have dreams about working there someday.

Flanda Castle's Café is a stand-alone building in Green Hills. The setting of the café is lovely. The restaurant, including the patio area, is large enough to seat maybe seventy-five. The décor throughout is simple and stylish. The patio area surrounds a giant sycamore and is enclosed by a rustic three-foot stone wall. Outside, each round café table is covered with a red- and white-checked tablecloth and surrounded by four white metal mesh chairs with plump red canvas cushions. Every table has a tall, thin glass vase of three golden daffodils. Red market umbrellas are scattered around the tables. The café sits across a large parking lot from a small strip center that is home to a grocery, hardware store, and art gallery. You can see the most popular bank in the area, People's Bank, from Flanda's front door. It's an easy walk anywhere. That is probably enough about Green Hills for now.

I parked my car in a space right at the front of Flanda Castle's Café. Satisfied that there wasn't a better spot, I got out of my car and went inside. Our aunt Minnie waitresses here but was nowhere to be seen. I walked through the café and took a table outside on the patio. It was refreshing to be in the open air after sitting in stuffy enclosed classrooms for so many years. This morning was particularly beautiful. It rained quite heavily last night. The rain cleared out, and the sky became the prettiest shade of cerulean blue I think I ever saw. Gigantic cumulus clouds floated by resembling enormous cotton balls that looked like giant cartoon characters. Maybe I've never had enough time to stare at clouds. What a joy they can be!

The air was slightly damp with a cool, gentle breeze that felt wonderful. Rays of brilliant sunlight came streaming down between the clouds, filtering through the leaves of the giant sycamore. The light created abstract patterns across the dark red market umbrellas and the maroon-stained concrete floor.

My sisters have always been my best friends; we three have been inseparable since birth. My middle sister, Sorina Luna, just finished a two-year stint at Belmont College here in Nashville. My youngest sister, Esmerelda Una, graduated from Hillsboro High last month. This was our first time at the café in a few weeks. We were meeting to celebrate graduations, my new job and just catch up on each other's lives and plans for the summer.

My sisters arrived. They were dressed in cute seasonal outfits. Esmerelda, the youngest, is gamine, like Audrey Hepburn pretty. She has very thick, straight, dark brown hair, which she wears in a bob with bangs. Her hair comes just below her jawline on the sides with a gentle under-flip. Esmeralda is our free spirit with a flippant attitude. She is definitely the most outspoken of anyone in our family. Today she was wearing her lightweight denim jumpsuit that zips up the front. It's her favorite piece of clothing; she's in it almost every other day. Today, she did not have on her normal white Keds, a forever staple in her casual wardrobe. This day she had unexpectedly chosen red leather sandals from out of the blue.

Sorina is the middle sister. Her significant stutter is the reason she remains quiet and shy. Sorina is a gentle person. With her feathery long blonde hair and beautiful blue eyes, she could easily be a model. She is rail-thin and has a delicate, milky complexion. Sorina has a calm nature and quiet mannerisms that I admire. Today she was wearing one of her favorite dresses, a loose, collared cotton peasant dress in a tan and cream batik print. She was in simple sandals, which she would eventually change out for tennis shoes when she got to her job at the cleaners. As she headed my way, she seemed to float through the air. She oftentimes reminds me of a star, someone like Mary Travers, Laura Nyro, or even Joni Mitchell.

And finally, me! I had on one of the new outfits I bought

especially for my new job. Most of my new clothes are from Castner-Knott, a local department store. Today I was wearing a lemon-yellow polyester pantsuit. The pants were lemon-yellow, gathered at the waist, and paired with a white collared blouse with yellow piping, a yellow pocket, and yellow cloth–covered buttons. The blazer was a yellow and white pinstripe seersucker. Naturally, I had added a matching lemon-yellow barrette in my hair. I have always loved barrettes. Always!

A waitress arrived at our table. She looked young enough to be in high school, so this was probably a summer job. She was dressed in a red and white candy-striped apron over a white button-down blouse and red Bermuda shorts. Once she had served the glasses of ice water from her tray, she asked, "Coffee?" We all replied, "Please, with cream." Sorina ordered toast and grape jelly. Esmerelda ordered an egg sandwich on white toast. I was too nervous to eat. I just needed my coffee!

After the waitress left the table, I held up my glass of water and said, "I propose a toast." Sorina and Esmerelda raised their glasses. "To summer and new beginnings," I said. We clinked our glasses and settled back into our chairs to chat.

As usual, I was the first to begin the conversation. I don't know why, but as the oldest, I have always felt it is my place to be the leader, to set an example. I already have my degree. At twenty-three, I've had the opportunity to travel around Tennessee, Georgia, Alabama, and Florida. I've taken maybe too much pride in being the first to holiday away with friends from university during spring and fall breaks. I'm the first to move out and have my own apartment.

As was my habit, my mind began to wander. For some reason, I suddenly thought of my grandmother. *As a child, I had worshipped the woman. She passed away when I was ten, and I still worship her memory at twenty-three. She was only sixty-three when she died. It was November 22, 1963, the same day President Kennedy was assassinated. She was struck by a city bus when she tripped and fell from a curb in front of Walgreens in Green Hills. I painfully remember that day like it was yesterday. I will never forget it. That day completely destroyed my mother. I don't think she and my father have been the same since. President Kennedy was shot around noon, and Lulu was struck down that afternoon. Sorina cried for days. Esmerelda, who had just turned five, was too young to completely understand the gravity of the situation. I just cried and cried until I didn't think I had any tears left in me. My mother, aside from losing her only living family member and best friend, also lost her beloved president the same day. It was the most heartbreaking day in her life.*

Lulu, as my sisters and I always lovingly referred to Grandmother, had schooled us in many of her personal beauty secrets. According to Mother, Lulu was a neighborhood beauty as a young woman growing up in Bucharest. Our great-grandmother had passed on her own daily beauty regimen to Grandmother.

Of all the inspirations I internalized from her personal tenets, one thing stands out: she always stressed to wash our hair only once a week. She believed that the once-a-week wash kept hair healthy and shiny because it retained its natural oils. My hair is straight and thick and ash-blonde. I keep it long enough to pull the sides back into a barrette, which means it's about five inches below the nape of my neck. On the days I wear a barrette, I usually match the color of the barrette with the color of my shoes or dress. There are other days when I just part my hair on the side and let it hang straight. My problem is that I know in my heart I don't wash my hair enough. Grandmother Lulu used to be so emphatic about her once-a-week hair wash plan. Since she passed, I've never dared change from her belief out of respect for her memory. I miss her every day and wonder what she would think now. But I swear, some days my hair feels so oily that I want to scream and throw it all up under a hat. When I look in the mirror, my hair seems sad and mousy. And then there's my skin. It's oily, too! I think it's because the oil from my hair oozes down my forehead. Pitiful, right? I will say my lips are pretty perfect. They're heart-shaped and plump. I think they are the focal point of my round face. My favorite thing at makeup counters is trying out different lipsticks. That for me is fun. Lipstick can change your entire appearance. A new lipstick will change your attitude. Then there is my eye makeup. I don't do much experimenting with that, ever. I'm happy enough with my eye shadow of azure blue. With a dab of black mascara, my eyes look fairly dramatic. But enough about me.

"So, Sorina, Esmerelda, what do y'all have planned for today?" I said. And then we were off.

The Social Scene

Flanda Castle, of café fame, and the Lapone girls' aunt Minnie had been best friends forever. Aunt Minnie is their father Frank's younger sister. Minnie and Frank's family emigrated from Italy to the United States before World War II. Frank's first name was originally Francesco. When the family arrived in the States, his parents shortened his name to the Americanized Frank. The two women met as children at Burton Elementary School. The very first day, something magical clicked between the two, and they have been each other's closest companion ever since. In high school, they joined the Nashville Young Women's Cotillion Club, more commonly known as the NYWCC; to this day, they continue to wonder why.

NYWCC members ranged in age from sixteen to twenty-one. More than anything, membership in the club was a local status symbol. The primary purpose of the club was to involve the younger members in the community through volunteer work. Every year in May, the club staged the debutante ball, and the oldest girls were presented to society. The event was held at Creekland Country Club, a private club responsible for hosting many local social events. The Cotillion Ball Committee selected forty young women for presentation at the annual gala. The girls chosen were from well-connected, elite, upper-crust "old" families; additionally, they had to meet all the rigid standards set by the committee. Many eligible-by-age girls simply did not get past the interview stage. Flanda and Minnie never bothered to apply. For the Lapone sisters, Cotillion Club was never on their radar.

At the ball, the girls dressed in the most elegant white gowns their family money could buy. It was no surprise for girls to wear creations by Halston, Cardin, or Chanel. The girls arrived early, before the banquet, for photographs with their escorts in front of the fireplace that anchored one end of the club. Above the fireplace hung a large oil painting of the club's founder, Mr. Harvey Pearson. The massive dark walnut mantel always held large brass and glass hurricane lamps at each end. The only thing that ever changed on the mantel was the dust and the flower arrangement for whatever event was on the books. The deb and her escort posed for a photograph. No matter whether for the Cotillion Ball or a high school prom, the pose was always the same. The smiling couple stood nervous and stiff, side-by-side, in front of the fireplace with Harvey Pearson gazing down from his frame. The Creekland Country Club's mantel was one of the most photographed backdrops in all of Nashville. Photos of a select few often accompanied the lead feature in *The Eye*, Nashville's weekly social events magazine.

Once photographed, the debs and escorts headed for their tables and the evening's meal. As the banquet wound down, the girls slowly disappeared with their escorts to begin lining up for the highlight of the evening: their presentation to society. The emcee for the evening was, most years, a local television news anchor or prominent political figure. As music played, one by one, on the arm of their escorts, the young ladies descended the stairs to the stage. After their presentation, they stepped down and stood before the audience until the last young lady was presented and joined the lineup. The final flourish was a curtsy, in unison, to the audience. When the band began to play, the debs enjoyed the first dance of the evening with their escorts. Each step of the evening presented a veritable feast of photo ops for images that would appear in the pages of *The Eye*. Flanda and Minnie found themselves caring less and less about the local social season as each year passed.

The Eye was owned, operated, and published by Charlotte Webber. Ms. Webber was also a guest columnist for the local evening paper, *The Nashville Post*. As a native Nashvillian and the daughter of Thomas and Delilah Webber, Charlotte attended an elite private girls-only school in the city, later graduating with honors from a prestigious university. As an adolescent, she took dance and etiquette lessons. Her mother hosted a tea for Charlotte every year on her birthday. Around the age of seven, with her mother's help, she began to cultivate the personality she would eventually realize: a self-appointed, somewhat autocratic town maven. Many townspeople became terrified of her. Many just could not stand the sight of her. Every important event was covered or mentioned by Ms. Webber somewhere, in either *The Post* or *The Eye*. No one ever knew where she would turn up; when she did, you could be certain someone or something would be mentioned in *The Eye*. For the most part, she was gracious and polite in her reviews. On the other hand, there were times when she was catty, spiteful, and just plain mean.

Among the numerous charitable events covered by *The Eye* was the annual pie bake-off competition in Green Hills. It was an extremely successful fundraiser for the benefit of the Nashville Children's Orphanage. The generous amount of money raised from the event helped cover an abundance of needs at the home. The competition usually had at least fifty participants, many coming in from surrounding communities. Each baker brought an additional four pies for a sale, adding greatly to the proceeds. Flanda and Minnie always had an entry in the contest. For many years, one of them won first place. Minnie's special pie was a sweet and savory pecan, and Flanda's a creamy, crackled chess. The women conjured some sort of magic to create the best pies, which for many folks had proved addictive. Townspeople always raved about their crusts and the delightful fillings, and yet there was always "something else" no one could name.

The yearly contest was always an important story for *The Eye*. Charlotte Webber seemed to deeply enjoy presiding as one of the judges. Each year, she used the event as a main article for the magazine, always commending the organizers and participants. The winning entrant each year received the Slice Award, a trophy of a sparkling brass pie slice atop a square cube of black marble. The trophy was always received with honor and good-natured humor. The recipient later received a brass plaque engraved with their name and the date of the event. Flanda and Minnie still proudly and prominently display their awards at the café for all to see.

Girl Talk

June 16, 1976

As we sat together talking at Flanda's Café, the morning was really warming up. I couldn't help but think, *I just feel like an oily mess. My face feels like it's melting, and my hair looks like a hot, greasy mop.* From my reverie, I blubbered to Sorina, "I am so nervous about starting my new job. I don't know anyone except Mr. Pangle, and I don't really know him! And then meeting all of those other people — how will I ever remember all their names? *Any* of their names? I will say, I am very excited about the prospect of touring homes listed for sale. *That* will be a lot of fun." After my little outburst, I quickly began to calm down.

Looking at me, Sorina giggled. "Why not let us ride with you to your new job? It's just a b-block away. We can walk b-back to our cars. No b-big deal."

"That sounds great. But I just thought of something. When I left the apartment this morning, I was rushing and dropped my jewelry in my purse. It's right here. Would you help me with the necklace?"

"Sure thing!"

As Sorina adjusted my necklace, I absentmindedly dug through my straw handbag for the earrings my parents had given me for graduation. The beautiful pearl and gold posts were still in the little black leather box from Gold Tree Jewelers.

On this hot, hot Wednesday, I feel like I just came out of a deep fryer. I can already feel my yellow pantsuit and white top clinging to every crevice and fold of my body. I like to think I'm fairly attractive. I don't know anymore. At five foot seven and 160 pounds, I'm no skinny mini. I know I need to lose weight. And right now, I could kill for a piece of Flanda's chess pie. Very, very bad idea. Already I buy everything new in a size 14 while I know in my heart this body needs an 18. Self-denial? Obviously! How I wish I had washed my hair this morning! It's time to let go of Lulu's "beauty secrets." It's high time I acknowledge I don't have the hair or skin of Lulu or my sisters. Sorina and Esmerelda ditched her regimens long ago. I have to start somewhere. A diet. I'll start a diet today, I swear. I am making a promise to myself right here and now to make changes in my life.

I know deep down that Sorina and Esmerelda are proud of me no matter what I look like. I'm still their role model, I think. I created a path that helped Sorina mature. When Esmerelda was younger, I was able to show her what feeling special can be like. I'm still protective of my sisters. Maybe I'm a fussy old mother hen. I'm okay with that, but at their ages, I'm sure they would be willing to let me out of the coop to fly free. My sisters are special for me and always will be. Family is paramount.

So here I am. I'm twenty-three and have never had a boyfriend, so my virtue is still intact. Good for me. Right now, I'm not sure I'll ever have a guy of my own. I'm strong-willed and can be bossy at times. I know my heart is in the right place. I'm kind and live by the Golden Rule. So here I am, out in the open, a protective, loving soul, ready for change and my own love.

Returning to my car and to earth from my trance, I offered, "You know, guys, this is pretty silly — both of you riding with me less than two blocks just to distract me from the inevitable. Silly or not, thank you. Seriously. I love your support."

"Not a problem," said Esmerelda as she got in my back seat. Sorina took her favorite spot in the passenger seat next to me.

Two minutes later, we were around the block and across the street. I turned into the lot that serviced three businesses. The parking lot for Hill and Garden Realtors was shared with People's Bank and Yannie's, a fast-food restaurant. I parked my car, only to realize I was nearer to the bank than to the realty firm.

Esmerelda made a sudden gasp from the back seat. Sorina and I both felt a quick chill at the sound of her distress. "Look over there," Esmerelda said as she pointed to a shiny black convertible Mustang that was pulling into a parking space. The car was spotless, with brilliant whitewall tires and chrome spoked wheels. It was in the next row of cars across the lot from us.

Still excited over the sighting, Esmerelda practically yelled, "Wow! What a cool car!"

A woman was driving the Mustang. She wore a red scarf wrapped around her head. It looked like a turban. As we watched, the driver's door opened. Seconds later, out stretched a woman's sculpted leg. As the second leg emerged, we saw a stunning woman dressed in black fishnet stockings, black patent leather high-heeled shoes, and a very short, tight red suede dress with black polka dots, cinched at the waist with the narrowest black patent leather belt. The front of the dress came to a strikingly low-cut V, revealing remarkably deep cleavage and a sinuously voluptuous body.

Sorina was flat-out gaping at the woman as Esmerelda said, "Get a load of her! Geez Louise! She must have those girls tucked into a 44E bra. That waist! It has to be, like, twenty-two inches? Her booty is near the same size as her boobs! My goodness. She's a billboard for something!"

Now standing and locking her car was none other than the illustrious and divine Helena Montgomery, widely known as one of the prides of Nashville. She turned and looked at her reflection in the window of her car. As she did, she reached into her small, quilted black leather Chanel bag, pulled out a lipstick, and proceeded to touch up her perfect lips. After a momentary pause, she deftly removed her headscarf turban, releasing a long, thick, wavy cascade of raven-black hair that fell just above her tiny waist. We continued to stare as Helena leaned back and shook her head. As she did, her hair and its waves fell into perfect position. Everyone in the city knew something of Helena, or at least thought they did. What was certain was that she had been the first runner-up in the Miss Tennessee pageant about eight years ago and a debutante presented by the NYWCC before that. Sorina knew she was only twenty-eight. Helena was one of the most eligible single women in town.

We tried not to stare, we really did. But we just couldn't help it. Then from somewhere else in space, Esmerelda's voice broke the silence. "I can't believe it! She looks like she's wearing an awful lot of foundation for this early in the morning! And hey! Those black fishnet hose? Give me a break!" Taking a deep breath, she continued, "The little mole on the right side of her face? See? Just above her chin? I swear to you, it was on the other side of her face last week and was higher up! I think she's wearing that new fad mole. You know, the one advertised in the back of *Beauty Today* as 'Move a Mole by Mary Lynn'? It has to be that! How dumb!"

We all nodded in unison.

Sorina started to sputter, "Will you l-l-look at her l-l-lips? Is she wearing a b-black lip l-l-liner around her red l-l-lipstick? In the morning?"

Helena Montgomery was a stunning woman, but she always looked the same, whether it was day or night. She always wore the same makeup, and she was always overdressed. By day, she worked as a teller at People's Bank. Thursday and Saturday evenings, she sang the blues and played piano at the Music Box down near Vanderbilt University. She had a smoky, moody voice, which drew a good crowd. The club itself was a favorite hangout for the over-twenty-one group.

As she walked away from her Mustang, she turned, patting a tissue between her cleavage, and noticed us looking her way. She smiled, waved, and said, in the oddest French-ish accent, "Bonjour, so waunderfool to see yous tress togetter. Eese not a booteeful dase, ooey?"

I waved back and said, "Helena, I haven't seen you in so long! You look great! How do you do it?"

"Teese nutting! All diette, diette, diettes and eggeresize."

Sorina chimed in, "It's great to s-s-see you too. I hope you are w-w-well."

Helena smiled and said, "Yous alla take goooood carr. I sam offfff to da wairk."

Quickly, I added, "I am just starting my new job next door to your bank. I'm working at Hill and Garden Realty. Let's do lunch sometime? Take care! See you later!"

Sorina whispered, "Puhleeze, I can't b-b-believe she still has that f-f-false French accent. Really! It's b-been years since she l-lived in Paris for that wa-wa-one and only s-summer."

I said, "Okay, girls, it's already quarter past nine. I'm supposed to be at work in fifteen minutes. That goes for you, too, Sorina. Thank you both for coming this far with me. I am actually feeling pretty calm right now. The time with you two and even seeing Helena really did the trick. This has been fun! We need to get together like this more often. Can we set another time now?"

"G-great idea. But I th-think maybe w-we should t-talk later. You're r-right about th-the time. Later, girls." With that Sorina turned, took a step away and stopped. "Wa-wait a m-minute! Esmerelda! W-will you l-look at that!" She pointed to a new Corvette pulling into the lot.

We waited and watched as the Vette stopped in front of the bank. Helena had come to a halt and was eyeing the car and its driver.

Esmerelda smiled at her sisters. "Oh, this ought to be good. Hold on, you two."

Johnny Montana

Already late, Helena proceeded toward work at the bank. As she reached for the door, a candy apple red Corvette pulled up to the curb directly in front of her and the bank. The Vette's door opened, and Helena gazed at the very tall, drop-dead-handsome man in his mid-thirties getting out of the car. He had thick, light brown, sun-streaked hair and was absolutely dashing in a navy linen suit, obviously designer. His height and broad shoulders made him a dead ringer for Troy Donohue. Helena stopped in her tracks, turned, and locked eyes with Johnny Montana, whose stepfather was president of People's Bank. Johnny had been promoted to the position of executive vice president of the same bank shortly after graduating with his MBA. Johnny enjoyed his work. He reveled in his time spent driving the Vette, going from branch to branch making surprise visits, evaluating personnel performance and the staff's daily responsibilities. When anchored to his desk, he felt like a paper jockey, poring over and double-checking applications for loans he might or might not consider as worthy risks.

Helena beamed a smile at Johnny and, raising her arm, gave him the same hand-cupped wave she'd mastered on the pageant circuit.

Responding with his own sun-blinding smile, Johnny said, "Good morning, beautiful! What's going on? Besides heading into work?"

At that, Helena gave Johnny her sultriest gaze and replied, in that oddest of accents, "Hey sere, John-ny! Indeet I ahm. Buht hows moan fauvoreet mawn dooing?"

Flustered, Johnny gave her a wink and asked, "Helena, why do you tease me? Will you ever condescend to go out with me? I'm getting tired of asking. C'mon. Give me a break. Pick a night, and let's just go out for a nice, quiet dinner!"

As she turned to reply, Johnny held up his right hand in that universal motion to stop speaking. "Helena, when will you realize I am serious about taking you out to dinner? Our age difference can't be a problem. It's not even worthy of discussion! How about dinner one night this weekend and then a movie? Are you free?"

Helena piped back in the raspiest, sultriest voice she could muster, "Okaya, wauht abou deese Fryda naut?"

Johnny smiled with a grin that said everything. "Friday it is! Great! Where do you live? I will pick you up at six thirty. There's a new restaurant in Franklin I've wanted to try, and we can catch a movie somewhere later. *All the President's Men* was just released. Any interest?" He paused and then, not waiting for a reply, said, "Oh, by the way, we need to keep this to ourselves. I'm not supposed to fraternize with bank employees."

Helena reached into her purse and pulled out her checkbook. She tore off the top of a deposit slip that had her address and phone number and handed it to Johnny. "Voila! Dis eese whar Ah leef, ant dona you vorrie, Ah can keep dah seecress."

Johnny's calm demeanor masked the ecstatic thrill he felt in his chest. He had wanted to go out with Helena the first time they met, which when he thought about it, he realized was nearly a year ago. It had taken forever to make this connection. *Well, there's no time to waste,* he thought. *Best to call now and make the reservation for 7:00 o'clock.* With only a twenty-minute drive, his punctually obsessive self would get them there with a few minutes to spare.

The Lapone girls were still watching from across the parking lot and had heard the entire conversation. Esmerelda, always quick with a remark, whispered, "She is such a hollow little tramp. How does she do it? I mean, first thing in the morning and in this heat!"

Sorina, looking first at Esmerelda and then to Schmellda, added, "Yeah, sh-sh-she sure knows how to p-p-play 'em."

Schmellda smiled at both of her sisters and said, "Remember, Lulu always said to look for the good in people. There has to be something in her we simply cannot see. Let's hope for the best for all concerned."

Schmellda began to reminisce to herself. *Lulu often babysat the three of us and was integral in helping to form and define our morals and personalities. While originally from Romania, she had adapted to the customs of the United States quickly. Lulu was a firm believer in reading. Early in our lives, she taught us the importance of literary giants, both past and present. She read William Wordsworth's lyrical ballads to us. She would ask us to describe to her what some of the lines meant to us, and then she would share her own personal interpretation of the writer's intentions. By the time I was ten, I could understand the literary intentions of many complicated essays and poems. Our vocabulary and grades in school reflected such early instruction. We were far more advanced than most of the other students in our classes. Lulu taught us so many basic life lessons. She instilled in us an understanding of, and the importance of, empathy in our lives. Then, suddenly, she was gone.*

We all learned to be especially empathetic to our classmates and neighbors who were singled out as different or odd or who were experiencing problems or difficulties. We were encouraged to be quick to notice and help guard the students who were teased — preteens and teens who were different or less fortunate. Too many classmates tried to single out others to taunt and tease, calling them names, such as "pimples galore," "geek of the week," "slut face," "school whore," and all the rest. We Lapone girls learned early on to be quick to befriend those who were teased and welcome them with kindness into our little circle.

Schmellda looked at her watch and saw it was 9:28 a.m. "Got to run, ladies!" She tore across the parking lot to the office of Hill and Garden Realtors.

Sorina Luna Lapone

Schmellda is off to her new job. I hope they're kind. She was looking a little slick from the heat. Don't get me wrong — I love my sister. She is my rock. Schmellda needs to learn to care for herself, though. Esmerelda is off to sell greeting cards in air-conditioned bliss.

Time for me to get myself over to the cleaners. This cannot last long. A laundry as a summer job? What specifically was I thinking? If you aren't hot and uncomfortable with the humidity outside, come on in here with me! Don't get me started on the smell of dry-cleaning fluid. Well, I dressed to stay cool today. I'll ditch the sandals for my tennis shoes. A girl can't be on her feet all day in no-support sandals. But enough about work. Now about me.

I know my sister has told you that I stutter. Well, I don't stutter in my head. And that doesn't define me, so let's start with the basics. I'm twenty years old. I'm tall and lithe (I prefer that term to "thin" or "skinny") with what others describe as perfect posture. My posture is Lulu's doing — "Walk like you're balancing a book on the tip-top of your head!" she used to say. My hair is blonde and long and always tied in a high ponytail, which of course accentuates my height. People say my blue eyes sparkle. I'll say they're pale blue. I wear clothes appropriate to my body type and age, always with an easy style. I wear enough makeup to accent my features, but nothing too bold. Without vanity, I will say guys find me attractive. Throughout high school, the boys would approach me with a smile or a joke to get my attention. A couple of them pulled off pranks for my benefit. I'd smile, but I couldn't laugh. I didn't find their immature antics funny. It wasn't a matter of being judgmental, snobbish, or unkind. It's just the way I'm put together. I didn't date much then. Still don't. I'll offer no opposition if the right guy comes along.

Now let's attack the roadblock ahead and get it out of the way once and for all time. Yes, I stutter. My stammer came on early. My parents tried desperately to find a cure with no success; there wasn't much help to be had anywhere. Exactly what is a speech lesson, anyway? I found it hard to answer the phone. The anticipation of saying "Hello" induced the most horrible dread — still does sometimes. If the caller waits long enough in patience, I might finally blurt out the word. Indeed, it is quite frustrating. I actually said prayers that teachers wouldn't call on me in class. It could be mortifying. The terror made it difficult to concentrate. I'm by no means stupid. Obviously, there were things I missed along the way. I'm a whiz at math and loved English. We had to write papers, not read aloud. I absolutely adore poetry. So I turned a little quiet, which most people interpreted as shy. Maybe I am.

The thing is, at some point I figured out I could sing without stuttering. I could do a lead-in with my harmonica and get a sentence out that didn't sound like a scratched record. My harmonica hangs around my neck on a chain. I joined the chorus in high school without difficulty. The chorus leader told me my voice was good but not exceptional from her point of view. I spent two years at Belmont's School of Voice and Music. The instructors there were wonderful. With their help, my voice bloomed into what I think might be special. Time will tell.

Since we've gotten this far, let's go for broke. At times, I think of myself like an artichoke. There's a tender heart in there, and I'll protect mine like the Hope Diamond. It takes time to peel away all the bracts and guards to get to the heart. Stutter as long as I have, and you'll build walls too. Children can be horrid, mean little creatures — nothing funnier than a stammer, right? With a little kindness, the petals start to peel away. All anyone had to do was listen, not interrupt, not finish my sentence to hurry me along. I eventually found some friends, in addition to my family, who could do just that. I could warmly embrace them because they had embraced me. My fluency did, and continues to, improve around those folks who take a breath with me and listen. Listen. I'll let you in.

Shy, introverted — pick your word. My speech therapist says that my stutter — she actually uses the phrase "speech fluency issues" — caused my introversion. Just because you're quiet doesn't mean your brain isn't bouncing ideas around in your head at the speed of sound. My imagination could run wild. I had the time to introduce myself to me.

Esmerelda

This has been a fun morning. No reason for me to rush to work. I think my personality is way different from my sisters'. I feel like I'm a full 180 degrees different from Schmellda. I admit to having a quick wit. I'm outgoing and nearly fearless. I graduated, with the other four hundred in my class, from Hillsboro High School, where I had a lot of friends. Without boasting, I can confidently say I was pretty popular. I was a cheerleader for both the basketball and football teams. Almost always on the Dean's List with As and Bs, I was also a member of the drama club and acted in several school plays. I even landed the role of Juliet in *Romeo and Juliet* my junior year. I tried out for a television commercial for a chain of shoe stores in Nashville and actually got the part. And there were the four years on the yearbook committee I can't forget. My absolute favorite classes were English, chorus, and dramatic arts. High school was fun! Oh, and educational. Perspective.

I have a boyfriend with whom I spend most weekends. (That's right. No dangling prepositions for this girl. Told you I liked English!) His name is Ricky Baker. I met Ricky in the middle of my sophomore year. Ricky is two years older than me, so he was already a senior. I almost hate to say this, but it really was "like" at first sight. He is so good-looking, so funny, and so sexy. Okay, he is *hot*.

There, I said it. I am one very lucky girl. Ricky is about six inches taller than me. I think he is six feet three — *tall.* He has straight black hair, the kind that, if he swoops his head just right, falls into place just the way he likes. His eyes are big, blue, and beautiful. He can outwit me sometimes, and the jokes he comes up with (almost) always crack me up. To his benefit, both of my sisters really like him, too. In school, he was a B/C student, my hero football player, and well, obvious or not, popular like me!

Our dating actually survived my last two years of high school, which were, of course, his first two out. We're definitely committed to each other. One of the reasons he didn't go away to college was so we could stay close to each other. Not sure how that'll work in the long run, but for now, we're good. He's working a job at a department store five days a week in the Boy Scout department. Seriously, yes, there is one. He sells and fits uniforms for newly recruited scouts. It is an odd job to be sure. He says most of the kids are on the chubby side. He jokes about his stint there, saying, "It feels like I'm serving time." The best part of this entire scenario is that the store is in the shopping center near school. After classes finally ended at three, and after cheerleading practice or drama club, I could walk over and wait for him to get off work

We might go for an ice cream cone or something or park behind the dumpster at Walgreen's and make out. I'm not sure how that sounds, but we always talk about our plans for the future, too. When we started dating, my parents were definitely not cool with the deal. They were leery of an "older" guy taking me out. It was difficult to say the least. It took some time to convince them that he wasn't some psychopathic pedophile. Maybe that's too strong, but my point is made. I think it was around the third date that he showed up at our house and rang the front doorbell. My father opened the door. Ricky held out his hand to shake with my father. As my father took his hand, Ricky stepped back and left my father standing there holding a fake arm by the hand. Ricky had come with a mannequin's arm tucked up his sleeve. Sounds stupid, but it worked! It was hilarious and still is a joke my father laughs about with Ricky.

Ricky has a master plan figured out for our future and says all he has to do is make it happen. And I know he will. He's keeping a secret from me that he swears will work in our favor. He promises that very soon he will fill me in on the secret. What I do know is that one morning every week, he spends about five hours in the workshop on his parents' property, which he guards with three padlocks. He won't let anyone near the workshop, including his parents.

My sister Sorina is great. She was in Ricky's class but did not know him until he and I met. Sorina was such a great help to me in school. With drama club, I had to memorize lines, and she would read the lines for the opposite character. As she read the lines, her stutter nearly disappeared. It felt like as she slowly read through the lines, her imagination took her into the character and out of herself. That said, I think most of the time she already had the lines memorized, which in turn caused her to slow her speech. The result was pretty amazing. I love to hear her words come without hesitancy.

We also love to share clothes — a lot. Sorina and I wear close to the same size. Without doubt, she's a bit more conservative in her choices. I, by contrast, gravitate toward what's trendy at the moment. Still, we always find things to swap from each other's wardrobes. She always has more shoes than anyone I know. It's actually kind of funny. Mother and I refer to her jokingly as Imelda Lapone.

Then there are Lulu's credos! She did preach. And I mean a lot. I know she made up some of the things that she told us totally on the fly. Who knows? She'd bore the life out of me sometimes and other times get me laughing until I nearly wet myself. The absolute craziest thing she ever told me concerned "necking" in the car. For starters, at four years old, I had no idea what she was preaching, but the message was clearly meant for all three of us. "Always keep one foot on the floor of the car — that way, nothing will happen." Yes, that is what she said. Who could forget? Some things like that stick with a kid, unfortunately. Schmellda remembers those credos to a tee and still reminds us, whether we want to be reminded or not!

Schmellda, despite our six-year age difference, was my best

friend during my early years. From around age seven until I was about eleven or twelve, she was a driving force in my life. There were many Saturdays when we would ride the bus from Green Hills all the way downtown (it felt like a long way then) and hop off at Church and Fifth. We would go into the four-story Cain-Sloan department store and ride the escalator all the way up to the third floor to The Iris Room. It was by far the nicest restaurant for lunch downtown. The Iris Room was fancy. Boy, did I ever feel grown-up. Once we were seated, with each step in our adventure, she subtly taught me the etiquette of proper table manners. She would motion for me to chew with my mouth closed and never to talk with food in my mouth.

Oh, The Iris Room was elegance itself, with deep red carpet and crystal and brass chandeliers throughout. Tables were draped in white tablecloths and held decoratively folded white cloth napkins. Each of the large round tables and smaller square tables spaciously scattered around the room held a floral centerpiece. The entire back wall of the enormous room was a gigantic mural of a map of Paris, France, with all the landmarks. The mural must have been sixty feet long by fourteen feet high. The food was dreamy. Sandwiches were served with crusts removed. I loved the pimento cheese on white bread with chips on the side. Schmellda would usually order a Waldorf salad. In the center of the room was a shiny black grand piano. Tuesday through Saturday from 11:30 a.m. to 2:00 p.m., Bradford Brockington played dreamy standards. It was completely magical. I felt so much older and more mature every time we were there. It's such a lovely memory. When lunch was finished, we would head back downstairs and walk up Church Street to the Crescent or Paramount Theater for the Saturday matinee. All in all, my oldest sister has been so wonderful to me. From her I learned manners, style, and how to be a lady. Thanks, sis!

Yvonna

My husband Frank and I have always been the glue holding our little family together. Well, of course, we have. Isn't that what parents do? It was November 1945 when I met Mario Francesco Lapone. I was twenty-one. By the time we met, he had already adopted the familiar American nickname of Frank. He and his family were originally from Torino, Italy. Frank, with his parents and sister, had immigrated to the United States in the early-1930s, a somewhat easier era to enter this country than when my mother and I immigrated toward the end of the war.

In early 1945, my mother and I had been living in America for only a few months. At the time we were staying with cousins from my father's side of the family whom we had not met prior to landing on these shores. Our first meeting with them had felt so very awkward. We were the new refugee immigrants stoically explaining our present situation. They could not have been more hospitable and kind, insisting that, as family, we stay with them until we could get our feet on the ground. To this day, I feel blessed by their compassionate gesture. Their apartment was in the same neighborhood as the Lapones', near the center of downtown Philadelphia. Frank's parents owned a small grocery, where he worked as a checkout clerk and bag boy. Mother had taken a job as a seamstress in a small dressmaker's shop on the same block as the Lapones' market. I spoke passable English, having studied it in my Romanian school as a required second language. I still had so much to learn to be fluent. Our neighborhood variety store took me on as a stockgirl. Sweeping floors, scrubbing the restrooms, opening shipments, tagging merchandise, and tidying the displays — I got to do it all. It took me about three months to settle into a routine. The bounty of goods was staggering, considering all that had not been available at home. Our jobs helped us move into our new future and away from our recent loss.

Eventually, Mother and I ended up renting a small one-bedroom apartment near our cousins. It was a nice-enough building, and the rent was reasonable. Having our own apartment was a momentous advancement in establishing our new life. Mother sold some of her jewelry, and with that added to the money remaining from what she had been able to salvage for our journey to America, we were assured some little comfort during the first period of our relocation.

Maybe six months after our arrival in Philadelphia, Mother asked me to stop by the market for a few things. I do not know how it was possible, but until that day I had never met Frank. Nor do I remember how our conversation started, but how glad I am that it did. After ten minutes, he was called back to his work, but before he left, he asked if he might call on me that afternoon. I told him where Mother and I lived. He asked if he could drop by around five, after he finished work. I hesitated and then agreed. When he arrived, we sat on my front porch and talked for an hour. He shared his life, and I shared mine. We very soon developed a more than casual relationship. Our love and happiness bloomed. We married in the fall of 1948.

By the time we were living in our first apartment, Frank's parents had expanded and renamed their grocery. The new Penn Market encompassed almost a half block of Second Street in downtown Philadelphia. Frank was able to take on management duties and received a regular salary. With partial ownership on the horizon and our future seemingly secure, it was time to start our family.

Schmellda

My First Day

The entrance of Hill and Garden Realty was grand. A pair of very large dark mahogany paneled doors made for quite a stately impression. I paused and took a deep breath as I adjusted my yellow polyester pantsuit and blotted the oil on my face with a wad of tissues. Unconsciously holding my breath to regain my composure, I entered the office of Hill and Garden Realtors with a beet-red face. I was quickly greeted by a woman I thought must be the other receptionist. She introduced herself as Donna Dixon and said, "Oh, you must be the new girl Mr. Pangle hired!"

I smiled and said, "Yes, I am! My name's Schmellda Lapone. Mr. Pangle told me you would be the first in to meet me this morning. He also said I'd be working with you. I'm so excited to be here!"

"Oh, he told me your name was Shoodle. I must have misheard. Now how do you pronounce that name again?"

"Sch-mell-da, S-c-h-m-e-l-l-d-a. I know — different. It's Romanian. Family name," I explained with a smile.

Donna looked a little more than just bewildered as she diligently repeated my name.

"Perfect!" I said to her.

It was probably just me, but "mysterious" was the first impression I had of Donna. I'm certainly not sure why. Maybe it was her narrow, gold-rimmed granny glasses with dark, smoky lenses that she did not remove even after she introduced herself. They seemed to be attached permanently to her face.

Donna said, "Let me show you around the office. There really is a lot to see, and the phones will start ringing before we open at ten. We'll be sitting next to each other over there."

As I followed her pointed finger across the reception area from the entrance, I saw two large office desks side by side, separated only by a middling sound partition. In the space between where we stood and those desks was a comfortable seating area with two sofas, six armchairs, and a few bunching tables covered with real estate magazines. It was all very stylish and modern in black, white, and gray.

"I am so excited that you'll be helping out with all of this. We're so busy right now, it's near impossible for me to handle it all myself. I was out on a short vacation when Mr. Pangle hired you. He said you and I will get along great, and I have no doubt he was right!"

Donna started walking and continued, "Let's take a quick tour of the office. And, like, I don't want to be weird, but I really think it would be great if you maybe abbreviated your first name. I'm pretty sure it might make it easier for all concerned, including you. So most of the agents call me Dede, instead of Donna. Have you ever used a nickname?"

I hesitated. I'd actually never had that question pop up. I almost felt like the odd duck. I had a fleeting thought and turned to Donna and said, "I guess that would be okay. It feels strange to start a new job and suddenly have a new name. It's almost funny. It feels like Hollywood. But in truth, I have been called Shell by a few people in my past. What about that?"

Donna perked up immediately and stopped me there. "Shell is a great name," she said. "Let's just do that. I love it and think it suits you well. I bet that the agents will have an easy time remembering Shell. Yes, I do. I like it very much."

After a quick tour through the large office, she took me to the breakroom, where she explained the honor food box: everything in the carton of snacks was twenty-five cents; employees were to drop their change in the jar on the counter. She showed me how to make coffee by starting a fresh pot, pointed out the tea bags, and made a real point that we were in charge of having a fresh pot of coffee at all times, with emphasis on "fresh" and "all times." Up next were the Xerox machines. This seemed like a no-brainer, but she said the guys seemed unable to figure out how to add more paper whenever the red light came on and their copy didn't appear. She pointed out the office supplies closet with everything anybody might need. There were pencils and pens, paper clips and staples, notepads, extra copy paper, phone message pads, reams of paper, and well, I got the idea. Part of our job also included making copies of anything the agents needed. Finally, she was faced with explaining the phones. She took me to my desk. The phones had twelve lines — press red, hit that, pass it along, or take a message. The directory of names was available, listing the different extensions for everyone in the office. I felt good. I felt anxious. Dede Donna had done her part. We spent my entire first day together.

I was pretty sure I'd been exposed to everything I needed to know to do my job on this first day. I just hoped I'd remember it all. I was introduced to at least twenty agents as they came and went throughout the day, and there would be more. My first day on the new job flew by, and suddenly it was 5:00 p.m. I thought, *Will every day be as madcap as this?*

I couldn't wait to get home. So much to do. I had boxes and boxes of stuff waiting to be unpacked. The movers supposedly brought all of my furniture from my parents' storage, things they'd saved over the years for the three of us. I was the lucky one to have first pick of what's available since I was the first to have an apartment. I was so excited that Mom came over while I was at work today to oversee the movers and arrange a few things to help me get started.

When I got home (I love the sound of that — *home*!), Mom

and Dad were waiting for me, all smiles. It was obvious how excited they were for me. When I entered, my mom had the apartment all together and looking so nice. They had placed their older sofa, chairs, and tables. The sofa was a little tired, so Mom had gone out and found a ready-made slipcover at Pier 1 that was as near to perfect as I'd get for ready-made. I was in absolute awe of how great everything looked. I also was dead-tired. I still needed to go to the grocery for a few things, come home, fix dinner (or something like that), and start unpacking boxes.

I am probably most excited about my second bedroom. It will be my craft area. In college, I amassed a sizable quantity of artificial flowers and greenery. Everything is still in boxes, ready to be unpacked. My plan is to open the boxes and stack them on top of each other with the open side facing out. I'll have access to everything as needed. I don't have shelving for the room yet, but I know I want to get back to my favorite hobby.

My parents left me almost as soon as I got there. I drove just up the hill to Cooper and Martin Grocery and loaded a shopping cart. As I was putting everything away at home, I studied just exactly what I'd tossed in that cart. Along with your basic milk and eggs, I had bought several Stouffer's TV dinners. I love those things. My favorite by far is Escalloped Chicken and Noodles, and it would be dinner tonight! After popping that in the oven, I had forty-five minutes until it would be ready. I hate that it takes so long. I heard there's this new thing called a microwave oven that cooks stuff in a jiffy. But they aren't sure if it might cause infertility. No rush. More unpacking awaited. I wanted to get through as much as possible tonight so I could begin to feel fully settled.

After my meal of chicken and noodles over a piece of bread and some canned peas on the side, I was still starving. So I decided to attack my half gallon of chocolate ice cream and big bag of good and salty potato chips. I love that combo. I fixed three big scoops of ice cream and crushed two handfuls of potato chips over the top. Yummy, yummy, yummmmy! *I definitely think I will start my diet tomorrow,* I thought. *Yeah, right. Didn't I tell myself that this morning?*

Schmell(a)/Shell

June 17–20, 1976

Thursday and Friday were much like my first day at work. I met more agents and began to solve the mysteries of the real estate business; it was pretty fascinating. But let's face it — there is still so very much I need to learn! Donna and I became fast friends overnight. She told me who was who and dished with abandon. Seems funny to be a part of something professional like this. The hierarchy, best this, better that, this week's BMOC in sales — it feels a bit like high school, only this time the games are played by adults. So all is good on the job front.

I've been getting to know my downstairs neighbor, and I find I like him quite a bit. He is a sweet older guy. Tallish, sort of thin, and with thinning white-blond Tom Petty hair, he always seems to be in a T-shirt and faded bib overalls. He asked me to call him Wally rather than Mr. Walloppe. According to him, he's also known as "the Inspector" among a group of longtime friends. It's a handle he admittedly enjoys, a souvenir of his career with the FDA.

The things he makes from twigs and tree branches are incredible. I've asked him to make a chair and ottoman for my living room. His stuff is so cool! I'm contemplating asking him to create a new coffee table base for me. I could buy a glass top at Pier 1 to finish it off. I have to hand it to him — he keeps our little yard neat and tidy. I think the gardening might even supplement part of his rent. Who knows? I feel bad sometimes that he's all by himself. He keeps a photograph of his late wife in a twig frame he made himself.

On Saturday afternoon, I was feeling pretty good about my apartment and my life. Everything had its place, including me. I heard an unexpected knock on my door. Peering through the peephole, I discovered Wally standing outside. When I opened the door, he held out a ceramic pot filled with the prettiest assortment of African violets, all finished with a silk ribbon.

Wally looked at me and said, "I just wanted to give you a proper little housewarming gift, that's all. I am so very happy to have such a lovely young lady like you as my new neighbor."

With no intention of letting a tear fall, I sniffled. "Aw, you are so kind, and this is so sweet and so unnecessary. Thank you so much!" With a deep breath, I continued, "Please, come in. I just made a pitcher of fresh lemonade. I can open a bag of pretzels. I want you to see what I've done with the place in the past few days!"

He stepped in, and I walked him around. He seemed genuinely impressed with what I'd done so far. I asked him to have a seat and sit a spell. I poured a tall, icy glass of lemonade for each of us, dumped pretzels in a bowl, and sat myself down. We gabbed and laughed for way over an hour, completely enjoying each other's company. It's definitely a good thing having a neighbor who's a solid friend.

The rest of the day seemed to slip away. I went back to Kmart and Pier 1 for a few more things. When I finished running around, it was suddenly 7:00 p.m. I was bone-tired and totally ready to get into my schlumpy lounging outfit. I love to hang out in my sweatpants and an MTSU tee shirt (I have many) when I'm home alone. A bug in my brain insisted there was so much more to do before I would be thoroughly settled and I should keep moving, but I wanted more to catch up on some TV. And it was definitely feeding time again. So once more, I pulled a frozen Stouffer's TV dinner from the freezer. I love their lasagna. It calls for fifty-five minutes in the oven, but I like it a little crusty around the edges, so I cook it for over an hour. Oh so tasty.

Shortly after I popped dinner in the oven, my phone rang. I answered and immediately heard the slight wheeze of a harmonica from the other end. Sorina. She can more easily start a conversation if she begins with her harmonica. Somehow a few brief notes help her glide into her first words, without stammering through them or blurting them out. Once she gets started, her stammer subsides, and her conversation becomes pretty fluid. The harmonica is definitely a crutch, but as long as it works for her, harmonica on. She usually wears one on a chain around her neck.

We stayed on the phone for two hours, talking about everything under the sun. I managed to eat my lasagna while we spoke, washing it down with a Dr Pepper. As we approached nine thirty, I signed off. Before disconnecting she asked me if we could meet at Flanda Castle's on Monday morning for coffee and muffins. I agreed and said, "Until then! Have a great day tomorrow, and I'll see you Monday. Same time and same place. Love you!" *Click*. Lights out.

Sunday was finally a day to myself. I have two main hobbies, knitting and making flower arrangements. I can spend hours poring over books and magazines on flower arranging. At the moment, I take great satisfaction in working with artificial flowers from my inventory. I fret that I've stockpiled way too many pieces and still spend much too much on all of it. But then I make something with it, and I'm happy, and the guilt passes. I subscribe to gardening and floral-oriented magazines such as *Scents into Cents, Flowers Today, Daisy's Daffodils and Dieffenbachias,* and *The Life of a Flower.* I've amassed seven years' worth of past issues of the things. Why I didn't just try to find a job working for a florist is beyond me. I do know why — I needed more than minimum wage to survive. And I want to do more than repetitious stock arrangements!

Helena Montgomery

Saturday, June 19, 1976

Last night was utterly dreamy. Johnny Montana is one of the finest men I have ever met, let alone gone out with. He is such a gentleman and looks like such a player. We went to this chic new restaurant down in Franklin. It only took twenty minutes to get there driving down Hillsboro Road. The name of the place was Paris á la Nuit — obviously, French cuisine. The waiters all wore black suits, white shirts, and black bow ties. Lighting in the oak-paneled room was dramatic and low, offering a tremendously intimate atmosphere. Tables were covered in white linen cloths, and the white linen napkins were folded like fanned peacock tails. Footsteps were silenced by the dense merlot-colored carpet. A recessed pin spotlight shone straight down from the invisible black ceiling, making each table feel cozy and private.

We had a wonderful time — or a *wanterfool teema*, I told him, maintaining my faux accent. One of these days I need to let go of all of that. Johnny and I talked nonstop for almost three hours. We missed the beginning of the movie he had wanted to see, so we decided to go to Baskin-Robbins for an ice cream instead. As he walked me to my door, he asked if I would like to go out again. I almost couldn't say yes fast enough. He gave me a quick good-night kiss on the cheek, turned, strolled to his car, and was off.

Once inside, I felt that odd emptiness that comes out of nowhere sometimes. I'd had such a magical evening with Johnny. It was hard not to show my giddy thrill at being with him. I made myself act *demure.* Guys can get weirded out when a girl is overly expressive. Anyway, that was our Friday night. I am home now with myself. I can just be me, not her, not *Helena*.

Shell

Monday, June 21, 1976

Since my graduation from college, all the days have seemed to fly by. I set my alarm for 6:00 a.m., and it never forgets to ring. This morning, I got out of bed and walked over to my window. The sun was already shining through my new white eyelet curtains. They had come ready-made with a rod pocket already sewn in, and I had picked up hardware with brass-plated café rods. I'd installed the hardware and then threaded the rods through the prefab pockets and hung them, proud of myself for a job well done. Easy-peasy.

I went into the living room and was disappointed to realize that I'd been so tired the prior evening that I hadn't put away my latest floral arrangement and the mess left from its creation. When I play with my artificial flowers, I do my best each time to come up with something new and unique. Last night, I'd imagined a piece for a huge entry table beneath a colossal crystal chandelier hanging from an eighteen-foot ceiling in a ballroom set up for a large charity auction. The arrangement before me from last night was enormous, maybe five feet around. It took up most of my living room. I had to laugh. It was actually quite good. Just one woman's opinion, but who else matters? So I took out my Instamatic camera and snapped a couple of pictures. With that done, I scrambled to disassemble the thing and put the flowers and greenery back into their boxes. It was time to shower, dress, and meet Sorina as planned at Flanda Castle's at seven thirty.

After a quick shower and a little makeup, I needed an outfit. I threw on my melon polyester dress, opened my accessory drawer and grabbed a matching melon barrette for my hair, then slipped into my white patent leather clogs. I love those clogs. The four-inch cork platform soles make me feel great. I can only wish I were that tall. I scoured the rest of the drawer and pulled out a white beaded necklace I made years ago. It was perfect, hanging below the gathered collar of the dress. The finishing touch was my wide white patent leather belt with the big brass buckle. I would have felt overdressed if not for the clogs.

I cannot wait for tonight. It's Monday — Wash-My-Hair Night. My hair is so nasty-greasy that I think tonight is definitely a triple wash-rinse-repeat kind of night! I have to get into a new habit of washing my hair at least every other day. Next wash, Wednesday! Sorry, Lulu.

The morning was so pretty, and the temperature for June so comfortable, that I decided to walk to work. It wasn't all that far, and Flanda Castle's was on the way. I went off down the sidewalk along my street and turned left onto Richard Jones Road and another sidewalk. All in all, the walk would take about fifteen minutes. My clogs were super comfortable, the walk was easy and pleasant, and this body always needs the exercise.

Midway up Richard Jones Road, a shiny black Mustang convertible approached, top down. It was Helena, driving with her classic "don't mess with the hair" black turban scarf wrapped around her head. As she neared, I could see she was wearing a black halter-top dress. This outfit, form-fitting as always, had a twist-top neckline with a center slit that cut from the base of her throat down, to expose a peek at the top of her black lacy bra. Welcome to cleavage city. She had a black feather boa draped over the passenger seat, restrained by a seatbelt.

Helena slowed down and pulled up next to me. "Dahleen, Ah neet to telt yous somting."

Like I was surprised to see her, I said, "Oh! Hi, Helena! What's up?"

Accidentally hitting her horn as she leaned and turned, and speaking rather loudly, she said, "Hawnee, yous neet to FTW." With that she honked briefly but purposefully and, full-throat laughing, drove away.

I looked and saw Esmerelda standing at the end of the block. She had seen and heard the entire exchange. She had spoken to Sorina this morning and decided to join us at Flanda's. I met up with her a minute later.

Esmerelda looked furious as she said, "I can't believe that sleazy little slut."

Truly puzzled, I looked at my sister and asked, "Why do you say that?"

Esmerelda, ever loving, looked at me and replied, "I guess you don't know what FTW means, do you?"

With a blank face I said, "Not a clue."

Esmerelda remained quiet and composed, then looked up at me, almost with pity, and said, "For your information, FTW is an acronym for 'Free the Wedgie.' Helena was intentionally being mean to say that to you, especially at that volume and in public!"

Pulling my dress away from my hips, I was totally flummoxed. I looked at my sister. "I guess she could have been a little more discreet. But honestly, I've never heard that term before. It's certainly kinda strange, don't you think?"

Turning to head to Flanda's, Esmerelda said, "Whatever. Helena just has no couth. I don't think she even knows the basic definition of manners. She's just another wannabe and a big slut to top it off."

The Lapone Family Home

Monday, June 21, 1976
8:45 a.m.

Yvonna and Frank sat at their kitchen table, finishing breakfast. Yvonna had prepared Frank's regular breakfast of bacon and eggs, two slices of rye toast, coffee, and orange juice. She was finishing up her normal bowl of cottage cheese and peaches. She loved peaches, especially the white peaches that were now in season. She'd picked them up, along with an assortment of vegetables, last Friday at the Amish produce stand in Green Hills, a regular fixture during the summer months. Breakfast had become a ritual for them. They would discuss each of their plans for the day ahead and what the girls had on their agendas. Sunday and Monday were Frank's days off from managing the grocery. Over the years, on his free days, Frank had been gradually getting up later and later. Yvonna was semi-retired from her years of door-to-door cosmetic sales. She had thoroughly wearied of the rejection, of people telling her to go away. Esmerelda and Sorina still lived with them, but at eighteen and twenty, the girls were pretty much independent and would grab a bite to eat on their way out the door.

Their kitchen was small but workable. The room was bright and cheerful in the mornings, with windows facing the southeast. The cabinets were white and needed painting. The counters were worn teal Formica, and the flooring a black-and-white checkerboard linoleum. The rectangular kitchen table with its white laminate top and chrome legs had easily seated six. The matching chairs had been part of a set and were now covered in an iridescent teal vinyl. A large wood-framed cork bulletin board was on the wall behind the long side of the breakfast table. It was covered with business cards, invitations, and a few postcards.

Yvonna got up from the table with a few dishes and headed to the sink. Frank followed with the remaining dishes then returned to the table with a bottle of Windex and a wad of paper towels to clean up. As he walked, he switched on the TV. *The Today Show* with Jim Hartz was still on as he increased the volume. Yvonna was gazing out the window above the kitchen sink. The hot water was on full force, bubbling with soapy suds. The sun was shining gloriously on this beautiful morning as she gazed across her patio.

As he stared at the screen, Frank mumbled something to himself and then said aloud, "I am so sick of hearing about all of this ridiculous news — Karen Ann Quinlan with her ventilator and Sanjay Gandhi's compulsory sterilization program. It really wears me out!" He continued to stare at the passing news.

Yvonna started, "Oh, look at this cute little chipmunk on the sill. I think he has a nut or something in his mouth. He's so—"

Suddenly, an explosion and ear-piercing crash broke the idyllic morning. Yvonna screamed, "*Aaahhh! Help!* I can't believe this! Frank! Look!"

The kitchen window was smashed to smithereens, and Yvonna was flat on her back on the floor, screaming, "Get this thing off of me!" Her screams turned to sobs as she angrily cried, "Frank, get this bird off of me! Now!"

Frank was momentarily transfixed as he stared at the implausible scene before him. His wife was on the floor, screaming and bleeding from her forehead, while over her lay a dead hawk with a deader chipmunk clutched in its beak.

Yvonna gingerly lifted her head and said, "Whaaaa ...?" and then, just as gingerly, laid her head back on the floor and was out cold.

Frank jumped to grab a towel from the counter and frantically soaked it with cold water from the tap. He dropped to his knees and, ever so carefully, gently laid the sopping cloth over Yvonna's head. He quickly opened the nearest drawer, pulled out a stack of kitchen towels, and placed them under her head. She had lacerations all over her face and neck. Blood was soaking her blouse, dripping down her neck and onto the floor. Frank was terrified; he jumped up and raced for the telephone to call an ambulance.

The woman who answered the call immediately responded, "Nine-one-one. What is your emergency?"

As fast as he could get the words out of his mouth, Frank explained to her what had just happened, where they lived, and that an ambulance was needed as soon as possible. The agent calmly asked several pertinent questions as Frank's anxiety flamed. While they spoke, she was signaling to alert the emergency staff. She asked Frank to hold for just a moment while she relayed the situation to the awaiting crew, informing them where to go and what to expect. The agent then told Frank that help had been dispatched and was already en route to his residence.

For a few seconds, Yvonna's eyelids fluttered. "Frank, what happ—" And as suddenly as the bird had crashed, her eyes flew open. She slowly whispered, "How long have I been down here? What happened? Was that a bird that flew through the window? Look at me! I am covered in glass!" With that, she closed her eyes and once again lay totally still on her black-and-white linoleum floor, breathing quietly.

Frank was sitting on the floor next to Yvonna when the doorbell rang. He yelled out, "Door's open! We're in the kitchen! Follow your noses around through the dining room!"

The two-man emergency crew came running into the kitchen about the time Yvonna began to come around. The scene was horrific. One of the crew ran back out of the house and returned with a gurney and a third medic. The first attendant was leaning over Yvonna, checking her vital signs. He made brief notations and quickly snapped a few photographs. The other two medics loaded Yvonna onto the gurney and wheeled her out to the waiting ambulance.

Frank breathlessly told the attendants that he wanted to ride with them to the hospital, that he was her husband. They pulled him in and sped off with sirens blaring to Vanderbilt Hospital.

In the ambulance, the two attendants in the back went to work. One hooked her up to oxygen and monitored her blood pressure and heart rate while the other attendant began gingerly removing small pieces of glass from her face and neck. With Yvonna now on oxygen, the first attendant pulled out a container of sterilized pads and began to lightly dab the splotches of blood. Yvonna was awake, quietly moaning in pain.

While Frank held her hand, his panic returned at the realization that their house had been left wide-open, and the window above the kitchen sink was smashed. Then the image of the dead bird and chipmunk on the floor by the kitchen sink made him twitch. The ambulance reached the hospital, and Yvonna was admitted through emergency. As the staff started triage, Frank used the pay phone to call his neighbor Ralph and explain the situation. Ralph and Karen had lived next door to them for twenty-plus years. He told Ralph about a roll of polyurethane he had in his workshop that could cover the shattered window if Ralph would be so kind, and he asked him to bag and toss the bird and then lock the house up. Frank knew it was a lot to ask. Ralph assured Frank he'd deal with it all — not a problem. Before signing off, Ralph told Frank that he and Karen were there if Frank and Yvonna needed anything — if there was anything at all, please just call them.

After the physician's examination, Yvonna was checked into the hospital and wheeled into a room on the second floor. She had suffered a very mild concussion and still needed more small shards removed from her face. She was prescribed medication for pain and prevention of other possible complications. The attending physician spoke to Frank outside of her room and told him Yvonna would need to remain in hospital for observation for possibly two days. While they were in the hall, a nurse assistant was dressing her in a drafty hospital gown and hooking her up to monitors and IVs for medications and hydration.

Charlotte Webber had made it her business and routine to stop by the hospital on a daily basis. She originally had gained entrance as a concerned citizen willing to volunteer to help with the morale of the injured and sick. This also provided her the opportunity to be ready to land and cover any story that might work for either *The Post* or *The Eye.*

Today, Charlotte Webber felt like she had won the prize. From the arrival of Yvonna's ambulance to her admittance to her room, Charlotte had followed the entire scenario. She always had a steno pad and pen at the ready. She had recently added a tiny Panasonic cassette recorder to her arsenal and had it tucked away in her purse. From the very beginning, Charlotte was there. Outside of the emergency room, she had donned a white doctor's coat over her street clothes and positioned herself in the hall. No one took notice while she leaned on her left shoulder, head down, and took copious notes on her steno pad. She followed Yvonna's gurney to the second floor and watched as Yvonna was wheeled into a room and put on her bed. She waited in the hall as the nurse finished and left. Charlotte knew Yvonna was still in a mild state of shock and it would be best to leave her alone. Tucking her steno pad and purse in her bag, she got on an empty elevator and removed the white coat, which she neatly folded and placed over her arm and purse. When the doors opened, she made her way back to the emergency room waiting area, where she took a seat, hoping for another jackpot.

June 21, 1976

9:35 a.m.

While Yvonna was being admitted to Vanderbilt Hospital, Helena was pulling her car into a spot across from the entrance to the bank. She had just left Johnny. They had met for breakfast at a Waffle House on Nolensville Road, a location far enough from any of the bank's branches to not risk his being seen fraternizing with a bank employee.

As she turned her car off, another automobile was backing into the spot next to her, bobbing up and down as it finally came to a shuddering halt. It was an old and dilapidated Lincoln Continental whose white paint had weathered badly. Dried mud flared up the sides from tires that had seen better days. The driver of the Lincoln wasn't in any better condition than the car but surprisingly could only have been in his early twenties. The poor thing was scrawny and had long, stringy brown hair and an immaturely thin mustache. His passenger looked equally bilious, but instead of gaunt, this one was pimply and plump.

With her eyes glued to the mirror and intent on freshening her makeup, Helena paid no further mind to the Lincoln's arrival. She required more foundation, and her movable mole needed replacing. The final act of this production was her hair, and for that she had to step outside the car. She walked around to the rear of the Mustang and opened the trunk. She reached for a small overnight case and popped the snaps. The inside was packed with beauty supplies and accessories. She grabbed the can of Aqua Net. She bent her head forward, flipping her hair over her face and letting her hair hang almost to the ground. She sprayed the can of Aqua Net for almost twenty seconds, thoroughly coating her long black locks. Snapping her head back, she vigorously fluffed her hair into place while the fog of the spray drifted and enveloped the Lincoln and its occupants.

Dumbfounded, their mouths agape, the two young men in the Lincoln stared wide-eyed at Helena. Straightening and standing tall and erect, she turned innocently, revealing her voluptuous profile to the occupants of the Lincoln. Dressed in all black, with her deep cleavage easily mistakable as the Mariana trench, she was a sight to behold. Helena had no doubts she had an amazing, shapely body; she worked at it. Once caught in her net, a man could not escape unless she cut the threads herself.

A little too loudly, the scraggly driver of the Lincoln, staring straight at Helena, mumbled to his cohort, "Damn, will you look at that?"

A startled Helena, now suddenly aware of her motley audience, turned toward them and smiled. Demurely cocking her head, she breathed, "Allo dare, fellose. Eese a booteeful dase!"

Mr. Scrawny behind the steering wheel grinned widely and said, "Excuse me, ma'am, but I do rightly believe you are the prettiest thing I have ever laid my eyes on."

Helena smiled back, thanked them, took a tissue from her purse, dabbed her wrist, and then tucked the tissue into her cleavage. She closed the trunk and walked to the bank with her hips swaying gently like trees in a summer breeze.

At this same time, the Lapone girls were across the street, paying for their breakfasts at Flanda Castle's. Over coffee, Schmellda had mentioned to her sisters that she had been given a nickname at

Hill and Garden: Shell. Sorina and Esmerelda had squealed with delight. They agreed that from that moment forward, they would forever call her Shell. Esmerelda thought the name so much more current. Sorina admitted that the name Schmellda, besides being peculiar, just didn't fit her personality anymore, if it ever had.

As Sorina opened her purse to pay, the phone next to the pie case behind the counter began to ring. Standing behind the register, Minnie grabbed the receiver. The three sisters saw her cheery expression turn to shock and concern. The girls listened intently to Minnie's end of the conversation: "What?" she exclaimed. "Is she okay?" Then they heard her mumble, "Yes, they're here right now, in front of me at the register."

As the phone call continued, Minnie interjected, "I can't believe this! It's just so strange! Yes, yes, I will tell them where you are and that Yvonna is doing well. Honestly, Frank, this sounds like it could have been a lot worse … Well, good for her. I will tell the girls right now!" After a few more "uh-huhs" and "okays," she disconnected, cradling the receiver.

The girls stared with anticipation at Minnie as she turned again to face them.

Esmerelda was first out of the blocks. "What happened? What has happened to our Momma?"

Shell chimed in as well. "Minnie, tell us! From the way you talked, it sounds like something horrible has happened to our mother."

Sorina started to stutter but then reached for the harmonica on the chain around her neck. She blew a brief note, and her voice glided into the conversation. "Where? What happened? Where is Mom? Is she going to be okay?"

Minnie looked at the sisters. "Girls, please calm down. Right now, it seems everything is okay. But it's just the darnedest thing I ever heard. Seems your mother was at the kitchen sink, washing up breakfast dishes, when a huge hawk came flying through the window after catching a chipmunk that'd been munching a nut on the kitchen windowsill. Stupid thing smashed the window, breaking it into a million pieces, then went on and crashed into your mother. It had the dead chipmunk in its beak, and the force knocked your mother to the floor. Apparently, from what your dad says, she was unconscious for a few minutes. She suffered a very mild concussion. She's doing better now. They're keeping her in the hospital at least overnight for observation, just as a precaution. She's going to be just fine."

Flanda, who had heard the girls' commotion from the kitchen, came out to the cash register to see what was going on. Minnie now repeated to Flanda her entire telephone conversation with Frank, adding more details about the emergency room, physician, and medications. The girls were silent and spellbound as they listened to the full scenario, including the part about claw marks on Yvonna's face and upper body.

When it seemed Minnie had nothing further to report, Esmerelda turned to her sisters and said, "I'm not just going to stand here and do nothing. I am going over to the hospital right now. There has to be something I can be doing for Momma. Sorina, you and Shell go on to work. Your jobs are much more important than my ditzy little gig at the card shop. They can get along without me. I'll call you both and let you know what's going on as soon as I can."

Minnie interjected, "Your father told me things are under control, but still, I don't blame you one bit for wanting to go. When you phone your sisters, please call us with any updates, too."

Esmerelda was the first out the door, followed by Shell and Sorina. Sorina walked with Shell to her office. They were both late, but that didn't bother either one a bit. Even though it was only her fourth day on the job, Shell knew Donna would understand. Last night while on the phone with Sorina, Shell had shared that she didn't think the receptionist job was really for her. She hoped she'd be able to last until she could find something for which she had more passion. As they walked, Shell went on again about how it was such a mundane situation lacking creativity, in an office environment that bored her to distraction. She told Sorina, again, that she would give the job two more months before she started looking in earnest for something else. The thing she liked most about her job, maybe really the only thing she liked, was getting out to see all the different styles of homes and interiors. She loved seeing the dramatic things people were doing with wall colors. She told her sister about one room she had just seen. It had navy-blue walls with white trim and ceiling. The upholstery was covered in a multicolored Matisse-like pattern. The area rug covering the hardwood floors was the newest rage, a natural grass woven into a herringbone pattern called sisal. When Sorina yawned, Shell switched tack and began to explain how Donna, her work partner, was teaching her how to compose fact sheets for the homes that agents had under contract to sell. It was a new responsibility that actually piqued her interest, at least a little. Donna had explained that when Shell was writing the fact sheets, it was very important for her to see the new houses in person so she could fully describe them on the listing documents.

It was a little past 10:00 a.m. Shell and Sorina were standing on the sidewalk across from the bank. Shell was wrapping up the conversation and telling her sister to have a good day. The hot summer sun was already burning down into the pavement. Shell's melon polyester dress was clinging to every inch of her body like plastic wrap. Her skin glistened from perspiration, and oil began to ooze from her every pore.

Looking across the parking lot toward the bank, she spotted the ratty Lincoln and mumbled to Sorina, "Will you look at that heap over there? It's a total land barge!" As Sorina glanced over, Shell continued, "And Helena's car is parked right next to it. Hope they don't scratch her paint. There'll be hell to pay."

Sorina knew she was late, and it was getting later, but she started chattering away about her job at the cleaners. She was a part-time cashier at New Colony Cleaners next to the Cooper and Martin Grocery up the street. She still wanted to tell Shell about the prissy woman who had come in the week before and complained about a dress she'd had cleaned. She had accused the cleaners of shrinking her dress. Miss Priss had put it on, and it was suddenly too small. Sorina giggled as she said to her sister, "Yeah, sure it sh-sh-shrunk. I think it might fit again i-i-if she had her j-jaws wired shut. My m-manager apologized because the w-woman was some big m-mucky-muck socialite."

As she babbled on about the woman, Sorina noticed that Shell was staring at something different from the car across the parking lot. As Sorina turned to look, the doors of the bank flew open, banging against their jambs. Without warning, a staccato of gunfire pierced the quiet — *pop, pop, pop,* in rapid succession. It sounded like metal was being hit. Shell watched two young men run toward the sad-looking Lincoln. One of the men clutched a blue duffel bag to his chest as he shot his automatic revolver into the air. At the same time, Sorina turned toward her sister, hand to her mouth, eyes wide-open, and began to scream. In a split second, one of the pops turned into a ping and then a clang. A bullet had hit the metallic "No Parking" sign directly in front of Sorina, dislodging it from its post. The sign rocketed the short distance and hit Sorina flat on the backside of her head. As she slipped to the ground, she saw the license plate of the fleeing Continental in the reflection off her sister's oily forehead. The Lincoln careened away, its squealing tires leaving black skid marks on the pavement. Sorina was now lying in an unconscious heap on the sidewalk. Shell screamed bloody hell.

As the Lincoln sped away, a bright orange and white Volkswagen van covered in flower decals, with "The Dancing Flower" in swirly script and a phone number on its sides, turned a corner and came rolling down the street toward the chaos. The van swung into the lot and pulled into a spot in front of where Shell was still screaming over her sister Sorina's inert body.

Eddy Francis jumped out of the vehicle and rushed to the girls. "What the hell happened here? This is nuts!"

Shell, in panic, introduced herself and frantically told Eddy what had just happened to her sister. She gently moved Sorina's hair off her face and heard her sister moan as her eyes began to open. Eddy was fanning Sorina with a newspaper and directed Shell to grab whatever she could find in his van that was flat and soft, to put under Sorina's head. He stressed "flat" in case she had a neck injury. He was smart enough to leave her exactly as she was until paramedics arrived and could deal with her injury properly.

Eddy said, "Make sure she can breathe. She's got a whopper of a lump on the back of her head."

Shell told him, "That's where the sign struck her after the bullet hit the post."

Sorina's eyes were open, but she was obviously dazed and bewildered. Tears streaming down her face, she looked into Shell's eyes and said, "Wh-what in the world j-just hit me? I know it wasn't a s-sudden thought."

That's when Shell began to sob. Uncannily, Sorina was trying to joke about what was truly a weird situation. Shell knew her sister was completely confused.

Eddy ran toward the bank to call for additional help. He bumped into Daisy Featherdale, the executive secretary of the bank, at its entrance. She was running to the entry doors holding a sheet of paper with "CLOSED" boldly hand-printed in letters big enough to see from a distance. Eddy told her about Sorina's condition outside on the sidewalk. Daisy let him know she'd already called 911 and the police. She taped the sign to the door and told Eddy to sit tight. As Daisy looked up the street and over at the situation on the sidewalk, her distress was obvious. She yelled to the three, "Help is on the way! We were just robbed, and we have injuries inside. I called 911 a while ago, and the police and ambulances should be here very soon. I thought I heard sirens when I was inside."

The once-quiet morning in Green Hills was penetrated by sirens wailing in the distance, becoming increasingly louder as they sped ever closer.

Shell yelled to Daisy, "I can hear the sirens now. You're wonderful! Thank you!"

On any normal day, the bank was a spotless and perfectly organized, smoothly running institution. At this moment, it was in shambles. The bank manager, John Dunkerly, and the bank guard were looking into Helena Montgomery's small teller cubicle. Each cubicle had an open area with a high counter facing the lobby. The cubicles' raised flooring allowed the tellers to sit and be at eye level with their customers. Each cubicle had two money drawers, each with its own specific cash distribution. The second drawer had a special stack of bills containing a red-dye bomb. Five minutes after removal, the dye bomb would detonate and stain the money, rendering it useless for the robber.

Helena's teller door stood ajar. John Dunkerly and the guard crouched in Helena's booth and began softly repeating her name. Helena's limp and lifeless body lay slumped on the floor, leaning against the wall of her workspace. One leg was tucked under her, the other projected straight out. Spittle trickled from her mouth and dripped down her chin. She would not be happy to be seen in this condition, hair and makeup in disarray, her dress disheveled. On the wall, a red smear streaked diagonally down and behind her head. Daisy, on the other side of the teller window, was telling Dunkerly and the guard that help was on the way. The other three tellers huddled together in a far corner of the bank, terrified and talking rapid-fire about what had just happened.

Dunkerly was trying to rouse Helena. "Helena, can you hear me? Give me a sign that you are okay, please! Helena, say something."

Daisy pointed to Helena and said, "Look at the wall next to her head! It looks like a bullet hole!"

John Dunkerly looked intently at Helena and turned to Daisy. "Oh my god, I think she may have been shot!"

"What?" Daisy screamed as she finally broke, tears starting to run down her face. "How did this ever happen?"

Hearing her scream, the other three tellers ran to her side.

Cathy Morgan, a teller in the cubicle next to Helena's, was still shaking and now began turning bright red. "Look!" she yelped, pointing to the top of Helena's right breast. "Look, there's a hole in her dress! It looks like a bullet hole."

Dunkerly went white as a sheet. He had been a branch manager for eight years, and this was his first robbery. He didn't know what to do at this point. One minute, it had been just another beautiful day, and the next, his bank had become a war zone. John said, "I wish I could get my hands on those two little shits! I would chain them to the back of my car and drag them to the police station! Where in hell are the police and the ambulance?"

The flesh around Helena's swollen right eye was slowly darkening to purple. The entire right side of her face had bloated such that her cheek was the size of a hen's egg. Her breathing was shallow. Dunkerly felt for a pulse. With the slightest hint of relief on his face and inhaling deeply, he turned to the others and sighed, "Her pulse is strong. Pretty sure she's okay for now."

Daisy, on the other hand, was not so stable. In fact, she was beside herself and nauseous. She kept mumbling and repeating, "I cannot believe this. How did it even happen? This is terrifying." Once again she looked around and took in the carnage. The bank was riddled everywhere with bullet holes. Glass was shattered. Sheets of paper, normally in their neat little piles, were strewn high and low like confetti. "Look up there! How did they manage that?"

All heads spun, and eyes focused up fifteen feet to the top of a corner window. A bullet had apparently dislodged one end of a drapery rod and left the rod dangling by one end. It would not be long before the weight of the drapes, which hung bunched to an end, would take down the other end of the rod.

With Helena temporarily secure under the watchful eyes of Cathy and the guard, Dunkerly darted to the front of the bank and surveyed the scene outside the open doors. What he didn't see unnerved him. There was not a cop or ambulance in sight, though he could hear sirens somewhere out there. Returning his focus back inside the bank, he spotted Daisy. When he came within earshot of her, he asked, almost pleading, "You did push the panic button?"

Daisy somehow managed to stifle her anger. "You know I did — *and* you know I called 911. I can't believe after all these years you'd even ask that question! They should all be here any minute! This really is all too much!"

As Daisy's anger flamed, the wail of screaming sirens came to an abrupt quiet as, one after another, police cars and ambulances came to a stop in front of the bank. Cops and EMTs scattered across the parking lot and into the bank. Yellow crime tape was quickly deployed to mark the entire crime scene. Outside of the taped area, folks from across the neighborhood, responding to the sound of sirens and the sight of patrol cars, began to congregate. Daisy peered out at the growing crowd. "Great! Lookie-loos!"

John Dunkerly ran directly to the first officer he saw. "We've been robbed, and they had guns! It happened about ten minutes ago, right after we opened. We have a casualty inside!" Dunkerly turned toward an approaching paramedic and said, "It appears to me that it might be serious." As he pointed to Daisy, "She will show you where Miss Montgomery is."

A voice was heard from the crowd near the sidewalk, yelling, "Help is needed over here! Quick! Can one of you please come?"

The crowd parted, forming an alley from the bank to where Sorina still lay in the middle of the sidewalk. Two paramedics from yet another ambulance rushed to Sorina. One of the paramedics shouted to no officer in particular, "We need more crime tape over here! Please stay back, people!" He was already checking her vitals.

As an officer ran to his cruiser to radio for additional police backup, he yelled back above the crowd, "Roger that! I'll be there as soon as I can."

Sorina tried to raise her head. "My head is killing me," she groaned. "Where am I?"

The paramedics secured Sorina's neck. Then, as gently as possible, they placed her on a gurney, rolled her to the waiting ambulance, and carefully loaded her in. As the doors were closing, she blearily looked out to Shell and whispered, "I'm gonna be fine. Don't worry." The ambulance sped away.

Eddy looked at Shell and said, "Come on. Hop in the van. I can take you to the hospital so you can be with your sister."

The inside of the bank was quieting, but still in chaos. It remained a mess, with papers and shards of wood strewn everywhere. As the interior looked now, it would be easy to imagine the robbers had used a machine gun. The police were questioning a bedraggled Daisy at her desk. The paramedics were hovering over Helena as they carefully placed her still-limp body onto a gurney.

Helena began to mumble something. At first, whatever she garbled was unintelligible. Then, clear as a bell and in the deepest drawl known to the South, she said, "What is happenin' here? Where'm ah? One minute ah was waitin' on a man; next thang ah knows, he's apointin' a gun or somethin' o'er my counter, sayin', 'Gimme all your money.' Then he hands over a blue bag and says, 'Fill 'er up, little sistuh!'" She took in a breath and a thought. "Oh shit!" she said as she realized she had spoken for the first time in forever without her Frenchified accent. She had slipped and drawled words, sentences even, out loud that people could hear, in her real voice. Then to herself, inside her head, she said it again. *Oh shit.*

Helena immediately began to fret and worry. She could feel her heart racing. She knew without knowing that she had to make an effort to compose herself.

As the gurney rolled, the paramedic saw her blood pressure rising as her heartbeat quickened. He said quietly, "Please, ma'am. Calm down. Just take it easy. You've been shot and lost a little blood. We've got you now, and we'll take good care of you." Though she was lying motionless on the gurney, he saw that her heart rate had spiked to 135 and knew he had to do everything in his power to calm her. He looked again at the small amount of blood that had now dried on the shoulder of her armless dress. Strapped to the gurney, Helena was wheeled out of the bank and toward a waiting ambulance.

The crowd outside the bank had grown, sizably, and was abuzz like a beehive, jabbering about what they had seen and "knew as a fact" or not. The doors of the bank were opening. Conversations paused. Bees must have flown. The paramedics were wheeling a body out on a gurney. The quiet was quickly broken by a woman standing in the very front of the crowd, nearest the bank's doors. "That's Helena Montgomery!"

Another voice piped in, "I wonder what happened to her?" The hive had been poked, and the bees were back, jabbering again.

Once in the ambulance, Helena was connected to an IV and fluids were started. She was awake and alert. She was not talking. Paramedics always want to get patients to the hospital as quickly as possible, and with Helena's elevated heart rate and loss of blood, they were moving as fast as they could. They were concerned there could be possible internal bleeding. Gunshots that showed no signs of an exit were dangerous and of major concern. The driver radioed ahead to Vanderbilt Hospital's emergency department to have staff waiting and ready for a gunshot victim.

At the Hospital

Registered-nurse sisters Octavia and Olga Nussell were pacing outside of the emergency department with several other emergency room staff. Both were ready for anything. They were always ready. They knew at the moment that they had a scheduled situation about to arrive. Too many times, a car would just pull up without warning, and the ER team simply sprang into immediate action. Speedy action, thoroughness, and knowledgeable quick-thinking were what the ER was all about. As the ambulance pulled in and came to a halt, its rear doors flew open, and Helena was wheeled out and taken to the first available room for triage.

Octavia unstrapped Helena from the gurney and, with the help of two technicians, slid the new patient onto an examining table, IVs still attached. A nurse assistant separated the wires from an EKG machine, and Octavia began applying the leads. Wide awake and alert to her surroundings, Helena lifted her head and, in possibly her worst Frenchified accent ever, said, "Whas yous doins?"

Octavia looked her in the eye. "Hon, you've been shot. We don't know yet how serious your condition may be. I will tell you that you're one lucky lady. We are here to help you. Please, just lie still and let us figure this out."

Dr. Fishman heard the conversation as he was entering the

room and stopped. He knew immediately that this patient needed sedation. He took out his pad and scribbled a prescription, which he handed to Nurse Olga. "Please get this immediately. I need her lights out before we proceed." He then stepped into the examining room.

Helena gazed at the doctor and said, "Ah doan sink anyzsing ees ron. Ah meense Ah feelse preeety goose. Wass averybodey worreese abu?"

It took only minutes before Nurse Olga was back in the room, prescribed liquid sedative bag in hand.

Dr. Fishman explained to Helena, "Don't worry, Miss Montgomery. You couldn't possibly have more competent care than you're already receiving from the Nussell sisters. And I've been attending physician in this emergency room for twelve years. You will receive only the best care this institution has to offer."

With that, Nurse Olga connected the bag of ketamine to Helena's IV. The general anesthetic would render her unconscious while her examination took place.

As she was going under the fog of the anesthesia, she once again raised her head and, addressing the entire group attending to her, said in her most southern drawl, "Hey, everybody, whars … the … fi-ar-ah?" And with that, she laid her head back, closed her eyes, and completely relaxed; she was off to dreamland.

Nurse Olga looked at Dr. Fishman. "I thought she was French. I think when they wheeled her in, she was speaking broken English with an accent of a peculiar French dialect. Then there was that. I honestly have never heard the word 'fire' spoken with three syllables."

Nurse Octavia began to undress Helena. She looked at the outfit and hoped to accomplish her task without needing to cut her clothes to remove them. While one of the assistants turned Helena on her side, the other unbuttoned the back of her black dress. They wanted to slip it off from her shoulders and then down, to expose what they anticipated would be a wound to her shoulder. No one in attendance had missed that Helena had the largest breasts they had ever seen in the emergency room. No one had dared say a word concerning their observation, but the glances between them spoke volumes.

Octavia's face silently reflected her shock as she ever so carefully pulled off the dress, exposing Helena's amply endowed bosom. She looked square at Olga and said, "I give. I know I should say nothing, but seriously, those girls are the biggest things I have *ever* seen!"

Octavia and Olga stood over Helena and just stared. They were in a quiet state of disbelief as a flesh-colored rubber bustier trimmed in delicate black lace was revealed. Tiny black seed pearls were sewn into the lace. The bustier was tight and perfectly form-fitting. Then they observed that she was wearing the new butt-lifting panties. Upon closer inspection, they discovered she had donned five pairs of the butt-lifting things to make her booty appear huge.

Olga was mystified. "Oh my goodness, I just can't imagine!" Olga blushed a nice shade of rose as she turned a puzzled face to Dr. Fishman, who was himself a pleasant shade of red.

Octavia, getting back down to business, pointed to an obvious hole in the side of Helena's bustier. "Look at that! I think that's where the blood was coming from." And there it was, the point of entry for the bullet.

Dr. Fishman stopped Octavia from undressing Helena any further. "Okay, everyone, we all need to mask up, and I'll want the magnifier goggles ready. We need to be ready for anything at this point. Once we unsnap this contraption, who knows how much blood could spew out of her. The rubber could be containing the wound like a tourniquet."

When the last snap of the bustier was finally undone, it sprang open to reveal a very large wire mesh bra. They unfastened the bra at its center, and no one was quite ready for what came next. It was akin to an apocalyptic plague being released. The immediate reveal was a mysterious and massive combination of rubber falsies, pliant gel-filled balls, and even a pair of athletic socks, folded neatly, under everything else.

The shock in the room reverted to stifled laughter. Not one of them had ever seen anything like this. Olga looked around to the others. "Can y'all imagine how much time a production like that would take every time the poor girl got dressed?"

Even Dr. Fishman couldn't help chuckling as he reached down and picked up one of the gel-filled balls. The thing was oozing the reddish liquid everyone had thought was blood. The bullet had penetrated the wired bra and come to rest inside one of the gel-filled balls. He held up the ball in amazement. "And here is our bloody emergency." He squeezed a bullet from the gel ball. "This looks to be a .22-caliber. It is by far one of the weakest bullets out there. Before you all lies one lucky woman!"

Octavia was standing over Helena, silently looking at her exposed chest. "My goodness. Poor little thing. She sort of missed out in that department, didn't she?"

At that comment, the room broke into full-out laughter. The tension from what they originally had thought a crisis dissipated. Helena was about as far from death's door as anybody could get. She was just fine and still sleeping. The elevated heart rate she'd experienced would have happened to anyone in that same situation. The assistants departed. With Dr. Fishman, Nurses Olga and Octavia settled arrangements for Helena to rest in a room until she came around. They'd check her vitals at that point and, barring any unforeseen circumstances, release her from the hospital's care.

Eddy and Shell sat in the waiting room while Sorina had a CAT scan.

The technician stepped into the hall, still in his lead vest. He walked over to the pair and said, "The scan looks good to me, but I'm only the tech. One of our radiologists will review her results and come to talk with you shortly." Tugging at his vest, he stepped back into the room with Sorina.

Shell turned toward Eddy. "I honestly don't know how to express my gratitude. You were more than kind to bring me here in the first place. But then to stay and wait with me all this time for support is, well, unbelievable. From my heart, I can't possibly thank you enough."

Eddy smiled. "It's nothing, really. And if I'm honest, I've seen you around and always wanted to meet you. That's the truth!"

Shell blushed. She couldn't help it. As a smile crossed her face, she looked at him and said, "I have always admired your work. I love flowers. I even took a short course on flowers at MTSU as part of my home economics major. The class was my all-time favorite during the four years I was in college. I actually wanted to apply for a job at your shop but didn't think I could possibly qualify. Your business is fascinating."

Eddy said, "There is a lot to love in flowers; they are fascinating to me as well. There are always new ways to do things with them. There's always so much you can add to an arrangement to make it different and more interesting. I absolutely love the creativity of the profession!"

The door to radiology opened, and out stepped a man in a white coat. He approached Shell and Eddy. "Hello! Are you the family that's here for Sorina Lapone?"

"Yes, I'm her sister, Shell, and this is Eddy Francis, a friend."

"I'm Dr. Zeus Cohen. I just read your sister's scan, and everything looks pretty good. I think she should be seen by one of our neurologists. Sorina may have a very mild concussion, and that department would settle that possibility. Otherwise, everything else appears to be okay."

Both Shell and Eddy breathed a sigh of relief.

Dr. Cohen continued, "It obviously could have been much more severe. I'm guessing that the flat surface of the sign was what hit her head. If it had been an edge, I'm sure things would be a lot worse. I'm serious when I say I want your sister to see a neurologist. We're in the process of assigning her to a room, and I've requested she be evaluated by one of the doctors on duty. I think she'll need to stay for a couple of days for observation."

It took Shell a while to settle down enough to consider that both her mother and her sister were now in the same hospital. She had no idea that Helena was there as well. Shell and Eddy went to the nearest nurses' station and asked if the attendant could find any information about her mother. The attendant found that Yvonna had been checked in and assigned a room, and she gave Shell the room number.

As Shell and Eddy made their way to Yvonna's room, Lawrence and Jayne Montgomery parked their car in the emergency department lot. Jayne and Lawrence, Helena's parents, were an attractive couple in their mid-sixties. Jayne got out of the car and flew through the emergency room doors. Lawrence trailed his wife at full speed.

Jayne went directly to the receptionist and said, "Excuse me. Helena Montgomery is my daughter. I was told she was brought here earlier. Do you know where I can find her?"

"Oh, honey!" the desk nurse told Jayne, "Your daughter was just taken to a room on the second floor. You'll find her in room 211. If she isn't there by the time you get there, just wait, they'll have her there soon enough. The room assignment posted only a few minutes ago, but I can assure you they're on their way."

Once on the second floor, Jayne and Lawrence started toward Helena's room. Jayne kept turning around. She felt like she was being followed. After her third twirl, she finally commented to Lawrence about her feeling.

Meanwhile, every time Jayne began to turn, Charlotte Webber either ducked into a doorway or did a 180 and stepped the other way. Charlotte had her tape recorder turned on and her Minox camera in hand.

Helena's quiet voice greeted her parents as they arrived in her room. They immediately noticed how groggy she was. "Mom? Dad? I am just so embarrassed. I mean, I don't know how all of this happened," she said as her head nodded.

Jayne said, "Hon, what in the world? When we found out, we were so upset. Sorry it took so long to get here. Are you okay? Daisy at the bank told us everything, or at least what she knew. She called us while you were on your way here in the ambulance. She wanted us to be sure to tell you all the girls would drop by to see you at some point. The police are still at the bank, questioning everyone.

Once they finish, John Dunkerly said he'd lock up and come over and check on you. He's awfully concerned, sweetie."

Lawrence chimed in, "Sugar, you know your mother and I love you and want you to get better quicker than quick. What can we do that'll help you, baby?"

Helena looked at her parents, her eyes half-closed, and said in her sleepy voice, "Please don't let anyone in here to visit. Please! I don't want to see anyone except hospital staff. Make the world go away." She started to tell them what she remembered of that morning. As she spoke deliberately and slowly, she kept yawning. Before they knew it, she'd fallen back to sleep before finishing her story.

Jayne and Lawrence knew their daughter all too well. They had seen her last Saturday night at Paris á la Nuit. Helena, on the other hand, had not seen them. The restaurant was so dark, and Helena had been facing away from their table. Her parents had been tucked away in a corner booth across the room. Lawrence and Jayne initially hadn't been really sure it was Helena based on the way she was dressed and carrying on. As they had continued to watch, they'd realized that Helena was acting out for her very handsome date. At one point, she had spoken loud enough for them to hear her false Frenchified accent. When they heard the voice, they whispered to each other, casting the blame for that farce on her summer at the beauty school in Paris, France. She had never been herself after she returned. That trip had changed her. The scene had disturbed them greatly. The moment their meal was finished and the tab was paid, they had made a quiet exit.

Now they were at Vanderbilt Hospital, looking at their daughter while she slept. They were finally realizing how troubled their baby really was. Her pretty face was without any makeup. Instead of her eye-grabbing outfits, she was in a flimsy hospital gown. This was the daughter they remembered — sweet, kind, lovable Helena.

Helena opened her eyes halfway and looked at her parents again. "Don't let anyone see me like this. Promise." And she was out again.

The Eye in the Lobby

Chaos had erupted in the lobby of the hospital. Outside she could hear sirens wailing in the distance while ambulances and patrol cars were coming and going in rapid succession. Charlotte was suddenly befuddled. She was madly scribbling notes and snapping pictures. Her frustration grew as she became aware that she hadn't the foggiest clue what was really happening all around her. In one conversation, she'd heard the snippet "bank was robbed." From somewhere across the lobby, someone had gasped, "Helena Montgomery?" Tidbits of exchanges and names were bouncing off the walls. As she overheard "Poor Sorina Lapone," she caught a glimpse of Shell and Eddy at the far end of a hallway. She tore off out of the lobby, running toward them as fast as she could go.

Charlotte came to an abrupt stop as she reached the two, taking a deep breath for composure as she quickly ran a hand down to straighten her skirt. "Excuse me!" she said. "I am so terribly sorry to bother you. I heard your sister's name mentioned and know her situation, whatever it might be, must be so very stressful for you, but what has occurred?" *Deep breath! Exhale!* "I really do so hate to intrude, but this is for *The Post.* I'm sure you know I work as a reporter for them as well as *The Eye.*" Without so much as a breath, she continued, "How is your sister? Sorina? What happened at the bank? And then I thought I heard your mother might be here too? Poor child! You must know I'm so very deeply concerned. What's going on with her? From what I've been able to surmise, today must just be awful for you. Truly, I am so sorry!"

From her expression, Shell was in obvious distress. She had started to tremble. She was speechless at Charlotte's barrage of questions. With his hand on Shell's shoulder, Eddy began to relate to Charlotte the downward progression of the morning.

Charlotte was shocked. She couldn't believe what she was hearing. "What? A bank robbery? In Green Hills? You're really saying there was a bank robbery? In Green Hills." Surprisingly, Charlotte actually looked concerned. "Helena Montgomery, shot? Sorina injured too? No, this really didn't happen!"

Charlotte asked a few more questions of the pair, thanked them, then turned and hustled toward the main entrance. She wanted more. She knew there had to be more dirt to be dug somewhere in this hospital. Charlotte was thinking of *The Post*, but far more than *The Post* were her blossoming ideas for *The Eye*, her own weekly publication. *The Eye* came out every Friday. With so much happening today, on a Monday, this Friday's edition had the promise to be her biggest ever!

Breathless from her short sprint, Charlotte had returned to the lobby. She stood at the information station, practically begging the attendants for any news with regard to all the recently admitted victims. No one uttered a word. Hospital policy strictly maintained patient privacy, and Charlotte was nobody's immediate family member. Charlotte was once again baffled. These people were treating her like the general public, not the star reporter she knew herself to be.

Room 216

Down the second-floor hall from Helena Montgomery, Yvonna Lapone was tucked into room 216. Frank and Esmerelda were there, keeping her company and tending to any request. At the moment, a floor nurse was in the room, once again checking Yvonna's vital signs. Startling everyone, especially the nurse, a hard-knuckled *knock-knock-knock* sounded on the door, which straightaway flew open, banging into the wall. Miss Charlotte Webber, reporter, had arrived. The nurse, who was still attending to Yvonna, was outraged. Her nostrils flared, and her face reddened in justifiably indignant anger. She knew of Miss Charlotte Webber's antics around the hospital and was not impressed in the least with this woman. She had absolutely no right, and certainly no business, barging in on the Lapones.

Esmerelda had concern in her eyes as the nurse began to speak sternly to the now surprised intruder. "Miss Webber, we all know what you're up to, and the Lapone family would appreciate your respect for their privacy at the moment."

Charlotte remained speechless as the nurse continued.

"You have no business barging uninvited into this room like this, or any other for that matter. You need to leave, now. If you do not, I will gladly pick up the phone, dial security, and have you physically removed from the premises. Now, please just go away, or security will be on their way."

"Well!" Charlotte was stunned. *The nerve of anyone to speak to me in such a manner! The sheer impudence of this woman to demean me, Miss Charlotte Webber, is appalling! I'll put her on notice!*

The nurse, maintaining her aggravation, began to walk toward Charlotte. "It's time for you to skedaddle!" She wrapped her arm around Charlotte's as she led her toward the door. "Please step outside." With that, the nurse nudged Miss Charlotte Webber into the hallway and kindly slammed the door, almost hitting Miss Charlotte Webber on her ample posterior.

The nurse walked back to Yvonna and finished her duties. "I do apologize for my outburst. Perhaps I was a bit too forward. However, you all deserve your privacy while in this hospital, and it is my duty to ensure that it is maintained."

With the warmest of smiles, Yvonna said, "I can't thank you enough. That woman can be as pesty as a horsefly. Job well done, miss."

"If you need anything at all, just give us a buzz." The nurse filled Yvonna's glass with ice water and left the room.

Esmerelda looked at her mother. "That lady, Miss Webber? She has about the biggest nose I have *ever* seen. It's big enough she could stow quarters in it!"

Yvonna looked at Frank, and they both laughed.

"Good one," Frank chuckled. They both looked at their daughter and laughed again. "Well, we raised her, and she's all ours. But honestly, Yvonna, I think she gets it from your side of the family!"

Esmerelda said, "Come on, y'all, you know it's true! She has a huge schnozzola. Stop making fun of me!"

"Oh, honey. We're not making fun of you. And we love your wit!" Then Yvonna turned and eyed Frank and said, "I am ready to get out of this place."

Frank looked back at his wife and said, "The doctors said they want to make sure you're stable. You took a pretty good tumble. It's important they get all that glass removed. Your swelling needs to go down too. I'm pretty sure you'll only be here overnight."

Esmerelda said, "The nurse said that the doctor would be making his rounds around three o'clock this afternoon. Let's see what he says."

"Fine." And with that, Yvonna settled back for a nap.

Lobby Workstation

Charlotte returned to the lobby mad as a hornet. She went to the pay phone in the waiting area to call her office. When someone finally answered, she asked for her assistant, Edna Graves. Edna answered, and Charlotte started. "There's a lot happening here at the hospital — too much to go into any detail now. I need your help. I want you to bring me some of the fancy notecards in my desk along with that special calligraphy pen. I'll be in the main lobby reception." With that, she slammed the phone back in its cradle and stomped back into the lobby. An idea was taking shape in Charlotte's conniving head.

Edna arrived thirty minutes later and helped Charlotte set up a makeshift workstation in a far corner of the lobby waiting area. Charlotte sat and began to write, in her most elegant penmanship, her special requests of Sorina, Yvonna, and Helena. The gist of each individual's note was an appeal for an exclusive interview. She also asked that if for any reason they did not wish to be interviewed, they please call her assistant at the office of *The Eye* and kindly leave a message. Charlotte went on to write how she deeply respected that they each needed their own time to recover. It would be most gracious of them if they would speak with her Wednesday morning, which would allow their stories to be told in Friday's edition of

The Eye. She assured them that the same article would most likely appear in *The Post* as well. Once she had completed the cards, she slipped them into envelopes and addressed them using name and room number. She handed Edna thirty dollars and asked her to run into the hospital flower shop and purchase three long-stemmed red roses and red satin ribbon.

Edna was quick and soon returned with the goods. As she started to hand over the change, Charlotte told her, "Thank you, dear. Just keep it. Buy yourself an ice cream. And don't leave quite yet." Charlotte wrapped each card in ribbon, tying a perfectly neat bow, then slipped a rose behind each bow. Satisfied with her work, Charlotte handed everything to Edna. "You'll take care of this, won't you, dear?"

Without a word, Edna set off to deliver each envelope and rose to the appropriate room.

Room 310

Sorina had gone through triage and had been admitted to the hospital's care. She was now the lone occupant of a very large private suite. A sign reading, "Limited Entry," was posted in the hallway on the suite's door. A uniformed officer had been stationed at the door and was now doing his best to get comfortable on a black metal folding chair. Anyone requesting entry to the suite was required to provide identification. For the moment, only hospital staff and family members were approved. Sorina was under full police protection. She was the primary eyewitness to that morning's bank robbery. Very few knew that in a fleeting moment, she had seen the getaway car's license plate reflected in her sister's oily forehead. Unfortunately for everyone concerned, Sorina now was experiencing temporary amnesia. She could not recall, no matter how hard she tried, an image of the plate or much about the morning in general. The police were eager to obtain any information locked in her brain. The theory was that if they kept her as comfortable as possible, she could relax, and her blurred memory might clear. It was already two in the afternoon, and *Days of our Lives* was on her television, making even less sense than reality. When she heard a knock on her door, she picked up her harmonica and played a short, lively melody and glided into her speaking voice. "C-come in."

A new white-coated doctor entered. He was not ugly. He was very tall and appeared to be in his early forties. His eyes met Sorina's as he smiled and introduced himself. "Miss Lapone, I am Dr. Reginald Rafkin. How are you feeling right now? Any immediate complaints? I understand you've survived quite a blow to your head after a rather harrowing experience this morning."

Sorina, confused, pulled at her harmonica. She gave it a little toot and glided into her answer. "I … I guess … uh, I mean, I really don't know what all the, uh, f-fuss is about. Um, right now, I c-can't remember what I saw … I mean, they want me, uh, to r-remember details that I just c-can't think of no m-m-matter how hard I try." Her eyes began to well with tears. "The police keep, um, c-coming in, and they k-keep, um, asking me over and over."

Dr. Rafkin pulled a chair around from the side of her bed and sat facing her. "Miss Lapone, I am a neurologist. I also specialize in hypnotherapy. I am here to do whatever I can to make you comfortable and will do my best to help you remember the events of this morning. I know you're exhausted from everything that's happened today. I hear it in your voice."

Sorina responded, "Th-thank you for your c-concern. Yes, it's been a really long day." Her face was flushed. She held her breath a moment and then, gradually letting it out, began anew. "I must have mumbled, uh, s-something to the paramedics while they were, um, bringing me h-here. I must have said, um, I saw the license, uh, plate n-number or something right before the, um, sign hit my h-head. And now I can't remember any of that."

Dr. Rafkin focused on the chromium harmonica attached to the silver chain around Sorina's neck. He was curious. "Do you use the harmonica to help with your speech?"

She answered, "Uh, yes, D-d-doctor. Yes, it's just a really stressful, um, t-t-time right now. I've been doing, um, pretty good lately, but, um, like especially today, my st-st-stutter has been p-p-pretty awful."

Dr. Rafkin said, "The mind is one huge labyrinthine catacomb. Sometimes it stores memories that we may not realize for long periods of time. Memories can hide forever, and then they can resurface when we least expect." He smiled and continued, "And then there are tricks that can help our memories resurface. That is where I have the opportunity to help."

Sorina looked intently at the doctor and said, "How do you … I mean, um, h-h-how can that h-happen? I guess I mean, h-how do you, uh, d-d-do that?"

Dr. Rafkin explained, "Aside from your mild concussion, which is why I'm here in the first place and the primary reason you will remain here for the next couple of days, the police have asked me to assist by attempting to use hypnosis to help you remember what you saw this morning. As for the concussion? With rest and a gradual increase in your physical activity, you will be as good as new in no time!"

Sorina smiled as she nodded her understanding. "So wh-when do, um, you th-think you will be able to d-d-do whatever it is, um, that you d-do to help me d-d-discover my forgotten, um, m-m-morning?"

Dr. Rafkin said, "We can try now if you'd like. It is an easy process. Actually, being mildly sedated as you are now will be perfect for our purposes."

Sorina spoke in a soft voice without the help of her harmonica. "I'm glad to, um, do anything th-that I can that will, um, h-h-help the investigation. I'll, um, sign a c-consent form if that's something you n-n-need."

It took no time for the room to be prepped for the procedure. Dr. Rafkin prescribed a five-milligram Valium, which his nurse had delivered. The shades were drawn and the lights turned down for slumber. Within a half hour, Sorina was perfectly relaxed and ready for whatever would come next.

He said, "This procedure will not take more than fifteen minutes. I promise you, if it is successful, we'll be done in no time." He paused and gazed directly and deeply into Sorina's eyes. He held up a black-and-white vortex optical of concentric circles in front of her. "I want you to relax. Breathe in and out slowly, very slowly.

You are feeling warm, cozy, and completely at ease. Concentrate on the image you see and follow the lines to its center." His soft voice slowly grew more and more quiet. "Imagine you are lightly floating through space to the center of the vortex. You're approaching the center. You have reached your destination."

Sorina appeared to have nodded off.

"Sorina, can you hear me?"

Her eyes fluttered, and Dr. Rafkin knew she had fallen under. Keeping his voice steady and low, he began to ask questions, slowly leading her back to the morning. After she had answered a few other questions about the day, he asked, "Sorina, what do you see when you look at your sister's oily forehead?"

Sorina mumbled, "I see a license plate. The numbers and letters are 733HE6. It's from Tennessee. It says Bedford at the bottom."

Dr. Rafkin had taken copious notes and recorded their entire session on cassette. He continued with other questions about that morning. Finally, he said, "Very soon it will be time for you to wake up. You will awaken when I gently touch your forehead and say, 'It's all right now.' You will then open your eyes and return to this present. Do you understand what I've told you, Sorina?"

Sorina nodded and said, "Yes."

Dr. Rafkin continued, "And once you are awake, you will slow your speech, and your stammer will begin to ebb. In time, it will completely go away. Visualize what you want to say from now on before you speak. Your speech fluency will improve over time." Dr. Rafkin touched Sorina's forehead and said, "It's all right now."

Her eyes opened, and Sorina breathed a deep sigh. She sat up and said, "Did you hypnotize me? I don't think it worked. You want to try again?"

Dr. Rafkin smiled. "You did great. I'll be right back." He stood, walked to the door, and stepped into the hall. He told the officer, "Please call your supervisor. Tell him I have all the information he has been hoping for."

The officer beamed, pulled out his walkie-talkie, and called dispatch at headquarters. "We have a breakthrough here at the hospital. The doctor just asked me to call for the chief. He'll probably want to speak to the doctor in person."

The chief, Nick Roscoe, and a detective arrived within fifteen minutes. They parked in front of the hospital and made their way to room 310. Dr. Rafkin was outside of Sorina's room, waiting.

As the two officers approached, Dr. Rafkin spoke. "This was a pretty easy one," he said as he tore a page from his notepad. "There you go. It's what she remembered. The license plate number is right there! I am so glad this was fast. I hope you catch the fools."

The officers thanked the doctor, and off they went. Back in their squad car, they radioed the dispatcher and relayed everything they had learned from Dr. Rafkin. An APB was released with the license plate info and a full description of the Lincoln Continental.

Inside room 310, Sorina was restless. She wanted to know what was going on outside of her room. She also wanted to see her family. She wondered about her mother. She wondered what had happened to Shell. She wondered what had ended up happening at the bank. And a lot more wonders just kept coming. *What a mess. I really don't like today,* she thought.

Telepathy between sisters works in strange ways. Shell was feeling the same as Sorina. Eddy, still at Shell's side, had accompanied her from office to office and from phone calls to meetings. He had even called her office at Hill and Garden to let them know what was going on. He'd called his own store and explained his absence, saying he'd check back later.

The Lapone family approached the door to Sorina's room and introduced themselves to the on-duty officer who had spent his day in the uncomfortable metal folding chair. Yvonna was in her green hospital gown riding in a wheelchair pushed by Frank. Shell, Esmerelda, and Eddy were following close behind. Frank knocked, and the sound of Sorina's harmonica called from inside the room.

Frank opened the door, and they all filtered into her suite. Frank rolled Yvonna straight to their daughter's bedside. Eddy stayed in the background while the family exchanged hugs and kisses. Looking around, he thought Sorina's suite was definitely lavish for a hospital and wouldn't be bad for a hotel either. He hadn't known they even had rooms like this. There was a sofa and three large lounge chairs, two big televisions, a desk, and a small dinette table. Sorina was still groggy from the Valium. With the aid of Esmerelda, she got out of bed, wobbled to the sitting area, and plopped down with her family.

The conversation was just starting to roll when there was another knock on the door. Frank got up from his chair and opened the door. Nurse Olga Nussell was standing there.

"Mind if I come in?" asked the nurse. "My sister and I have been fretting over y'all since you passed through our emergency room this morning. I just wanted to do a quick check-in. Oh, and by the way, Mrs. Lapone? You need to return to your room. Doctor's on his way for that three o'clock checkup. I apologize. He's obviously running really late. Been one busy day — like I need to tell you! Glad you're all coming along so well. I'll be on my way then. Y'all take care." Olga opened the door and was gone.

Esmerelda looked at her big sister and leaned over and whispered, "Don't you think that woman has about the biggest nose you've ever laid eyes on? I think it's even bigger than Charlotte Webber's honker."

Eddy overheard the comment, and his eyes rolled along with Shell's. Shell whispered back to Esmerelda, "Why are you always such a little twit?"

Shell paused and turned to Eddy. "I can't believe it's this late and you're still here. I've enjoyed your company and thoroughly appreciate all you've helped me through today. I really have to say that the only good thing about today is that we met. Anyway, I just want to thank you once again."

Eddy smiled and said, "I always like to help when I can. Today was definitely different." When he glanced at his watch, he was shocked at the hour. "Shell, it's actually close to five o'clock. I have to go by the shop and check in on Gladys — help her close up the shop, just make sure everything is okay. Mondays may be our slowest day, but we get a lot of telephone orders for the upcoming week."

Shell looked back at Eddy and, with a serious look on her face, said, "Eddy, if you ever have any openings at your shop, please think of me." She smiled. "I hope to see you soon."

"I'm sure you will." Eddy got up from his chair, said goodbye to all, and left.

Frank and Yvonna looked at Shell after Eddy left. Yvonna said, "Shell? I think I can get used to that. I guess Schmellda was maybe a little too old-country."

Frank said, "I like the nickname — Shell." He smiled and continued, "Are you still interested in the floral business? If you are, let's check into it. You know you have to pave your own way on this road. I've always thought that way about life. My mother used to tell me the old cliché, 'You need to follow your heart. It will always lead you in the right direction.'" He paused while Shell thought over his last comment. "If it's something that you really want to do, I'll help you any way I can. Now, Yvonna, we need to get you back for that doctor."

A knock came at the door again, and Frank once again responded. Eddy was standing there. He looked at Frank and said, "I'm sorry to interrupt. I have one more thing to say to Shell." He took a few steps in and looked at Shell. "If you're serious and want to come work at the shop, let's give it a go. Let's at least talk about the possibilities. There're a few things you need to learn first, and classes are available at Nashville State Tech that cover the business side of the floral industry."

Frank grabbed Eddy's hand and thanked him. "We appreciate you coming back. Your offer could mean the world to Shell." He then turned to her and said, "Did you hear all of that? If you want to risk it, you have my complete support."

Eddy said, "Mr. Lapone, you all have a lot going on right now. I will speak to Shell later. I just wanted to throw it out there. Y'all have had more than enough to deal with for one day." With that said, Eddy turned and walked down the hall toward the elevator.

And Frank rolled Yvonna on back to room 216 as fast as he could.

Room 211

Jayne and Lawrence stood flanking either side of Helena's bed. Jayne felt deflated. Her eyes were weary as she took in the sight of her recumbent daughter. "Honey, you know we both love you so much! All we care about and hope for is your happiness. It's all that matters in life."

Her father said, "Really, baby girl, I've never been able to figure out why you care so much about what other people think of you. This is *your* life, it's not some dress rehearsal. Why do you always struggle to be someone other than your true, beautiful self? I have no idea how you ever arrived at the notion that you aren't good enough. How did you ever set your standards?"

Helena knew where this conversation was going. The three had had it before, on too many occasions, in her estimation. She couldn't have been more thankful when a gentle knock on the door interrupted her parents' sermon. Her tone was deadly serious when she said, "Don't let anyone in here other than staff. No one I know can see me like this!"

Jayne stepped to the door and opened it enough to slip out and into the hallway, where she faced a most handsome young man clutching a generously large bouquet of red roses. She saw his surprise and said warmly, "Hello! I'm Jayne Montgomery, Helena's mother. And you are?"

"I'm Johnny Montana. It's a pleasure to meet you, Mrs. Montgomery. I brought these for Helena. I'm hoping she's able to have visitors? We work at the same bank, but I'm at the main office. I was in a meeting with our branch manager in Knoxville this morning when I heard the news. As soon as my meeting ended, I jumped in my car and drove straight here. I know Helena and think she is truly special."

"My daughter has asked not to see anyone for the time being. She's still so shaken up. I think it's best for her to just stay quiet for now. But I can tell you without a doubt, red roses are her all-time favorite. She'll just love these!" Jayne continued to eye Johnny. She noted that he was dressed conservatively: navy sport coat, blue oxford cloth shirt, tan slacks, cordovan belt, and wing tips.

Johnny continued, "I understand. If something like that happened to me, I think I'd be of the same mind. But is she okay? How serious are her injuries?"

Jayne looked at him. "Physically, she is in very good shape. Her injuries are minor. However, mentally, she will need time. Thank you so much for coming by. I'm sure she will be elated you did, and she will just *love* these beautiful flowers!"

Johnny handed her the vase of flowers, and she turned to the door. Then she looked back and said, "Johnny, it was so nice to meet you. I will look forward to seeing you again."

"The pleasure was all mine, Mrs. Montgomery. Please give Helena my best?" Johnny smiled, turned, and headed to the bank of elevators.

Jayne opened the door to Helena's room and realized why Johnny had seemed so familiar. She had seen him last week at Paris á la Nuit. *He* had been Helena's date! She closed the door and held the bouquet toward her daughter. For maybe the first time since she and Lawrence had arrived, Helena smiled. Jayne began to relay the conversation she'd had with Helena's handsome visitor.

The girl was all questions. "And then what did he say?" "What else?" "Isn't he nice?" And on it went.

Jayne continued, "He was terribly concerned about you. I told him you needed time to recuperate, and you were not up to seeing anyone quite yet. He completely understood and said he'd most probably feel the same way if the roles were reversed. In any case, he sends his best. And that's about it."

Jayne turned to Lawrence. "Dear, I'm famished. Let's go down to the cafeteria and get something. Helena, would you like us to bring you anything back?"

"Thanks, Mom, but I ordered my dinner a couple of hours ago when the nurse was here. They said it's usually served between five and six. So I'm good. Y'all enjoy yourselves."

Jayne and Lawrence walked down the hall to the elevators and began the same conversation they had had for years. How in the world were they going to help Helena this time? The girl's life had begun with so much promise. She had started piano lessons when she was three. By nine, she had been playing the classics with an affinity for Mozart's études. She had memorized Beethoven's Moonlight Sonata for her last recital and wowed the audience with its beauty.

Then something in her had changed as she approached her teens. At eleven, Helena and two of her friends were arrested for shoplifting. The girls appeared before a juvenile court judge known for firing off fire-and-brimstone reprimands, hefty fines, and substantial sentences. Her parents paid the fine. Helena and her two friends spent a weekend in juvenile detention and worked off fifty hours of community service in order to have their records expunged.

Then at thirteen, she'd managed to get herself pregnant and ended up in a maternity home for seven months. Jayne and Lawrence paid for her stay and added a sizable donation on top of that. When it came to telling her parents the irresponsible father's identity, she went mute as a stone. She gave birth to a healthy boy and just as quickly gave him up for adoption with no perceivable regrets.

Helena managed to graduate from high school and started college in the autumn of that same year. This turned out not to be a great investment for Mom and Dad; by the middle of her sophomore year, she was a dropout. After an overabundance of coercion, her parents finally relented in the face of her pleas to attend fashion and beauty school in Paris, France, for a year. They paid all her expenses for that adventure as well. When she returned from her year abroad, she began telling stories about an imaginary boyfriend she'd left in France. She described him in great detail. Of course, he lived in Paris and came from great wealth. At that point, Lawrence felt compelled to begin consultations with psychologists and counselors. He and Jayne both knew they should have started Helena in counseling long before this last incident, but they had been sure after each mishap that their beautiful daughter would come around. The Paris episode was the finale. Helena was lost in her new dreamworld, and without her participation, counseling wasn't going anywhere.

As they walked and remembered, Jayne said, "This feels different from any of the other times. Remember when she entered the Miss Tennessee pageant after being crowned Miss Davidson County in Nashville?"

Lawrence smiled at the memory. "Yes, of course I do. It's almost as clear as yesterday. We thought that pageant would make a real difference for her. She shined! I was so excited. She was prettier than so many of the girls, and her genuinely sweet personality came through loud and clear."

When they reached the cafeteria, they picked up trays and utensils and proceeded along the buffet line to make their selections. They paid and sat down at a table near a large window with a view into an exterior courtyard and idly began their meal.

Jayne put her fork down and dove back into the beauty contest. "Remember how she and I had to make her evening gown? Crazy regulation of a handmade gown by mother and daughter. Pre-sketches and photos of progress along the way. I think that dress took us three weeks." Jayne laughed. "We bought the pattern from the fabric store. Helena insisted on a jade-green satin top with jade-green and turquoise sequins sewn onto it. The skirt was the same jade green in velvet. We attached all those peacock feather tips from the costume store. We must have hand-stitched three hundred feathers to that thing. Oh my god, I just remember snipping and sewing all those nights. It was stunning under the lights. The field of contestants was narrowed down to five, and Helena's name was called third. Then they were into the talent competition. Remember that?"

Lawrence said, "I wish I could forget it. Our daughter was a virtuoso pianist, and instead she decided on that majorette act, tossing three batons. Was she ever even a majorette?"

Jayne shook her head at the memory. "I'll admit she surprised me with that baton thing. I mean, I had no idea she was that good. No idea where it came from. I was just terrified for her!"

"Yeah," Lawrence sighed, "the outfit! Where did she ever dig that up? Tight red- and white-striped sleeveless top, red miniskirt with white stars—and all of it sequins! Plus those white patent leather go-go boots. She was a sight. And you know? She did fine until near the end, when that one baton went sailing out into the audience, and the fellow in the third row caught it. Poor thing was mortified. She turned almost as red as that damn outfit. But she just kept going. She recovered nicely and finished her program with the two batons. I genuinely think she handled it perfectly. But then she was followed by the last contestant, that Tanya Simplestone. A ballet piece from *Swan Lake*. Wow. She was truly spectacular."

Jayne continued, "Oh, remember the final portion of the competition was the interview — remember that?"

"I thought that was perhaps the best of the evening," replied Lawrence. He continued, "The emcee asked Helena to recite two of what she considered the most memorable quotes she had heard up to that point in her life. She paused for a few seconds, smiled, and looked out into the audience and said something like, 'I have two that I love. I hope that you will love them too.' Then she quoted the one by Albert Camus from his novel *The Plague*, which I remember to this day: 'There are more things to admire in men than to despise.' I couldn't possibly forget her second one either. It was from an Ann Landers column: 'Hanging onto resentment is letting someone you despise live rent-free in your head.' Where did *that* girl go?" Lawrence added, "I thought she did well. Where she came up with those two quotes is beyond me. But the last girl won with a touchdown."

Jayne replied, "Tanya Simplestone. The emcee asked, if she could name one word to unite the world, what would that word be? And she had to explain herself in two short sentences. Poor thing looked stunned. Remember, Tanya looked at the audience and just said, 'Hope.' She continued with something like, 'Hope is an aspiration.' Oh, what was it? *Oh*! 'Hope is an aspiration that every living person carries deep inside. Hope is real, hope is honest, hope is genuine.' Remember that? I thought she was brilliant."

Jayne continued, "I didn't think the other three held a candle to Tanya or Helena. Then they brought all five back out and eliminated three, one by one, until it was only Tanya and our Helena. They were just standing there with stars in their eyes, holding each other's hands, when the emcee finally announced the first runner-up, Helena Montgomery. Tears were streaming down both their faces. You remember, don't you, Lawrence? Tanya was crying from pure happiness, and Helena was crying because she believed that from that point on she was and always would be a loser."

Lawrence and Jayne absentmindedly finished their meal and started back to Helena's room. Lawrence ventured, "We have to find somewhere, someplace, that we can send Helena for diagnosis and treatment. There has to be some professional out there who can get through to her. Jayne, our girl needs some serious help. We can't save her anymore by throwing money at her problems and mistakes. And our love is obviously not enough. I'll start making calls in the morning and find out all that I can."

Jayne looked at Lawrence and said, "I agree. There has to be something or someone that will help her get back to the real genuine self that she's run so far from and buried so very deep. We've seen her honest and compassionate soul. It's just been too long ago."

When they reached Helena's room, she was fast asleep. Jayne left a short note with their love and promise to return. Helena's parents left the hospital for a silent drive home.

Shell

Late Monday and Early Tuesday

Geez, she thought as she climbed the stairs to her apartment. *This was the longest day in history! Definitely the longest I've ever experienced. I am so glad to be home. I can't go to work tomorrow. I just can't. I'll have to call Donna first thing in the morning. Gosh, I cannot wait to wash my hair! Ugh! My hair smells like a hospital. My clothes smell like a hospital. I smell like disinfectant! My hair is totally gross and definitely oilier than normal. Tomorrow when I get out of bed, I begin my own regimen. I will wash my hair every morning. Forget Grandma's beauty secrets! Sorry, Lulu! But tonight! Tonight I will have a long soak in a very hot tub and wash my hair while I soak. I will wash away this horrible, horrible day!*

As she walked into her apartment, the first thing Shell noticed was the flashing light on her answering machine. As she listened to the messages, she fixed herself a nice, big bowl of ice cream and topped it with crushed potato chips. The only person who had left a message that really mattered to her, at that moment, was her downstairs neighbor, Mr. Walloppe. His voice expressed the worry he had felt all day. Hearing him on tape, she knew she needed to tell him that she had made it through this wretched day. She picked up the receiver and dialed. "Mr. Walloppe! This is Shell! I got your message. Thank you for checking up on me." She went into great detail between spoonfuls of ice cream explaining everything that had happened on this most awful of days.

He listened intently and frequently interjected with short responses, "Oh my goodness," "Uh-huh, uh-huh," "Gosh," and finally, "I am so glad you and your family are okay. At least you made it home safely." Shell knew how very deeply he cared. She thought, *Is there a nicer neighbor anywhere?*

After a long enough conversation to settle his worries, Shell said, "Mr. Walloppe, I need to get off the phone. I just need to be quiet for a while. I'm going to take a long, hot soak and try to forget about this entire day." *Well, maybe not Eddy. No, definitely remember Eddy!*

He answered, "Please stop calling me Mr. Walloppe. We've been through this already. You will call me Wally. Enough with the mister stuff."

Shell answered, "Well then, Wally, thank you! I'll see you tomorrow. Have a lovely evening and sleep well."

Shell hung up the phone and went straight into the bathroom and began filling the tub. She poured in probably too much liquid bath soap and let the tub fill with water as hot as she thought she could stand. She tossed her clothes into a pile and slowly lowered herself into the bubbles and steaming water for a good, long, relaxing soak and possibly the most pleasurable shampoo of her life. She put her hair through three wash-rinse-repeat cycles. It was squeaky clean when she was done. The clock was ticking toward eleven. Shell wrapped herself in her still-fluffy pink terrycloth bathrobe, wrapped a yellow towel around her head like a turban, and sat down to her kitchen counter. She was feeling much better after a most miserable day.

She opened the drawer at the kitchen counter and retrieved a folder containing information she had accumulated on floral schools. She shuffled through the file and finally found the catalog and application for Nashville State Technical Institute. After perusing the catalog for floral classes, she zeroed in on one particular class that piqued her interest: *Blooms of Life: Flowers are Exploding*

Everywhere. "In this class," the description promised, "you will learn how to arrange and adapt with an attitude that shows in every design. You will learn the basic principles of color, proportion, scale, balance, and harmony. Completion of the curriculum prepares and qualifies the participant for floral certification and subsequent licensing in the state of Tennessee." The full description of the program was intense and interestingly short.

The brochure covered everything Shell needed to know about the class. The curriculum for floral certification was explained. Required materials were included. It described rules and regulations as well as several design competitions and awards. Participation was limited to twelve candidates. The term would last sixteen weeks. Shell was so excited about the possibilities, and with class size so limited, she decided to call her father that very moment. She knew that he would be asleep, but what the heck. This was her life they were talking about.

"Dad," she said when he answered, "I have something that I have to talk to you about. I know it's really late, but sorry, this can't wait until tomorrow. I want to take you up on your offer for floral school." She explained everything in as much detail as possible. The school's conveniently close location was a big plus, as was its affordable tuition.

Her father yawned heavily and said, "I'm happy you've made this decision. I will back you completely. You will stay in your apartment; we will figure out an allowance. Maybe you can work part-time at The Dancing Flower with Eddy Francis."

Shell gave a little moan. "Yeah. I will have to quit my new job. I doubt they'll let me work only twenty hours a week. I'll deal with that in the morning. I won't keep you any longer, Dad. I'm about to burst and just had to let you know my plans. Thanks, Dad! G'night. Sleep well. Love you."

She received a quick sign-off from her father as he returned to dreamland.

So I've gotta think about this. First thing tomorrow, I need to get over to the school and see if the class is full. I'll do that before anything else. The course starts Monday, July 12. Oh my god, I am so excited! I hope that it's not full already. Be calm. I have my bachelor's in home economics; that's gotta count for something. I've had one class in floral already. I just have to be better qualified than most for the class. I just have to be.

The next morning, Shell went to the school first thing, as planned. She wanted to submit her application in person. She tracked down the instructor's office and found him already at work. She gave him her full story and shared her transcripts from MTSU. After reviewing her application and discussing the course and her obvious qualifications, he welcomed her to his class. He gave her a wide smile. "See you on the twelfth!"

From the pay phone in the lobby of the admissions office, Shell called Hill and Garden Realtors. Donna answered. Shell immediately went over the previous day with her. Donna told her she was pretty much aware of everything that had happened and was glad to know Shell's family was doing well. Donna had even called the hospital and found out about Shell's mother.

Shell said to Donna, "There is something else. Strangely, it's a result of yesterday. I won't bore you with all the details, but I need to quit my job there in a couple of weeks. I've been thinking about this a lot and finally decided I want a different career. I want to be a florist. It's my passion. I'm so sorry, Donna. You have been so kind. I can stay through July 10 if you want. But on July 12, I begin an intense course to become a licensed florist."

As usual, Donna was more than accommodating. She said, "I need to talk to Mr. Pangle and see what he'll want to do. Will you be able to work this week? I mean, it's only Tuesday."

Shell paused to think and then said, "Let me get my mother and sister situated. I think they're both being released and going home today. Do you mind if I call you later in the day?"

Donna answered, "Of course, hon, by all means. We'll just plan to see you Wednesday. If that's too soon, then Thursday. Just let me know. Oh, and I am so glad that things worked out well with your family. We were all worried sick. Talk to you later. Bye-bye now."

Shell was ready to go!

Room 211

Wednesday Morning, June 23, 1976

On their Tuesday morning visit, Jayne and Lawrence had arrived with a change of clothes for their daughter's eventual release. Lawrence had then ended Tuesday evening consulting with his daughter on her hospital room phone. They had come to an agreement. As the sun began to brighten the sky on Wednesday morning, the door to room 211 slowly opened, and an inelegant female figure slipped out the door. She was wearing a formless, inexpensive black peasant dress. Her face was hidden behind extravagant YSL sunglasses, beneath an enormous black floppy sun hat. Spike-heeled black pumps clacked on the linoleum as she crept toward the elevators. Meanwhile, in front of the nurses' station, Olga Nussell was running a final check of Yvonna Lapone's chart and watching from the corner of her eye as the figure approached and tapped the elevator button. Helena Montgomery was busted.

Olga called out, "Miss Montgomery! I was unaware the doctor signed your release order."

Helena spun around on one heel. "I … I just need to go! I … I cannot stay here another minute. We all know I'm fine. Please tell everyone thank you for me. Two days are enough."

Helena was blushing crimson, feeling like a little girl caught with her hand in the proverbial cookie jar. She wasn't stupid. She knew hospital procedure. She knew she'd been caught leaving the hospital without being officially released. Olga could only smile as the doors slid open and Helena walked into the elevator.

As the elevator doors closed behind Helena, Olga turned to the woman sitting behind the desk. "Please make a note on Miss Montgomery's chart that the patient has released herself. She was in 211. Probably a good idea to note as well that both you and I witnessed her departure."

Emerging from the elevator on the ground floor, Helena ran out of the hospital and jumped into a tan Buick Electra with her father behind the wheel. The Electra rolled away.

As they ambled toward Hillsboro Road, Helena looked at her father. "Thanks, Dad. I'd have gone completely mad if I had to spend another day in that room. I can't be around anyone right now. Maybe I could hide under a rock somewhere. Maybe I need to go away for a while."

This had been the gist of their conversation last night, and Lawrence could feel his daughter's anguish. Helena had finally admitted to her parents, but more importantly to herself, that she needed to get some help. "Dad," she said, "what do I do? I think we've agreed that the best plan is for me to disappear from here for a while. I need to go somewhere and find where 'me' went. I need a readjustment. My soul compass needs a reset. I'm sick of the act I've been playing and want to change. I met this great guy. Well, Mother met him too … he brought me those roses at the hospital. I like him a lot. I want him to know the real me. From the way he treats me, I know he recognized something special in me beyond the boobs and booty. Oh god, my mouth! Sorry. I heard about a place in South Carolina that's supposed to be really good with helping people deal with problems like mine. I want professional help this time."

Her father looked at Helena, slumped in the seat next to him. "Sweetie, your mother and I will do anything possible to help you. We want you to be happy with your life again. We've always been there for you, and we won't abandon ship now. Keep your chin up. We'll do this together." And then they rode in silence.

Same Morning

Other Rooms

As Helena and her father drove away, Frank and Esmerelda were heading into the hospital. They'd received a call at sunup saying that Sorina and Yvonna were both being discharged after breakfast. Frank went to Yvonna's room. Esmeralda headed to Sorina's. She cheerily greeted the good-looking cop on the metal chair as she opened the door to find Shell already there. Shell had arrived earlier with fresh clothes for Sorina and had helped her dress.

Sorina perked up and looked at both her sisters. "Oh, I didn't tell you, did I? They caught the two b-bank robbers! They were hiding out in a R-Ramada Inn down I-24 in Manchester. Seems they ch-checked in under their real names and used their own credit cards. Brainiacs, right? Little did they know, the police had their license p-plate number, thanks to moi! Smart as they thought they were, the m-morons drove all of s-sixty miles from Nashville in the same car and figured they could hide in plain sight at a m-motor inn. Like nobody was looking for them. Smart, huh? Oh, and l-l-lest I forget, Charlotte Webber from *The Eye* is c-coming by here before we leave. She should be here any m-minute. She wants to interview m-me! Can't imagine that'll take very long, but c-can you even believe it?"

Before Sorina had finished her sentence, Frank and Yvonna entered the room, followed quickly by Charlotte and her assistant, Edna Graves. And if the room didn't already feel filled to capacity, they were trailed by three police officers, accompanied by police chief Nick Roscoe, nurse Octavia Nussell, and last, but by no means least, Sorina's own Dr. Fishman. It seemed like every one of them had their own conversation to start and, unfortunately, at the same time. The noise level was reaching its limit!

So Charlotte Webber, who knew she could be the loudest, chose to be and spoke over everyone. "Can I get a photo of all of you for *The Eye* and *The Post*?" Pointing at the hospital bed, she said to Sorina, "Dear, I realize you're all dressed and ready to go, but would you mind slipping back into bed? Just cover yourself up to your chin so the photo looks real. And would the doctor and nurse please join our city's finest on her right? The family can gather on the left. This won't take but a minute or two of your time. One quick photograph. Now, please, if you all would stand a bit closer together. No! Closer! This will be simply marvelous for the papers!" As was typical for Charlotte, the way she barked orders like a drill sergeant had everyone in place and at attention, ready for the production to be over.

With the groups assembled and Sorina in bed with the blanket pulled up to her chin, Edna rushed over, Nikon in hand, and began snapping frame after frame, all the while chirping, "Smile at the camera! Look at me! Smile! Oh, say cheese! Smile!" She must have taken twenty or more shots by the time she was finished.

Charlotte looked at the police officers and hospital staff and forced what she thought was her best warm and gentle smile. "Please, just one moment more. I will need to get everyone's names."

Sorina tooted on her harmonica and said, "Yay! Al-m-most outta here!"

Chief Roscoe looked at Sorina as she slipped out of the bed. "Miss Lapone, it looks like I have a little news for you and your sister that I'm sure you will love to hear."

Sorina looked at him quizzically. "What are you s-s-saying?"

Roscoe continued, "Unbeknownst to you, there was a substantial bounty on the two men we arrested last night." He and Sorina made use of the lounge chairs and sat to face each other. "The two men we arrested have been wanted for a string of bank robberies in three states. They have also committed a few felonies along the way. They had a hostage situation occur during one of the robberies. You'll be pleased to know there are a lot of folks out there who are really happy those two are behind bars. The reward moneys are substantial. On the last wanted flyer I saw cross my desk, the reward was up to fifty thousand dollars, and that was a couple of weeks ago."

Sorina did a hum on her harmonica and with a huge grin said, "Really? Th-th-that is wonderful! And for Shell t-t-too. It's hers as much as it is m-m-mine. If it weren't for Shell, this could n-n-never have happened. I would have n-n-never seen the license plate number!"

Shell squealed, "You aren't serious, are you?"

Chief Roscoe said, "As serious as a weather report!"

Listening in, as if they could help themselves, Charlotte and Edna were all ears. Edna began snapping photo after photo once more while Charlotte madly scribbled notes. Charlotte attempted to interrupt the chief, as was her practice, but Roscoe had no intention of letting her have the floor.

Chief Roscoe continued, "Will you ladies be able to come by my office this afternoon? Around four, perhaps? I would like to go over a few things with you and then help you fill out the papers for the reward. My secretary is most likely at this very moment compiling a list of the rewards that have been offered from the different sources. There are so many, many people and businesses that are absolutely delighted with what you have done. Even if unintentional, your efforts are still very much appreciated!"

Sorina looked to Shell, then back at Chief Roscoe. "To answer your question, I don't see w-w-why not. We can come to your office anytime. Gosh, th-th-thank you s-s-so much. I mean really, this is amazing! Well, b-b-beyond amazing, really!"

Esmerelda was thrilled for her sisters. She grabbed Shell in a bear hug and gave Sorina a thumbs-up. She asked Chief Roscoe, "Do you mind if I come along? I promise I won't get in the way. I mean, the three of us are sisters. And to tell the truth, I have never, ever been in a police station. I think it would be so cool."

Frank and Yvonna had listened intently to Roscoe. Hearing Esmerelda's request, Yvonna blurted, "Me too!"

Chief Roscoe answered, "Absolutely! Of course! Why not? We can have a little party!"

Charlotte walked to the front of the room in order to address them all at the same time. She always felt good — well, better than good — at taking command of any situation. "The news coming from this room is monumental. I mean, what happened and how it all came down is something Nashville has not experienced before. This story will make headlines! It'll be breaking news across the media."

Seemingly ignoring Charlotte, the crowd began to disperse. The policemen were the first to leave, followed by Dr. Fishman and Nurse Nussell. Charlotte and Edna were lingering, waiting for more.

Esmerelda, noticing their hesitation to depart, stepped over to Charlotte. "Ms. Webber, my family and I need some alone time right now. I'm sure you understand. You understand etiquette. It would be so considerate of you both to just go away. You can get anything more that you think you need from us later today, as if you don't have enough already."

Flustered, Charlotte replied, "You may be correct. Oh, I suppose, yes, you are right. I thank you all. I believe everyone already agreed to meet in my office around three today? I'll most likely have only a few more questions. Again, thank you. See you then. We will take our leave." She smiled and turned to Edna. "C'mon, let's go."

As she stalked out of the room, the family all smiled.

The door finally closed, and the family were at last alone. Esmerelda looked at her parents and sisters and said, "I guess the witch left her broom outside in the hallway!"

Yvonna looked at Esmerelda and said, "Now, dear, she's just doing her job."

Esmerelda grimaced. "Yeah, sure, whatever. Anything at the expense of others." She began to mumble, "She is such a snot-faced little ..." Then her mumbling became so low and quiet that no one heard the rest of her little rant.

As they rode the elevator down to the lobby, it was already getting close to eleven. Frank suggested, "Let's all of us go over to Flanda's for lunch. It'll be great. We can all tell Minnie and Flanda the whole story, from start to finish."

The family agreed to meet at Flanda's Café in thirty minutes. Frank said to the girls, "I know y'all will get there before us. We need to make a stop at the pharmacy to pick up your mother's antibiotics. We'll see you there."

Sorina, Esmerelda, and Shell headed off in one direction to Shell's car, while Yvonna and Frank set off in another for theirs.

As Shell was pulling out of the hospital in her Le Mans, she began telling her sisters about the new path she had chosen for herself. "I want to be a floral designer instead of just a businesswoman." She started flying. She went on about her class, Eddy's offer to work at his shop, and her plans to finish her work at the real estate office.

Esmerelda and Sorina were shocked to hear Shell so talkative. Neither sister could recall her ever being so off-the-cuff and vocal about her thoughts and plans. They simply weren't accustomed to her speaking so freely.

Shell kept talking as she drove. "This is something I have always wanted to do. Flowers! I'm going to work with beautiful flowers. These last few days, I came to the realization that I need to live my life for myself, not spend it working and living the way I think the world expects me to. Does that make sense to you guys?" She didn't wait for a response. She was on a roll. "Oh! Best of all, the school has a health club available to all students! Once a person is enrolled as a student, they are automatically given a membership to the health club. There was something about it also sharing a presence with Nashville State, which I'm not real clear about. Whatever. But they offer diet programs, too! How cool is that?"

Her sisters were elated at the future Shell had described for herself as she parked in front of Flanda Castle's Café. Shell, Sorina, and Esmerelda watched in surprise as their parents pulled up behind them before they'd even had a chance to open a door. Esmeralda, quick as ever, said, "Must've been the new drive-through, or Dad's grown a lead foot!" And they laughed their way into the restaurant for lunch.

Vacated

Room 211

Charlotte knocked on the door to room 211 so hard that it swung open without so much as her touching the knob. Charlotte and Edna stepped into an empty room. The bed was still unmade. The closet was open, exposing empty hangers on the rod. A hospital gown had been dropped on the cold floor. The trash bin was overflowing with tissues smeared with a woman's dried-up foundation and mascara. Helena was gone. She had flown the coop without an interview, not that she'd ever RSVPed one way or the other. Out of habit, Edna began snapping pictures of the empty room. She was a little compulsive that way, she knew.

Charlotte looked at Edna. Miss Webber was not happy. "Wonder where in hell she's gone off to?" she said as she returned to the corridor outside room 211.

Charlotte spotted Nurse Olga and called to her quietly. "Psst, Olga. What happened to Helena Montgomery? When was she released?"

Olga's nostrils flared a bit at the memory of that morning, watching Helena slip into the elevator. She thought she saw Charlotte's nostrils flare too, but that seemed wrong. "Miss Webber, it seems that Miss Montgomery discharged herself early this morning. No doctor involved."

Olga had easily piqued Charlotte's interest; it didn't take much. She suspected something a little irregular in Olga's tone. Edna, ever ready, sensing a story in Olga's comments and a change in Charlotte's attitude, had pen and pad at the ready. Olga began to say something and then stopped herself abruptly.

Charlotte, smelling dirt, zeroed in on Olga and said, "You were about to say?"

"Well," Olga started, "if I told you a little fairy tale, you wouldn't think anything about it, right? 'Tis only a tale." She gave Charlotte an exaggerated wink.

Charlotte pursed her lips. She nodded as she squeezed her eyes nearly shut with eager anticipation. "Hmmm. So I guess you're speaking of no one in particular!"

Olga continued, "We absolutely respect patient privacy here at the hospital. But if you are up for a fairy tale, I have one to share that I'm pretty sure you'll enjoy. Mind you, I need to keep my name out of this. Are we clear on that?"

"As crystal!" Charlotte purred with a snarky sneer. "I love fairy tales."

Olga commenced. "Okay, then, here it is: Once upon a time, there was a nurse that worked in a hospital emergency room. The paramedics wheeled in an unconscious woman. She was voluptuous — ab-so-lute-ly stunning, even with her eyes closed. Admission came as a result of a gunshot wound. The poor victim had a bullet hole through the left side of her dress into her left breast. There was very little blood, yet her breast continued to ooze … something."

Edna broke into the story, "Give me a minute. I'm taking notes. My finger cramped, and I need to catch up with you."

Olga paused for a minute, until Edna nodded to her to continue. "And so, as this tale evolves, the person shot was immediately undressed on the examining table. As it turned out, she had been shot through her false breasts."

Charlotte, stunned, almost couldn't speak. "Whaaat did you say?"

Edna said, "You aren't serious, are you? This didn't really happen, did it?"

Charlotte said to Edna, "Edna, it's a fairy tale. Pay attention. But we can't ever divulge this tale to anyone. We could incur all sorts of legal troubles if it ever leaked. No pun intended." She smiled. Charlotte turned to Olga and, nose to nose, said, "Really, how close was the bullet to being embedded in this person's actual flesh?"

"A few inches." With a tight smile on her face, Olga continued, "I mean, when the dress came off, it was amazing. First, the damsel in our tale wore a black rubber bustier, under which was a lacy black wire mesh bra packed with a pair of falsies, two large gel-filled balls, and a neatly folded pair of socks — mind you, all inside that bustier. Oh, and then there was an emery board stuck in her cleavage. It was equally shocking and hilarious at the same time. All five in attendance felt amazement, disbelief, relief, and well, you name it, for this fair damsel."

Olga continued, "A pin could have been heard dropping in that room for at least a minute. Then all attending the fair damsel broke into the biggest grins and smug chuckles. But lo, one attendant was suddenly struck by embarrassment for this poor character."

Charlotte looked at Edna and then to Olga and said, "I think I may write a real fairy tale along the lines of yours — maybe name it something like *False Fronts*. It will certainly pay to wait a few months. I will use one of my pen names and publish it in *The Post* as a short story. It's a little too much to risk at *The Eye*. I promise you, Olga, the story will be extremely obscure. It will sound as if it could have happened anywhere — maybe another planet."

Olga smiled and said, "I am so glad you understand. Oh, and by the way, I don't often read *The Post*. Let me know when it comes out? I love the way your articles are so visual."

Charlotte smiled. "Thank you, dear. Keep up your blessed work." And with that, she and Edna headed toward the elevators.

A Family Lunch

The Lapone family had gathered at a table near the center of Flanda Castle's Café. It was a busy lunchtime as each family member pored over a menu — quite needlessly, really, since they practically knew it by heart.

Minnie came over to the table and patted Sorina on the shoulder. She said, "Sweetie, you have been through a lot this week. How are you dealing with all of it? I hope you're well and have gotten past the stress. I would have had a real hard time myself."

They all concurred. Sorina had been through the wringer and had to be exhausted. Yvonna smiled, put down her menu, looked up, and gave Minnie her order. The others followed suit.

Minnie said, "No problems there! I'll get this into the kitchen and be back in a second with your waters. I have to say, after everything that's happened, it is so nice to see you all together."

As the family dove into conversation, Shell excused herself to powder her nose. As Shell backed her chair away from the table, Esmerelda, with a smirk, started to make a little beeping noise, much like a commercial truck's warning while moving in reverse.

Shell, standing, put a hand on her sister's shoulder, bent toward her ear, and whispered, "Stop referring to my butt as a wide load."

Esmerelda started laughing so hard that she had tears in her eyes. Sorina went red as a beet from anger. Yvonna and Frank tried their very best to contain their smiles as Shell slipped away from the table and headed to the restroom.

Esmerelda jumped up and ran after her sister. She whispered in her ear, "You know I mean this nicely, but truly, sis, as Helena said the other day, FTW." Esmerelda let out another giggle.

Shell tugged at the back of her white cotton parachute pants, freeing the fabric from her clenched cheeks. Her yellow off-the-shoulder polyester blouse was too tight, her pants way too loose and baggy. She realized the ensemble screamed "wide load." Shell looked at her sister and said, "Just go away. You're too old for me to tell you to go outside and play in traffic."

The conversation lulled as lunch was served. The topic soon turned to the reward money. Sorina disclosed that she was going to use some of her money to take voice and speech lessons. She didn't know where she would be doing any of this, but it was something she both wanted and needed to do. Shell confirmed her desire for floral school and reported that she had given notice at Hill and Garden. She said, "The best thing that happened during my brief stint in the big bad world of real estate is my short, cute nickname. I just love being called Shell."

Shell and Sorina put their heads together, whispering to each other.

Yvonna looked at them with some irritation and said, "Do I need to remind you ladies that it is rude to whisper at the table? There are no secrets within family."

Sorina grinned, nodded to Shell, and addressed the table at large. "Shell and I have a little announcement. We've decided to share some of our reward with the brat. Yes, you, Miss Esmerelda. As much as we feel you are one big baby, we'll each share a portion of our money with you."

As the four of them looked at Esmerelda, Shell spoke. "Esmerelda, Sorina and I have decided to each give you five thousand dollars.

We think it will help you get on your feet. We know from experience that it'll make it easier for you to get your footing."

Esmerelda jumped up from the table and ran over to her sisters to give them each a hug. Successfully holding back tears, she shrieked, "Oh my god, you guys! Who even does that? You are so sweet. I am just so lucky! That's a lot of money. I promise I'll be really careful. And I promise to use it wisely. There is no way I can thank you enough! Oh … my … *god*! Shell, I promise, I will never, ever refer to you again as my 'big' sister!"

Everyone at the table had a collective chuckle and continued on with their meal.

Friday's Eye

Charlotte worked on Friday's edition harder than any other she had ever published. She was in her office until 3:00 a.m. every day, all week long. This week's issue would be her crowning achievement. She planned to mail copies to the editors of larger publications. She visualized accolades pouring in from everywhere and could not help expunge the thought of a Pulitzer as Edna addressed and mailed the large manila envelopes. Staring at Edna at the postage meter, Charlotte dreamed up hordes of photographers coming to Nashville to take her picture. She gloated over her inevitable forthcoming notoriety.

On the front page of the week's edition was a photograph of the entrance to the People's Bank about thirty minutes after the robbery. It showed the crime tape, the handwritten "CLOSED" sign, the crowd of people outside, and a corner of a gurney. The photograph definitely captured the essence of the chaotic scene. The caption below the photo read, "Robbery Awakens a Sleepy Nashville." The article itself described the bank robbery with its gunfire and multiple injuries, singling out Sorina Lapone and Helena Montgomery as the victims.

The bottom half of the second page showed a photograph of the Lapone family huddled around Sorina's hospital bed. The caption under the picture read "Sorina Lapone's One Glance Captures All." In the accompanying article, Charlotte explained how Sorina had viewed the license plate of the fleeing vehicle in the reflection off her sister's oily forehead. The article went on to relate that once at the hospital and stabilized, Sorina had been placed into a hypnotic trance by an expert local neuro-hypnosis doctor, who had been able to extract from her subconscious her suppressed memory of the license plate number.

Page 3 carried a complete profile of the robbers. Charlotte Webber had wasted no time driving to the Manchester, Tennessee, jail to interview the two criminals. Both men were in their mid-twenties and from a neighboring small town, Bell Buckle, Tennessee. One of the young men was named Freddy Bilco, the other John "Two Wrong" Delgin. Two Wrong and Freddy had been friends for years. They had committed minor and major crimes throughout their teens, and though caught before, they had never been convicted. Charlotte had obtained their mug shots and published those alongside the article.

The rest of the paper captured the essence of Nashville during its time of turmoil. Charlotte and Edna had clenched interviews with numerous individuals who were directly or indirectly connected to the events of the day. The most interesting interview was on page 5. The title of the story was "Nurse Olga Nussell Exposes a Little Something." Olga had been photographed in her uniform, standing by a vacant hospital bed, smiling into the lens of the camera. The article was vague and alluded to a mystery unveiled in the emergency room. Another story addressed the chaos in Sorina's room, with the police and the guard by her door.

Yet another article described the events that had taken place at Sorina's parents' home before the bank robbery. Charlotte explained in detail how a hawk had crashed through the window above the kitchen sink where Yvonna was standing, washing breakfast dishes — how it had collided into her with such force that she was knocked to the floor unconscious, with lacerations and glass embedded in her skin. Charlotte even added how Frank had been across the room at the breakfast table and had sprung into action, calling 911 for paramedics. She went overboard conjuring the eerie nature of the incident as a strange and enigmatic omen.

The entire city of Nashville had heard about the events that had played out that Monday morning, and residents were all too ready to land a copy of *The Eye* and relive the harrowing incidents in detail. To Charlotte's glee, she was forced, by pure demand, to print a large additional run of *The Eye.* She fell all over herself when asked to autograph a reader's copy of the paper. Charlotte grandly attributed the popularity of the issue to everyday, run-of-the-mill, standard journalism as she strutted her stuff around Green Hills. And in her mind, she, Miss Charlotte Webber, reporter, was the absolute first-rate, most significant social columnist the city of Nashville had or ever would have — Miss Charlotte Webber, *star* reporter.

Not Quite the Ritz

Rumor quickly spread around town that Helena Montgomery was away at a spa in the West for much-needed rest, relaxation, and recovery. In truth, Helena was destined for a stay at a rehabilitation center for personal adjustment in the opposite direction. The center's name was fitting: the Personal Alignment Center for All Human Beings. The center was fully staffed by one psychiatrist, three licensed psychologists, two clinical social workers, and an entire staff of generalized caretakers. The motto for the center was, "We help you rediscover your inner self and provide you with the tools necessary to realize your full potential and establish healthy personal boundaries." Jayne and Lawrence Montgomery had received the referral to the center from the hospital's Dr. Fishman. During his visits with Helena in room 211, Fishman had quickly recognized a number of the issues troubling their daughter and had great confidence in the abilities of the staff at PAC, as it was more commonly called. The doctor had proffered the possibility of visiting Helena at the center during her stay. He'd enthusiastically expressed his belief in the center as a viable clinical option to resolve her search for wholeness.

PAC's publicity brochure, which both Helena and her parents had read and reread, advised that clients should anticipate discovering their core selves and recognizing their ultimate life goals. Clients, the brochure read, would participate in organized group sessions in addition to their one-on-one visits with a personally curated therapist. The brochure implied a great emphasis on self-expression and exploration of feelings. Clients would leave with a mastery of their own truth and reality.

The center was located just up the road from the very small town of Elloree, South Carolina, a little over fifty miles northwest of Charleston. Elloree's claim to fame was also its main attraction, the world-famous Teapot Museum. An age-old roadside attraction located near the heart of the quaint rural village, the museum was home to the "World's Largest Teapot," which stood some twenty feet high and rested on the roof of the museum for all to see. Folks motoring through Elloree on their way to and from Charleston often made a point to stop and ogle the giant blue and white teapot looming in the open air. The museum itself housed thousands of teapots in every imaginable shape and size. Entrance to the museum was free; however, a sign noted that "Donations Are Encouraged and Most Genuinely Appreciated" — but not tax-deductible.

Jayne and Lawrence wasted no time in completing their "due diligence" research. Upon further investigation, they had discovered that Helena's health insurance through her employment at the bank would cover the significant costs of her stay. The Montgomery family jointly had arrived at the decision that PAC was the road to Helena's successful rehabilitation. Helena was accepted into the program based on an application she had submitted along with a referral letter from Dr. Fishman and a heartfelt letter from her parents. The brochure had informed them that program duration was three or six weeks. There was no hesitation by Dr. Fishman or her parents in choosing the six-week session. Helena, on the other hand, had some trepidation, but she was ready for a cure, and if that would take six weeks, she was fully on board. The impending start date was next Monday, June 28.

Jayne and Lawrence helped her pack for what they had dubbed her sleepaway camp. During the preparation for her departure,

Helena's mood bounced back and forth between distress and solace. Six weeks was a long time to be away from home, work, and Johnny. She eventually settled on solace; treatments would bring her peace.

Helena wrote Johnny a long letter explaining her six-week retreat. She adjusted some of the facts, just a little. Helena was otherwise completely honest with him. She understood, clearly, her need to resolve some mental health issues to allow her to cope with life. She wrote from her heart, exposing her deep feelings for him and the joy she had experienced on their two dates. She sent him her love, wished him well, and signed off with "XOXOXOXOXO!"

With bags packed and a reservation for Jayne and Lawrence made at a Holiday Inn near Elloree, the family set out. At the end of their five-hundred-mile journey, the Montgomerys' Electra pulled through the gates and up the tree-lined drive of the Personal Alignment Center for All Human Beings. They stopped in front of what easily could have been an attractive English country house, climbing roses and all. Lawrence took Helena's luggage from the trunk, and the three walked to the entrance. As they approached, the massive wooden doors opened. They were greeted by a porter, who took the bags and ushered them into the reception area and up to the check-in desk. On the wall behind the desk was a large plaque that read, "Be yourself; everyone else is already taken," with attribution to Oscar Wilde below it. The gentleman behind the desk greeted them with a cheerful, welcoming voice. He provided the family a bit more paperwork, with admission forms to complete. He offered beverage refreshments and directed them to a comfortable seating area that Jayne found quite pleasantly decorated. They each took a seat and worked through the papers, eagerly awaiting the next steps, whatever they might be.

Across the room, a door opened, and out walked a middle-aged man and woman, nicely attired in everyday street clothes. They introduced themselves to Helena and her parents as Stanley and June, members of the staff. June asked, "Well, Miss Montgomery? Ready to start?"

And with that, Helena hugged both her parents and followed her hosts back through the door from which they had entered. As she walked away through the doors, Jayne and Lawrence both gulped some air and waved, knowing their daughter would not be coming out of those doors for six weeks. There was nothing more for them to do. They thanked the gentleman behind the desk and left the building. Lawrence asked Jayne, "Perhaps the Teapot Museum?"

PAC was an outstanding institution that had received praise from both the American Medical Association and American Psychiatric Association. It was a coed institution that could accommodate at most thirty clients. Almost all clients chose to participate in the full six-week program. Participants were evaluated during several private sessions by different professionals. Over the course of the initial sessions, the individual's presenting issues and desired results were discussed. Inevitably, other, more subtle, repressed issues were discovered during these same sessions. Individuals were assigned to small groups with other patients of varying personalities. Once the target issues were defined, a course of action was prescribed.

Dr. Theodore Beane was PAC's lead psychiatrist. Oliver Constantine, PhD, was the primary psychologist. Protocol had been created by Beane. Once he had reviewed a person's primary issues, Beane required the patient to do several things. Following Beane's protocol, when an issue was categorized, any solid object peripherally corresponding and relatable with the patient's problem was physically loaded into a small grocery cart, sometimes a wicker basket. Beane's type of aversion therapy worked well for most individuals.

Helena's cart included a few batons, some melons, a jar of foundation, socks, gel-filled balls, several pairs of padded underwear, a photograph of Raquel Welch, and an Edith Piaf greatest hits album.

Helena entered a small group of diverse patients. One individual was a man who had enrolled for several reasons. He became bad-tempered when he drank alcohol, which he did in excess. Additionally, he had a history of uncontrollable rage and used extremely foul language in the most inappropriate circumstances. His basket was filled with empty liquor bottles, a skeletal plastic shoulder with chips along the edges, several 8x10 glossy color photos of himself exposing a variety of his ugly moods, and last, a mini-cassette player looped to continuously play him ranting through his own vulgar tirades.

Then there was Muffy, a young lady of about eighteen. She was there because she was an incorrigible brat. She came from a wealthy family with good looks right out of a *Town & Country* ad. She tended to be catty and two-faced with schoolmates. She would do anything, literally anything, to feel superior to her peers. Muffy loved to flaunt her privileged birth and elicit the green eyes of envy in others. For her most recent birthday, her parents had given her a brand-new white Cadillac convertible. She adored driving the car around her small town to flaunt her good fortune at those less fortunate than herself. Still, she was clueless as to why she had no close friends, boy or girl. Her basket was filled with rotten eggs, lemons, and ragged, secondhand clothes that she was expected to wear in rotation. She was not allowed any makeup or style enhancers. Her task was to always smile in public and preface any conversation with a compliment to the individual she addressed. If and when she sneered, didn't smile in public, arched an eyebrow, or skipped a compliment, she was instructed to sit in a corner and suck on a lemon.

Among the rest of the participants was a girl who seemed to scare everyone for no definable reason. Her first name was Tammie. She had a basket full of cucumbers and pomegranates. No one dared ask why she was at PAC. Tammie was only allowed to participate in all-women groups. She was not allowed to even come close to any long blunt objects.

Evening socialization between patients was discouraged. The reasoning was that they were always together during the day, save for their individual sessions. Dr. Beane wanted some self-involvement, some ego building. He believed his patients should learn to follow a steady regimen in which they could be alone with themselves and find entertainment in reading, writing, doing puzzles, or even creating art projects. Television was not allowed; it was simply a distraction. Beane believed in the importance of becoming your own best friend. When a patient became their own best friend, they would know confidence in their independence and be able to fly with their imagination. Perhaps most importantly, a door would finally open in themselves allowing them to experience empathy and kindness and, in turn, find the capability within to be their best selves with others.

For Helena, the days and weeks flew by. She had met a fellow patient who, to her delight, was in a band back in the outside world. She and Tyler had become friendly on that basis alone. During their daily free time, Helena would play the piano or sing, and Tyler would play along on his guitar. At one point, Helena and Tyler put together a performance for residents and staff.

Time would tell whether the treatments were successful. Helena's stay had come to an end. She was anxious for her parents to arrive and take her home. On August 7, 1976, Jayne and Lawrence Montgomery were introduced to a new person, the actualized Helena. Their little girl who had been lost for so many years was found. Here stood a realized woman, happy in her own skin, able to cope with whatever the world might throw her way. Change was good.

On her release documents, along with suggestions for reentry into her everyday life, Dr. Beane had included two encouraging quotes. Helena felt most grateful. The first read, "It's never too late to be what you might have been," written by the English novelist George Eliot. The second quote he offered was, "Keep your face always toward the sunshine, and shadows will fall behind you," a quote sometimes attributed to the American poet Walt Whitman.

Facing the sun, Helena said, "Daddy? Let's go home."

Ricky Baker

I am in love with Esmerelda Lapone. Honestly? The only thing I don't love about her is her first name. I have been calling her Esme for the past two years. It just fits her so much better than Es-me-rel-da. I guess I first read the name Esme in J. D. Salinger's short story about a young orphaned girl who befriends a man going into combat. She is not anything like the character in that story, but no matter — the name fits her. I love Esme!

I was born and raised in Nashville. I was born in the spring of 1955. I'm twenty-one now, if anybody can't do the math. By the time I was thirteen or fourteen, I was popular — not to brag, just a statement of fact. I was the cool guy, tall with the kind of looks and hair that all the other guys envied. Again, not to brag, just a statement of fact. I have the ability to flick my head to the right and have my hair fall into perfect position. To myself, I always have been, always will be, just your normal Joe. To others, I have been the "I wanna be like him" guy. Go figure. School was a breeze. I have a brain and use it. Again, not to brag, just a statement of fact. It was pretty easy for me to maintain good grades, oddly, while having as much fun as my parents allowed.

Speaking of my parents, they were cool, too. Both Stella and Max were fairly strict. I'd started calling them by their first names around the time I was twelve. It was novel at first, but the fact that I called them by their first names slowly grew on them. They eventually embraced it.

Both of my parents work. They work hard. My mother is a beautician and owns a small beauty parlor in Bellevue, which is about twelve miles from Green Hills. My father is the manager of a hardware store in Green Hills. My mother had more flexibility with her job while I was growing up. She picked me up from school and brought me back to her beauty shop for the rest of the afternoon or until my father came for me, which he often did. I helped around the shop. I swept up hair and took towels out of the dryer and folded them. I spent a lot of time doing my homework. When I worked, my mother paid me a dollar an hour, which was great because getting all that money early on taught me how to save and not spend too recklessly. My childhood was a happy one. I love my parents.

I used to watch my mother cut and style women's hair. Sometimes she would take them into the back room, where she waxed them in private. I didn't know what waxing was until I was about thirteen. Once I knew, my interest was piqued. The whole idea of waxing hair off of individuals' bodies — fascinating. I asked her what it was for, and she explained to me that some women grew hair above their upper lip, and waxing was a clean way to remove it. One day, I was in the waxing room by myself and decided to experiment on my legs. At first, it hurt like hell. I think I got the wax too hot. Anyway, I learned how it worked without too much study. Then at fourteen, out of boredom at the salon, I began to thumb through her beauty magazines. I learned that waxing was fast becoming quite the rage. Waxing also involved other parts of the body — the personal parts. I remember there was one day right before I stopped going to the salon after school, when a lady came into the salon, and I overheard her conversation with my mom. She asked my mother about a bikini wax. Being fifteen, I was savvy to what she was asking about. I just thought and thought about that for days. At that point in my life, I had joined the track and basketball teams, and I had practice after school, which ended my afternoons at the salon. It was definitely much more fun to be running or shooting hoops with my friends. But the more I thought about that lady's request, the more I thought about all of the parts of a body that could be waxed. Again, fascinating.

From that point on, my thoughts kept wandering back to waxing. Then, on one exceptional day, I had an epiphany, and my imagination kicked into high gear. I think I was maybe eighteen or something when it hit me. I envisioned the concept for a possible invention. It happened while I was in the Wilson-Quick drugstore. I was standing in front of the magazine rack when I noticed a women's magazine. In the bottom corner of the front cover was a little blurb about waxing the private parts of the body. I picked up the magazine and subtly read the article. I desperately hoped no one was looking. It was as bad as when I was a kid sneaking peaks in Playboy. It was at that precise moment that an idea hit me like a tornado. It took me about a year after that to process my idea into a fully developed thought. I contemplated the mechanics of waxing. I read all that I could. I would sometimes ask my mother off-the-cuff questions about her work and the salon — you know, showing an interest in her business — then slip in a question about waxing. Anyway, I had something serious on my mental to-do list.

The most exciting moment of my life — well, up to that point — happened only a month later. Okay, this has nothing to do with waxing. It was my eighteenth birthday. My parents, or actually, my father, gave me my dad's 1968 yellow Pontiac Tempest convertible. It was a gift to celebrate my upcoming graduation from high school. He was ready for something new. Instead of trading in his car, he wanted me to have it — a convertible in immaculate and perfect condition. He said I had earned it. He said one reason I got it was because I was happily graduating with a solid B average. And the other reason was simply that I was such a great son. And fortunately for me, Mom agreed with my father. Fascinating.

Ricky and Esme

Thursday, July 1, 1976

Ricky drove to Esme's house around 9:00 a.m. and picked her up. They had both taken the day off from work. Ricky was finally going to show Esme what he had designed and been working on for so long in secret.

Esme asked, "So where are we going? You have been so mysterious about this whole thing lately. It's not like you to keep something from me."

"Well, for starters, we're going to my workshop. I'm having something delivered this morning, and once we uncrate it, I'll be able to explain the rest."

As Ricky drove, Esme sat in silence with thoughts bouncing in her head. *What in the world is he doing?*

Ricky pulled into his parents' driveway and drove to the back of the property to his workshop. Parked right in front of the door to the workshop was a large U-Haul truck. The driver was leaning against the driver's door, smoking a cigarette.

Ricky got out of his car and walked over to the driver and said, "Dex, sorry I'm a little late. Thanks for waiting."

Esme got out of the car and headed toward the two. Ricky

made quick introductions. "Esme? This is Dex. Dex? My girlfriend Esme." Ricky continued, "Esme, I met Dex when I drove to Chattanooga a few weeks ago and bought what he has in the truck." He turned to Dex and said, "Hey, by the way, I was able to borrow two four-wheeled dollies from the place where I work. I think they'll help a lot."

While Ricky was talking, Dex opened the back of the truck and climbed in. Dex yelled out, "Lucky for us, I was able to find a U-Haul with an electric lift tailgate. Unloading this thing is gonna be a piece of cake."

From inside the truck, Dex pushed the crate to the tailgate platform and slowly lowered it to the pavement. Once it was down, Ricky and Dex wiggled the crate onto the two dollies and rolled it into Ricky's workshop. Ricky went to his worktable, picked up an envelope, handed it to Dex, and said, "Thanks so much. It's been a pleasure doing business with you."

With that, Dex turned to Esme and said, "It was nice to meet you, Miss Esme." Then he turned to Ricky and said, "Ricky, thank you!" He shook Ricky's hand and said, "If you need any more of these guys, you know where to find 'em." Dex walked out of the workshop, flipped the tailgate back in place, got into the truck, and drove away.

Esme asked, "What in the world was that all about? And what is with this crate? What's inside?"

"Okay, okay. Yes, I have been keeping a little secret. If I'd told you before, you would have thought I was nuts. Remember how I used to hang out at my mother's beauty parlor? All those days when I was a kid?"

Esme answered, "Sure, but what has that got to do with anything?"

As he walked toward his tool cabinet, Ricky said, "First, just help me open this thing. Then I'll fill you in. Let me get my drill and put the screwdriver attachment on. Power will make this process way easier."

Drill in hand, he began to undo the screws from the crate. One by one, they fell to the floor, until one side was completely exposed. The object inside was big and covered in sheeting that made it impossible to figure out. All Esme could decipher was a logo across the bottom of the hulky thing. "WINNER" was all it said.

"Here," Ricky said to Esme. "You just push from back here. I'll shove from there."

Together, the two managed to manipulate the object out of the crate. Once it was out and on the concrete floor of his workshop, it was time for the unveiling.

Ricky stopped to collect his thoughts. "Esme, you have to be completely open to what I have planned. I've studied how this can work from all sorts of angles, including electrical, mechanical, and practical. This is an invention in the making. I really want you to like my idea."

With that, he uncovered the object.

Esme covered her mouth and laughed out loud. "What were you thinking? I guess, why — no, what are you doing with that here? Seriously, Ricky, this warrants explaining."

The purchase Ricky had revealed was a brand-new dime-store horse, the kind that children rode outside of grocery stores. "WINNER" was imprinted on the side of the base. It was an exact replica of a real western horse, complete with saddle, bridle, and reins. It had a coin slot and a control for the type of ride desired. This was the top-of-the-line model.

With a concerned and an inquisitive look, Esme eyed Ricky and asked, "What do you plan to do with this?" She was still trying to control her shock and not burst out laughing.

"Okay, so here's my plan." He explained to Esme all he had learned from the beauty parlor his mother owned. "I researched everything I could find about waxing a body. The last few times I worked at the beauty shop, women were coming in to have their private parts waxed. I finally figured out what it was all about. It nearly always took my mother over an hour to provide most any service requested. I figured if I could invent a way to get this waxing thing done faster, then besides freeing up time, it could be a real moneymaker. I just had to figure out how to construct the thing, how to make it work, and then apply for a patent. I think people will like it. Selling it will all be in the marketing. And that's the reason a dime-store horse is here."

He continued to explain the process he had come up with to make it work. "In plain terms, the horse is made of fiberglass resin, much like the body of a Corvette. The horse is hollow on the inside, and the shell of the horse's body is pretty much indestructible. My plan is to drill small holes into the saddle. Then I will create a flap that can open and close. Open, the flap will expose the hollow interior on the underside of the saddle. I'll figure a contraption that can attach inside that'll hold molten wax. The molten wax will be extruded through the holes of the saddle and onto the underside of a naked person sitting up there on the horse. Once the person is covered with wax, a large sheet of epilating fabric will be placed under the naked person on the saddle. The fabric will be attached to the saddle with some kind of sturdy clip. Then the beauty operator flips the setting for the horse to 'Gallop' mode, and the customer bounces free of the saddle, leaving fabric and hair behind."

Esme's eyes were huge. She was laughing so hard that her laugh turned into snorts. "Are you out of your mind?" she exclaimed. "You seriously think that this will work? Have you even thought who in the world will buy this? Or how?"

Ricky wore his most serious of serious faces. He began to laugh with Esme, and suddenly, they were both snorting and laughing hysterically. "Stop! Yes, I really do think this will work! I still need a little more time to work on it and iron out the wrinkles — fine-tune a few things. When it's ready, I'll need a few volunteers to try it out." He took a deep breath. "And I know where I can sell the first one. It's a shoo-in, I promise. Just give me a few weeks! This whole thing is a major step toward achieving our goals." He led her out of the shed, gave her a wink, locked the shed, and headed to the car.

Going Away

The relationship between Esme and Ricky continued to blossom. By midsummer, the two were inseparable. Early on a Wednesday afternoon, Ricky and Esme nervously asked Frank and Yvonna if they had time for the four of them to have a little chat. Ricky had been at the Lapone home earlier in the day, and Yvonna couldn't help but notice that he and Esme both seemed anxious. She knew something was up but didn't have the slightest clue what that something might be. But knowing her youngest daughter as she did, she knew a "something" with her could be just about anything on this earth.

"No problem," said Frank. "Maybe around four?"

So at 4:00 p.m., the group convened in the Lapones' living room. Yvonna and Esmerelda sat on the sofa directly across the coffee table from Frank and Ricky, who had made themselves comfortable in the leather club chairs.

Esmerelda jumped right in. "For starters, Ricky's been calling me Esme for more than a year. Do you like it? Can you live with it? I really like my name shorter, just like Shell. I would love if you'd call me Esme from now on. It's a good nickname. Seems funny to think of using a nickname after eighteen years. Thing is, I love it. Think of all the ink I'll save."

Yvonna was the first to respond. "I thought I'd heard him call you that. Never really sank in. But you know what? I like it, too. Esme."

Frank joined in. "I happen to agree completely. But you called us here for something else. I've got a feeling you must have more on your minds than just Esmerelda's name. Let's have it."

Esme looked at her parents and then at Ricky. "Ricky, don't you want to go first?" She took a quick breath. Ricky didn't have time to say a word before she dove back in. "Oh well, I opened my mouth. Might as well keep going. Mom, Dad, we want to go away — together. I mean, like really away. The move may not be permanent, but then, it might be."

Ricky was flushed and obviously eager as he said, "Esme and I have been seeing each other for almost two years. The fact of the matter is we are in love — with each other! We want to go away and build a life together. We want to build that new life in Los Angeles. And while marriage isn't on the top of the table right now, it is definitely a regular topic of conversation.

"We both chose LA because it has so much to offer — the glamour of Hollywood and Beverly Hills, Santa Monica's and Malibu's beaches, the boardwalk and canals of Venice Beach. And there're Studio City and Sherman Oaks and the rest of the San Fernando Valley. Did I forget Pasadena and San Marino? The entire Los Angeles area is such a great place for young people like us. Esme wants to keep going forward with her acting. She's good. She'll be able to audition for roles. I want to take a stab at acting, too. And I have another opportunity I'd like to pursue, which I'll explain to you both as it develops." He was on a roll now and kept talking.

"I've been saving from my jobs all my life. I've actually built up a decent nest egg. Esme will have her money as well. She has everything she's stashed away, and with the reward money Sorina and Shell gave her too, she has a nice little cache. Between the two of us, we'll have close to forty-three thousand dollars. We harbor no illusions. We know we'll both have to find jobs. We'll keep what we've saved as our cushion and only use the minimum we need to get started out there. We want to do this. I know it's a shock to both of you. Just know we've been discussing this for months and given it serious thought." He stopped and began to breathe again.

Esme took up their cause again and said, "Mom and Dad, I hope this isn't too much all at once. Is it? I mean, I want this as much as Ricky. Any adventure is scary and has its roadblocks. But I think if I don't take control of my life now, when will I ever? For both of us, this is a chance worth taking. I've come to the realization that everything in life is temporary. We have to follow our hearts and dreams. Life shouldn't be a pile of regrets about what a body should have done or could have been."

Ricky took it from there. "Who knows? Esme could become a famous movie star. I could too, although I ultimately see myself as a salesman for that project I mentioned earlier. I'm not putting you off about what I'm doing. I assure you, I'll tell you more when I'm further into development."

"Remember, Mom, you've always told me, 'You are the one and only person who can choose your destiny. You're the one who has to live with yourself.' Ricky and I are making a good choice, even if it doesn't work out but I know in my heart it will. Chances are rare, change is valuable." Esme rested her case.

Yvonna smiled and looked at Frank. "Esmerelda." She paused and started again, gazing at her daughter. "Esme, your father and I have raised you to be independent. I stand by what we've done. In other words, what I mean to say is, I think both of you are doing the right thing." She paused again, composing her response. She continued, "If I were to disagree with you, it would only drive a wedge between us; that is the last thing I would ever let happen. So with all of that, yes, I am all for it. In fact, your and Ricky's plan sounds really quite exciting."

Frank was smiling as well and said, "Honey, I too am excited for both of you. As to the financial part, to help you get on your feet, your mother and I will chip in some cash to help you start your life out there. It's the very least we can do to show our encouragement. Plus, once the two of you are settled, we would love to come out there for a visit. Neither one of us has ever been to any part of California. It's a dream trip that, for whatever reasons, never happened."

It was settled — the Lapone parents were on board with the idea. Now it was time to go talk with Stella and Max. Ricky asked Frank, "Want to join us for the chat with my parents? We're headed there now. My dad can be stubborn, but Mom is much more open to change."

Yvonna rolled her eyes as she looked at Ricky. "I think you both need to do this yourselves. Just start the conversation the same way you presented it to us. I feel certain your parents will be agreeable. Having heard you out myself, I can't see how they won't agree with your plans. You don't need us there. Our presence would be, well, let's just say … awkward."

Nashville State Technical Institute

Six weeks had now passed since the first class of Shell's program at NSTI. She had signed up for the complete four-month term. She had decided that if what lay ahead in those four months was what was required to become a certified floral arranger in the state of Tennessee, she was in for the long haul. Every state had a different registration process for becoming a certified floral designer. Passing the classes she was taking would ensure her certification in Tennessee.

This school was different for Shell. The class load was extremely regimented. Her school day started at 9:00 a.m. and lasted until 3:00 p.m. By 3:30 p.m., she was in the school's sports center, sweating it out with her new, very own personal trainer, Anita Mintz. Shell had a list of reasons to go to the gym. Her primary reason was weight loss. Next on her list was to improve muscle tone and strength and flat-out get her body into shape. As she saw it, she was well on her way to middle-age at twenty-three. It was now or never. She'd seen herself in the mirror enough times to know her body was losing its fight with gravity. If she didn't deal now with the droops, rolls, and sags that had begun to appear in too many places between the top of her head and the soles of her feet, there would be no dealing ever.

So every Monday, Wednesday, and Friday afternoon at three thirty, Shell went to the women's locker room, changed into her workout clothes, and went in search of Anita. At each of their sessions, Anita worked with Shell one-on-one for the first hour and gave her instructions for activity during the second hour. "Intense" and "tyrannical" were adjectives commonly used to describe Anita. She herself was in perfect physical condition. Shell came to her sessions ready and eager for anything Anita had in store. Shell was determined to shed twenty to thirty pounds. With help from Anita, she gained dietary and nutritional knowledge. She knew she had been on the wrong track all her life. Armed with this new knowledge and working through aggressive physical conditioning, Shell would lose twenty-two pounds by end of term and be proud.

Shell had found the very first day in her floral class to be a life-changer; the first hour had been her turning point. Her instructor, Professor Benjamin Blondell, had introduced himself to the class and then said to everyone, "Please, let's get to know each other. We can start by just going around the room, and each of you can briefly stand and say your name." This wouldn't take long with only twelve students.

When the time came for Shell, she stood and said, "Schmellda Lapone." For the life of her, she couldn't figure why she had done that. Looking at the perplexed expressions around her, she quickly recovered composure and said, "But please call me Shell!" And for the remainder of the term and her life, she would welcome being known by her nickname.

Benjamin looked at Shell and said, "I don't think I've ever heard that name before. It's really quite interesting. Is it Italian?"

Shell blushed and told him, "Oh, no. It's Romanian. I was named for an aunt who died during World War II."

All of Shell's classes were geared exclusively toward floral certification. There had been fees, and she'd bought a stack of texts at the school bookstore. Fortunately, the school provided most of the tools, containers, and flowers, both artificial and real, for each student.

The curriculum was broken into four parts. Part one had started with a brief but important introduction to botany. The intro was more thorough than Shell had thought possible. They'd gone over plant function and appearance, the relationships between different plants, where various species grew, our use of plants, and plant evolution. After the intro, the course studied the wide variety of flowers, the selection process based on seasonal availability, texture, color, handling, maintenance, scale, dealing with wholesalers, and even a little vase work.

The second part of the course was titled "Foliage, Greenery, and Fillers" and covered exactly what its title said. The students discovered the vast variety of foliage used as fillers in individual arrangements and what to use for best effect. Students learned about period styles from the Renaissance to the present and about specialty arranging such as the Japanese art of ikebana. During this portion, the class was taken on field trips to the landscaped gardens of a few local grand estates.

Part three was possibly the most diverse segment of the class. The title of this segment was, oddly, "Make Believe." It covered weddings and funerals. So students studied altar flowers, tabletop wedding specialties, bouquets, boutonnieres, cake decor, and lighting, right alongside wreaths, sprays on stands, and casket sprays. Each student participated in mock weddings and funerals. The funerals were particularly difficult and challenging. The student first posed as a grief-stricken mourner and then, switching hats, became the consoling floral designer. To aid with this role-playing, Nashville psychiatrist Dr. Henderson Palms was brought in for a few sessions. Dr. Palms's specialty was grief counseling, and he was the noteworthy author of several books on grief. His second book, *Grief Is Hard to Grab,* had made it to the number 3 spot on the nonfiction bestseller list. The volume was widely used in university psychiatry courses. Dr. Palms talked with the students about grief, the need for empathic consolation, and things you especially didn't want to say to a mourning client. Shell would keep that last one close to her chest.

After Dr. Palms spent three days in the classroom in lecture and roundtable discussions with students, Professor Blondell introduced Ms. Joan Delarue at the podium for the remaining two days of the week. Ms. Delarue was a professional acting coach. She was brought in by Professor Blondell to develop and improve the students' emotional response to the myriad emotions expressed by participants in weddings and funerals and to then teach them how to use those newly improved responses in their sales. Ms. Delarue began each class session with some quick improvisation. She then led them into a cold reading of dialogue from a movie or play in which the students needed to dig deep and read the parts using tremendous emotion. Most of the scenes were centered around some crisis like an overdose or a car accident or an event such as a wedding or a funeral. A few of the scenes she chose were actually upbeat; one involved the emotions of a bride with a bridesmaid while another portrayed a first-time father pacing the floor in a maternity ward. Shell wasn't thrilled about Ms. Delarue's contribution. She believed honest emotional responses would come from the heart.

After Delarue's departure, Professor Blondell continued with role-playing exercises. The impromptu sessions involved normal transactions between clients and staff working in a flower shop and also staff reactions to phone calls from customers who were either crying or happy. The takeaway from these sessions was how to remain calm and composed at all times and put the client at ease, no matter what was required. The students had the option of getting into costume for these exercises, picking from the wide variety available from the drama department, which was right down the hall. Nashville State was known for these classes. The program's reputation was strong and positive, and it was well known for turning out thoughtful and creative florists.

Shell thought that one student in particular had too much

fun with this portion of the class. His name was Ned Fulcher, and he was six feet seven and thin as a reed. In one of these real-time sessions, he returned from the dressing room carrying a walking stick and wearing a black three-piece suit, a starched white shirt with floppy black bow tie, and a wide-brimmed black fedora, with a single white rose boutonniere pinned to his lapel. He had rouged his cheeks and donned a fake handlebar mustache. This boy got into it and pulled off the ruse without cracking a smile. He hobbled to the counter. Using the walking stick as a gavel, he rapped on the counter to get the "florist's" attention. He feebly leaned over and spoke to the attendant. Staying in character, he sniffled while madly obsessing over what sort of floral arrangements would be appropriate for his own funeral. This was a preorder, thank you. The class roared with laughter. Shell thought Ned should maybe switch to the drama department as fast as possible.

Part four of the semester was divided into two sections. For the first part, each student would design and construct a scale model of a float for the Pasadena Rose Parade. This would turn out to be an actual judged competition, in conjunction with Springs Academy down the road in Memphis, Tennessee. Springs Academy had a corresponding program that was planned and executed in the same manner as Nashville State's floral certification class. Each school had the same number of students. The instructors were using the same curriculum. The floats were to be constructed to one-third scale and should be no wider than eight feet, no longer than sixteen feet, and no taller than ten feet. The two schools' projects would be judged together, and a winner would be selected from the combined pool of students. Additional information would be forthcoming.

The second and final project of the fourth part of the class required each student to create a floral design for entry in the state competition. Two competitions were staged yearly, each coinciding with the end of a school term. The winner of the state title received a cash prize, a plaque, and recognition across all forms of Tennessee media — print, radio, and television. In addition to the students' submissions, entries would be submitted by professional florists from across the state. Some of the professionals had been working in the floral business for years. The chance for the students to compete at this level offered tremendous opportunities for their futures.

Sorina Goes to Stuttering Camp

I have wanted help to conquer my stuttering for as long as I can remember. In their search for help, my parents were told it was something I would eventually grow out of — wrong! Nothing they tried ever worked. They didn't understand why. We tried speech lessons — waste of time and money. There's no blame to be laid. Anybody who knows me knows about my use of the harmonica hanging around my neck — blow a little tune, glide into words. This year, I tried something totally different. I went to sleepaway camp for the first time in my life.

On July 6, I found myself at a stuttering camp, or maybe the better term is a camp for those with speech fluency issues. Camp Mouthoff is located down the interstate, just south of the Tennessee state line, in Dalton, Georgia. It's a six-week experience. Parents, my mother and father included, were required to attend the first three days and then return for the last two days of camp. The staff explained to everyone that therapy needs to be a process shared between parents, family members, friends, and their stutterer. One of the first things we learned at Mouthoff is that friends and family too often unwittingly contribute to the stutter. It isn't their fault. No one ever told them that trying to help by finishing words and sentences when their stutterer stammers only compounds the frustration. The youngest camper attending was six years old. I was one of the oldest at twenty. I know — that's quite an age span. Believe me, everything was geared to be age-appropriate. The counselors were college-age students of speech fluency; almost all were working toward their master's degrees. Certified speech therapists were on staff to supervise and provide one-on-one sessions. I was given the opportunity to help with younger campers if I wished.

When the parents or friends left, counselors divided campers into groups of eight. The eight in my group were eighteen to twenty-one. Every Monday a project was assigned to each group to work through that week. Over the course of the entire six weeks, assignments rotated between groups. Any project could be as elaborate or as simple as the group wanted. Projects ranged from creating a play to be performed the following Friday to pretending to be salespeople giving their best pitch to make a sale. The classroom project sent shudders down my spine. Everyone in the group had their turn to be the "teacher" while the other campers remained "students." The teacher asked questions, and the students responded. You want to talk about flashbacks? Happily, for me, in this place, it was of no concern how long a question or answer took to get out of my mouth. For a lot of us, this was possibly our first time experiencing a completely nonjudgmental environment in reaction to our stammers. Stammer on, my friend, stammer on. We're all listening to you. We can hear you.

We had a silly thing once a week called "camp talks." It reminded me of the game Gossip or Telephone that we played as kids. The general idea was similar. A counselor would gather his or her group into a powwow circle. They were surrounded by all the other campers. The counselor would make up the beginning of a story, and then going around the circle one by one, each camper would add their own two lines to the story. We older campers were advised to behave. After eight campers' additions to the rambling dialogue, the laughter that arose at the ridiculously incongruous story was the real prize. Laughter constantly rained buckets around the camp. I can tell you from experience, laughter is healing.

We had lectures. We heard tales of famous people like Mel Tillis, Marilyn Monroe, Winston Churchill, and Carly Simon, all of whom had speech problems. The counselors told us that stuttering is just an interruption of speech, experienced by many from time to time. We stutterers just have the experience more often. The speech therapists provided exercises we could practice on our own, after our sessions with them ended. As individual stutterers, we were not alone in this world.

I had several memorable and productive sessions with my therapist. In one of our earliest meetings, she said, "Tell me about yourself, Sorina." I stuttered through the story of my family, my grandmother Lulu, and my sisters. I stuttered when I told her about school. My stammer eased up when I gave her an earful about my love of music and singing. I explained the harmonica around my neck, my likes, my dislikes. I gave her my best Autobiography 101.

In one of our later sessions, she said again, "Tell me about yourself, Sorina. Who are you? What makes you you? What do you find special in yourself?"

"Wow. I sp-sp-spend a lot of t-time in my o-o-own head. I h-have a few close f-friends. Enough acquaintances. I'm probably closest to my sisters. My speech fluency issues made me an introvert. I'm okay around people. I'm better by myself most of the time. I've cultivated my imagination. I'm especially fond of poetry. When I embrace a poem, I can go into myself and be completely comfortable. There is so much about poetry to relish, alone. You take the poets of the Romantic era: Shelley, Wordsworth, Byron, Keats. They take a little more time to understand. Part of it is that language itself was so different then. It seems complicated and intense. And then I just sort of fall into their world. So much seemed tragic and beautiful. Then I come through time to Dickinson, Millay, Eliot, and Frost. Modern times? Some of their poems seem so facile on the surface. But the poems are like roses, beautiful in and of themselves. Each line is like a petal with its own color, nuance, interpretation, and pleasure. I especially love Millay's "Dirge without Music" and Frost's "Stopping by Woods on a Snowy Evening." They're quite different in tone. Taken slowly, each line has its own angle, magnitude, and depth. Interpretation depends on the reader. Reading a poem can be work. Maybe that is how life itself is meant to be viewed — challenging if one is willing to accept the challenge. Oh goodness, my time's up. I hope I haven't rambled on too long."

"Did you hear yourself while you spoke? You were sure of yourself and your thoughts. Your stammer was almost completely absent. Good work, young lady. I've enjoyed our time today, Sorina. I'll look forward to our next session. You're making excellent progress."

Several days before the end of camp, my parents returned to fulfill their obligation. They joined me for all our activities, including the performance of the last play. I was able to introduce them to my therapist, and they very happily joined in my last session. In separate meetings, all parents were introduced to practices and given options for how to positively interact with their stutterer to help further improve their fluency. Those last two days were a cram course for the parents.

The six weeks at camp passed quickly for me. I was delighted with my progress. The improvement I made in my speech fluency felt profound. I left with exercises and tools to further improve my stammer. Best part? The speech therapist I saw at camp lives in Nashville! I would be able to continue sessions with her.

The three of us drove back to Nashville. Mom and Dad both thought they noticed a new confidence in me. They knew I was on my way to becoming a better speaker. Summer's end was around the corner, and it was time to think about fall. I could actually visualize the beginnings of my new life. Best. Camp. Ever!

Twelve Weeks After the Robbery

Charlotte was perched in a chair behind her desk, surrounded by her current staff of eight. Fortunately, no one suffered from claustrophobia; space was tight and the air was close. Ever since the edition of twelve weeks ago covering the robbery, she had never been busier. She had hired a part-time reporter to take care of "the little stuff" and now had a total of three staff members dealing with printing and deliveries. She had taken on two commissioned sales agents as advertising sales grew alongside increased circulation. The magazine was now at least fourteen pages long every Friday. Gradually, after the robbery issue, Charlotte had been advised of or invited to more events whose organizers wanted her coverage in *The Eye.* Organizations and social clubs were calling for her to do more interviews. More opportunities were heading her way every day. It had all dominoed into more than she possibly could have imagined. Meanwhile, Charlotte's executive assistant and prodigy Edna was still plugging away, working tirelessly, and tagging along after Charlotte as needed. For people looking at Edna constantly putting in the hours, it was hard to believe this was the first and only job she'd ever had.

With the meeting set to begin, Carmen, Charlotte's manicurist, arrived. She squeezed her way through the assembled staff, took a seat next to Charlotte, and began work on her nails. Charlotte sat erect in her chair like a princess. Sitting on her lap was Teenie, her pet chihuahua.

These weekly Monday morning meetings were fairly simple events. Actually, not a whole lot ever came from them. The employees were all professionals and knew how to do their jobs. Charlotte led the meetings with her usual, toxically caustic personality. In her own head, she was, as ever, a tenacious and significant reporter, much sought-after, and admired as a businesswoman with tremendous acumen. To her staff, including Edna, she was none of that. Her employees saw the real Charlotte, an obnoxious and insecure condescending micromanager. Where she saw herself as a shrewd entrepreneur, they saw a delusional snipe. The increase in business and accolades had gone straight to her already swelled head. Today, after suggesting several benign strategies, Charlotte surprised everyone when she excitedly professed, "I think now is the perfect time to pen my memoir."

Edna simply stared at her in amusement. No one else could reply. Carmen laid the final coat of polish on Charlotte's nails and began packing up her equipment; she was ready to go.

The meeting was coming to its usual end. Once again, nothing substantial or pertinent had been learned or imparted. It was just like every other Monday morning meeting. They were leaving a room that smelled strongly of nail polish and chihuahua farts. The entire staff filed out, heading to accomplish real work in fresher air. Temporarily satisfied, Charlotte remained, with her constipated thoughts and vainglorious dreams, still sitting erect as a princess, staring into space. Edna gave her a nudge. No one was left in the room except Charlotte, Edna, and gassy Teenie. Edna, ever efficient, reminded Charlotte of several outside appointments and columns to be written. Charlotte locked Teenie in her crate and headed out with Edna.

As they drove, an announcement came over WKDA, a local and wildly popular pop radio station in Nashville. The owner of the Music Box had just announced an exceptionally special event coming up this Saturday evening at his bar and grill. Joni Mitchell would be performing in the round at the popular venue, accompanying herself on acoustic guitar and piano along with her traveling band. The club had a capacity of three hundred, but at the back of the room, double garage doors rolled open to the enclosed patio, doubling capacity. As industry news had it, Joni was in town to record a new album with some of Nashville's undeniably incredible musicians. She had offered to play the famous venue and sample a few of her new singles as well as a couple of her standards. She had requested that the Music Box bring in a local up-and-coming talent for her warm-up act.

After the owner of the Music Box sent queries throughout the local industry in search of a performer, he had settled on a local who already had proved herself at this very place: Helena Montgomery. Locals already enjoyed Helena's blues nights at the club, but now, as a bonus, she had recently added a partner. The newest addition would remain a mystery until the performance. Helena's mystery partner would join her for a couple of numbers and then perform solo, using her three-octave range to cover songs penned by Laura Nyro.

Call it what you will — fluke, serendipity, or pure luck — but the stars had aligned for Helena and Miss Mystery, quite by accident, to bump into each other in the women's department of Cain-Sloan a few weeks prior. They had started talking and, before they knew it, decided to go for coffee. Over a delightfully long and congenial conversation, their shared talents and affinity for music had come up. They told each other about their respective summers. They considered the possibility that their individual musical talents might mesh and planned to meet up and give it a shot. It took no time to discover that what they had together musically worked. So besides being new friends, they were a new musical duo ready to take on Nashville.

When the news of the concert had finished, Charlotte turned to Edna behind the wheel. "Why didn't we hear about this any sooner? How did I not know Helena Montgomery was back in town?" She mumbled, "The little tram —" Stopping herself, she continued, "That little fake. What is she doing back in town?" She snickered, a little too loudly, and said, "I cannot wait to see her!"

Edna piped up and told Charlotte, "I saw her at the grocery the other day. She looks great! Completely different. Honestly, she had this weird, kind of angelic thing going on. She has changed so much. She looks like a totally different person. Maybe she had a lot of 'work' done. She was gone long enough. Maybe she just lost a lot of weight? I can't put my finger on it."

Charlotte glanced over at Edna. "Righto — she goes away for a few months, and now she is completely different. I have to see this!" She rolled her eyes a couple of times. "You have to finagle a couple tickets to that show for us, Edna! Go for backstage passes if you can. We have to remember to bring the Minox."

They drove on to the luncheon at the women's club.

Labor Day Weekend

It was Thursday, September 2, 1976. Shell had an end-of-summer break from classes. Only one more month to go. She lifted her head from her pillow, saw it was only 5:00 a.m., rolled over, and immediately went back to sleep. As she slept, she drifted farther and farther away into the deepest of sleeps and landed in her childhood. Her father was telling her another one of his own wildly imaginative fairy tales. This particular tale was a favorite and always a comfortable landing pad. It was a tale about Mr. Moonbeam and what he was doing. Mr. Moonbeam Man was an imaginary person her father had used in a variety of stories he made up just for her when she was very young. Mr. Moonbeam was a hero who saved all children from their nightmares. All they had to do if they were being chased by an ogre or a dragon was open their eyes, stare up at the ceiling of their room, and wish. Mr. Moonbeam Man would be there, shining down from space with his silvery arms, holding them tight and safe from horrible things. The beams from his arms were as bright as the sun. They would stream down in a small tunnel of light, pick up their nightmare, and transport it far away, to a place where it would never be seen again. That was all a child needed to know. Mr. Moonbeam was easy to find and would always come when needed. If children wanted to visit with him, all they had to do was climb onto the beam of light from his arms, and he would transport them to the moon.

Once on the moon, the children were greeted by a welcoming committee of small creatures and tiny beings. The welcoming area was filled with lots of colorful balloons, candy canes, and ice cream cones. Mr. Moonbeam Man would soon be joined by his wife, Princess Aurora de Borealis. An angelic silver halo flowed about Princess Aurora's head. She had silvery hair that was a reflection of magical glistening light. Her hair was as white as the most brilliant sunlight. The princess had a beautiful, sparkling magic wand with a heart-shaped tip encrusted in diamonds. One gentle tap of the wand on a child's head would instantly make the child's nightmare disappear. Once the nightmare was erased from the little one, light telescoped back into the arms of Mr. Moonbeam Man, and the child was taken back to earth and tucked safely into their own cozy bed. As a child, before she went to sleep, Shell had always known that she would be protected. Mr. Moonbeam Man was watching over her. Deep in her heart, she believed in Mr. Moonbeam Man.

The alarm clock blared next to her bed; it was 7:00 a.m. She turned it off and smiled as she thought of her dream and was comforted by the innocent dreams of her past. It had been ages since she had reveled in the past. This morning she lazed in bed for a few minutes longer, thinking of the years that were really not so long ago.

Today was a special day she had planned all for herself. She'd have her hair done at the salon, get a massage and a facial, and then have a little lunch and do some shopping. Anita, her trainer, had become a monumental influence in her life. After all her hard work with Anita and after sticking with her diet, she could reward herself and spend a day like this. Her first appointment was at Snips, the hair salon, at 8:30 a.m. She was getting the works. The next appointment, at eleven, was at Perfectly Smooth, a facial salon. Lunch and shopping would follow. The finale of her delightful day would be at four o'clock with a massage.

The hair salon turned out to be pretty intense. The stylist and Shell decided she needed a solid trim, light blonde highlights, and a new hairstyle that would involve a new technique called crimping. First things first — deep cleansing of her hair and scalp. Oil from her scalp, diluted with water, flowed down the drain of the sink. After what seemed an exhausting two hours, she thrilled at the results. At the register, she bought all sorts of new hair products. Out the door she went with the goods and a list of suggestions from her stylist for a personalized daily regimen.

Next, the facial. After wrapping Shell's new hairdo in cellophane to protect it, the aesthetician introduced herself and had Shell lie on a white padded table that was draped in a soft white sheet. She dimmed the lighting, covered Shell's eyes with a comforting mask, and started the facial. As the work began, Shell became aware of the soft, light music floating through the room. A warm mist blew and lightly covered Shell's face. She felt warm, damp gauze strips being applied to her exposed skin. After a few minutes, the strips were removed, and the suction and extraction process began. This was a new experience, and Shell had no idea what to expect. The process took nearly an hour, and she felt her skin being poked and gently jabbed time after time. The aesthetician commented in a soothing voice that she had never had so many extractions from one person. This was followed by a soothing, cooling treatment of creams and liquids that all smelled like cucumber. It felt like layer after layer was applied and then removed. Next up, her face was gently wiped down with some new thing that was again cool and very soothing. At last, the aesthetician removed the eye covering and helped Shell down from the table. Looking in the mirror, she saw that her face was a little pink, but it glowed. She felt wildly fresh and clean.

Shell looked at the woman. "I am so sorry. I don't even remember your name, but this was a fantastic experience! Thank you so much. I feel great!"

The woman looked back and said, "My name's Connie. I think you'd benefit if you came to see me every six weeks. You had so many extractions. I won't even tell you what could be done with them. In any case, if you will do this regularly, you'll achieve a balance in your complexion that I think you'll appreciate. You can see for yourself; you actually have been hiding quite a lovely complexion. You just need to deal with it. Now then, tonight and tomorrow your face will be a little pink and splotchy. Don't worry. Neither will last. And I'm happy to suggest some products we have available that you can use at home between sessions."

With that done, Shell paid and walked back to her car with a small bag of facial products.

She really did feel like a new person. Now it was time for a small lunch, then a little shopping for new clothes. Something was stirring in her that she hadn't experienced maybe ever. Her life was falling into place in a good way. She was confident and self-assured. She was determined to continue taking care of herself. She would complete her studies. She would become a certified florist.

After lunch, she drove to the shopping center. Her first stop was the Gap; she'd go down her list from there. After a few hours, she was lugging four big shopping bags, brimming with new purchases, back to her car. It was approaching four — massage time. She had booked thirty minutes specifically for her neck and shoulders. It was a lovely thirty minutes.

By evening, she'd made it home, freshened up, and dressed in one of her new outfits. Now she was waiting. She had dinner reservations with Esme, Ricky, and Sorina. They were meeting Shell at her place and were running late. She heard footsteps coming up the stairs and opened the door.

Esme shrieked with joy when she saw her sister. "Wow! You look fabulous! I mean, what a change! You seriously look like a different person. Really!"

Ricky was staring in amazement. He had never seen Esme's sister look so good. For once, he was speechless.

Sorina blinked and blinked again and smiled. "You are stunning. What a difference since forever! We've missed you. I'm so glad you have a break. We'll have lots of fun tonight."

Shell had been a hermit since starting her courses. Between school, the gym, and her projects, her days were filled to overflowing. Every day seemed to launch at dawn and was a marathon until she left the gym around 5:30 p.m. She'd made a habit of grabbing a quick something to eat and then either returning to school to work on her current project in the lab or running home to collapse in front of the television. There'd been no extra time in her days.

At any rate, her two sisters were still staring at her. Although they all spoke on the phone almost every other day, if only briefly, Sorina and Esme had never stopped to think what Shell was really going through with her diet, school, and the gym. Now they saw her and the results of her time underground for the first time. They were most happily surprised.

A Cookout at the Lapones

Friday, September 3, 1976

The three sisters, Ricky, and Ricky's parents, Max and Stella, were all heading to the Lapone home for a Labor Day weekend cookout. It was late afternoon when Ricky steered his Tempest into the Lapones' driveway, followed by Max and Stella in their new vehicle. Frank had been home from work only about thirty minutes; Yvonna was in the kitchen, busily preparing food and getting everything ready for the cookout. Sorina and Esme were both upstairs, primping and talking as they changed in preparation for the soiree. Shell had called to say that she was running a little late and would be there by five thirty, no later.

Ricky and his parents went straight to the kitchen to hang out with Frank and Yvonna.

Ricky commented, "I was shocked when I saw your daughter Shell yesterday. She looks great! Have you seen her yet?"

Yvonna looked up from making hamburger patties and said, "I have seen neither hide nor hair of that girl in at least eight weeks. All she does is study, work on her projects, go to the gym, and get home late. She calls at least every few days just to check in and let us know she's alive, but that's about all. She does talk about her neighbor, Wally, sometimes referring to him as the inspector or something like that. Seems they often have dinner together. I think that is the only person who has seen her these last few months."

"Yeah," Ricky said, "I think they are like really good friends now. She loves the twig furniture that he makes, and he likes all the artificial flowers that she assembles. She told us last night that he likes to come up for dinner. Seems some evenings he'll bring takeout for them both to eat, and then he'll sit and watch her create things for her school projects."

Frank smiled. "It sounds like a really nice scenario. She is so lucky to have such a pleasant person for a neighbor. I mean, I've only met the man twice, and I think I would enjoy time around him too. He has such a warm and kind heart."

Yvonna mumbled, "At least someone sees her and knows she's okay. It's good, and I'm really very glad she has someone watching out for her."

Shell was pulling her car into the driveway about the same time the girls came downstairs. All three converged in the entry at the same time.

When Esme looked at her big sister, she squealed again. "I cannot believe this change in you, Shell. Just wait until Mom and Dad see you. You haven't seen them in a few weeks, have you?"

Shell beamed with pride and answered, "More like two or three months."

The three broke free of their conversation and walked through the dining room into the kitchen, where their parents were talking away with Ricky and his parents.

Shell was the first to open her mouth. "Hi, everyone. Guess who's home?"

Yvonna turned all the way around from her kitchen counter. The expression on her face was one of utter shock and disbelief. Her mouth dropped open. Then a broad smile crossed her face, and she said to Shell, "You come over here right this minute and give me a hug, skinny girl."

Shell grinned and walked over and gave her mother a big hug.

She followed with the same for her father and said, "Can you believe it has been almost three months since we have seen each other? I only live three miles away!"

Sorina piped in, "Shell, what are you going to do with all your old clothes? Oh, I know. You could have a tent sale."

The group broke into laughter. Esme picked up the conversation from there. "Mom, we saw her last night. Doesn't she look great? I mean, she is unbelievable."

Frank was quick with a solid "Absolutely!"

Since this was the first time both families had been together in such a long while, Sorina and Shell stepped back a bit and just listened, laughing and smiling, interested in following all the conversations.

Sorina said to Shell, "I am so proud of you. It takes guts to go through what you have just done in three months. Really."

"And I have one more month of weight loss in my book. I hope to lose another six pounds, or maybe even seven, by mid-October," Shell responded.

Esme joined the mix and began telling all of them about the plans she and Ricky were making — California, acting, and a passing reference to something she and Ricky just didn't want to discuss. Sorina and Shell were surprised. This was the first they'd heard about Esme's plans. They listened intently with sadness on their faces, thinking about losing their little sister, as Esme continued to detail their plans, still completely avoiding the topic of Ricky's invention.

Shell looked at Sorina and then to Esme and said, "I will be so sad to see you leave home. But your plans sound solid, and if that's what you both really want, I say go for it!"

Sorina hesitantly agreed and said, "I too will be really sad to see you go. I'm so used to you being across the hall. It'll just be so lonely here without you." Sorina turned to Shell. "Can you tell my speech lessons are working? My vocal instructor is amazing to work with too. He's actually impressed with my vocal abilities. It's kind of shocking to me."

"So when are we gonna get to hear you sing?" Esme asked, but she didn't wait for an answer. "You just won't believe what Ricky has done. He has a couple more weeks of work, and then he'll show you all what he's been up to. His project is the reason we're delaying our move to Los Angeles." Esme looked at everyone and said, "I really think that this might be a big deal."

The Lapone and Baker families were all together at last. Max and Stella were a perfect mix with Frank and Yvonna. They had discovered they shared any number of interests. Yvonna had the group move out of the kitchen to the living room, where Frank offered up cocktails, wine, or beer for all — even Esme! They all laughed and talked about their summers while Yvonna served a variety of tasty hors d'oeuvres.

Around 7:00 p.m., Yvonna announced that dinner was almost ready. It was time for everyone to move out to the patio. She was grilling hamburgers and had barbecued a good deal of chicken. Over the past couple of days and into this morning, she had prepared coleslaw, potato salad, baked beans, corn on the cob, and cornbread. It was going to be a true pig-out — for everyone except Shell, anyway. She stuck with her diet and ate small. Frank had his portable Sony stereo cassette player turned on and played a cassette that was a compilation of favorite hit songs. The conversations continued over dinner. Shell spoke of her school and all of the events that were happening there. She explained that the next several weeks were going to be her most intense yet. She told everyone about the floral competitions and each student's involvement. She said, "I'll be back underground for the next few weeks."

Sorina interjected, "There's something special happening the evening of Saturday the eleventh at the Music Box. You all need to keep the date open. For now, part of it is a secret, but Joni Mitchell will be the headliner. And it'll be a really big surprise you'll enjoy. I promise I'll tell you everything soon enough. I just don't want to jinx it and spill the beans right now. Just keep next Saturday night open!"

Everyone was having a great time. It was ten thirty before anyone realized. Max and Stella were the first to thank Frank and Yvonna for a lovely evening. Stella said to them, "It's at our house next time," before they headed out to their car.

Ricky and Esme were the next to leave. When Yvonna asked where they were going, Esme turned to her mother with a smile. "We're just going out for a little while. I'll be back."

Sorina was going with Shell to spend the night at her apartment. The two of them had not had any girl time together in a very long while. On their way out the door, their parents overheard Sorina saying to her sister, "No matter what, I am not telling you what is happening next weekend. You'll just have to wait." And off they went.

Saturday, September 4, 1976

Morning arrived at Shell's apartment. The girls were both up and out by eight. The family had agreed to meet for brunch at Flanda's Café at nine, and Shell wanted to stroll the streets of Green Hills before they met up with everyone else. The September sun was still very hot as the two sisters, both dressed in shorts and colorful T-shirts, aimlessly walked the streets. They came to the spot where both their lives seemed to have been changed forever. They looked over toward the bank and real estate office. This was their first time back here together since that awful day.

Sorina uttered, "I wonder what happened to everyone. I … I mean the rest of everyone in the bank and the robbers and stuff."

Shell mumbled, "I really wonder whatever happened to Helena — all that stuff going on in her head. I heard a bunch of rumors and wonder what, if anything, is actually true. Who knows? Why should I care? But I really sort of do. She was always nice to me."

Sorina felt uncomfortable knowing what she knew and not being able to say anything to her sister. So like any person with a brain, she changed the subject. "I heard the robbers are in jail. They'd done all sorts of other bad things, as we well know. Someone told me they were sentenced to twenty-five years because they used a gun on someone."

The conversation continued, with Sorina steering it toward

Shell's hibernation and her experiences at school. Shell was truly happy when she talked about her trainer, her professor, her beauty operator, and the things she was learning about life in general.

The girls arrived at 9:00 a.m. on the dot. Minnie came running down the steps to give Shell a big hug. Sorina followed as Minnie led Shell inside, but just as Minnie started to chat them up, Flanda came flying out of the back room to give her hellos. They had managed to draw the attention of the entire restaurant, who were left to wonder, *Why all the commotion?*

Regulars began filling the restaurant. One of those regulars was Wally. Shell beamed when she saw him, smiling from ear to ear. She walked over and gave him a big hug. It seemed everyone was into hugs this Saturday. Shell's family had all met Wally on only one or two sporadic occasions. He had ambled in wearing his signature uniform: faded blue overalls with ink stains at the bottom of the chest pocket and a white T-shirt. Shell invited him to join the family for breakfast.

By around 9:45 a.m., Sorina began looking ill at ease. She finally stood. "Sorry, everybody. I need to excuse myself. I need to be somewhere by ten. Love you all!" It looked like she was leaving as fast as her feet would move. Not a one of them knew what was going on in her life that would be so important to make her just up and leave.

Over brunch, Shell, Esme, and Ricky decided to drive the twenty minutes to Smyrna to check out the new outlet mall. They were all looking for any bargains they might find. Ricky wanted to visit the day spa in the mall, just to check out some products. Autumn was quickly approaching, and his and Esme's plans were falling into place for the move to California. Ricky had already written a letter to a salon in Los Angeles, requesting an appointment with the owner to demonstrate his invention. He still had research to complete before he could finish his project. The mall spa was as good as any other spa for his purposes.

So after brunch, the three set off, singing along to the radio as they tooled down the road.

The Mall

The sisters had talked all the way to Smyrna. Shell had gone on at length about the trials and tribulations of her classes. She talked a blue streak about her workouts at the gym. Her trainer, Anita, had been a stern taskmaster through all of Shell's personal sessions, but hadn't that turned out well? Shell lamented how, at the outset, she had struggled and left the gym achy and dripping with sweat. The torture had eased with her weight loss. It was all worth the effort.

Esme had been able to share little more about her and Ricky's plans in between Shell's amicable rants. She decided enough had been said at the cookout about Ricky's "secret project." She described to Shell how Ricky had started mapping out plans for the drive to Los Angeles. The Tempest was getting a trailer hitch, so they'd be able to get a U-Haul to hold their gear and paraphernalia for the trek. It turned out, it was easier to let Shell talk. Ricky drove with his own thoughts bouncing between his ears.

"Hey, you two! We're here!" Ricky pulled into a parking spot near the entrance to the Smyrna mall.

The doors of the car opened, and one by one, out stepped Ricky and the girls. They headed toward the mall. The exterior of the place was generic enough.

Shell was still talking as she and Esme made their way toward their first shop. "I hope this place has outlet stores for the Gap, Banana Republic, and Ralph Lauren. Those are my absolute favorites right now. You looking for anything in particular?"

Although the machines were fading away by the mid-1970s, Ricky was happy to see a mechanical horse by the entrance to this mall. It was the first thing he'd noticed when they got out of the car.

Esme looked at the horse and winked at Ricky. As they passed the mechanical beast, she said, "Oh my gosh! It still only costs a dime to ride and be Dale Evans!"

Ricky held the door for the girls while they stepped through the main entrance of the monstrous new Smyrna mall. Shell turned when her eyes were magnetically drawn by a glimpse of Eddy Francis. She had not seen him since the day at the hospital. The two had had only a few phone conversations while she was snowed under with her class and projects. Shell definitely missed him, even though they had spent only one traumatic day together, and that had happened only by accident. Eddy's eyes locked onto Shell's. They both broke into broad smiles as they walked toward each other, eyes fixed. Shell felt like she was in a slow-motion movie and couldn't figure what had happened to the violins. When they met up, she felt his breath as they both started to speak at once. An unanticipated giggle slipped from Shell, opening the door for Eddy to speak. They were rapidly in deep conversation. Esme and Ricky, only a short distance away, found themselves just staring at the two.

Twenty minutes later, Shell and Eddy were still hard at it. Esme, though she'd been willing to wait briefly, had grown restless and now was fully agitated. She had come here to shop. She walked over to her sister. "Hi, Eddy. It's great to see you again. I hope all is well at the flower shop." And then to Shell she said, "Ricky and I are going to go on and start checking out the stores. Do you want to just meet us somewhere in, say, thirty minutes?"

"Just give me a couple more minutes." Shell realized as she said it that she'd already spent much more time in conversation with Eddy than she'd thought. "I'll be right there."

Shell started her goodbye, but Eddy interrupted and said, "You want to go out tonight? Dinner? No big deal. Just the two of us."

"Oh, I'd love that!" Shell said without pause.

"Great! I'll pick you up at your apartment around seven? And now you had better get back with your sister before she blows a fuse. See you tonight!"

Shell smiled as they both turned to walk in opposite directions.

Esme glared at her sister as she approached. As they walked, Esme whispered to her sister, "Couldn't you have done that in half the time?"

Shell smiled and, ignoring the question, looked at her sister and said with excitement, "Okay, where are we going? I know I'm going out to dinner with Eddy Francis!"

The three laughed and began their expedition. Before long, Ricky said, "I saw a couple of men's shops back there I want to check out. How about I meet you two at the food court in thirty minutes?" The bit about the men's shops was a lie. He had reconnaissance to do.

Esme replied, "The two of us have a lot of ground to cover. Let's say an hour instead."

The girls went on their way. Ricky headed straight to the day spa located at the far end of the mall.

The First Date

Saturday Evening, September 4, 1976

Shell had not been on a date since high school. Truth be told, she was nervous. She had never thought of Eddy as a possible suitor. Then again, that prospect was exciting. She had no idea where they were going, nor did she know what to wear. Her options for clothing were limited. She had either the new things she had bought on her "me" day or an outfit from the outlet mall she'd picked up earlier today. Between her diet and exercise during the past three months, her body had changed so drastically that her options were minimal. Realizing that she was genuinely limited in her choices in effect made her final choice easier; she'd wear her new black capri pants with the loose off-the-shoulder blue knit blouse and black espadrilles. She was set. Crisis averted.

After more than an hour spent bathing and washing her hair, she began the process of applying her new makeup. She had not bothered to paint her face this much in, well, at least the last three months. It really had been a long time. Plunging in, she started with a powdery light foundation and went from there. When she was finished, she stood back and looked at herself in the full-length mirror on the back of the bathroom door. She smiled. She sincerely approved of the new Shell.

The knock on the door of her apartment coincided with the click of the hands on her shelf clock. It was seven on the dot. Eddy had arrived precisely on time as promised. Shell opened her front door. Eddy was standing there, gazing at her like he never had before.

This was the very first time Eddy had seen her put together. She was radiant. He noticed that she was even wearing a little makeup — not too much, just enough light blue eye shadow to accent her eyes.

Eddy continued looking at Shell, completely enthralled. "You look beautiful! Let's go. I made reservations downtown at a new restaurant, Zero's. It's only been open two weeks, and it's supposed to be really good. I hope you don't mind — it's being new, I mean. One of my favorite things to do is try out new places in town."

"Zero's? I haven't heard of it, but the name is certainly different."

"It's supposed to be nouvelle French cuisine, except with a drawl. It sounded interesting to me. One of my clients opened it. He has a couple other restaurants in town. He dropped off a menu the other day at the shop. Choices look great."

The restaurant was on the west side of downtown Nashville. It was in an old church that had been converted into an intimate café and bar. The moment they walked inside, Shell found the interior elegant. The space had the special feel of a country home furnished with lots of antiques and old Nashville memorabilia. The light fixtures were bell jars with electric candles. The pine tables were brand-new but finished to appear old and gently distressed. The floor was the original tiled floor from the days when the building was an operating church.

They were seated immediately and began talking — and continued talking, nonstop, for almost three hours. To break any ice that might still remain, their conversation started with flowers and the floral business itself. Warmed up, they talked about their personal lives and pasts. They spoke of family matters, friends, and even their high school and college days — and their dreams.

They both thoroughly enjoyed their meal. Eddy had steak au poivre. Shell had a beautiful filet of salmon with sauce béarnaise. Both Shell and Eddy had begun their meal with something entirely new for them both: salade Lyonnaise — frisée, crisp bacon, barely cooked egg, and a warm vinaigrette. They agreed it was one of the best things they had ever put in their mouths. The portions all had been reasonably sized, so they splurged and split a warm chocolate soufflé.

In the blink of an eye, it was already 10:30 p.m. The table had been cleared, and it was time to go. The drive back to Shell's apartment was quiet; they had talked non-stop through their meal.

As Eddy pulled up to Shell's apartment, she said, "Thank you for tonight. It was lovely. I've had the best time. Any chance you'd like to go with me to the Music Box next Saturday night? Joni Mitchell's performing in the round. I love her music, especially her lyrics. I can't explain why, but for some curious reason, Sorina, who has no connection to the club, invited the entire family to the show. She promises a surprise. Who knows what? It'll be fun."

"I would like that very much. Thank you. I'll pick you up at eight?"

At the door, Eddy kissed Shell good night. The kiss took her by happy surprise.

Back in her apartment, Shell could not wait to tell Sorina about her evening. Sorina was bunking with her sister for a few days, and when Shell came through the door, she found Sorina up watching television. Shell went into luscious details all about the restaurant and Eddy. She told her sister they had a date for Saturday night's concert and Sorina's surprise. Shell reminded her sister she'd need an extra ticket.

The girls stayed up talking until two in the morning. They laughed and yacked while Shell made a pile of clothing to take to Goodwill. The night ended when Sorina promised, "You and Eddy will have a great time Saturday night. You'll be shocked when my secret is finally out." With that she gave Shell a peck on the cheek and wished her sweet dreams.

Ricky's Workshop

Sunday, September 5, 12:30 p.m.

Ricky Baker's favorite pastime had always been making things out of random pieces of wood. One time during his teens, he'd taken sections from a fallen tree, worked the pieces into manageable sizes, and carved each one into a different face, full of expression. He was a master with wood and could do almost anything with the right tools.

On the far reaches of the five-acre Baker property stood his workshop, a converted tractor shed. Last year, Ricky had finally decided to invest in a space heater for the large space. He owned almost every tool imaginable. The space, roughly fifteen by twenty feet, suited him perfectly.

In the middle of the workshop, he stood proudly admiring his newly completed invention. He had been successful in adapting a coin-operated mechanical horse into something entirely different. With the help of an electrician he knew, he had been able to achieve his desired final result. Ta-da! The Waxing Pony. Except for his electrician, Ricky and Esme were the only people alive, or dead, who knew anything about it. Esme was on the fence, both apprehensive and hopeful for him and his project. His parents hadn't the vaguest idea what their son had been up to in his workshop for so long.

Ricky was now waiting for Wally Walloppe to arrive. They'd had many conversations over the past few months. Ricky had met Wally when Shell first rented her new apartment, and Ricky and Esme were helping move boxes and furniture upstairs. It had taken little time for the two men to form a bond. Ricky felt lucky that Wally had been retired for several years; at sixty-five he had been looking for a project when they met. He was game for anything. It turned out that in his youth, Wally had been a bit of a rebel. During the time of hippies and love-ins of the late '60s, Wally had surprised his wife and peers by letting his hair grow long but always hiding it under a cap at work. His hair was still almost to his shoulders. The youthful blond of his twenties had turned white over time, but the unruly, natural waviness had persisted. Ricky couldn't help but notice that Wally had an exceptional amount of body hair. Sticking out of his T-shirts, Wally's arms and neck were thick with coarse, curly gray and white hair. Ricky could only imagine the hair covering the rest of the man's body. Ricky had pondered, sleeplessly, over and over for weeks, how best to approach his query. Mustering all his fortitude, he had swallowed the proverbial bullet and asked Wally straight-out if he would be a guinea pig for an experiment. Then he had explained the experiment like the salesman he hoped to be. He'd assured Wally it would be safe. Ricky would do a run-through in advance to demonstrate how his creation worked. If, after seeing what was involved, Wally wanted to back out, fine, no problem. Ricky's utmost concern was that what they were doing be kept secret. Wally, in his typical laid-back way, had figured, "What the hell?" and agreed to participate. Today was the day for the premiere beta test run.

Wally arrived at Ricky's workshop at the agreed time of 1:00 p.m. Ricky walked him inside and said, "Hey, Wally. Welcome! Well, this is my workshop. And that, over there, is my dream child. I can't thank you enough for helping me with this project."

The Inspector, as he often referred to himself, stood in the doorway, hair askew, wearing his signature faded blue ink–stained overalls and white T-shirt. Wally always looked like he was somewhere between the edge of homelessness and just being a really cool old dude.

Ricky dove in. "I'm so glad you're willing to help me test this. I think you're a perfect candidate for this experiment. I know it will work. And I know it probably feels odd to be here. So I have to tell you again how much I appreciate your participation. And yeah, I'm a little anxious. I don't envision you actually wanting to have this done monthly, like my ultimate target market. Thing is, like we've talked about, you have the right amount of hair for me to prove whether or not this will work like I think it will."

With that, Ricky walked Wally over to the dime-store horse and showed it off. He explained again what it would do, what it would be used for, and how it would be used, like he was speaking to any future client.

Wally took notice of all the debris around it. "Looks like you just finished this puppy."

Ricky said, "You don't even know. With the exception of Esme, this has been my entire life for the past year. The planning took so long by itself. Then I had to find where these machines were sold. After I found out how much they cost, I had another small hurdle. I have been saving money all my life. Parting with it is another thing. Suffice it to say, it is here, and I am pretty sure it will work. If it does what it's supposed to do today, I will consider applying for a patent!

"So you understand what needs to happen? I will insert a block of wax into the underbelly of the horse and turn on the warmer. It takes about ten minutes for the wax to get to the proper consistency. When the wax is molten, that's when you strip and get on the horse. Once you are on the horse and comfortable, we'll begin. The first switch will be the horse going into a slow rocking motion. As that happens, I'll flip the next switch. That second switch releases the hot wax, which will ooze through the holes I drilled in the saddle. After you start feeling the warm liquid, let me know, so I can turn the speed of the horse to an easy trot. While all of this is happening, the wax will continue oozing out of the saddle. After about sixty seconds of the slow trot, I will stop the horse, and you'll stand up in the stirrups. While you are standing, I will place a large sheet of epilating fabric on the saddle and secure it. With that in place, you'll sit back down onto the fabric that is covering the saddle. You will remain there for another minute. Then for the last step, I'll turn the horse up to a gallop. Shortly after that, you'll be rocked off the horse. What happens at that point will take your mind off of anything else. Once you're off the horse, I'll be able to show you what we've accomplished."

Wally took a long look at Ricky. He started laughing. When he was composed enough to speak, he said, "Has anyone ever told you you're one idea short of being looney tunes?"

Ricky laughed. "I think I'd have to welcome the comment. You know, I started dreaming this up when I was thirteen while I helped my mother in her beauty parlor. Women began showing up for personal waxing. I didn't know what that meant until one day I peeked in the room when my mother and her customer were there. The lady had come to my mother for a little personal wax. My mother always took them into the back room. I knew the wax was there, but I really didn't know what or how or why. Boy, I sure found out fast. And then one day when no one was around, I experimented on my own leg. I was fascinated by the way it worked."

"Son, I have never done anything like this in my life. Do you think it's gonna work? How bad will this thing hurt?"

"Wally, I have tried this on myself. The hurt is temporary. I think the results are, and will be, amazing." In all truth, Ricky was suddenly concerned.

Ricky lifted the side panel and loaded the wax block into the horse's underbelly. He flipped a switch. "This will take about ten minutes."

Inspector Wally began to climb out of his overalls, his T-shirt, and finally, his undershorts. Ricky gave him a sheet to cover himself.

While the wax was heating up, they talked. Wally told Ricky about his wife, how they'd met, and how deeply he missed her. Ricky was telling Wally a little about Esme when the timer's buzzer went off. Ricky looked at Wally and said, "It's time to begin," and helped him up onto the horse. "This will be over before you know it."

Once Wally was comfortable, Ricky flipped a switch, and the horse began slowly rocking back and forth. As it did, the warm, molten wax began to ooze through the multitude of holes Ricky had drilled in the saddle.

Wally felt the wax spreading around his crotch and between his hips. "This feels a little nasty." He smiled and, not being one to complain, sat tall in the saddle while the horse continued to rock, and the wax flowed into the cavity between his hips.

The rest happened just as Ricky had described, to a point. Wally hadn't expected, as a finale, to be thrown off the horse. Toward the end of the treatment, Ricky accidentally turned the canter to "high," and the horse bucked Wally off. Wally landed, wobbly, on his feet, stunned by the whole experience. The shock of the landing erased any pain that he might have felt.

Ricky thought, *I need to work on the dismount!*

Wally eyed Ricky. "Son, you are demented. So did this do what you expected?"

Ricky smiled and said, "Lookee here," as he pointed to the saddle. The sheet of cotton fabric was still there. It was covered in a disgusting mass of gluey hair. "How do you feel? Be honest, Wally."

"Gooey. Airy. Slimy. How do I get all this stuff off of me?"

"I do have something for that. It's a combination of baby oil and alcohol. Just go in the bathroom over there. I left a bottle and paper towels by the toilet. Soak the paper towels with the liquid and wipe the stuff off. The wax'll come off easier and faster than you think."

Wally wrapped himself tightly in the sheet and grabbed his clothes. He sidled over and into the bathroom, closing the door behind him. Wally cleaned himself up, dressed, and after a time, emerged from the bathroom.

The first words out of his mouth were "I will say, I do feel different. It actually feels kinda good down there. It's nice and airy in my underwear, for sure. I think I could get used to this." Wally scratched his head. "You know, Ricky, I thought this was a nutso idea, and you might be just a little crazy, but you've got something here. If I were you and had made this thing, I think I'd follow my heart. Do what is best for you. What's the worst thing that can happen? You realize it was a mistake? If that happens, remember not to beat yourself up. If you don't at least try something, you'll never know what could have been. Some of the craziest ideas seem to just fall from the sky."

Ricky thanked Wally for being so agreeable and encouraging. They shook hands, as always. Wally opened the door. "I won't tell a soul about this. You need to apply for that patent — and pronto, my friend. Oh, by the way, I will see you next Saturday night at the Music Box. Shell invited me to come along with her and Eddy. I don't want to be a third wheel, so I told her I'd meet everybody there. It sounds like it'll be fun. And I love the mystery part." He winked at Ricky with mischief on his face. "Now, you aren't planning on trying something funny like this there, are you?"

Ricky cracked up laughing and said, "No way! See you later."

Holiday Inn

Friday, September 10, 1976

Joni Mitchell's tour bus pulled into the parking lot of the Holiday Inn, announcing her arrival. A special parking area had been prearranged in order to keep the bus out of the public's view. She arrived with a small entourage. Traveling with Joni were her manager, her personal assistant, and a small group of band members and sound technicians who all worked full-time with her, in her hometown and on the road.

A few hours after their arrival late Friday afternoon, the lobby was a beehive of activity. This Holiday Inn wasn't an ordinary motor inn. The hotel had eleven stories and was well equipped to handle visiting celebrities. Joni's group checked into half of the rooms on the tenth floor. It was standard procedure for everyone to stay close together and out of the public domain. The hotel offered the benefit of a private dining room and grazing area available for the duration of their stay. The dining room served until 10:00 p.m. The grazing area, arranged in the same location, remained fully stocked for them around the clock.

Charlotte Webber had been stalking the Holiday Inn for a while. She and Edna, as always, were all ears and eyes. Charlotte had brought her ace part-time reporter, Tim Tedd, along for the ride. In her way of thinking, he was young and handsome and could somehow improve their chances of landing a coveted interview with the revered singer-songwriter. Charlotte wasn't the only one stalking the place. Other news outlets also had set their sights on the Holiday Inn as a possible landing spot for Ms. Mitchell and were poised and ready.

Charlotte had been an acquaintance of the Holiday Inn's owner, Don Sims, for years. She decided that this situation would be the perfect opportunity for her to become better friends with him. Nothing ever stopped her from getting what she wanted. She waltzed into the lobby and approached the front desk. With her head held high and her inherent attitude of entitlement, she asked the front desk clerk, "Is Mr. Sims available? Miss Charlotte Webber." She'd added her name just in case this young lady lived under a rock.

Sophie, the front desk clerk, wobbled on her heels and said, "I will see if he is in his office. I am so sorry — I missed the last part. What is your name again?"

Charlotte now stretched her neck, throwing her head higher than a fetching swan, frosted hair perfectly coiffed, and answered with obvious indignation, "Miss Charlotte Webber. I am sure you know who I am. I am owner and editor of *The Eye.* Mr. Sims and I are very close." At this point, she was glaring down at Sophie through her silver-rimmed eyeglasses.

Sophie, scrunching her forehead, looked up with sassy brown eyes and said to Charlotte, "I will see if he is not too busy." She smiled through clenched teeth at Charlotte as she slowly backed away.

Charlotte huffed, "One moment, young lady!" Leering sternly at Sophie, Charlotte winked, dangled a crisp new twenty in the air, and said, "Missy, I am quite positive that he is not too busy to see me."

Sophie snapped the twenty out of Charlotte's grasp, saying nothing. The young woman slinked toward a door behind the front desk and leered at Charlotte as she closed the door behind her.

While Charlotte waited for Sophie to return with Sims, a few of the band members happened into the lobby. Edna came running to Charlotte's side, steno pad in hand. Charlotte put on her pleasant, as-laid-back-as-possible face and attempted to feign unawareness of who they were. She and Edna inched toward the members.

One of them turned around to Edna. "May I help you with something?"

Edna stumbled over her words as she said, "My boss — I mean, the person that I work for — wants me to ask you 'pretty please' for an interview."

She turned to Charlotte, who now stood ten feet away, leaning against the front desk in an effort to appear casual and nonchalant.

Charlotte smiled. "I am her boss. Do I look bossy?"

The group erupted in a solid chuckle. One of the guys casually said, "Sure, what is it you want to know?"

Charlotte tilted her head slightly to the right and with her most inviting voice said, "How about I spring for a round of drinks for a quick chat?"

Another member of the group piped up. "We would all love that! Thank you. Let's head to the bar, gentlemen." He pointed straight to the double glass doors.

Charlotte laughed. "Anything you all want. All I need is about fifteen minutes of your time. The entire tab is on me."

The crew slipped through the doors and into Holiday Sippers for a cocktail, with Charlotte and Edna in tow. Don Sims and Sophie no longer mattered in the least.

The group settled into a back corner. They were joined by a few more members of Joni Mitchell's crew. Now there were seven ready to go on Charlotte's tab. The waitress came over and took their orders. As it turned out, the bar also served food — sad news for Charlotte because each one of the boys was hungry. The menu offered a diverse list of goodies. Four of the guys each ordered a three-pound lobster, three ordered prime New York steaks, and to a man, they all ordered special top-shelf call drinks.

Charlotte was shocked at the thought of the total cash she was laying down for a fifteen-minute interview. "Do you all mind if I turn on my tape recorder?"

The person who appeared to be the main guy said, "No problem, ma'am. Have at it."

By the middle of Charlotte's interview, her personal, most burning question had been answered: she wanted to know how in the world Joni Mitchell had come to have Helena Montgomery as her opening act. It was fairly straightforward. Joni had requested somebody local, and the owner of the Music Box had checked around with his Nashville connections and ended up with a performer he already knew. He sent over a demo tape to Joni's people, they liked it, and the deal was done. She was the opening act. Simple as that, Charlotte had the answer to her gut-churning question, and it only cost her over five hundred dollars.

Charlotte and Edna lingered until the guys finished their meal and drinks. As Charlotte was paying the bill and watching the group leave, their manager approached Edna, handing her backstage passes to the show for both her and Charlotte.

Edna was thrilled. "Oh yes! Thank you. We will be there. You can count on us! Oh, Miss Webber will be so delighted."

"My pleasure. Here, write your names down on this napkin. When you get there, show the guys at the door you have backstage passes. Your names will be on a list up front."

Edna did as she was told and handed him the napkin. He folded it and slipped it into his shirt pocket. Edna couldn't believe it. She hadn't even had to grovel. They were set for the evening. *Backstage passes for Joni Mitchell! Oh, Charlotte is going to love this!*

Saturday, September 11, 1976

Across town, early Saturday morning, things were in high gear at the Music Box. Tickets for that night's show had been sold out for two weeks. The venue planned for the maximum six hundred patrons that evening. The Music Box was known for hosting exceptional pop-up events on an irregular basis. It was a popular spot for recording artists visiting Nashville to stop by and perform in the round. Tonight was one of those nights. Joni Mitchell was headlining. A local, Helena Montgomery, would be the warm-up act. Tickets for tonight cost twenty-five dollars a person with a two-drink minimum. Employees had worked both yesterday and today in preparation for tonight's show. The owners, Ched and Mary Ann Meade, were maniacally running around like chickens with their heads cut off. The small back room of the Music Box had been closed off for rehearsals; still, music reverberated through the walls for anyone working to hear. Everyone thought it sounded like Helena, but then it didn't. Odd.

It was a beautiful summer's day. The manager had rolled up the back wall's garage doors to open the enclosed patio. A round stage was being constructed in the center of the expanded space, placing it just inside the opened back wall. Everywhere, wires were camouflaged under rubber walk-over strips. A large upright piano was moved into place on the stage, along with the amps and mics. Lighting was being tested, rearranged, and adjusted. Tables and chairs were being set up according to the prescribed plan.

Ched and Mary Ann held a short, impromptu meeting with all the employees. They announced that Helena Montgomery would be joined onstage by her previously unnamed new singing partner, Sorina Lapone, for the opening act. Helena was no surprise. They were all familiar with her regular gigs at the club. But no one had ever even heard the name Sorina Lapone. The staff could only wonder about her talent and vocal ability. They were all in agreement that Helena was a great fit as the opening act. She had not been around for a few months, and consequently, all were excited to hear her new music.

At the end of the meeting, Ched said to his staff, "Please keep Sorina's addition to the bill inside these walls only. She specifically asked us not to mention her name in advance of the performance. She wants to surprise her family, all of whom will be in the audience. Also, you all need to know that Helena has been away at a health spa for a few months. She looks completely different, and I mean that in a very, very good way."

With the meeting concluded, Ched sent everyone back to work. The addition of this Sorina had everyone talking among themselves. No one had ever heard of Helena performing with someone else. None of them had the slightest clue until today that the two had been practicing together in the rehearsal room of the Music Box during off hours. Helena and Sorina had been working with each other ever since their run-in at Cain-Sloan. The show looked to be a fun experiment for both.

Sorina's stutter disappeared completely whenever she took to the stage. Slowly, her stammer was disappearing in her day-to-day conversations as well. Helena's and Sorina's voices complemented each other nicely, and their harmonies were magical. They had recorded a few of their songs on tape, which Helena had sent to Ched and Mary Ann. She had wanted them to hear their combined voices as well as propose that Sorina join her for the upcoming show. Both owners had been sufficiently impressed with the duo and had given their approval to add Sorina for the gig. And tonight, they were opening for Joni Mitchell.

Ched and Mary Ann peeked into the back room while the two were hashing out a few last-minute changes. Ched's eyes fixed on Helena for a minute, and then he said to her, "I've meant to tell you. I've seen you lately, but only briefly and peripherally. You really look different, but I can't say how. I mean, you look great! But those few months you spent away at that health spa seem to have made a tremendous difference for you. I have to say, Mary Ann and I would benefit from something like you must have experienced. You just look so rested."

Helena winked at Mary Ann and with a big smile said, "Thank you, Ched. You're so sweet to say that. I have lost some weight and packed and unloaded a lot of baggage." She chuckled, smile still on her face, and redirected the conversation to her concerns for tonight's performance. "When do you think we'll be able to do soundchecks?"

Ched glanced at Mary Ann with a questioning expression and got nothing. Returning his attention to Helena, he said, "Soon, I would expect. Very soon. Have you settled on a set list? When we heard those tapes, we were blown away. I loved the mellow songs in particular, especially with Sorina playing acoustic guitar while you were working the piano. You two are such a nice combo. You'll be great as an opener for Joni tonight! I'm excited for you both."

Mary Ann piped in and said, "I'm pretty sure the sound techs should be ready by now. Let's all go see."

The four of them walked out of the rehearsal room, bound for the stage. All the stagehands did double takes of Helena and Sorina as they passed by. Today, both girls were rehearsing without makeup and in everyday clothes. The guys were stunned. These two were natural beauties; it wouldn't matter what they wore, with or without makeup. Sorina wore a light-green T-shirt under her favorite baggy denim overalls, her hair tied into her normal high ponytail with a blue scrunchie. Helena was walking around in blue jeans and a white open-collared, untucked, loose-fitting pinpoint oxford blouse.

Ched, who had gone ahead of them, finished talking to the lighting technician. He turned to Helena and Sorina and said, "Five more minutes, and they'll all be ready to work your soundcheck."

Shopping

Saturday, September 11, 1976

Shell and Eddy had been out on two more dates since last Saturday night. Tonight was the "something special" that Shell's sister Sorina had set up for the two with the entire family included. Shell was on edge, wondering and worrying about what her sister had in store. *Anyway,* she thought, *que será será.* Oh, how she loved Doris Day. Tonight would be her fourth date with Eddy Francis. She found herself, once again, beside herself.

Today, Esme and Shell were happily shopping together again. This morning they would go to the stores in Green Hills. It had been a while since the two of them had spent a day solely in each other's company. Shell filled Esme in on school with tidbits of what she was doing in lab and described some of the new friends she had made while there.

Esme inquired, "How's it going with Eddy?"

Shell replied simply, "It's developing. Tell me about you and Ricky!"

Esme spoke at length about her relationship with Ricky and their plans for the move to Los Angeles. Esme said, "I'm excited, apprehensive, and scared, all at the same time. I'm totally comfortable with our relationship. Ricky's the only reason I can keep it together and not completely freak out." As Esme's last sentence trailed off, it occurred to both of them that Shell would graduate from her program just about the same time Esme and Ricky were heading to California and their new life on the coast.

Esme looked at her sister with sad eyes and said, "I just don't know what life will be like without you. Honestly, you have been my role model, crutch, confidant, and best friend as long as I've been alive. You practically raised me."

Shell looked at her, with those motherly eyes Esme was already missing, and said, "To be truly alive, you have to realize that as you age, change is the only thing that remains constant. Being able to be flexible and adapt to those changes is called living. Once you accept the constancy of change, living becomes easier, and then time begins to fly. At least that's what I've come to believe."

Like all the times they spent together, this day began to slip away. They stopped at the jewelry counter at Castner-Knott for twenty minutes to try on necklaces and earrings, then headed to the skin care and hair product area. Shell had become obsessed with new shampoos and skin treatments now that those products were suddenly on her radar. She spent quite a bit of time with one salesperson, who walked her through the different brands. The woman filled a bag with free samples and gave it to Shell with her card. Shell knew she'd be back.

Lunchtime rolled around, and they were both hungry, so they left the department store and went next door to Cross Keys. Cross Keys was a dinosaur of Nashville luncheon establishments. It had been around since the early 1950s. The menu never changed. Many of the people who ate there looked like they had aged right along with the restaurant. The staff was always welcoming, and the food predictable. It was a comfort going there for lunch. They both enjoyed an hour of more talk and local gossip. The mystery surrounding Sorina continued to seep into their conversation, and together, they finally decided to drop the unsolvable dilemma. They would know the answer soon enough.

Shell perked up and said to Esme, "I need some more clothes to perk up my wardrobe. My closet is still half full of fat clothes and just a smattering of new stuff. I have already worn every new thing I have in the past week because all of it is just really casual."

Esme smiled and said, "I can help you fix that! Let's walk down to China's. She has a lot of things that will look good on you. I think she has some of the most current women's clothes in the city."

Esme was referring to the hottest store in Nashville. It had been open for only a few months, and the owner, China Desmond, was a new Nashville resident. She and her husband, Dr. Freemont Desmond, had relocated to Nashville for his oncology residency at Vanderbilt. She was originally from Chicago, where she had graduated from Northwestern. China Williams had met her future husband-to-be on the first day of her freshman year.

After entering the store and poking around a bit, Esme noticed how bewildered Shell looked. Esme went into action and began pulling things from around the shop for Shell to try on and model for her. An hour later, Shell emerged from the dressing room with an armload of things she was ready to take home, and they checked out.

As they left the store, Esme said to her, "I have never seen you this excited about clothes in my entire life."

Shell said, "I wear a size eight now. Can you believe it? I love all these things. Now my problem will be deciding what to wear tonight. I love solving that kind of problem!"

Esme said, "You bought that Lady Battaglia dress. It looked great *on* you, and you looked great *in* it! Why not wear that tonight? It's all cotton, not too dressy, not too casual, not too sweet. I think it's perfect for tonight."

Shell laughed as she said, "I guess you settled that in a hurry. It's almost two thirty. Let's go to Flanda's for some coffee and people-watching for a little while. We have plenty of time."

The pair walked toward the café. Shell, with her shopping bags, definitely had an extra little skip in her gait.

As they entered Flanda's, Esme caught sight of Minnie and

yelled to her, "Wait until you see Shell's new clothes! She just bought about five new outfits at China Desmond's."

The café was pretty quiet this Saturday afternoon. Flanda and Minnie followed the girls and their shopping bags to a corner table, where Shell showed off her new clothes. Minnie and Flanda were excited for her. They enthusiastically commented on everything she'd bought. Esme took it all in with joy as she stood by her big sister.

After coffees and chatter with Minnie and Flanda, the time had come for Esme and Shell to go back to Shell's apartment and prepare for the evening's adventures. They wanted to enjoy a little downtime, and Shell was wild to try on all her new clothes just one more time.

Saturday Evening

Esme and Shell went back to Shell's apartment. The two sisters had planned on dressing together before being picked up by their dates. Sorina had opted out and was nowhere to be found. She had left a note on the kitchen counter saying that she would catch up with everyone later.

Esme looked at Shell and said, "Hmm, the mystery deepens."

Shell laughed and just said, "Whatever."

It was already four thirty, and Shell needed to unpack her shopping bags and organize her new things. With Esme standing by with scissors, ready to cut off price and product tags, the two of them went to work. After a half hour of snipping and cutting, Shell began to fold and hang her new clothes.

There was nothing left now but to put themselves together for the evening. Esme had brought a small overnight bag with her cosmetics and an outfit for the night. Shell turned on the television while the two began primping and preening for their dates. Ricky and Eddy were both due at eight to pick them up. They had plenty of time to prepare.

Meanwhile, Yvonna and Frank, Flanda and Earl, and Minnie and Tom, on Shell's recommendation, had made early reservations at Zero's for a five-thirty dinner. From what Shell had told them about her experience there, Minnie and Flanda thought going to a new restaurant in town would be fun and a nice change of pace after their hours at the café. Sorina had provided tickets to everyone for tonight's concert at the Music Box. She had stressed to them, and they knew, that they needed to be there and seated by 8:30 p.m. for the 9:00 p.m. show. The three couples thoroughly enjoyed their meals as well as their delightful conversations. The close friends agreed that they needed to meet for evenings like this much more frequently.

Minnie mentioned, "I am looking forward to meeting the young man that Shell has taken a liking to. I'm so happy for her."

Yvonna smiled and said, "He's such a polite young man. I'm happy for them. At first, I thought they were moving too fast. Then Shell reminded me about the day the two spent together following the robbery. They hadn't seen each other again until last Saturday. Apparently, something struck a chord that might turn into something between them. I hope so."

Back at Shell's, she and Esme were still dressing when there was a loud knock on the front door. They looked at each other with question marks in their eyes. Esme broke their quiet and said, "Who could that be? It can't be Ricky; he is never early. It's only seven-something."

Shell said, "I hope it's not Eddy. I'm not even close to being ready."

Esme strolled over to the front door and opened it.

Standing outside on the landing was Wally, looking a little bewildered. He had a sheepish look on his face as he asked, "Is Shell available?"

Esme replied, "She is, but she's getting dressed for her date. Actually, we both are."

Wally said, "Do you mind if I come in and sit a spell? I had some kind of a different week. I think you must know what Ricky and I were up to last Sunday. I'm feeling a little anxious. I really just want to be around someone right now, even if y'all are in the next room."

Esme called out to her sister, "Inspector Wally's here."

Shell came out of the bathroom in her pink terrycloth bathrobe. She obviously had been applying makeup; only one eye was done. She looked at Wally and said, "Hey, what's up? You are still meeting us at the thing tonight, right? Eddy and I are going to be there about eight thirty. He'll be coming here to pick me up at eight. I think your ticket is at the reservation desk. We're all at the same table. I'll save you a seat next to us."

Wally walked toward the sofa. Shell noticed he had a bit of a limp. He turned to Shell and said, "I'm pretty sore. I went horseback riding the other day. The horse got spooked and threw me off. I still ache." He sat down with a strained look on his face. Almost immediately he got back up and said, "But I suppose I should go downstairs and get cleaned up. It's getting late. I just heard you up here and wanted a little company before I got started. The last few days have been kinda rough. I'll tell you the whole story sometime."

Esme smiled; she knew what he was referring to as she said, "Ricky will be here in a little while to pick me up, too. You two had that meeting, right? I heard it went really well."

Wally replied, "Yes, it did. Certainly, for Ricky, it went very well. I can say with all honesty, it was not like any meeting I have ever had or even dreamed I might have."

Shell had gone back into the bathroom to finish her other eye, and she called loudly to the living room, "See you there. Stay as long as you want. Just don't be late."

Wally said, "Oh, I'll be on time. See y'all in a little while."

The Inspector went out the front door, and as he gingerly stepped down the metal staircase, he made a slight moaning noise that echoed up the stairs. Esme looked over the railing to be sure he made it down okay. She smiled to herself, relieved that he hadn't spilled the beans to Shell about Ricky's successful trial run with the Waxing Pony.

Esme returned to the bathroom and started back with her makeup. Shell finished her make-up. Esme was quick to follow.

As they slipped into their outfits, Shell said, "I wonder what all that was about. Did he say anything more to you about how he was thrown from a horse?"

Esme looked at Shell and said, "We'll talk about it later. C'mon, we need to crank it up. There is still a lot to do, and the boys will be here soon."

The girls finished dressing.

When they were ready, Esme looked at her big sister and said, "Shell? You are absolutely stunning in your new Lady Battaglia dress — not to be a name dropper. Seriously, you look fab!"

They both stood fidgeting by the kitchen table, gazing at *The Jeffersons* on the television in the living room. The kitchen clock read 7:45. Shell fixed them each a glass of water. After a few sips and a number of deep sighs, they began to relax.

At 8:00 p.m. on the dot, a knock came at the front door. Esme opened it. Eddy was standing there.

He said, "Oh, hey, I didn't expect you to answer the door, Esme. How are you? You look great! I mean, the only times I've seen you were at the mall the other day and the hospital a few months back. For a little sister, you clean up good." He laughed at his own sarcasm and continued, "I hope I'm not too early. Is Shell ready?"

About that time, Shell walked out of the bedroom, adjusting her earrings. Seeing Eddy, she said, "Oh, hey there. I'm ready." She turned and looked at Esme. With her big-sister voice she said, "When you and Ricky leave, please don't forget to lock up. We will see you at the show."

"Don't worry. I promise to lock up and leave a few lights on. See you all there."

Palindrome Man

Ricky had stopped at a red light at the intersection of Woodmont and Hillsboro Road in his Tempest when he spotted Otto. Otto was standing on the corner, holding one of his latest signs, another palindrome he had drummed up in his weird little head. This one read, "Go hang a salami, I'm a lasagna hog." As usual, he flashed his sign, grinning ear to ear. Ricky laughed so hard that he had to pull over and stop — nailed again by Otto, the town oddball.

Ricky waved and said, "Hello! Your sign made me laugh hard enough I had to pull over." And there he was, once again, face-to-face with Palindrome Man, trapped and in a hurry and already running late. Esme was probably pacing by now, waiting for him to arrive. Ricky always had to pull over for Otto; it was in his chemistry. So many simply drove by as quickly as possible. He told Otto, "Man, I'm sorry I can't stay and talk. I'm late to pick up my girlfriend. But I had to let you know I like your latest sign. Very funny stuff, man."

Otto stood proudly by the car, preening with his latest achievement. "Thank you, Ricky. Have a nice night. Bye-bye."

And Ricky was off.

Otto was known as a nutso around Green Hills. His first name, his first palindrome, was well known. He was generally regarded as a nice and simple person. Otto wouldn't hurt an insect. People often spoke to him honestly, with concern and care. Many wondered if he might be schizophrenic, and some thought he would be better off in a mental facility. It was a constant topic of discussion. He'd be seen walking down the street, mumbling palindromic words to himself. Quite recently, he had decided to climb a church steeple, equipped with climbing gear, including ropes and pulleys. Once he reached the top of the steeple, he had quite a crowd below watching. The crowd was terrified for him. Once he was standing in his climbing shoes at the pinnacle of the steeple, he began screaming, "My steeple's bigger than your steeple!" He continued to ramble on and on about "too many steeples in Nashville" until the fire department arrived with their ladders. He voluntarily came down via the pulley system he had rigged to the top. Once down, he said nothing but repeatedly mumbled to himself, "It's all just steeple envy," until something else crossed his horizon, and then he moved on to other meaningless snippets. When he got a little too bad, his parents came running. In the end, he was harmless to everyone but himself. He was just there on the corner with his signs, his grins, and his waves.

By the time Ricky finally arrived at Shell's apartment, Esme was waiting outside. It was eight forty-five, and she didn't want to miss anything at the Music Box. She looked at Ricky and said, "We need to hoof it so we actually get our seats."

Ricky said, "You know these things never start on time. I bet they won't begin until nine thirty. Hop in. By the way, you look great! You should get dolled up like this more often."

She answered, "Give me a reason, and I will."

"Okey-dokey then."

Esme was not a happy camper as he sped away toward the Music Box.

Surprise! The Show Really Starts at Ten

Parking for the Music Box was utter chaos. This was nothing new. Cars were parked on both sides of the surrounding streets for blocks. A long line had formed of people waiting to get into the venue. Ched and Mary Ann stood at the front of the line, taking tickets and stamping the tops of patrons' hands with a "Paid" stamp in magenta ink. The hostess, Betty Sue-Donna, was welcoming guests at the door and seating VIPs. She had been hostess at the Music Box for as long as most could remember. She was accompanied, as needed, by the bouncer Hugo, who would and could — again, as needed — become a human blockade. Betty Sue-Donna was glad she had assistants helping with seating tonight. It was just that kind of crazy night. Every seat in the house was sold.

The interior lights of the Music Box were slowly dimming. It was close to nine, and the summer sun had faded. The feel of fall was creeping into the evening air. The change of seasons was beginning. Change was the key word for the evening. The girls, their families, and their friends were about to view a most unexpected transformation.

Ched and Mary Ann had wisely hired extra staff for the event.

The laughter and chatter of the patrons penetrated the atmosphere of the bar and restaurant. Waiters and waitresses were running into one another as they secured orders for all their tables. Everything was going as smoothly as possible.

Two trailers were parked near the kitchen and employee entrance in the adjoining alley. One had been divided into two dressing rooms; Joni and her assistant occupied one, Helena and Sorina the other. The second trailer was being used entirely by Joni's band and staff.

The round stage in the center was elevated about four feet and ready for performers. Final soundchecks were being made by all of the managers. The stage lighting was set. All technical aspects for the evening were ready to go.

A small commotion was brewing at the entrance. Betty Sue-Donna and Hugo were having issues with two women whose admission was being denied. Betty Sue-Donna had been in complete control of the line until the point when these two appeared. She pushed them aside for Hugo to deal with, to avoid a complete bottleneck.

The two women were Charlotte and Edna. Charlotte Webber was being herself — loud, pushy, and obnoxious. Anyone near the door could hear her saying, "Sir, excuse me. I don't think you know who I am!"

Edna chimed in, "We're from *The Eye* — we're here to review tonight's performances."

"We have backstage passes!" Charlotte snarled as she held them up like they were her own personal copy of the Bill of Rights. "I don't understand your problem. Just show us to our seats!"

Hugo, who had the looks and physique of a Greek god, was dressed in a tight-fitting navy-blue T-shirt and jeans. His massive upper arms were the size of most folks' thighs. As a dues-paying member of Mensa International, he had a brain as big as his biceps. Hugo was completely at ease as he said, "I have no problem. I am sorry to stop you. We need identification, and we'll need to check the contents of the tote bags you're both carrying. You need to pay for admission like everyone else here, even with those passes. Backstage passes are just that and do not cover your admission. Tickets are twenty-five dollars each, and there is an additional two-drink minimum." He held his ground, continuing to block Charlotte's and Edna's path with his intimidating frame.

Glaring at Hugo, Charlotte said, "Hon, you obviously do not understand. We are the press! We are always allowed unfettered entrée to what we want, when we want!"

Hugo, unmoved, said, "Madam? You are mistaken in this instance. That may be true for other events and venues. But the Music Box is a privately-owned establishment, and we have our own established procedures and rules." Offering direction with his hand, he added, "If you would please go over to that corner and wait, I will find the owners and have them personally discuss your situation with you." As he pointed to the dark corner by the front door, he said, "I'll find them. Until then, you need to calm down, or I regret that you will be asked to leave, backstage passes or not. I have the authorization and will do what is deemed necessary to resolve this unfortunate situation. Now go over there and wait." He gestured again to the dark corner.

Ched and Mary Ann had been away from the door only a few minutes when the ruckus started. From across the room, Mary Ann had taken notice of the altercation and started her trek through the crowd back to the front. She approached the four of them and said to Hugo, "What seems to be the problem?"

"Your boy won't let us through," Charlotte snapped. "I think he must be lacking something upstairs," she added as she leered at him. "We have told him who we are, and he insists we pay full admission. He wants us to show our IDs and let him search our bags. I have never in my life!"

Mary Ann's face went blank. "Hugo is absolutely correct. He is following our protocol. I regret I was not here upon your arrival. We could have avoided this unfortunate situation entirely. I would have been happy to escort you myself." She eyed Hugo with a smug smile. "You both have your paid tickets with you?"

Charlotte said, "We have backstage passes given to us personally by the manager of Ms. Mitchell's band!"

Mary Ann, with a gleeful smirk, said, "I'm afraid this venue is in the round; there is no backstage for this concert. You are most welcome to stand by the bar over there." She pointed to the area available. "You will each need to pay the twenty-five-dollar admission and conform to this evening's two-drink minimum. Given your behavior, I don't think requesting an additional ten dollars each to ensure your minimum is out of the question. Your payment is the only way I can possibly offer admittance. And just between us girls, so you are clear, Hugo is not 'our boy,' and he is by no means mentally deficient. Hugo works for us as a courtesy among friends. If you choose to make another scene, we will quite simply ask you to leave. There is enough going on here tonight. I don't want a reason to call the police. Furthermore, I believe an apology is in order to both Hugo and Betty Sue-Donna. They are doing their jobs and doing them well!"

"Okay, okay," Charlotte said. She looked at Hugo and Betty Sue-Donna. "I am very sorry for the way we have behaved. I admit I was possibly a little pushy. It's just, for us, tonight's show is of tremendous importance. Joni Mitchell rarely does a small venue such as this!" Charlotte exhaled and waited for her nose to grow the length of Pinocchio's.

Hugo smiled and said, "I normally don't even listen to excuses. However, in this case, I will let it fly. We accept your apology and appreciate your honesty. Let's just start fresh."

Hugo led Charlotte and Edna away to the corner of the bar. He accepted their payment and very graciously secured a bar stool for Charlotte to perch upon. Everything covered, he introduced them to their bartender and said to him, "Chip, these two ladies have prepaid their first two drinks. Any additional, please start a tab."

Charlotte turned to Hugo and said to him, "Thank you, you sweet thing."

Hugo, managing not to gag, excused himself and went back to the front desk to join Mary Ann and Betty Sue-Donna.

The large table that Minnie and Tom, Flanda and Earl, and Yvonna and Frank all shared was located in a prime spot next to the stage. There were only a few of these select tables set up around the stage. This would be a great evening, for sure! As they sat waiting for the rest of their crew, they jabbered away, eyeing the crowd as it settled around them.

Minnie spotted Shell and Eddy on their way to the table, with Wally following on their heels. She stood up to her full height in her towering heels and waved them over. As they took seats, she asked Shell, "Where're Esme and Ricky? Didn't they ride with you?"

Shell responded, "No, they wanted to come by themselves. Ricky hadn't arrived before we left. They can't be too far behind."

Flanda soon spotted Ricky and Esme rushing to the table. As they reached the table, she said, "We were worried that y'all were going to be late. I think they close the doors once the show starts."

Ricky laughed. "You won't believe why we're so late. I'll fill y'all in later. I'm glad we made it, too. Esme's already upset enough I was late. Has anyone ordered cocktails yet?"

At that moment, as if he'd conjured her, a waitress appeared and took their drink orders.

Flanda looked at the girls and then leaned into Yvonna and said, "Your daughters are stunning. Where do you think Sorina is? I don't think I've ever seen her miss a family function."

Yvonna mumbled something unintelligible to herself and looked at Flanda and said, "I have no idea what is going on with that girl. She's beginning to make me a little crazy. Anyway, thanks for the compliment. You can't help but know Shell's been on a diet the past few months. She has lost so much weight! I'm so very proud of her. We all know how hard it is to do."

Meanwhile, Minnie stared in wonderment at Shell. "Honey, you look absolutely beautiful tonight! Your dress is perfection. I am going to miss you when you're back in classes. I swear, you barely come up for air when those things are in session. It'll all be over soon enough though, right?"

Shell answered, "Oh, thanks, Aunt Minnie. I'll miss you, too.

I'm back at the grindstone Monday. These next few weeks will be intense. I am sure they'll fly by." She leaned toward her and whispered, "You know, I really like Eddy a lot. He is the first man I have ever truly cared about." She stammered a little. "I mean, this is only our fourth date. But we get along so well and have so much fun together. I won't be able to see him these next few weeks either. I know we'll talk on the phone some, but it's just not the same. We'll see each other soon enough."

By now, the venue was almost filled with eighteen-year-olds to fifty-somethings, including a wide mix of local musical talent. The entire branch of the People's Bank in Green Hills was there to support their former co-worker and teller. They had not laid eyes on Helena since the day of the robbery. At this late hour, their table still had two empty seats. The bank employees could almost touch the Lapones' table from their own.

Ched Meade dashed up the stairs and onto the stage. He had changed from his earlier jeans and polo into a navy suit, white oxford cloth shirt, and white Converse sneakers. This outfit was quite a departure for him. This night was obviously special. Ched was playing host and emcee for Joni Mitchell.

He took a mic in hand and, with suave finesse, opened the evening. "Welcome! Welcome, everyone, to the Music Box! This is an exceptional night for us. Besides very special guests taking our stage, this is the Music Box's eighth anniversary!" The crowd erupted in applause. He waited for the din to subside before continuing. "We have quite a show for you all tonight. As you know, our own Helena Montgomery will open the show. Helena will be joined, for the first time on our stage, by her new singing partner. Following a brief intermission to reset equipment, our guest headliner will take the stage — the incomparable Miss Joni Mitchell!"

This time the crowd rose and exploded with applause and shrill whistles.

Ched finally announced the required precautions. "Everyone, please pay special attention now. I need to talk to you all about safety." As he pointed, he said, "We have eight emergency exits. Be aware of the exit nearest you." At that point, the eight fire exit doors were opened by staff members. "Please, folks, there is no smoking at your tables; you may smoke either at the bar or outside. We are here to have a good time and enjoy some great music. Again, welcome, and have a great evening. Let's start the show!"

Johnny Montana came rushing in and took his seat at the People's Bank table. Daisy raised her glass of wine toward Johnny and gave him a wink and whispered to no one in particular, "Cheers to Helena!"

As applause slowly waned, the lights of the restaurant grew dim, and the tight stage spotlights began to glow. A chair, two microphones, and an acoustic guitar were positioned with a black upright piano and microphone. The stage was set; the audience was silent.

The Show

As the spotlight grew ever brighter, a figure with waist-long, dark, wavy hair walked onto the stage. It was Helena Montgomery. The audience erupted in applause, hoots, and hollers. The light made her red lipstick glisten. Her pale skin looked almost translucent and silky soft. Her blue eyes sparkled like brilliant sapphires under her perfectly arched eyebrows. Her face was void of her trademark mole and heavy foundation. She stood gracefully, wearing a simple black silk satin gown, with all its edges detailed in black rhinestones, the front featuring a narrow slit down the middle to just above her navel. Helena basked in the spotlight's glow. She unfurled her arms from her sides and held them out, embracing the crowd. She remained in the spotlight. Her eyes gradually met those of the audience, one by one, as she slowly spun and scanned the entire venue.

While all eyes were fixed on Helena, soft whispers spread across the tables. Flanda leaned over to Yvonna and said, "She has changed. I mean *really* changed! Something about her is so different. What is it?"

Yvonna nodded and leaned back and whispered, "It looks like she's been on a diet."

Flanda looked back at Yvonna and said in a whisper loud

enough for the entire table to hear, "I didn't know you could put your breasts on a diet by themselves."

The entire table quietly snickered as Helena began talking to the audience in a perfectly articulated soft voice. As she spoke, the footlights came up softly. Her band started playing at low volume, somewhere in the darkness.

Esme quietly muttered to Shell, "Where is her Frenchy accent? Or did that stay wherever she went?"

Shell looked at Esme and put her finger to her lips, signaling her to be quiet. It didn't seem to work at all on her little sister.

Esme continued, "And the mole — where is that thing hiding?"

Esme smiled and leaned toward her sister. Cupping her hand around her sister's ear, she said, "Where is Sorina? Didn't she say she'd be here?"

Shell shrugged and once again put her finger to her lips.

From her newly found center, Helena courageously spoke. "Many of you all know that I have been away; actually, I was away for almost two months. Some of you only know me through my music here at the club. Many of you know me quite well. I have something to tell you all. Changes have been made. And they are permanent."

The crowd cheered.

Helena continued, "No, really." She laughed and said, "I had a self-revelation while I was away. I have gained some things, and ... and well, I have lost others. While I was away, I spent a lot of time pondering my life and happiness in general. I spent some time writing songs — songs that reflect life, peace, and contentment. Tonight, I'm going to do a few songs from my previous repertoire and several songs from my new collection. I also have a little surprise for everyone. It's a big deal for me. As Ched mentioned earlier, I have added a member to my solo performance. We will perform as a duo from now on. I'm confident you'll agree with me. My performance is truly enhanced by her musical skills. I will introduce her shortly."

After all of that, the crowd was eager for the show to start.

Helena turned to her band and raised her right arm. With her right forefinger extended, she said, "Okay, boys, let's go!"

Donny Dixon was on the drums. His command of drumsticks and wire brushes was amazing. He started on his cymbals, building the sound, and then changed from the wire brushes to drumsticks. The patter and the tempo were soft, even, and seductive. About the same time Donny started on his drums, Bill Hegley began strumming his upright double bass.

Helena turned again to the audience as she said, "This song is a new one. I wrote it eight weeks ago while I was away. Strange things happen when you are all alone. It's called 'Changing Ways.' I hope you like it."

The footlights dimmed as the beam of the single spotlight was once again directed at her. She knew she was more than a performer in this light; she knew people were meeting the new Helena Montgomery. The background music began to grow as she seated herself at the piano and pulled the microphone toward her mouth. The room was silent as everyone eagerly awaited her first song. Helena bowed her head and began to play a riff while Donny and Bill followed, blending with her melody. She slowly lifted her face toward the microphone and began to sing, her voice ever so soft.

> "I've changed my ways,
> Had to do it, had to do it
> I've found a new me, a real me
> All that is me, and was hidden beneath …"

The further and deeper she got into the song, the fuller and stronger her voice became.

As she sang, the pulley operator offstage began to do his intricate job. Donny was making a quiet repetition on his drums that, ever so softly and slowly, grew into a melodic, syncopated pattern. The sounds of the drums covered the noise of the pulleys. A clear plexiglass platform was being lowered from directly above the stage. A second spotlight beamed onto the descending platform, revealing a stunning blonde figure in a flowing white gown, floating down through the air toward a spot next to Helena and the piano. The only lights in the room were the two spots, one shining on Helena, the other on the angelic female figure descending from above. As the platform came to rest onstage, Helena sang her last note.

As the audience responded with applause, Helena stood and said, "Ladies and gentlemen, I would like to introduce you to my brand-new singing partner."

Danny did a drumroll for a short ten seconds and then stopped.

Helena said, "Please, everyone put your hands together and give a warm welcome to Sorina Lapone."

The crowd applauded loudly as Sorina stepped off the platform and onto the stage. The spotlight followed her as she joined Helena. There they stood, hand in hand, Sorina and Helena, center stage. Sorina looked like she never had before — with the exception, of course, of her signature high ponytail holding back her long, baby-fine, white-blonde hair. The audience appeared hysterically happy. The cheers and applause continued while Sorina and Helena bowed in unison to the audience all around the stage.

Sorina blushed as Helena once again began to speak into her microphone. "Ladies and gentlemen, this is my little surprise." She looked at the audience and said, "We actually bumped into each other about four weeks ago after we both returned from vacations. We had a good, long conversation over coffee, and the next thing we knew, we found ourselves meeting here several mornings a week, singing and playing our instruments together. It was an odd coincidence we even met that day. Truly a twist of fate. We think, and those who have heard us play together agree, that our voices and music blend well. We'll let you be the judge."

Sorina smiled and took a deep breath as she nervously addressed the audience. "A few of you know me and are familiar with the fact that I play the harmonica. Many also know that I learned to play that instrument to help a stutter that affected my speech. The harmonica is not a proven treatment, but I found that it helped me. It was a great instrument to learn too, because I became a pretty good harmonicist. With that out in the open, what many of you do not know about me is I also play the acoustic guitar. With Helena's encouragement and her piano skills, we have formed our duo." As she turned to Helena, she said, "I think it's time we show 'em what we've got."

Helena took to the microphone and said, "Sorina and I want to play this first number for you because it is one of our favorites. It was written by Carole King and Gerry Goffin in the early 1960s and has been sung by many different artists. Our favorite rendition was performed by Laura Nyro. The name of this song is 'Up on the Roof,' and it goes like this."

Sorina picked up her guitar and sat in the chair by Helena's piano. They both adjusted their microphones while Helena situated herself at her keyboard. The two of them began their song as they were joined by Bill and Donny.

> "When this old world starts getting me down
> And people are just too much for me to face …" [1]

As the last part of the melody ebbed, and Sorina and Helena reached the last notes of the song, the audience applauded with wild enthusiasm, eventually rising for a standing ovation.

The lights in the Music Box were now brightened ever so slightly, enough for the women to see the people seated at the tables around the foot of the stage. While Sorina was smiling at and absorbing the proud expressions of her parents, sisters, and friends, Helena took notice of the People's Bank table and locked eyes with Johnny, and *zing* went the strings of her heart. There he was, seated with her former co-workers.

Esme was trying to contain herself. She was astounded. She had been totally unaware of Sorina's talent or ambition. Shell stared with joy at her sister onstage, thrilled by Sorina's perfect surprise. Ricky was mesmerized. Eddy silently took Shell's hand in his.

[1] *From this writer: To capture the mood, I would encourage you, the reader, to listen to this song by Laura Nyro.*

Esme whispered to Shell, "I am so shocked! I mean, who would have ever thought that sister Sorina was friends, much less secretly rehearsing, with that … that thing!"

Shell put her forefinger to her lips as she turned to Esme and said, "There's a logical explanation. I mean, this is so not what I expected to see tonight either, but you need to hush, they're starting again."

Everyone else at the table was still whispering when they realized the show was continuing. Helena and Sorina sang a wide variety of pop songs written by various artists, along with their own songs.

Esme was twirling internally. She continued her quiet tirade, whispering to Shell, sitting next to her, "I just can't believe her. That damn mole is gone, too."

All the while, Shell continued to hush her sister.

Helena and Sorina were beginning the final song of their last set. Helena said, "This is the most recent of my new songs, and it is for someone very, very special."

Sorina began an opening riff on her guitar. Helena joined her on piano. Helena began to sing as Sorina sang backup harmony. Helena could only think of Johnny and cast a momentary glance his way as she started.

"I'll sing a song for you, for
you are always in my dreams
We will drift among the clouds …"

After they hit their last notes, Sorina put down her guitar, Helena slid back from the piano, and they both stood. They were joined by Bill and Donny, and as an ensemble, they took a bow. The audience stood and applauded as Helena walked back to the piano, grabbed her microphone, and began to speak to the audience.

"We are so grateful to be here as the opening act for Joni Mitchell. She will be up here after this intermission in about thirty minutes. She is my favorite songwriter and performer; we are so beyond thrilled to have had this opportunity. You all are in for quite a treat. I've heard tidbits of her rehearsals. I would like to thank her for choosing us, over so many others, to be her opening act tonight. And Joni, I think you can hear this in your dressing room — thank you from the bottom of our hearts. Your songs all mean so much to us, and your talent is endless. I can't wait to hear you in person. Again, thank you!"

The audience applauded. Helena took Sorina by the hand, and they stepped down from the stage together. Helena sat down next to Johnny in the last remaining chair at the People's Bank table, and Sorina joined her family and friends. They were all feeling festive and exhilarated.

Sorina's family and friends had been thoroughly and completely astounded by the magic that she and Helena had just performed. She was bombarded from all sides with question after question, and she answered each in its turn. The consensus was that they were all happy, proud, and over the moon for her.

Esme said, "I can't believe that you kept this a secret for this long. I was so shocked I almost fell out of my chair. I mean, you and Helena? How did you ever do this? I have to say you both were amazing — absolutely unbelievable."

Sorina smiled as she sat with her perfect posture. "Remember in high school I was in chorus? And remember it was one of my favorite after-school activities? Well, when I was at that stuttering camp, it kind of came back to me; when I sing, I don't stutter. So while I was there, the counselors and I figured out the rest. I kind of sang my way out of the camp, and then I happened to bump into Helena a couple of weeks after I returned. One thing led to another, and you just heard the results."

Shell had to ask, "How did you ever strike up a conversation, much less a friendship, with Helena Montgomery? I mean, she is your complete opposite. I mean … well, you *know* what I mean."

Her parents felt they had waited long enough and broke into the conversation. Yvonna began, "Sweetheart, you were just wonderful. I had no idea you had a voice like that. And you were stunning up there in the spotlights. Your skin, your hair, your everything was runway model–ready. I am so proud of you; I just don't know what else to say."

Frank said, "Sorina! I am so … well, proud doesn't even describe it. You were fantastic! You have blossomed into the most beautiful person, from inside all the way out. I never in my life dreamed you'd be performing onstage!"

The buzz continued until Sorina mentioned Helena's name again. They piped down and tuned into Sorina like they had just sat down for the season premiere of *M*A*S*H*. Right off the bat, she explained their friendship, both its origins and its depth. With that out of the way, she dove into Helena's adventure in Elloree, South Carolina. She gave them just enough particulars to sate their curiosities. Sorina rightly considered that some things just needed to remain private. And how could you bring up Elloree without at least a mention of the world-famous Teapot Museum? It turned out, Sorina explained, that Helena's only liberation from the center during her stay had been a field trip to the museum. Two counselors had arranged for her group to go off-grounds for an afternoon. As Helena had described it, the entire escapade had been hilarious, and she had the photograph of herself, with the giant teapot looming overhead, to prove it.

Sorina had about talked herself out. "The way Helena told the story, it seemed funnier. Her version made me nearly pee my pants. I hope you all will get to know her like I have. If you do, maybe someday she'll open up to you completely about her stay in Elloree." With that Sorina was finished, and the rattle of conversation resumed all around the table.

As she approached the bank group's table, Helena had worried that the group might have an exclusive and clubby feel. After all, they were her *former* co-workers. But as it turned out, it was a lighthearted and friendly crowd who welcomed her with open arms. Everyone had heard her sing at the club in her former life, as she now thought of her life before the center. John Dunkerly and his lovely wife Edweena were in agreement that tonight's performance had been indisputably sublime.

Miss Montgomery was now the center of attention, free of her former pretensions and facades. Helena smiled. She addressed the group in a calm voice, articulating her words. "I am so happy you all were able to be here to see Sorina and me. I need to admit to all of you, I know now what a hot mess I was when I worked with you all. The rumor is I spent my summer in a spa out west. Not even close. I went to a rehab facility in South Carolina to get myself back on track. I needed help to believe in my own self-worth. My self-esteem was in shambles, and I needed to get it back. Truth is, I needed to rediscover my core and reestablish my true and honest self. It wasn't easy. Each day there was a challenge. Each day remains a challenge. I'll be working on me for the rest of my life." She paused, releasing a slight chuckle. "The place was a center for personal alignment. And you thought that alignment was only for tires! Boy, little did I know what else that word can mean. I'll just say I am back, happy, and content. Oh, and by the way" — she looked at Johnny, who nodded to her — "I guess I can tell you all something else since I am no longer working at the bank. Johnny and I are dating!" She leaned over and gave Johnny a quick peck on the cheek. She actually made him blush.

"Yes! And I'm happy to confirm it's all true," he said.

Esme heard Helena laughing. "I have never heard an honest expression from her! That laugh sounded real," she said, pointing in Helena's direction.

The strangest falsetto giggle came out of Shell's mouth. She said to Esme, "Same here. She certainly looks good." And to Sorina, Shell said, "Why not get us all together sometime? I need to thank her for her FTW input. Pretty sure that comment helped push me into my diet!"

Eddy was talking quietly with one of the cocktail waitresses. Everyone else at the table was involved in conversation. The waitress left, only to return quickly with another waitress, each carrying several bottles of champagne. They stood between Sorina's and Helena's tables. The original waitress announced that Eddy had ordered the champagne for both tables.

Eddy stood. He first looked at Helena and then swiveled and nodded to Sorina. "I thought you both were brilliant tonight! I cannot think of a more appropriate time to celebrate! And I mean celebrate everything!" He looked to the waitresses, who popped the bottles and poured glasses at both tables, as appreciation was acknowledged back and forth. Once everyone had a glass in hand, Eddy raised his own and toasted, "So cheers to all and cheers to change!"

With champagne bubbles tickling their noses, everyone settled back in their seats in eager anticipation of the evening's star attraction.

Wally finally spoke across the table to Shell and Sorina. "Girls, thank you so much for including me in all of this. I'm having such a good time. And I just have to tell you, I love Joni Mitchell. Did you know she's been labeled the female version of Bob Dylan? I mean, how many people can write and perform like the two of them? Personally, I like Joni more. I can't tell you how excited I am to be here. I was in my fifties when they started performing."

Sorina spoke up and said, "Wally, I know what you mean. She is finishing up her latest album. It's titled *Hejira*. If you don't know the meaning, it refers to a journey from a troubled environment or land. The lyrics and songs are so good, they take your breath away. I don't know how she does it. She's working on her last two songs here in Nashville, and then her album will be complete. Her record label is planning to release it in late November."

Wally replied, "*Blue* is my favorite album of hers, and next would have to be *Court and Spark*. When you analyze and focus on the words in conjunction with the music, she is undeniably one of the best songwriters ever. Her music makes me feel twenty years younger."

Meanwhile, back at the smoke-filled bar, Charlotte and Edna were busy making copious notes. Charlotte kept complaining to the bartender that the smoke was too thick. Edna just stood, staring out into space with watering eyes, thinking, *Why did I ever go to work for this woman?*

Joni

Ched once again took center stage. With microphone in hand, he began speaking. "The Music Box is proud, and so deeply honored, to introduce Joni Mitchell as our special performer for tonight's show."

The applause was mind-blowing. It seemed to go on forever. When it finally began to ebb, the spots were dimmed, and in the middle of the stage stood Joni Mitchell in a simple black scoop-neck silk blouse, ikat-print mid-length skirt, and soft leather knee boots. She picked up her guitar and started plucking strings. She began to sing as her eyes scanned the room.

The audience cheered in recognition as she floated through her first song. They sat rapt, intoxicated by the lyrical tone of her contralto melody. Hypnotized by the lyrics, they were all transported to places and scenes they knew personally. They loved her for her music and the stories she told of deepest feelings, hurts, and joys. Her words played magically with each audience member through each mesmerizing riff. She paused to tune her guitar.

Sorina whispered to Esme, "I just explained to Wally, her new album is titled *Hejira* and due to be released this November. I've heard her sing one from it already. I think she calls it 'Coyote.'"

Esme quipped, "Why 'Coyote'? And what is a hejira?"

Sorina smiled. There were times she had to wonder where her sister's head disappeared to. Esme had been right there when Sorina had explained the same thing to Wally. "The definition of hejira is a journey, exodus, migration, like a lost soul escaping a troubled land. As for 'Coyote'? It covers too many bases to worry about right now."

Esme had a contented smile on her face as she said, "She is just a pretty incredible writer and performer. I can't wait for the rest of her set."

With her guitar retuned to her satisfaction, Joni began again, playing and singing through seven more songs, until thirty-five minutes had disappeared like a dream. What a glorious evening. She'd covered selections from her memory books — *Court and Spark*, *Blue*, and *Ladies of the Canyon* — and from the smiles on their faces, it seemed the audience could not be happier.

Focusing, the audience realized she had finished her first set already. Suddenly, Ched was onstage, saying, "We'll take a brief break, and Joni will be back with more."

Shell, Esme, Ricky, and Sorina soon were in a heated conversation. The excitement was interrupted by Helena and Johnny, who came over to their table to say hello. The six of them got into a heavy discussion that became a retrospective of the past few months.

"Do you all realize that everything that has happened was because of that bank robbery?" Shell asked. "I mean, if it weren't for that, we would be bumbling along with our humdrum lives, and nothing would have changed. I don't know about you, but I was bored out of my mind. Look at all of us now! It's just weird that so much good has come out of a bank robbery."

Helena laughed and said, "If it weren't for that robbery, who knows? I could have upgraded myself to basketballs." They all laughed. Who knew Helena could be funny? "No, what a turning point, what luck, if that's what you want to call it. I am just so thankful everything has worked out so well for everyone! Just you wait a few months." She paused and looked at Sorina. "Sorina has so much talent. Her voice is so strong and versatile. I really think we may actually get somewhere with her on board. You all have only heard a hint of what she can do. Remember, we've only been rehearsing for a very short time."

"Helena, thank you for your kind words," Sorina said, beaming from the compliment.

Helena turned to the others and said, "This girl can say and do the funniest things one minute and then be on perfect pitch in a song the very next. She is such a great mentor and duet partner."

Esme chimed in, "I am dumbstruck. That's all I can say."

Ricky and Johnny both nodded. Johnny added, "I saw right through Helena the moment we first met. I didn't know how to peel away the surface." He laughed. "No pun intended."

With a round of laughter, the group dispersed toward the bathrooms and bar. When they returned, they retook their seats, ready for Joni's next set.

With Joni back onstage, the evening become even more magical as she sang through her repertoire, even taking a few requests. As the evening drew to a close, the audience gave a few more standing ovations before Joni did one last song. She and her band all took a bow before leaving the building. The crowd began to break up. People were heading for the exits.

Charlotte and Edna were among the first to depart. Both reeking of smoke, they agreed they'd had their fill of cigarettes for a lifetime. Charlotte joked about it to Edna. "They tried to smoke out the press. But we didn't let 'em."

"I just hope after tonight I'm not addicted to nicotine. Really, a friend's mother just died of lung cancer." Edna was so upset she was close to crying.

Shell and Eddy

Shell and Eddy lingered at the table a while longer. On Monday morning, Shell would be back at the grind of school for one more month. She had projects that she both dreaded and felt excitement for. Upon completion of her projects, she would be done with classes at NSTI.

With school and projects at the forefront of her mind, Shell looked at Eddy and said, "I am going to miss you. I mean, I'll miss you a lot. Do you realize we have been out four times in the past week?" She paused. "That just hit me today!"

"I know. I'll miss you, too." Eddy's face was full sad-sack. "Thing is, you have got to do this. Would you mind if I stopped by one or two of your classes over the next few weeks?"

Shell looked at him and said, "That'd be fine with me. I don't think my instructor, Mr. Blondell, would care. I'll just be working on that float. Well, the float and my contest entry. The float gets graded by a rep from the actual Rose Parade people."

Eddy said, "I can't believe you have to do a small-scale model float for the Rose Parade. Do you have any idea what you're going to do?"

"I've got some ideas I've been mulling. Mr. Blondell has alluded to a surprise he'll announce on Monday." Shell was sounding tired.

"I have no idea what or who it could be. At any rate, it's time to head home. Let's get outta here." Out they went. As they reached the car, she said, "Oh, you want to join us all at Flanda's for brunch in the morning?"

"Of course!" he replied as they got in.

Eddy drove them back to Shell's apartment. He walked her to her door, and this time she received a long and passionate kiss before he left.

Sunday, September 12, 1976

Eight o'clock in the morning had arrived just as fast and early as it had for the last twelve weeks. All three sisters had spent the night at Shell's — Esme on the sofa, Sorina with Shell in her bed. The girls had risen with the clock and were now up and dressed. They were meeting their parents, Eddy, and Ricky at Flanda Castle's for brunch at nine thirty. It was going to be a fun get-together that would include Minnie's and Flanda's husbands. It was another beautiful morning in Nashville. The girls decided to walk to brunch rather than drive. The weather was too perfect not to be outside in fresh air.

As was her usual practice, Flanda had arrived at her restaurant at the crack of dawn. This morning she had something up her sleeve. She had gone out and purchased a large amount of tacky plastic flowers. She did her best to arrange the ugliest, most gargantuan arrangement she could possibly muster. She planned to act like she thought it the most gorgeous thing she'd ever seen, just as a joke to get a rise out of Shell. She couldn't wait to see the girl's reaction. The arrangement ended up being so large that it took over the table and so high that no one would be able to see across to the opposite side. When Minnie had arrived at eight, she'd screamed with laughter and begun to set the table in preparation for the group to arrive. When Minnie was finished, all the family had to do was get there. It wasn't long before she heard the first car pull up outside.

Yvonna and Frank soon came through the door. Yvonna caught the joke immediately and laughed. Frank took one look at the monstrosity and said to Flanda, "Don't you think the flowers are a little big for the table?" He was clueless.

Yvonna explained. Then Frank laughed. Earl and Ricky followed the Lapones and got a chuckle when they saw the thing.

The girls strolled up after most of the family. Eddy was just pulling into a spot. Eddy joined the girls, and the four ambled in together. Esme squealed. Sorina smiled. Shell's mouth dropped open as she stood with Eddy, transfixed in a mild state of shock. Flanda came out of the kitchen and over to Shell and said, "I did this especially for you, honey. Nice, huh?"

Shell was speechless, thinking of what to say. Eddy continued to stare. The rest of the room watched for Shell's reaction, doing their very best to hide their laughter. It only took Minnie to give the joke away. She couldn't hold it in anymore and doubled over in hysterics. The rest could only follow her lead and broke down laughing.

With everyone in the room in tears and with peals of laughter ringing, Shell asked Eddy, "Did I mention my family is possibly certifiable?"

Hearing that, Flanda clutched a fist to her heart as if crushed, inched over, and removed her masterpiece, chuckling all the way.

Everyone headed to the table. When they had all managed to pick their seats, conversation picked up from the night before. A palpable energy remained from the phenomenal experience of the previous evening.

Eddy announced, "I had never heard Helena sing before last night. She's astonishing. I had no idea she's such an accomplished vocalist."

"She was pretty good. I'll give her that much," said Shell. A bit of sisterly pride was rising in her. "On the other hand, it didn't hurt one bit that Sorina joined her and lit up the stage, quite literally! I really think the new duo is so much better than Helena as a solo performer. I also think Helena believes that to be true as well."

After lively conversation and an impeccable meal, the group scattered to the four winds.

Monday, September 13, 1976

Shell arrived at school early and made her way to her classroom. Several students had already arrived and begun discussing the possibilities for Mr. Blondell's surprise. The consensus seemed to be that they already had enough on their plates. So the question remained, what did he have brewing? It was simply too close to end of term to add anything more.

Shell's remaining classmates filed in, trailed by Benjamin Blondell. The students sat at their desks as Mr. Blondell made his way to the lectern and began to speak. "Class, welcome back from your Labor Day break. As I told you all when you signed up for this series of classes, there will be something different about our last four weeks.

"You are already aware that our Rose Parade project is being conducted in conjunction with Springs Academy down in Memphis. My surprise is that to facilitate the process, construction and judging of your final scale models will all take place in Memphis. The facilities available in Memphis are much larger than what we have here in Nashville. Both schools have been granted permission to work on the campus of Memphis State. Arrangements have been made for a warehouse on that campus for our use. It has been filled, by donations, with all the materials you'll need to complete your floats. Lumber, wire mesh, tools, and a myriad of objects and odds and ends have been provided for you. You'll have colored tissue, butcher paper, and newspaper to create your flowers. You can pick from an entire wall of spray paint to add color to the papers. Anything in that warehouse will be fair game for use on your projects.

"We will travel as a class to Memphis this coming Sunday for seven days. The construction will commence on the following Monday, and you will be finished by the following Saturday afternoon at 5:00 p.m. Final judging will be the following Sunday, the twenty-sixth. I am aware and completely understand how this affects your lives. Schedules need to be rearranged, and personal arrangements need to be made. For that reason, we'll break at lunch today and reconvene here tomorrow. You'll at least have this entire afternoon to start preparations.

"Let me wrap up the remaining details for our week away. We'll travel together by bus to Memphis. All expenses for lodging, meals, and transportation are included. You'll be staying at a Howard Johnson's near campus. Healthy snacks will be available during the day. Each of you will be assigned an assistant with carpentry skills to help with construction and cleanup. Days can be as long as you wish. If you want, bring a sleeping bag for naps or downtime if you pull an all-nighter. Take pleasure in and enjoy this challenge. You'll present your floats in Memphis State Auditorium. Two judges from the Rose Bowl Committee will be on hand to assess your entries and make award presentations.

"Let's talk a little bit more about your actual projects. If I missed this earlier, you are required to create an index listing the names of the real flowers your designs represent. But today, I'd like to spend a little time with each of you, separately, to discuss where you are with ideas and plans. Any questions?"

Was he crazy? Any questions? Apprehension and anxiety had flooded the room. Blondell was immediately bombarded with a barrage of questions. He calmly provided an answer to each question in its turn and slowly quelled the commotion. The class settled in to ponder the final objective of this journey: certification.

Mr. Blondell gave a short intro to a slideshow of Japanese ikebana and other "high design" floral arrangements. He explained as he walked that the syllabus he was distributing provided numbered descriptions of the works on the correspondingly numbered slides. He set the carousel projector on auto-play and hit start. Each beautiful example slowly lit the screen. With the slides captivating the class, Blondell had a brief conference with each student about their ideas for their project, offering his observations and providing suggestions. By the time class finished at noon, anticipation was beginning to build among the twelve classmates. Everyone was becoming excited about the trip.

Busy as she was, Shell still made it to the gym for her daily exercise routine. Over the months they'd worked together, she and Anita had become close, even spending idle hours together. The two enjoyed talking over a glass of wine from time to time or meeting for the occasional dinner out. Anita had taken a special interest in Shell, whose determination she found inspiring. Shell had shed close to twenty-five pounds since she began training with Anita. They made a perfect team.

Shell had formed congenial relationships with several of her classmates, most of whom were a few years younger than her. It was easy to form bonds with people when you spent every day together in such a small group. She had established closer friendships with two of her classmates, Ned Fulcher and Dixie Calhoun.

Ned was a couple of years older than Shell and hailed from Atlanta. He had a pale complexion and dark hair, was thin with toned muscles, and at a height of six feet seven inches, was hard to miss, anywhere. Immediately likable and funny, he had a quiet demeanor. Ned too had successfully graduated from college. His bachelor's degree was in business administration. Since graduation, he had tried several office jobs, none of which he'd found satisfying. He had an itch to try something totally different, maybe something in the creative arts. The business world had proved smothering.

Ned had discovered the floral program at Nashville State quite by accident through a friend of an acquaintance. The next thing he knew, he was enrolled in the school and playing with flowers.

Cultivating a friendship with Ned had taken time for Shell. She had thought at times that he was shy. With his home base being Atlanta, she'd wondered if a friendship was worth the effort. Class would end, and they'd lose touch. What she'd found was a friend who would always be there when needed. Ned was comfortable in his own skin, and his confidence had worn off on her. He had opened up to Shell and shared that he had a boyfriend, Philip, down in Atlanta. Going home for weekends had become a given. Small things never got under his skin. He told Shell he felt blessed and lucky to have been raised by parents who had instilled in him both independence and self-assurance and embraced his dreams as well as his life with Philip.

Where Ned was big-city, Dixie Calhoun was definitely small-town. She had been born and raised in Calhoun, Georgia, about fifty miles north of Atlanta. Her family had been living there since the late-1800s. The Calhoun money — and Shell got the idea they had plenty — came from peach plantations in southern Georgia.

Dixie was younger than Shell by a few years. She qualified as petite. Auburn-haired, she was overly polite, perky with a good sense of humor, and a southern belle to the core, with a delicate drawl to prove it. Dixie had been raised in privilege and knew it. When she acted out with airs, Shell wanted to smack her. But Shell had been raised with the Golden Rule and thought, as their friendship had developed, that maybe some of her was rubbing off on the oblivious side of Dixie's personality. It seemed Dixie had always had an affinity for floral arranging and intended to become an expert designer. Her aspirations were many. Her primary objective had become to attain such fame that she'd move to New York City and become one of the most desired florists. Dixie had always known of the school and had planned to attend from an early age. She had originally signed up for two four-month terms; this marked her second and final.

Shell had learned from Dixie how to pamper herself. Their friendship had been cemented early in the term. From Dixie, Shell had learned the nuts and bolts of personal care she'd not been exposed to before. It was because of Dixie that massages, facials, manicures, and pedicures were becoming part of Shell's regimen. Toward the end of term, the two were enjoying massages and mani-pedis after a few of the longer days in classes. Dixie was the one responsible for Shell learning to pamper herself without guilt.

All three enjoyed one another's company. Theirs had become an easy friendship, in which they shared hopes and dreams alongside problems and disappointments. The three talked away the days, fussing with their projects. Shell couldn't have been happier.

The Dream

Eddy drove Shell to the bus station on Sunday, September 19, at 7:00 a.m. Her bus was scheduled to leave at 7:30 a.m. They were greeted at the curb by Professor Blondell, who helped unload Shell's luggage and assorted paraphernalia from Eddy's van. Shell thanked Eddy for the lift, and they shared a quick kiss. He got back into his van and, starting to pull away, yelled back, "Have fun! I hope you're the winner!" Then he was gone.

Mr. Blondell took Shell and her luggage inside the terminal to an area where the other students were beginning to assemble. Six of her classmates already were sitting there, chattering about the week ahead. Excitement spiked the air. They all shared enthusiasm for the beginning of the end of their four month term. The rest of the class, including Dixie and Ned, were trickling in.

It wasn't long before they piled into the private bus that would take them the three hours down the highway to Memphis. A cheer went up as the bus began to rumble from the terminal. Shell had made herself comfortable, settling into an empty row of seats that would be her home until they reached their destination. A blanket from home and a stack of new magazines sat beside her.

She gazed out the window as the bus ambled away from the terminal. As it climbed the interstate ramp, she felt sleep creeping up on her. The low, monotonous drone of the bus's engine, the hum of its tires on the open road, and the cozy warmth of her blanket soon lulled her into a deep and heavy sleep. Once she was asleep, snoozing like a baby, her mind wandered into the labyrinth of her subconscious.

Shell was standing in an endless field of yellow daffodils. The fields undulated over rolling hills as far as her eyes could see. In the very farthest distance, she saw an enormous white castle, a building so tall and grand that it reached into the sky, touching clouds. She started in its direction, and after walking and walking for what felt like hours, she found herself standing at the base of a vast white marble staircase with a huge structure in the near distance. To her right was a white podium holding an enormous guest book. Hanging from the podium was a sign that read, "Please sign in before entering." With pen in hand, she wrote her name and address in silver ink, then started the climb up the stairs. With her first step she began a count. She climbed and climbed. She lost count after one hundred and continued to climb. Suddenly, Shell thought, how perfectly odd. She was lost and completely unaware of any place she could be as she continued to climb the blindingly white marble stairs. At last, after what must by now have been at least a thousand steps, her legs felt as light as feathers. Looking up, she discovered she had reached a pair of enormous doors. The massive doors, made of the same white marble as the stairs, shined with beauty. Each door had to be at least ten feet wide and a hundred feet tall. Peculiar as it all was, directly at eye level was a small bronze plaque that read, "Push to Open." She thought that perhaps, maybe, she needed to go into whatever awaited beyond these doors. She looked at herself. She looked up at the doors. How was she ever going to find the strength to open these massive doors? She had no choice. She felt a force drawing her in. She must at least make an attempt. Standing aslant toward the doors, she positioned herself with both hands on one of the marble doors; then with all of the strength she could summon, she pushed and pushed and pushed. She pushed with all the strength in her being. The door began to slowly budge. Slowly, slowly, inch by inch, it gave way and opened with a whoosh that blew her hair.

She tiptoed into an enormous vestibule that appeared as the light passing through the doors made the space brighter and brighter. She stepped hesitantly forward and became aware that she now stood at the beginning of an immeasurably long and wide corridor. Everything inside the hall gleamed radiantly white. It was all constructed of the same white marble as the stairs that had brought her here, the same marble that made up the exterior of the castle and the immense entry doors. Along the corridor walls appeared an infinite number of more enormous doors, placed roughly forty feet from one another. The doors continued as far as she could see.

Shell walked to the first door. On it was, again, a small bronze plaque, attached at eye level. It read, "Department of Fairy Flies." She thought, How odd. She continued walking and walking and came to the next door. It again had a bronze plaque at eye level. This one read, "Department of Bee Hummingbirds." As she strolled the hall, she began to wonder about the labels on every door. In complete clarity, she knew the names were for living creatures behind those doors. After walking and reading signs for what seemed forever, she realized that all of the signs had been growing in size with each new door. It occurred to her that as the signs became larger, the creatures listed on the signs, living behind the doors, were likewise becoming larger in size. Odd it was. She had traveled from Bee Hummingbirds to a door that now read, "Cats." As she raised her eyes, the hall appeared to have grown even longer than it had been at the beginning. This was exhausting. She turned around, squinting, trying to see all the doors she had passed, but they were long gone. And when she turned back around to go forward and looked ahead, it was still the same door after door, fading into a vortex of infinite space.

She stopped again and turned and looked across the hall. She spotted a bench that resembled a throne not far in the distance. But how far was "not far" in this odd place? Then she was there, at the bench. It was made of white marble and was two-sided. She walked up to the bench, thinking she needed to sit for a while and collect her uncollected thoughts. Where am I? She sat in a deep state of wonder. A soft, angelic voice emanated from ahead, uttering nothing she could understand. She looked as hard as she could but could still see no one. Tired and bewildered, she screamed out loud, too loud, "Where am I? All I want to do is find my way out!"

She was now sobbing, feeling helplessly alone. There she sat on a marble bench in the middle of nowhere, in a place that felt like an infinite mausoleum of curiosities. When she looked to her right, sitting on the white bench next to her was a small white purse. Filled with curiosity, she picked it up and unclipped the clasp. Perhaps, just somehow, what was inside the purse might hold the answers to her fears. To her dismay, inside of the bag were only buttons, buttons of all shapes and sizes, just like her button jar from childhood! Except these were all pearlescent. She began to pick them out of the purse, one by one, studying each as it sat in her hand. She realized that the buttons all had a strange and curious facade. Each button had humanlike features, and upon closer inspection, she found that the facades were faces of people she recognized from her life. She turned the purse upside down and poured the buttons out onto the bench. She desperately wanted to see what was at the bottom of the purse. Hundreds and hundreds of buttons spilled onto the bench, many too many to have been in such a small purse. Shell was suddenly scared. She'd never get them all back in. The button pile was now ten times larger than the purse. She'd reached the bottom of the purse and found nothing. The pile of buttons had grown so enormous that they began falling to the marble floor, where they scattered. Bouncing buttons with faces began to surround her, all landing faceup with big, big smiles. She began to weep. She was so lost. She only wanted to be back in her happy home.

She pulled herself together, got up from the bench, and continued her trek down the hall. In the distance, Shell could see an intense beam of blinding white light. The closer she neared, the brighter the beam became. How curious. This mysterious light appeared to have come from nowhere, and magically, she was drawn toward it. The pull of the white light felt magnetic. She felt powerless. Shell could hear a voice emanating from the light. Coming into view and descending from above was an effervescent, willowy, shapeless image. She strained to focus her tear-filled eyes on the light. Shell was standing face-to-face with Princess Aurora de Borealis. The princess's right hand held a wisp of a silvery wand with a heart-shaped, diamond-encrusted tip. In her left hand, she held a fan of most delicate rose petals and freesia blossoms, which she gently waved toward Shell. The aroma of the princess's fan quelled Shell's fear, and her tears stopped flowing.

Shell knew her. Her father had always told about the princess in bedtime stories when she was a child. She'd seen the princess sitting on the foot of her bed, smiling back at her. Shell was so happy and warm. She gleefully smiled and said, "Princess, I never in a million years thought that I'd ever, ever get to really meet you. I thought Daddy made you up!"

Princess Aurora, with her angelic and comforting smile, said, "Oh, but indeed we do exist. My husband and I have been busy for millennia. My dear, you are not supposed to be here. We have come to guide you back to your home."

Tears of elation welled in Shell's eyes as she trembled and said, "I have never been happier to see anyone in all of my life. What is this place? Where am I? The last thing I remember is the white marble hallway. This is such a strange place."

Princess Aurora stood next to Shell and took her hand in her own. She aimed her wand toward a brilliant beam of light far, far away and said, "Dearest, I need to move us to the light. Please, you mustn't let go of my hand." And a moment later, they were effortlessly flying through billowy clouds.

In a blink, they were in the presence of Mr. Moonbeam Man. His head and eyes were focused upward, and his arms were opened to Shell. Princess Aurora let go of Shell's hand, and the last thing Shell heard was a whooshing sound.

Shell opened her eyes to see a gentleman standing directly in front of her. He was dressed in a gray uniform and wore a black and gray newsboy cap. He was the bus driver, rousing her from an obviously very deep sleep. They had reached Memphis. She had slept the entire trip, a ride that had ended up taking a little more than four hours.

For a split second, Shell was lost and disoriented. It had been a long and deep sleep that felt like only a moment. Her dream had seemed so real: the stairs, the gigantic white marble castle, the doors, the bronze plaques listing living creatures, the endless hall. She remembered the long bench and all the buttons with familiar faces. She realized that she had never reached the end of the hallway. The princess and Mr. Moonbeam — were they real or just her imagination?

The bus was parked in the main terminal at gate five. She was the last one off. She scooted down the aisle and the three steps to her awaiting class. Together, they all left the station. Waiting outside was a much smaller bus that transported them to the Howard Johnson's motor inn where they unloaded their luggage and walked the short distance to the Memphis State Auditorium. All of them hoped there would be enough time for fried clams and sweet tea.

The Judges

It was four fifteen in the afternoon of Saturday, September 25, and the TWA 747 from Los Angeles had landed at Memphis International Airport. As the passengers began to deplane, Benjamin Blondell waited patiently at gate A-16. He heard his name called from somewhere among the crowd of passengers entering the airport from the tarmac. "Benji!"

Benjamin looked around and finally spotted Horace Donavan and Chuck White walking down the ramp toward him. Horace always had his assistant Chuck by his side. The two were known to anyone involved with the Tournament of Roses Parade. Horace held the final stamp of approval for any applicants hoping to participate in the parade come New Year's morning. He came to Tennessee twice a year to see his oldest friend, Benji Blondell, and judge his students' faux Rose Bowl floats as a favor.

Horace was the first to speak. "Ben, it is always such a treat to come and visit with you, whether here in Memphis or up in Nashville. It is such a delight to reminisce with you during these stays. And this biannual float contest of yours, I will tell you, is the most entertaining escape. I enjoy it immensely."

Benji responded, "We have some wonderful and overachieving students this term. I can't wait for you to see and meet them."

Horace smiled. “We’re looking forward to your students’ creations. Your pupils have had some of the most innovative ideas I’ve ever seen. Hey, Ben, let’s go out for drinks before you take us to our hotel. It will be like old times. Besides, no one needs us right now, do they?”

Chuck said, “This is how this always begins with you two. Let’s make sure we’re at least near our hotel before we get started. Better still, since we are staying at the Peabody, let’s just check in, dump the luggage there, and go downstairs to their restaurant for dinner. It would be nice to have a walk afterward and go for a drink or two somewhere else. Now, who doesn’t think that’s a great plan?”

“Chuck, that sounds fine to me too,” Horace responded. “Why don’t we get settled in and cleaned up? Benji, what do you think about that? We can grab a taxi, the three of us, and head to the Peabody. You can continue on to your place. I understand it’s fairly close. It’ll give you a chance to freshen up and change if you want. When you’re ready, just come back to the Peabody. We’ll take Chuck’s suggestion and dine in this evening. Chuck can make reservations with the concierge at the Peabody’s restaurant, Chez Philippe. Let’s say for seven thirty? Good?”

Benji smiled and said, “I think that is a stellar idea! Chez Philippe is still one of the best restaurants in Memphis. And with you staying at the Peabody, we should be guaranteed a table.”

By now, it was close to five. The trio hopped into a waiting cab, and off they went to the hotel. When they arrived at the Peabody, the driver and bellman helped with Horace and Chuck’s luggage.

Benji called to them, “Back in a flash!” and continued in the cab back to Howard Johnson’s.

All three of them looked forward to these get-togethers. They enjoyed each other’s company tremendously. They had been meeting like this for almost ten years. The judging had become a ritual they prized. Chez Philippe was a grand restaurant. Tonight would be no different from most. They would dine on good food and good wine over rapid-fire conversation. After dinner, they would head for an out-of-the-way piano bar for drinks and more heart-to-heart talk, as was their custom. Anticipating their evening, Benji already had planned for them to take a short, leisurely stroll to a quiet piano bar called the Club Car.

Dinner at Chez Philippe was perfection, as expected. Now it was time to enjoy the music of Angus Kahn at the Club Car. Angus, middle-aged and originally from New York City, was a fixture at the Club Car. He had been the main attraction for years. Angus sang standards and favorites while accompanying himself on the keyboard. His voice, a raspy baritone, set the mood in the popular venue. He had studied music and voice at several noted academies abroad. He had honed his talent catching gigs in cafés and bars wherever and whenever they'd have him. Recently, Angus had recorded his first album, live, at the Club Car. The newly released vinyl was getting good airplay on the radio. Angus's stage personality was infectious; to hear him was to love him. He invited Club Car guests with any vocal ability to get up and join him in song. Angus welcomed the interaction with his audience. After a few drinks, with their self-reserve on standby and confidence bolstered, singers would join him, and at that juncture, the club was hopping and would continue hopping long into the night.

Horace, Benji, and Chuck were all having an absolutely wonderful time. The rest of the evening went as expected. Benji and Horace pulled their usual stunts. After drinking a wee too much, they were up on the stage, singing their favorite sentimental songs, swaying at the piano with Angus. At 2:00 a.m., with all three of them singing "Cherish," the manager of the Club Car began turning up the lights ever so slowly, signaling that last call had already passed and the bar was closing.

The three walked unsteadily back to the Peabody. Ever the gentleman, Benji escorted his friends back and up to their rooms. Plans were made to meet up in the morning about eleven, there at the Peabody. They would have brunch in the hotel, then proceed to Memphis State Auditorium to judge the contest. Benji went back downstairs, hailed a cab, and was off.

The Competition, or Judgment Day

For their entire cab ride to the auditorium the next morning, Horace and Chuck had ribbed Benji about his vocals the night before. As they exited the cab, Chuck was still laughing about Benji duetting with Angus. "So you wanna be a torch singer, Mr. Blondell? Nice thought, but I would tell you to think again!" Chuck zipped it on that one.

Horace and Benji were both laughing when Benji said, "Horace, you aren't quite that good yourself. I mean, my friend, when you sang 'Misty,' it brought tears to my eyes only because your sound hurt so bad!" He took a breath. "It could be we're all just tone-deaf when it comes to singing. Who knows? Best to keep at what we do best." They all had a last laugh before they entered the auditorium. The time had come to be serious grown-ups.

Shell, along with most of her class, had pulled an all-nighter putting final touches on their floats. The class from Springs Academy had become equally frantic. Everyone had made their last tweaks. Their projects were completely ready as the judges arrived at 1:00 p.m. Some of the individuals still lingering at this point were representatives of the companies these mock floats were representing.

Anxious parents and friends of the students were filing into the venue with eager anticipation. The twenty-four floats were ready for their close-ups. Without doubt, this project had been the students' most arduous project thus far. For the students from both schools, today's arrival brought momentous relief.

The three judges continued their quiet conversation as they mounted the stage. Unbeknownst to the students, they were still snickering about the night before, especially when Chuck said, "Both of you could have roused the dead with your renditions of some of those songs. Benji? Horace? Neither of you should ever tell anyone that you know how to sing. Statements like that could be used against you."

When the judges turned to the assembled group, their cheery faces had gone serious. They took their seats on the stage and were immediately joined by the professor from Springs Academy, Jonathan Duet. Jonathan quickly introduced himself to the out-of-towners and took his own seat next to Chuck. The program would be starting momentarily.

Meanwhile, a car was turning into the parking lot of the auditorium. The white Fleetwood Cadillac pulled into a parking space. Behind the wheel? None other than the Wicked Witch of the East incarnate, Miss Charlotte Webber. Always first to exit the car, she was dutifully followed by her entourage of one, Edna Graves, her faithful assistant.

Charlotte said, "C'mon, hon, we need to hurry. We can't miss another second of this. It's not every day we get to see a mock parade with make-believe mini-floats!"

Charlotte was walking as fast as her little legs would carry her. She clutched her chihuahua, Teenie, to her chest as she tromped toward the auditorium. Her reading glasses, dangling from a chain around her neck, bounced about, persistently hitting little Teenie in the head. Edna opened the door to the auditorium for Charlotte before following her in. They strutted in like they owned the place. Once inside, they found themselves standing next to the stage, only feet away from the two judges and two instructors. Charlotte immediately took the opportunity to introduce herself — and oh yes, Edna — to the four men. With introductions made, they looked over to the floats still shielded from view. The overwrought students milled around their works nervously.

Charlotte walked over to Shell and said, "We can't wait to see this. We drove all the way down here this morning to photograph everyone's work. I'm planning to use some of today's shots with an article in the upcoming issue of *The Eye*. Aren't you excited?"

Shell replied, "That's nice. These have taken us all week to finish. We've all worked eighteen hours a day to complete them in time for this very day. We're all exhausted. I am so anxious for you to see what we have accomplished."

Charlotte gave Shell a little wink and said, "I'm sure what you've done is pure genius. Aside from all of this, I mean, just look at you! Wow, what a transformation you've had over the past few months. You are looking great!"

By now, everyone who was coming had arrived and was settled inside the auditorium. Everyone was seated, facing the stage, as Professor Blondell took to the podium. He faced the expectant crowd and spoke into the microphone. "Hello, everyone, and welcome! My name is Benjamin Blondell. I am the professor of floral studies at Nashville State Tech. We are here today to view the finished floats by the students from our two schools, Springs Academy of Memphis and Nashville State Technical Institute. Joining me onstage is Mr. Jonathan Duet, the professor of floral studies at Springs Academy here in Memphis. We also welcome our guests, Mr. Horace Donavan and Mr. Chuck White, our primary judges. They have come all the way from Los Angeles, California. Mr. Donovan and Mr. White are the parade masters for the Tournament of Roses Parade.

"The twenty-four students assembled today have made these floats as a part of their final project for their school term. Both of our schools follow the exact same curriculum. This competition is one of our students' last projects and is produced by each class at the end of their term. Today, the judges will choose a winner and a runner-up. The winners of this competition have happily alternated between our schools over the years. I know the class I have instructed this term has been one of my best. I look forward to viewing Mr. Duet's students' works as well.

"The parameters for these floats are as follows: Each model float must be made to one-third scale. The finished sizes can be no wider than eight feet, no longer than sixteen feet, and no taller than ten feet. Of course, wood, mesh, wire, and rope play a huge part in their construction. In lieu of fresh flowers, tissue paper, spray paint, newspaper, seeds, and dried vegetables, such as corn and beans, are used as simulation. Each entry must be accompanied by a legend matching the faux flora to its correlative living flora. Each contestant has received assistance from a carpenter in the construction and completion of this undertaking. Due to our somewhat limited space, the floats will remain stationary during judging. Jonathan and I will unveil each float as we make our way past the entries. Once the tarp is removed, our judges will make their inspections. When we reach the end, and the last float has been revealed and reviewed, our judges will discuss their opinions and make their final decisions. They will provide me with the winners' names in sealed envelopes."

Benjamin and Jonathan descended the steps from the stage and walked to the first float to be unveiled. It had been created by a Springs Academy student. The anxious young man stood by as they approached. Benjamin had the honor of unlatching the first tarp curtain. The tarp fell to the floor and was promptly removed. The float was clearly visible. It had been named "A Scene from a Playground" and had been created for the Memphis parks department. The float carried a large swing set made of wire and wire mesh. Covering the apparatus was green tissue paper in varying shades, which the legend stated represented different varieties of ivy. The girl on the swing was lifelike. Her wire mesh base was covered with tissue paper. Some tissues were striped, others solid; all were in yellows and whites, depicting daffodils, carnations, and daisies. The swing moved back and forth while music played. The base of the float was covered with wads of green tissues in varying shades, simulating grass. All in all, the young man had made a solid effort. He had done a good job within the limitations of materials. His float was maybe not a showstopper, but definitely deserved a passing grade.

Moving on, more floats were revealed and judged. None of them completely wowed the judges or even the audience. Too many were rather crudely constructed. The eleventh float was the creation of one of Shell's besties, Ned Fulcher. His float brought the spectators to their feet in applause. It depicted an art deco Erté painting. Portrayed on his float were three Russian wolfhounds leashed and walked by a woman elegantly dressed in deco garb. Most of his float was done in browns, blacks, grays, and whites. He had been most innovative with the darker colors. His legend listed and defined his tissue creations as woodland mushrooms and different varieties of fungi. The whites were carnations. Ned had paid particular attention to the details of his realistic Russian wolfhounds; they were a definite showstopper.

After viewing a number of unexciting entries, the judges came to number nineteen — Shell's float. As the judges approached, Shell was not standing by her own creation. Professor Blondell was visibly perplexed. He looked at her carpentry assistant with ashen pallor and whispered, "Where is she? Please find her and get her over here. Pronto!"

The assistant, bewildered as well, answered, "She'll be back any minute. She asked me to tell you to just go on with the unveiling. I assure you, she'll be here any second."

On that assurance, Shell's instructor began to unveil her float. Off came the curtain hiding her finished masterpiece from the world. Her float's fictitious sponsor was the Shell Oil Company. A loud round of applause followed the unveiling. The work was stunning, perhaps even shocking to some. Front and center on the float was Shell herself, standing in the center of an open clamshell situated in the middle of her float. She was draped in a loose and billowy, white sheer fabric. Her face, neck, hands, and hair were all sprayed with a white flour paste that, if real, would have been hundreds of petals from white roses. Shell was posed as Venus, goddess of love, beauty, and desire, with one hand covering her right breast, the other covering her genitalia. She had replicated to perfection the likeness from the 1484 painting by Sandro Botticelli, *The Birth of Venus.*

Surrounding her and covering the floor of the float were wads of blue tissue paper tipped with white paint for the ocean. She had constructed clouds from gray and white tissue paper that hung from nearly invisible wiring that her assistant had rigged above the entire area of the float. The legend referred to the clouds as carnations and pieces of ash bark. The clamshell was made from a variation of papier-mâché. She had used torn paper and a mixture of glue and water to create the form. She'd finished it off by spray-painting the shell in different shades of white and tan. It was sturdy enough to be the base on which Shell stood. Theoretically, the shell in reality would be covered in varieties of rice and other small grains.

The applause from the audience rose when all four judges joined in. Charlotte and Edna were both busy. Edna was snapping photographs while Charlotte scribbled away, her nose buried in her notebook. The entire time, Shell stood motionless, occasionally blinking, staring straight ahead. The two reps from Shell Oil were obviously happy, as they stood on their chairs, clapping and whistling.

Two more floats were shown, their creators deflated after Shell's masterpiece. Dixie's was next, the twenty-second float and one of the last to be revealed. It was good, but it was not the crowd pleaser she had hoped it would be. Her imaginary sponsor was the Colgate Palmolive company. Her float featured a giant tube of Colgate toothpaste and a toothbrush. It was all resting on a simulated bathroom countertop. She and her assistant had rigged the float so that the cap of the tube would come off and then go back on. In the background, a musical recording played; she had written and recorded an original jingle to the tune of George Gershwin's "I've Got a Crush on You," changing the words to "I've got a brush on you, yummy, yum, yum." The spectators unfortunately did not respond to her attempt at a pun and reserved their applause.

After Dixie's float, the final two were revealed. Neither float wowed the judges or the instructors. The judges made one more complete walk around the floor before disappearing. With the show complete, the floor was opened for thirty minutes of audience perusal while the judges conferred. Shell allowed her mind to relax. But sadly for her, she had to remain standing in the shell for another thirty minutes. If she moved too much, her white makeup would crack. Her arms were getting tired, very tired.

After half an hour, Jonathan and Benjamin returned to the stage with Horace and Chuck. Jonathan announced, "We are all pleased with this year's results. They all took significant effort, and we applaud each and every endeavor. Each student has shown immense originality with their creations. The limitations of the use of certain items in place of living plants was in itself a hurdle many could not have fathomed. I think this show has achieved its purpose and highlights the visions of these true artists in the creation of something from virtually nothing."

Horace stood, crossed the stage, and handed Professor Blondell two envelopes.

Professor Blondell thanked him and turned to the audience. "These envelopes represent first- and second-place winners of this competition. The four of us are in consensus — each entrant did an outstanding job and will receive a passing grade. These envelopes hold recognition for two special students." He looked over at Jonathan and said, "Jonathan, will you please make the announcements?"

"It will be my pleasure." Jonathan smiled and took the envelopes. Stepping up to the microphone, he opened the first envelope and read aloud. "Second place this year is awarded to Mr. Ned Fulcher from Nashville State Technical Institute."

Cheers and whistles followed. Ned stood and waved to the audience in thanks.

The audience applause subsided as Jonathan composed himself

and readied the next envelope. With Benjamin by his side, Jonathan tore open the first-place envelope. He smiled. "It is my pleasure to announce that the first-place winner of this year's competition is — and excuse me, but I have to say, we were all amazed by this entrant — Ms. Shell Lapone."

Shell was still standing motionless in the middle of her clamshell. Her face broke into a huge smile, and tears began streaking her pasty makeup. In her head she thought, *What a thrill!* Dixie jumped up and onto Shell's float, gave her a big hug, and helped her maneuver out of the clamshell and down to the auditorium floor.

A catered reception followed. Dixie, Ned, and Shell felt the pure relief of total exhaustion and thanked their stars the float project was finally over. Only two weeks remained until the end of the program, with one significant project lurking in their minds.

Los Angeles, Here We Come

Shell had been back in Nashville since Monday. She suddenly found it was already Wednesday afternoon, and she and her family were gathered at her parents' house. Of course, Ricky, Eddy, Wally, Max, and Stella had joined the small party. They had come together to celebrate, or mourn, with a farewell barbecue for Ricky and Esme. A little later, once they'd closed the café, Flanda and Minnie would be by with their husbands. Esme and Ricky had planned this date for about six weeks. On Thursday, September 30, 1976, they were leaving for Los Angeles. The tone of the group had bordered on somber until a few drinks were served, after which the mood had become more festive and the party much livelier.

Beneath their calm surfaces, Ricky and Esme were scared to death about the move. Holding them together was the knowledge they had each other for support. Everything was set. Ricky had the trailer hitch attached to his Tempest. He had finally replaced his car's aging white convertible top with a fresh new one. Ricky had even sprung for a professional service and oil change. Once he was satisfied that the Tempest was ready for the trip, he had gone to a U-Haul rental center and found a medium-sized utility trailer he'd figured would do the job. The U-Haul sat out front at the curb, attached to the new trailer hitch, ready for the Tempest to roll. Esme and Ricky had spent all of yesterday and most of today loading the trailer with all of their clothes and sacred possessions. How they had managed to squeeze all of their belongings around the Waxing Pony was nothing short of a miracle. Ricky had already made several appointments with salons in Beverly Hills. He was ready to show off his new invention that, proudly, was now "patent pending." Being the diligent businessman he was, he had contacted the dime-store horse manufacturer. They'd agreed on arrangements for Ricky to purchase units of the horse at wholesale if and when the time presented itself.

Esme was most excited about all the possibilities available and waiting in Los Angeles. She figured at worst she might have to waitress for a while until they got settled. Wasn't that what all struggling actors did in LA? It might be a while before they started bringing in an income, but they both knew they would eventually. The reality was, they were not poor or needy by any stretch of the imagination. With what Ricky had stashed away and Esme had saved, they were secure financially. Just as important, they were secure with their own instincts and dreams.

Kisses from their family and friends were in no short supply for Ricky or Esme. She had been hugged so many times that she laughed and said, "I'm gonna be bruised for at least a week from y'all's hugs!"

It was true. Everyone was sad to see them go. Ricky and Esme even became a little melancholy. But no matter how sad anyone became, they had made their decisions. The motion of change had begun.

The barbecue lasted until around ten that evening. Ricky's and Esme's plan was to begin their journey before seven the next morning. After tearful goodbyes from everyone, Esme and Ricky went upstairs to her room, physically and mentally exhausted from the past few days. By eleven thirty, they were tucked in tight. Their first big driving day was Thursday. The plan was to drive the longest distance that very first day. Interstate 40 was the logical main route Ricky had chosen. Getting past Oklahoma City the first day was his intention. In his estimation, the first leg of their journey would take close to thirteen hours of hard driving.

The morning of their departure, the road to the interstate was nearly vacant. When they reached the interstate from the on ramp, traffic was easy and consistent. Adrenaline kicked in at the first sign reading "I-40 West." Esme was at the helm of the eight-track tape player. She managed to play a big enough variety of tapes the first few hours to keep them both entertained. She started with America, segued to the Little River Band, and then landed on Led Zeppelin. Esme was quite the disc jockey those first few hours, and when she tired of changing the tapes and took a look at their surroundings, she immediately realized they were already crossing the Mississippi River. Happy to be moving farther along, she settled back into her seat and fell soundly asleep.

She woke when Ricky pulled off the interstate and into a truck stop for gasoline and a bathroom break. It was close to 1:00 p.m. He needed some coffee and water and seriously wanted a cheeseburger. By the time he pulled up to the pump, Esme was wide awake and eager to drive. Satisfied after burgers and coffee, and with water for the road, they switched places and hit the highway. Esme was headed to west Oklahoma City or thereabouts. The western part of Tennessee had bored her to sleep. The wilds of Arkansas, she had found, were not a lot better. Trees and other foliage were changing colors and varieties. The view out the windows into the distance was meager. Foliage was high and dense and the land so level that there was not much more to be seen besides the colorful landscape. The only thing to see through the windshield was more open road. So she drove, and drove some more, taking what joy she could from the scenery and happily imagining the new adventure they were beginning.

It was close to six thirty and still daylight as they approached Oklahoma City. Because of the time of day, traffic was light as they sailed through the middle of town. Esme drove about twenty-five miles past Oklahoma City to the small town of El Reno, where Ricky had planned to stop overnight. As they exited the highway,

Ricky spotted what looked like the perfect place for the evening. Esme was still focused on the road. Ricky navigated her into the parking lot of the Jones Family Motel. As she pulled up to the front office, six middle-aged people sat rocking in chairs directly in front of the office.

Esme parked and waited while Ricky got out of the car and headed inside to inquire about a room for the night and the safety of the area. As it turned out, Mrs. Jones herself was behind the front desk. She welcomed Ricky like he was her own son, assuring him the motel was indeed safe. She instructed him to park the car and trailer right in front of their room. Feeling completely at ease and assured, Ricky filled out the registration card, listing their names as Esme and Ricky Baker.

Mrs. Jones handed Ricky the key. "Here you go, honey. Room 10. It's good and quiet. Highway noise kicks down early around these parts. Now, the restaurant is open till nine. My daughter and son-in-law have been runnin' it for a coupla years now. The food is simple country cookin' and down-to-earth delicious."

"Thank you kindly, ma'am," he said in his best southern voice. "I'll look forward to that homecooked dinner." This was perfect! Her straightforward kindness had made all the difference in the world to him. He thanked her once more and went back to the car. He directed Esme to their room from the passenger seat, telling her all that Mrs. Jones had conveyed while he was renting the room. When he had finished, she too was ready for some home cooking.

Esme backed the trailer into the designated spot that led up to the door of room 10. Silly as it seemed to both of them, they were excited about their first motel room and couldn't wait to check it out. It was charming, with all the comforts of home. The walls were painted a pale blue, and the shag carpet was the color of red wine. The odd thing about the carpet was that it didn't stop at the baseboard because, well, obviously, closer inspection revealed, there was no baseboard. The carpet continued straight up the walls about two feet. The bed, with its white hand-crocheted bedspread, looked comfy. Next to the bed was a table skirted in a floral fabric that matched the blue and red of the room. The lamp was a reproduction of an old oil lamp. Across the room, they had a small club chair, a floor lamp, and a chest with a TV on top. The room passed their close inspection.

Now they faced the first perplexing dilemma of their trip — should they or should they not unpack the entire car? They were convinced that the convertible top made their belongings easily accessible to thieves. They had to decide. Everything? Essentials only? They went with their natural instincts and completely unpacked the entire car.

Once that chore was done, they took the short walk down to the restaurant. Even before they opened the door, they could tell this little place was all about family. Ricky and Esme felt comfortably at home while they feasted on the fine meal provided from the kitchen by Mrs. Jones's daughter and son-in-law.

Totally stuffed, they returned to their room. Exhaustion and contentment settled in quickly. And just as quickly, Esme became paranoid. Being a genetically programmed worrier, she was afraid someone was going to break into their room while they slept and steal everything they had.

Ricky, worn out from the drive, said, "Esme, stop worrying. These are really nice people. We are lucky to have found this place. It feels to me like we have found ourselves in our first home away from home."

"Whatever," she said. She insisted they move something in front of the door, even if it was only the club chair and suitcases.

Ricky conceded. He was too tired for discussion and always went along with anything she wanted anyway. A chair and their suitcases would save them tonight. Esme turned on the television, and Ricky set the alarm clock for 6:30 a.m. After a short passionate tumble, they both fell asleep, the TV still flickering. Esme woke at two and turned it off.

The next day, Friday, October 1, they followed the same pattern as the day before. Ricky started the day driving, and Esme played DJ. Today, Ricky had Flagstaff, Arizona, on his mind as their next destination. The day continued much like the prior one. What changed dramatically was the scenery. They passed through vast and rolling desert. Approaching the border of New Mexico, the road became a steady rise. When they reached the peak of the rise, they looked out to the horizon and the undulating highway. It was time for a game, and they began to clock the miles between rises as they came into view. For most of the ride, it was at least five miles between hilltops. Esme, still playing disc jockey, kept finding the perfect songs, providing a great soundtrack for their wandering imaginations.

The stop that evening in Flagstaff was not a lot different from their stop in El Reno the night before. Their Arizona motel was a little tumbledown but again was family-owned, by folks who were as nice and kind as the Joneses the night before.

The next morning, Saturday, October 2, 1976, they began the final stretch of their drive to the Big Orange, Tinseltown, the City of Angels — Los Angeles, their new home! Interstate 40 would take them to Barstow, California, where they would pick up Interstate 15 for what, at this point, would feel like a short ride to somewhere between Fontana and Ontario, where they would switch to Interstate 10, which would take them straight into Los Angeles. Ricky expected and hoped that this last part of their road trip would take only eight or nine hours of travel. *California, here we come!*

Benjamin Blondell

The Next to Last Week of School

Let's chat. I always get a little maudlin the final two weeks of my class terms because I come to care so much for my students and their futures during our time together. To them, the last two weeks are the most exciting. Their most arduous study is behind them. At times, some of them become a little melancholy themselves. They, too, have spent long stretches of time together, learning about each other's dreams and forming solid bonds of friendship. I know some of those friendships last forever.

Today, we met up at a flower shop called The Flower Master. I have always thought of this place as more of a floral factory than a shop. It employs over thirty certified florists. They advertise that they deliver throughout the state of Tennessee on a daily basis. With sixteen air-conditioned delivery vans, I am sure they do very well. The byline below their logo is, to me, well, strange. On the sides of each van is written in big, colorful script, "The Flower Master" and, below that, "We Whip Our Flowers into Shape." See what I mean? A funny thing about the place is that generally, nobody talks about price. The owner has always been known for fair prices. In the same breath, I'd tell you to be aware. Order some of the over-the-top designs with exotics, and your bill can go over the top, too. Just saying.

The business's retail showroom is surprisingly large. In addition to retail, The Flower Master sells wholesale to individual floral shops throughout our metropolitan area. The retail staff probably adds another thirty full- and part-time individuals who are all deeply and passionately in love with the floral industry.

Almost everyone in the shop is acquainted with me, if not from my visits here with my students, then from eleven or twelve years ago, when I worked at The Flower Master part-time as a designer in their retail department. Many of them even call me by my nickname, Benji, because they are previous students or long-timers I worked with. I like bringing my class here. The visits expose them to the retail environment in which they eventually hope to work. I arrange for my class to come and observe for three days. I walk them through everything that happens on a daily basis, from orders, sales, and stock to retail gift items, arrangements, and deliveries. They also see staff–client interaction and transactions, which I feel is extremely important.

Over the years, I have become friends with the owner, Frank von Schmittou. He was my mentor many moons ago in another shop, during another life. I originally came to him for a part-time job that I could work during breaks from teaching my floral classes. Through that apprenticeship I became known as a more than competent floral designer. I worked as a professional florist for about five years and during that time made my decision to teach full-time. I had found teaching significantly more rewarding. Interacting with my students has been far superior to standing on my feet all day, working with flowers.

I looked around and my students had arrived and appeared quite happy to be out of the classroom. They were still exhausted from last week in Memphis. As we gathered in the main atrium of The Flower Master, and before I could even begin my intro, we were startled by a loud crash and then a screaming, X-rated tirade by a male voice. The outburst of profanity had originated from a far corner. We all stood speechless. I could tell by the voice that it was one of Frank's top designers — Valise von Schmittou. Valise was Frank's favorite nephew and was known among staff as 'the Chosen One.' From where we were standing, none of the other staff seemed to have bought into his drama. Maybe this was just an everyday occurrence. From what we heard, he was ranting because another designer had left her scissors and some stem cuttings on his worktable. Apparently, the crash was a heavy cut crystal vase he had smashed on the concrete floor. When we could finally see him, his anger had made him red as a beet. Shards of glass and broken flowers lay all around his work area. A pall had come over the workroom, and it had grown silent. My class was completely dispirited. This was not what we had come for.

He didn't stop. "Can't you keep to your own worktable? You are a stupid imp! I pick up your shit all day long! I am sick and bloody tired of cleaning up after you!"

Satchel, his sister, was by his side now and pleading with him. "Val, you need to calm down. Stop sweating the small stuff!"

The floral designer who was the object of his tirade had collapsed in a heap at the end of the work table. She was sobbing, and her face had gone blotchy. The poor thing tried to talk, but tears stopped her.

Valise continued his insulting rant. "You need to go somewhere else — somewhere where white carnations and baby's breath are the only flowers available because you are incapable of working with anything else!"

We had all become uncomfortable with the outburst, and I motioned for my students to follow me to a far corner. I decided that it was time to explain what was going on, even though it was obvious. "Class, you have just witnessed a prima donna in action. It's never a pretty sight. Please remember that you never want to be that person."

Around that time, a dinging sound came from Valise's table. He had tapped a metal object on a water glass. When he had the attention of everyone who was going to listen, he started. "I know

I just made a jerk of myself, but I am tired of everyone getting in my space. Please, just let me be alone to work in my corner. Please accept my apology if I may have upset anyone."

I looked at my class and explained that the business was not normally like this.

Ned from the class asked, "Are we going to be working in that room with all of the others?"

I answered, "Yes, you will. I am sure you will be assisting more sedate designers. I will be here the entire time you are here. I'll watch out for you, trust me."

Dixie chimed in, "Professor Blondell, how long will we be here anyway?"

I scanned all of my students' faces as I answered. "We will only be here three days. I want you all to take notes and watch, learn, and listen to everything that goes on." I continued, "After Wednesday, we will be moving on to another venue."

The three days proved to be both fun and interesting for the students. The class was broken up into four groups. Each group was assigned a designer to shadow for the duration of our time there. The designer mentored them through a normal day and guided them through the ins and outs of the business. Each student was given a task to complete for a customer from start to finish. Once they had finished their task, they were instructed on how to write up a sales ticket and how billing was established in accordance with time and materials.

Thursday arrived, and we were back at school. It was time to concentrate on the students' final project. I announced to the group, "Class, we will not be going to another florist. It's time to zero in on your last project. We discussed this earlier in the term, but let's go over it again for the books. Your last project is a floral entry at the Tennessee Floral Design Competition, maybe better known as The Iris Bouquet. It's the largest competition for florists in the state. The grand winner, as we've said, gets the state title, a cash award, and — let's not forget — an engraved plaque you'll stick on a shelf and forget. The competition has been set for October 8, the very last day of class. All I can say is the contest is an excellent opportunity to show yourself, each other, and the entire floral community what you're capable of. This one is entirely up to you. No parameters.

"All right, class, our last week together is approaching. I get a little sentimental at this point each semester. I know, you'd think I'd get over it, but you all will be going your own, separate ways soon. To celebrate, I would like to invite you all to my home for dinner this coming Sunday evening. It will be just the thirteen of us. Believe me when I tell you, this class has been one of my all-time favorites. I will be honored if you'll join me."

Everyone looked stunned. Shock turned to excitement, and the entire group eagerly accepted my invitation. Yelps of "What can I bring?" made the rounds. Dixie offered to bring yeast rolls, Ned wine. Shell wanted to bake a cake.

I smiled broadly. "You're all very nice to offer. This may come as a surprise, but I actually prepare the entire meal myself. I enjoy cooking, and to my chagrin, it's usually for one. As a lot of you may know from experience, cooking for yourself isn't exactly the joy of cooking. It is my pleasure to do this for the twelve of you. Each one of you has been a delight to instruct. And no joke, I think I've had as much fun as each one of you. Come around six. We'll have drinks and sit down to dinner around seven. Sound good?"

Professor Blondell's Dinner Party

Sunday night rolled around. Shell, Dixie, and Ned had decided after class Friday that they'd ride together. They were the first to walk up the stairs to the door of Benjamin Blondell's condominium. In true southern tradition, they did not arrive empty-handed. The three strolled through the door bearing chocolates, wine, and a huge bouquet of the last sunflowers of the season. When they stepped into Mr. Blondell's home, their initial reaction was awe, and they had to remind themselves not to gawk.

The place was huge. The walls in the entry were twenty feet high and appeared to be limestone, though closer inspection revealed that the limestone was actually masterful faux painting. The entire space was done in taupe and creams with touches of black. There was a definite vibe of European elegance. His living room sofas were covered in a cream-colored chenille damask. A large square iron-based glass-topped coffee table separated the sofa from two oversized, pickled French fauteuils in black suede. Antique tables and a chest sat where they might be expected. At its far end, the room was set off by draperies in Jim Thompson Thai silk that reached the full twenty-foot height of the space. Mr. Blondell had some kind of taste! Or a premier interior designer.

The dining room didn't change their opinion. Centered in the large room was a triple-pedestal mahogany dining table surrounded by Chippendale chairs to match. The table was banded in rosewood and satinwood and rested on a low-piled black and tan Wilton area rug that covered an honest-to-goodness limestone floor. The table could seat sixteen comfortably; their group of thirteen was not an issue. An enormous antique mahogany breakfront cabinet sat to the right of the table. Hanging over the table was a gilded chandelier, dripping with antique rock-crystal prisms. The table was set with glittering crystal and fine china, with the host's chair at the end and six chairs down each side. The centerpiece was stunning. While they gawked at the interiors, the other nine had made it through the front door.

As the students did their level best not to stare at the surroundings, Mr. Blondell said, "Okay, guys. Welcome to my home! From now on, please think of me as your friend and call me Benji. Enough with addressing me as mister or professor. And to relieve any further stress, I'll let you know right now, you all have passed with flying colors."

To that, they all cheered.

"You still are required to finish with an entry in The Iris Bouquet. That is our finale as a group. Have fun with the challenge and enjoy yourselves this week. Students, my friends, remember to take some time to utilize our classroom and the library to research opportunities available to you with your new certification. The school library has all sorts of resources available that will help each and every one of you identify job possibilities. It's time for you all to focus on your lives. That ends my paternal prodding and any school discussion, and I thank you. Now! It's party time. Cocktails, anyone?"

Dixie, of course, was the first to speak up. Dressed in a little, scoop-neck, black velvet dress and reflective, silver-beaded, sky-launching pumps, she said, "I would like a gin martini with two olives, very dry, please." Miss Calhoun rides again!

Ned piped in and said, "Make that two."

Everyone else followed suit and ordered the same icy cocktail. Benji was glad to have laid in extra jars of succulent Santa Barbara martini olives and an abundant supply of gin. With drinks dispersed all around, the jovial mood of the evening soared. It was a flawless party. After another cocktail, or two for some, Benji sounded the dinner bell and the group sat down to dinner. Everyone furiously devoured their meal and delighted in conversation that never lagged.

To Shell, this was real magic; something special was happening. Bonds were forming, and friendships were cementing between twelve students and their mentor. The connections made could span their lives. The blissful evening danced on until after midnight.

Benji slept that night a very happy man.

Los Angeles

Driver responsibilities switched at Barstow. Esme was now the navigating passenger feeding directions to Ricky, who was clutching the wheel. At Barstow, she'd maneuvered him from Interstate 40 to Interstate 15 South for the relatively short distance to Interstate 10 and all points west. After eight hours of travel, they exited Interstate 10, with relief, at La Cienega Boulevard and headed north. As they passed along surface streets, Esme played the part of tour guide as well as guide dog. Sights from novels and films that had taken place in and around Los Angeles were appearing directly in front of their faces. As they headed up the boulevard toward the hills, the Hollywood sign appeared bigger than life. This was the home stretch and their final day of travel.

Ricky and Esme, with their U-Haul trailer in the rearview, lumbered up La Cienega. They passed signs for Wilshire and Beverly Boulevards. Wide-eyed, they zipped across Melrose, through the large intersection at Santa Monica Boulevard, past Fountain Avenue, and up a hill steeper than anything in Nashville, hoping to emerge onto Sunset Boulevard. As they waited at the light, Ricky felt the weight of the trailer pulling on his Tempest. He felt relief when the light went green, and at Esme's instruction, Ricky turned right, away from the Playboy Club he'd spotted to his left. Heading east on Sunset Boulevard, they passed the famous Comedy Store and the turrets and balconies of the Chateau Marmont. Sailing along, they passed through an intersection where up the hill to their left was Laurel Canyon and down the hill to their right was Crescent Heights Boulevard. Now that felt like home! Safely across Crescent, they both spied Schwab's Pharmacy on their right. Esme knew all the stories about the fabled Schwab's soda fountain. Early on, it had been a hangout for Hollywood actors and aspiring wannabes. At sixteen years of age, Lana Turner had been discovered there by Mervyn LeRoy. Esme wondered if stuff like that still even happened. While the Tempest cruised down Sunset, the sights and sounds were everything the guide books had foretold and their imaginations had envisioned. Palm trees were everywhere. This was a real and living fantasy world. Now they were crossing La Brea Avenue, leaving West Hollywood and entering the magical world of the real, honest-to-god Hollywood itself, the land where Ricky and Esme hoped their dreams would come true. There were odds — they hoped in their favor.

Esme told Ricky, "We're getting close. We're coming up on *The Hollywood Reporter* building on our left, just up here. Once we pass that, it's another block on our right." Sure enough, ahead on their right they spotted the Sunset Court Motel. "Ta-da!"

"Great job! Perfect directions!" Ricky proclaimed as he pulled into the motor court and up to the entrance of the office.

The size of the motel did not come as a surprise to either one of them. It was on the small side, very similar to the Jones Family Motel back on that first night in El Reno, Oklahoma. It could have been the Jones's motel identical twin. Before leaving Nashville, Ricky had made reservations for today, October 2, for an open-ended stay at this location. "Be prepared" was not bad advice. Check-in was easy. The desk clerk was extremely helpful. He was putting them in the largest room of the Sunset Court's twenty. With the open-ended booking, the clerk felt that their extended stay warranted, and they would appreciate, the larger room, which he was providing at the lower price of a regular-sized room. He suggested that Ricky could unhitch his trailer and leave it in the large parking spot across from the office, near the motel's entrance. The clerk assured him this was the safest location available. At night, a streetlight kept the spot illuminated. The desk clerk handed them keys for room 14 and welcomed them to Hollywood.

Together they worked to unhitch the trailer, then parked in front of their room. When they opened the door, they were very pleased with what they saw. The clerk had been kind. The room was huge. Along with a small sitting area, it had a tiny kitchenette, complete with a mini two-burner stove, toaster oven, coffeemaker, sink, and small under-the-counter refrigerator. They had arrived. This was it, and it felt like home. Esme and Ricky immediately dove into making trips back and forth to completely unpack the Tempest and parts of the trailer. They were happy, after two thousand miles of highway, to have landed on solid ground on this fine, sunny Saturday.

By the time they'd emptied the car and organized a bit, it was late afternoon. They were beyond exhausted and knew that if they sat, they might not be able to get up again for a very long time. So out the door they went, around the corner to the neighborhood grocery the nice clerk had mentioned. They filled their cart with milk, eggs, bread, margarine, and everything else they thought they might need. At the checkout, Esme spotted what she had been lusting for: *Backstage Magazine*, *Variety*, and *The Hollywood Reporter*. All three were film industry magazines with ads for casting calls. She grabbed them and tossed them into their cart. Checkout complete, they headed back to Sunset Court, lugging four full bags of groceries. They spent the rest of the afternoon and evening organizing and setting up house for at least the next two weeks. Esme made ham-and-cheese omelets for dinner and served them with steamed broccoli and warm toast. It was satisfying to be able to relax after their trek. Tomorrow was going to be their first big day exploring their new city.

Sunday, October 3, 1976

The weather during the month of October in Southern California was always picture-perfect, and you could take that to the bank. The morning air was cool, and the sky was blue. The pair got into the Tempest, and Ricky put the top down. They had decided today was strictly a day for exploring. First things first, Ricky needed to find the shopping area of Beverly Hills. As he had told Esme already, he had his first important appointment there on Rodeo Drive at nine thirty on Monday morning. And, he reminded her, it was pronounced ro-*day*-o, not ro-dee-o.

As Esme followed the city map with her finger, she guided Ricky as best she could. While they might not be getting to their destination by the most direct route possible, she would get them to Rodeo Drive. She knew she needed to get them back through West Hollywood. She thought their best bet was to use streets that she had already heard and read about. So they turned left out of their motel and headed down Sunset. She told Ricky to take a left on La Brea. Passing A&M Records, they turned right onto Melrose Avenue. Both of them had heard of Melrose. It was a hip street filled with trendy clothing, cool jewelry, art, and some fine restaurants. What they found on Melrose was not what they'd expected. Shops dotted the street, but there were a lot of empty spaces for lease. It seemed pretty boring. When they crossed Fairfax, things began to change. They passed what looked to be a very cool clothing store, Fred Segal, and a restaurant with outside dining called Moustache Café that looked expensive. It seemed the closer they got to La Cienega, the nicer the shops on Melrose became. They passed some seriously fancy restaurants and shops. Once they crossed La Cienega, Melrose did not disappoint. The stores and cafés looked even more intriguing. They passed a huge, shiny, royal blue glass building that was definitely space-age. Easing left at Santa Monica, they drove past a smallish brown shield of a sign announcing Beverly Hills.

Esme breathed a sigh of relief. She had found Beverly Hills. They made the first left they could off of Santa Monica Boulevard. This was nice. When they came upon a Thrifty drugstore, they pulled over and parked. This was it. Ricky and Esme got out of the car and walked the eight-square-block area that composed Beverly Hills' shopping district. While they strolled the sidewalks, they passed Bentleys, Rolls-Royces, Lamborghinis, and other expensive and exotic cars, more than they had ever seen. Esme thought there might have been one Rolls in Nashville, maybe. Turning their attention back to the shops around them, they saw that all the famous stores they had only ever heard of were right in front of them — and to the left and behind them as well. Dizzy with amazement, they turned a corner onto Rodeo Drive.

Once they were on Rodeo Drive, it didn't take them long to spot the location for Ricky's appointment the next morning. After taking note of the exact location, they did a little daydream window-shopping and headed back to the car. They got back into the Tempest and headed to Santa Monica to see the Pacific Ocean for the very first time. Cruising along Santa Monica Boulevard, they passed Beverly Hills City Park on their right, where it seemed the residential neighborhood began. The towers and wide boulevards of Century City they passed were simply mind-boggling.

In an easy twenty minutes, they had reached the cliffs of Ocean Avenue and the very edge of the Pacific Ocean. They parked at a meter and took a stroll on the grass among the palm trees. The scent of the sea was in the air. Walking over to the edge to get a better view, they discovered the Pacific Coast Highway below and, to their surprise and delight, a pedestrian walk-over to the beach. Esme and Ricky both wanted to wiggle their toes in the sand and at least touch the water. So, decision made, they started descending what seemed to be a hundred stone stairs to the walkway that crossed over the highway and down to the beach. Santa Monica Beach and the Pacific Ocean were waiting to welcome them both. Hand in hand, they rushed and jumped to put their feet in the waters of the vast Pacific and just as quickly jumped right back. What a disappointment to find the ocean was ice-cold. Well, they hadn't planned to swim anyway, so they walked the beach until it was time to explore more of this unbelievable dreamland.

At Patrick's Roadhouse across the street from the beach, they sat at the counter and ate burgers and fries. Esme pulled out the map to the stars' homes that she had grabbed at the motel. They spent the rest of the day winding through Holmby Hills and Bel Air, past the Beverly Hillbillies mansion and Jack Benny's home on Charing Cross. Esme pointed out Hugh Hefner's Playboy Mansion, where the gates were wide-open. Ricky headed for the gates, then swerved away, figuring it was too early in their stay to risk being arrested for trespassing. They drove up Benedict Canyon past Harold Lloyd's old estate to Mulholland Drive with its views of the San Fernando Valley on one side and Los Angeles Basin on the other. They careened down Coldwater Canyon and then past more massive homes along Sunset Boulevard back toward Hollywood to explore Laurel Canyon. Eventually, after they had driven past and gaped at so many beautiful homes and gardens, the cityscape they had seen began to blur into a jumbled memory.

Before they realized it, it was nearly 5:00 p.m. They decided it best to head back to the comforts of their motel room. When they returned, they popped by the office and asked their new friend behind the desk for a good restaurant nearby. He recommended an authentic Mexican restaurant, Lucy's El Adobe.

"In LA, Lucy's is an institution and known to all," he said. "It's directly across the street from a Paramount Studios entrance. The restaurant has been owned by Lucy Casado since 1964. The food is the best, and because of the studio across the street, you'll often find celebrities dining there as well. Lucy doesn't take reservations, but the wait goes pretty fast. I know you'll enjoy it. Have a margarita for me!"

Well, dinner was decided. They went back to their room, cleaned up, and drove to dinner at Lucy's, which they discovered was only about a half mile from their home base.

Stuffed from dinner and still excited from the wonderful day, they returned to the motel and had some fun with each other. Esme perused the magazines she'd found at the grocery. Down in the ads, she found something that piqued her interest. She showed the ad to Ricky. He agreed it was something she needed to check out. Esme's Tuesday was all set.

They set the alarm clock for 6:00 a.m. If Ricky could be early for his meeting, that would suit him just fine. He didn't mind waiting in the car until the clock on the dash told him his time had finally arrived. All would be good. He could feel it in his bones.

The Last Week of School

Shell's alarm sounded to announce Monday morning, October 4, 1976, 5:20 a.m. She jumped out of bed and went into autopilot mode. She splashed her face with cold water and brushed her teeth. After slipping into her head-to-toe running gear, she threw her hair into a high ponytail and was out the door. This new routine had started about three weeks ago. She was in her car and on her way to meet Anita at the entrance to the park at six for a five-mile run. Aside from great exercise and the exhilaration she experienced from the run itself, these runs meant a couple more pounds were history.

Shell arrived at the park a few minutes early to find Anita already there and waiting. The two began to chat as they ran through the series of stretches Anita had laid out for them on their first run. The pair would, more often than not, run and talk the entire time. Shell had gotten into a habit of reminding Anita to look up and through the trees, to see the hills across the way and enjoy sightings of deer and the wide variety of birds they encountered. Anita was always so focused on the task at hand, in this case the details of a good run, that she never took the time to enjoy life in the minute or the horizon out in front of her. Today's run would be the last that Shell would be able to enjoy until the end of her class. School was rapidly approaching its end. This coming Friday was the last requirement before certification. She knew all too well her participation in The Iris Bouquet competition was her last day of school.

The time passed quickly on their runs. They were usually back at the entrance for a cooldown in a little over an hour. It was 7:15 a.m. as they walked to their cars. Still chattering away, they decided on a nearby café for coffee and a bit of breakfast. The Bottomless Cup was a popular spot within the running community. Every morning from 6:00 a.m. until 9:00 a.m., the restaurant was packed with patrons still in their running gear. So the place was predictably crowded when Shell and Anita arrived at the Cup. A hostess directed them to one of the few remaining tables, which happened to be in the front window of the café. Once seated, they each ordered a coffee and croissants with jam. This day was off to a great start.

During this last week of school, Shell was spending most of her evenings with Eddy. With class time so flexible and uncomplicated, she had no projects to keep her late on campus. She had all the time in the world to do whatever suited her fancy during her evenings. The more time they had spent together, the stronger the bond between them had become. In Shell's mind, he was the one. In Eddy's mind, she was the one.

Preparation for The Iris Bouquet

The floral students from Springs Academy were once again joining Professor Blondell's class from Nashville State Tech for a contest. The graduating floral novices were going up against roughly sixty professional florists descending on Nashville from across the state's ninety-five counties. The professionals had already been named winners within their own divisions, several of them multiple times. The students from Nashville State Tech and Springs Academy in Memphis were the only amateurs allowed to enter the contest. The students' participation had been going on as long as the schools had offered their courses in floral design. Over the years, both schools and their professors had come to be highly regarded and respected within the floral community. After much deliberation, this competition had been added to the curriculum as the final requirement for students in their quests for floral certification. And although all agreed that competition at any level was a great learning experience, neither school had ever had a finalist.

During what remained of their last week, the class spent their time receiving pointers and counsel for the approaching Friday's competition. All the students were dumbstruck when they were eventually informed, in detail, of the contest's procedures and how everything would actually be conducted. The fact that the judges would be twelve randomly selected professionals from the Tennessee floral industry was no surprise. But the full description of The Iris Bouquet told them this was not their mama's state fair bake-off. This competition was, without doubt, more like a pop quiz. Design tasks would be impromptu creations, drawn from a hat, on-site. Shell, Ned, Dixie, and the rest could only imagine and ponder the myriad possibilities and different categories that could be presented to them come Friday — and hope for the best.

The Contest

October 8, 1976

Shell's morning passed quickly as she madly packed her duffel. What to bring with her today had baffled her the entire week. She had stuffed the bag with odds and ends of clothing, parts of ensembles, complete outfits, and different shoes. Benji had encouraged his students to bring an assortment of clothing that could be mixed to create different costumes appropriate for any category that they might be assigned. Shell had ensured she had a variety of makeup items. She had even thrown in a crocheted tablecloth. This was a crapshoot if ever there'd been one. Anything and everything was a possibility for this competition. Shell realized there was no point where she would feel "done," and there was certainly no reason to get excited. She called "time" on herself. At this point, it was what it was, and now it was time to make her way to Nashville's Municipal Auditorium and sign herself in for this schizoid contest.

After parking in a lot as near as she could get to the venue, she got out of her car, pulled out the leaden bag, and began the trudge to the auditorium. She walked, huffing, into the facility at 11:30 a.m. Wild hordes of people were already milling around the auditorium's vestibule. The inner entry doors would remain closed and locked until exactly 12:00 p.m. At the crack of the noon bell, Shell heard the click of locks, and the doors flew open. Contestants immediately poured through and into the inner sanctum.

As the crowds filled the inner hall, a voice from above, in stereo, requested that all contest participants please advance, in orderly fashion, to the front of the stage, draw only one envelope from the enormous, clear glass bowl, and then please step away. Feeling like just one more lemming, Shell made her way to the front. The voice continued, over the shuffle of feet, that within each envelope was a color-coded card. The colors corresponded to one of the following categories: bridal, funeral, decor/centerpiece, beauty pageant, and get well/best wishes. The color legend would be revealed once everyone had their envelope in hand. The shuffling continued until the last participant to draw raised his arm into the air to announce the last envelope had been drawn, which the voice in turn confirmed to the assembly. As entrants nervously anticipated the result of their draw, the color legend was revealed. At that moment the voice instructed competitors to open their envelopes and discover their fates. Heavy sighs rose through the crowd. The voice loomed, instructing participants to please proceed to the flagged tables corresponding with their card color and register with that table's proctor. The participants slowly scattered to their appropriate tables for registration within their category.

Upon registration, each participant was assigned an individual workspace within a larger area specified for all the participants of the same category. Each workspace was surrounded by rolling partitions, which, joined together, provided complete privacy around an area measuring approximately ten feet by ten feet. Each space was equipped with two 3'×6' folding tables. All designers were provided the same tools and accoutrements, including, but not limited to, wire, scissors, floral sticks, florist's foam, and tape.

Shell's card was pink, which, happily for her, corresponded on the legend to the bridal category. Dragging her duffel, she made her way around the room to register with the proctor at the pink-flagged table. As she walked, she passed Ned settling comfortably into his booth in the blue area, with a small trunk stacked in a corner atop a large suitcase. Continuing on, she saw Dixie looking thrilled and smug in a booth in the yellow section.

The beginning segment of the competition would provide participants forty-five minutes to shop products. Each contestant was given five hundred dollars in play money to use. A large wholesale store had been created at the back of the auditorium expressly for this purpose. The abundance of flowers was staggering. Each contestant was to purchase whatever they needed to complete their entry. Particicpants eagerly filled their shopping carts to the brim. A few competitors went back several times for goods. As the forty-five minutes slipped away and participants sped about, Shell could only think of the scene as organized chaos. The voice eventually made the announcement that the store was closed. The stragglers at the register were allowed to check out. It was showtime.

With contestants settled alone in their booths, all of the individual workspaces were closed off. Anyone looking at the booths from the outside could see only the designers' feet moving back and forth in their areas. The room was nearly silent; the only sounds were those of snipping scissors and stems, twigs, and florist's foam falling to the floor, along with Mozart and Bach the organizers were playing softly through the overhead speakers.

Located away from all of the competitive activity, a lounge area stocked with refreshments and reading materials provided a quiet area for the judges and press to congregate. Representatives from local television stations and other news outlets had been invited and were now sequestered in the area.

Charlotte and Edna, as always, had made sure they would be noticed. They had both arrived clad in flashy sequined cocktail dresses. Charlotte wore black and Edna was in a shimmering fuchsia. There was always a method to Charlotte's madness, and they purposely had overdressed because of Charlotte's idea that by overdressing they would stand out among the press, be noticed by the judges, and thus be selected to get the first big scoop.

Among the organizers and judges, Eunice Wentworth was the

first to take notice of Charlotte's and Edna's glitter. She quietly gasped so deeply that she inhaled a small fly. After a coughing fit, her voice raspy from hacking to clear her throat, she said to Charlotte, "My dear woman, this is not a formal affair. And the sun is still high."

"Oh, I know. We are simply with the press and must be ready for what the day may bring," Charlotte said while she blushed, attempting innocence.

Edna, ever the perky prodigy, said, "We just want to have the first opportunity to speak to the winners and get their stories. Honestly, I just love sequins, don't you?"

Eunice stood looking at the two women. She was dressed in her regular attire, appropriate for lunch at the club or bridge with the girls. Eunice was always in vogue. She was a walking fashion plate of high style and jewelry. Through a clenched smile, she said, "Yes, but it is the middle of the afternoon. You are —" She cut herself off as she thought, *I had no idea this woman was so tacky.* "Well, I suppose whatever makes you happy, but really," she said, recalibrating her approach, "perhaps the sequins could pass, but the pearls and tiara — just a bit much for day. I'm sure your intent is well meant. You, of course, know we like the press here, covering our event. We're most glad to assist in any way possible to ensure everyone gets a story." Eunice walked away.

Charlotte smiled and pulled Edna close to her and whispered through clenched teeth, "Hon, it's time to hold our heads high. We are proud swans. Our work is ahead. Do not fear what others may say or think, and never, ever look back."

The floral designers were all busy in their individual stations. In hers, Shell was putting the finishing touches on a large centerpiece that would be placed on an imaginary entry table, in an imaginary church, to greet wedding guests. Next on her agenda were a bridal bouquet and the bridesmaids' nosegays. Her job, in her opinion, was a breeze. From her early teens until now, she had dreamed of her own wedding and the flowers she would want to have at her ceremony.

Ned was in his booth, happy as a lark. His blue card meant he had to design an arrangement for a funeral. Upon learning his category, he had muttered to himself, "Great, at least I am ready for this one!" In his space, he had artfully crafted a four-foot round wreath of white lilies and roses mixed with willow, with a wide black ribbon woven between the flowers and the willow. Ned had made one of his worktables look like a casket by covering it with arched chicken wire, which he had then covered with brown chintz to resemble wood. He was wrapping up his work on a large funeral pall with an abundant spray of giant yellow sunflowers, mixed with large yellow roses interspersed with yellow and white dahlias.

It was 4:00 p.m., with an hour to go. Dixie was still bubbling with excitement over her assignment. She had drawn a yellow card, which corresponded to a beauty pageant. Dixie knew beauty pageants like the back of her hand; she'd been in enough of them growing up. She had entered the circuit as a toddler and had kept on through her late teens. Her booth was full of red roses, rubrum lilies, pink tulips, and magnolia leaves. She was almost finished with her arrangements of a pageant winner's bouquet and a pair of floral displays on easels for either side of the pageant stage.

The warning bell sounded. It was 4:50 p.m. The participants had only ten more minutes before everyone had to stop their work and be ready for judging. The front panels of every station were going to be wheeled away at 5:00 p.m.

Mrs. Eunice Wellington Wentworth, III, gracefully mounted the stairs to the stage. She held a bell she began to ring. She announced, "Ladies and gentlemen, it is precisely five o'clock. Please stop whatever you are doing. Time is called. Prepare for judging."

As the panels were rolled away from the front of the contestants' workspaces, Mrs. Eunice Wellington Wentworth, III, stood noncommittally upon the stage. She was motionless in a cream silk skirt suit — the jacket double-breasted à la mode, the skirt accordion-pleated. Her crested brass buttoned jacket covered an off-white blouse of indeterminant fabric, its flat, point-tipped collar buttoned at the top. Eunice was an attractive woman of an age (as people were wont to say in polite southern circles), with a whipped froth of frosted hair and a too-long-in-the-sunbed tanned complexion accentuated by a double-strand necklace of marble-sized pearls and a discreet, emerald-cut diamond tennis bracelet. Regrettably, when she raised the microphone to speak and the beam from her spotlight caught the ten-carat solitaire diamond riding on her finger, half the crowd could have been blinded. When the final panel had been wheeled away and the last workspace exposed, Mrs. Eunice Wellington Wentworth, III, spoke into her microphone to cheerily welcome, once again, all the participants, applauding their accomplishments of the day. Her introductions of the judges blessedly and finally began. As today's master of ceremonies and presiding chairperson of the Tennessee Floral Association, she was enthusiastic throughout her time with the microphone.

The twelve judges were seated, with six on either side of Mrs. Wentworth's podium. Each one stood as she announced their name and provided a brief description of their accomplishments, merits, and credentials. Perhaps saving her favorites for last, Mrs. Wentworth giddily introduced the eleventh judge, Frank von Schmittou, effusively reading a brief bio of this man whom everyone knew. Then the name of the twelfth judge was read: Mr. Eddy Francis. As her cousin Mitzi might say, Shell about done fell out, which was to say, she had never known of Eddy's involvement with the competition. She nearly tipped out of her chair in surprise. Eddy stood tall, suave as usual, in a navy blazer, khaki slacks, and a starched white oxford cloth shirt, while Mrs. Wentworth spoke of his experience and achievements, offering accolades to his creativity. With a nod to the audience, Eddy sat, looking more uncomfortable than Shell had ever seen him.

Due to a nondisclosure agreement signed by all of the judges for the event, none had been allowed to divulge their participation on this year's panel — not to a spouse, a girlfriend, parents, or anyone else breathing. His selection as a judge had occurred months before he met Shell. Eddy's relationship with Shell was a secret to no one. He simply had never been able to work out just how or when to explain his awkward situation to the committee. It seemed the time was nigh.

The first area up for judging was the funeral division. Frederic Chopin's funeral dirges quietly played, the sound subtly permeating the area. An aura of sadness and helplessness hung in the air; it was that first step into a mortuary. The floral designers were costumed appropriately to project sympathy and grief. As the judges walked around, assessing the sixteen completed projects, they came upon a very slender and extremely tall woman perched on a folding chair, wailing into a monogrammed lace handkerchief. The judges turned their attention to the wreath and pall upon the makeshift coffin. The floral arrangements were magnificent, both precise and distinctive. Then they were drawn back to the sobs. Upon closer inspection, it rapidly became obvious that the woman was a man done up in drag. The man beneath the costume was none other than Ned Fulcher.

Ned was sitting next to his arrangements, sobbing into his lace handkerchief, which his own mother had monogrammed. He wore a violet-colored cotton crepe housedress with a poorly handmade black knit sweater, buttoned to his neck. For shoes, Ned had glued five inch cork wedges to the soles of sandals, spray-painted them glossy black, and created elevator clogs. He had donned an orange orphan Annie wig and covered his face with pancake foundation thick enough to cover the stubble of his five o'clock shadow. Shaving his legs on-site had left an untidy mess all over the floor. Fake nails in blood red were glued to his fingertips. His lips were glossed in the same blood red. Thick black eyelashes were extra-long and caked with mascara. Heavy black eyeliner framed his eyes. To finish the look, he had applied dusty-blue eyeshadow from his lids to his eyebrows. He had transformed himself into a lonely, grief-stricken widow, quite believable in his sorrow. Ned stood, his clogs pushing his natural six-foot seven-inch height to a full seven feet. Sobbing into his handkerchief, he approached his flower-draped casket. Now, fully into his portrayal of the sorrowful widow and still sobbing, he threw himself over the flower-draped coffin. He had played his part perfectly and to the hilt. The judges had enjoyed his performance and smiled as they departed his area.

After viewing all the entries, the judges conferred and made their final tabulation for the sympathy area. It was complete. They headed next to the bridal competition. The judges would have sixteen entries to observe in this area as well. They made their rounds. Shell's station was last. As the judges approached her booth, Shell stood nervously patting a few errant flowers into place. The judges had almost reached her station when they paused and began a quiet conversation. Whispering, they scurried to a nearby corner. During what appeared to be heated discussion, heads turned at times to look in Shell's direction. Mrs. Wentworth was called over to the huddle by Frank von Schmittou, who was acting as captain of the judges' quorum. A brief discussion ensued. With an apparent end to the conversation, Eddy Francis walked away from the group, having recused himself from judging the bridal portion of the contest.

Shell had constructed a spectacular centerpiece that was arranged in a two-foot round glass bowl. The judges immediately noticed her use of lemons and green Granny Smith apples to anchor the bowl and an arrangement that rose three feet or more into the air. Shell had used yellow and white roses, sunset-colored tulips, dinner plate–sized dahlias in varying shades of yellow, white peonies, and interesting greenery. The rest of her bridal arrangements were beautifully and tastefully done. The bridal bouquet consisted of yellow and white roses and white tulips and freesias, with a few magnolia leaves. The nosegays were simple tight French-style bouquets of baby-yellow rosebuds and tiny yellow and white freesias.

The judges continued through the remaining sections of decor/centerpiece, beauty pageant, and get well/best wishes. When the last booth had been considered, the judges retired to a private room to discuss all the entrants and make their final decisions.

Mrs. Wentworth returned to the stage with the twelve judges. As the judges took their seats, she approached the podium with envelopes in hand. Mrs. Wentworth began her final act of the day by thanking all of the entrants for their participation and commending them for their fine work in completing the competition. Looking across the faces in front of her, she confirmed she held the names of the finalists and a short list of honorable mentions. The names of the winners were read. No different from years past, not a single student from either school had won in any of the categories. But reading through the list of honorable mentions, Mrs. Wentworth announced Ned Fulcher's name in the funeral category. Ned was in blissful shock as his classmates cheered him onto the stage. The sight of Ned's skinny seven-foot frame, still in full costume, jigging onto the platform for his award sent the entire house into hysterics. As he took a small bow, he ripped the wig off his head and threw it into the cheering crowd that was still raucously applauding his victory.

Eddy found Shell at the edge of the crowd. She had taken not winning in stride, proud of what she had accomplished, not only in the competition, but also in her own life during the past months. When Eddy reached her, they threw their arms around each other and had a celebratory kiss that seemed to last forever, their embrace a welcome sight to all.

Ricky and Esme

Monday, October 4, 1976

The phone rang in their room at 6:00 a.m. It was the front desk clerk with a wake-up call. But Esme and Ricky had taken no chances this morning; they'd set their own alarm for 5:30 a.m. They were already out of bed and diving into the day. While Esme brewed coffee and fixed a light breakfast, Ricky showered and dressed. His day had arrived! The long-awaited appointment with a prospective buyer about his Waxing Pony would happen.

As they cleared their breakfast dishes, Ricky said to Esme, "I need to go connect the car to the trailer and get it closer to the room to unload. It'll be much easier to get the rest of our personal things out of the trailer and into the room if it's just outside the door. If everything works out this morning, I found a U-Haul place where we can return the trailer. I found it in the Yellow Pages and then checked out the address on the map. It's on Sepulveda Boulevard not far from where we'll be in Beverly Hills. We just head toward the ocean down Santa Monica Boulevard, and Sepulveda's right there before you go under the highway."

Esme said, "When you get the trailer over here, wait for me to help. I want to at least try to organize stuff as we bring it in — you know, so we have some semblance of order in here."

Ricky heard both hope and worry in her voice.

"Today is so exciting," she continued. After taking a deep breath, she went into the bathroom to clean up and get ready for their big day.

Ricky went outside. It was another perfect, blue-skyed Southern California day. The morning temperature was around sixty-five degrees with almost no humidity. The air felt almost cool. He backed the Tempest around and connected the hitch to the U-Haul trailer. Maneuvering around the lot, he backed up until the trailer doors were facing their room. Ricky unlocked the trailer's doors, swung them around the sides and latched them in place. The back of the trailer was wide-open. He sat on the chair outside the room and waited for Esme. Best to have her directing whatever she had in her head. It was not a long wait.

Ten minutes later, she was outside and ready. Perky as ever, she said, "Clean as a whistle. Let's get started, pony-boy!"

By eight thirty, they had emptied the entire trailer of personal belongings, including a few pieces of furniture Stella and Max had insisted they take, as well as boxes Esme's mother had added to the mix. Ricky closed and locked the doors to the trailer. He was ready to roll.

"Well, let's get started. I would rather be too early than late," he said to Esme.

Esme agreed. "Ricky, I want you to look at the street map with me before we leave. You need to have an idea where we're going. I've studied this thing. It'll be easier for you to handle traffic if you understand the way. We don't want a problem in the middle of the drive."

"Good idea," he agreed.

Esme opened the map on the car hood and laid out the route.

The second they turned left out of their motel and headed west down Sunset Boulevard, Esme went into navigator mode. She advised Ricky to stay in the right lane. They knew traffic in Los

Angeles was always heavy, but this was their first experience with it on a Monday morning. They were once again passing Schwab's Pharmacy. They crossed La Cienega Boulevard and recognized the Chateau Marmont on their right. As they tooled along Sunset past Holly's Harp and Cyrano's restaurant, Esme directed Ricky to the middle lane, to be ready for a left onto Doheny Drive.

As he drove, they couldn't help but take in the panorama on their left. It was a surprise to see the ocean sparkling in the distance. When they reached Doheny, Ricky turned left and ambled down the steep hill. Ricky noticed they had crossed Santa Monica Boulevard. Soon enough, they were on the other side of Beverly Boulevard, and after a few blocks more, Esme was telling Ricky to turn right onto Burton Way with its beautiful grassy median. It wouldn't be long now before they'd be in the heart of Beverly Hills. Burton Way transitioned into Little Santa Monica Boulevard as they crossed the border. The shops of Beverly Hills were now all around them. Esme guided him only a few more blocks to Rodeo Drive, where he knew to turn left. After two blocks, they had reached their destination, 325 North Rodeo Drive. As he pulled to the curb in front of the store, Ricky read the writing on the door. Large, clean printing announced "Vivienne Fontaine et Associés" and, below that, "Luxury Facials, Skincare, and Waxing." It was 9:00 a.m. The shops on the street did not open until 10:00 a.m. Parallel parking was pretty simple. With the trailer, they filled two metered parking spaces. Esme, who had anticipated this, had her roll of quarters at the ready.

Esme hopped out of the passenger's door and looked at the meter. She yelled to Ricky, "Holy cow! It's a quarter for every twenty minutes to park here. Pricy street! You think the salon has parking in the back? You know, we'll be here for a while. This could get nuts."

They looked around at the expensive shops and cafés on the street. Esme was anything but speechless. "Look, over there's The Daisy, Cartier, and Georgette Klinger. This is amazing. And look, this side of the street has Gucci, Giorgio's, and Jerry Magnin. I can't wait to be able to shop in these stores. Fun! And probably dangerous, too."

They walked through the entrance of Vivienne Fontaine et Associés and were immediately greeted by a stunningly beautiful receptionist with the most perfect skin Esme had ever seen in her life.

"My name is Ricky Baker. I have a business appointment with Ms. Fontaine at nine thirty. I'm aware we're early. We'll be glad to sit in the waiting area."

The receptionist smiled, putting Ricky at ease. "I know she's expecting you. I'll advise Ms. Fontaine you have arrived. Would you care for a coffee? Or water, perhaps?"

"Thank you, kindly," Esme said, suppressing her anxiety. "We're fine."

Ms. Fontaine appeared rather quickly, out of what seemed to be thin air. "You are, of course, Ricky! I am Vivienne Fontaine. It is so nice to finally meet you! Welcome to our salon. I am thrilled you have chosen us as your first stop. I cannot wait to see what you have. If it turns out to be all you say it is, it will be a fabulous addition!"

Ricky smiled and said, "It is my pleasure to meet you, Ms. Fontaine." Turning to Esme, he said, "This is Esme Lapone, my other half." He continued, "One thing before we get started. Do you happen to have a back door to the salon? It would be a real advantage if I could pull my car and trailer off the street." He turned and pointed to his Tempest and U-Haul trailer through the salon's glass doors.

"Oh yes, of course. And please, call me Vivienne. Just go to the end of the block and turn right. You will see an alley on your right. Just pull into it. I will be waiting at our back door and can direct you to the perfect spot. I actually reserved a space for you. You'll see the orange cones my receptionist put out to save the area."

"Terrific," Ricky replied.

As Ricky left to drive around to the alley, Esme walked with Vivienne to the rear of the salon. Esme complimented her on the salon. "Your decor is so luxurious. It's so calming."

Vivienne thanked Esme and opened the back door. A man came out of a side room and asked, "Ms. Fontaine, do you need me now? I have the dollies ready, and I'm glad to help roll in whatever you're expecting."

"Oh, Carlos, why yes, now is perfect. The fellow just pulled up."

Carlos and Ricky unloaded the pony and wheeled it into the back of the salon. There Ricky unveiled the horse. It was a solid, high-gloss black. Esme had no idea when Ricky had spray-painted over the "WINNER" logo and the cutesy, kiddie-ride colors. It looked high-style.

Vivienne smiled and started to laugh. "Oh, it's simply wonderful. I absolutely love the black! You do know, this area is a destination for bachelorette weekends. If this is a hit, we will become *the* destination for facials and waxing for all those girls."

Ricky situated the horse and plugged it in as she spoke.

"I have someone at the ready for the experience," Vivienne said. "She has not had a wax for four months and is more than eager to give your pony a whirl."

Vivienne and Ricky chattered away until a woman came through the door. Chloe de Marco had arrived. Vivienne and Chloe traded a few words and a round of laughter as Ricky loaded a wax block into the belly of the horse.

"Okay, kids. You'll excuse me while I go get naked and grab a robe. I'll be back in a New York minute! Can't wait to try this contraption!" Chloe's heels clicked away as she headed off to prepare.

Chloe returned sooner than Ricky expected. Ricky gulped, "Uh, Miss de Marco? I kind of need to be here for part of the process, if you don't mind. I can make arrangements for your privacy. You wouldn't have to be naked in front of anybody."

Chloe laughed and said, "Sweetie, that's nice of you, but don't you worry about me. People see me naked all the time. Doesn't bother me in the least. And for heaven's sake, call me Chloe."

Vivienne whispered to Esme, "Chloe is a porn star. Adult films? She's accustomed to cameramen, lighting techs, entire crews being around her all the time while she is nude."

With the wax warmed, it was time for Ricky to show off his wares. Chloe dropped her robe, and Vivienne and Ricky helped her up onto the pony. Ricky said, "Okay, Chloe, just settle into the saddle like you're riding a real horse. I will walk you through the remaining steps."

When the ride was over, Chloe was shocked and hiccup-laughing as she said, "That was different! It's a funny thing! I honestly enjoyed it. And best part, it worked! Look at me, Viv!"

Vivienne was equally impressed. Chloe slipped into her robe.

Ricky, ready to evaporate in embarrassment, managed to speak. "Vivienne, if you want to buy this, I'll be happy to put your logo across the base of the horse. All I need is a template and paint."

Vivienne, enthused, said, "Yes! I really must have this in my salon! Let's go into my office for a chat." To her friend, she said, "Oh, Chloe, thank you so much for being our test girl. Luisa will finish your session and get you cleaned up in her booth. Your next three visits are on the house! I can't tell you how much I appreciate your help! You are such a dear."

Refreshed, Chloe bid her adieus and went through the door.

Vivienne escorted Ricky into her office. They sat down, side by side, in front of her desk. Esme followed and sat on a small love seat to the side.

Vivienne said, "Ricky, what you have made is amazing. I think you said that your charge for one of these horses is six thousand dollars. Am I correct?"

Ricky nodded in agreement. "Yes. This is my prototype, and you're welcome to it."

"Wonderful! Now, Ricky, I think three more would make sense for the salon. But I need you to swear in writing that you will not sell this same product to anyone else in Beverly Hills." Vivienne paused. "I'm sure you can understand why. I want the exclusive. We talked about bachelorette parties already. The girls usually stay down the street at the Beverly Wilshire. I know in my bones they will love the ponies. It'll become a regular part of their spa day in between shopping and lunching at The Daisy. My salon will be a real destination. Georgette across the street has nothing like this. And she won't!"

Ricky beamed with pride. Esme could only try to contain herself. Ricky answered, "Yes, to all of the above. I am in total agreement with you. I will sign anything you want. We can write a contract right now if you'd like, just the two of us — a simple non-compete agreement. The only other places I want to go with this product right now are Santa Barbara, maybe Malibu, Coronado, and Palm Springs, and eventually on to other major cities north and east. I think it could be a big hit in Dallas — and Miami for sure.

"I've told you already how my interest in this came about, as a result of my mother's professional salon. I spent a lot of time there as a kid. Beauty and grooming products are a serious market, as you well know. What I haven't mentioned to anyone is I've been doing some research" — he looked at Esme — "and Esme doesn't even know this, but I think I've developed a formula for a line of moisturizers that will help with crinkly, aging skin. Thing is, I need to confirm everything with a chemist to help me finalize my work."

Vivienne offered, "It's your lucky day. I happen to know a chemist who just might be able to help you. I would be happy to introduce you to her. She lives not far from here."

"That would be lovely and very much appreciated." Ricky sighed and smiled.

Vivienne walked around her desk and pulled out a checkbook. She said, "Let me pay you for this horse. My branding on the horse needs to be the same yellow as my logo." She reached inside her desk and pulled out a paint chip and handed it to him. "Get whatever you need. I'll get in touch with my printer and order a spray template for you. I'll call when I have it, and you can come back and finish the job. Work for you?"

Ricky said, "Definitely. And so you're aware, Esme and I will be looking for a place to live in the next few weeks. Here is our number until we're permanently settled. We're staying on Sunset at a little motel. We had to find a mom-and-pop place so we could park the trailer. You'll be the first to know our new phone number and address when we have them. I cannot tell you what a pleasure you are to work with. Vivienne, you are the epitome of kindness. I appreciate your willingness to give me the chance to prove myself."

Vivienne smiled and said, "Ricky, how do you think I started out in this business? I was nervous as hell! We all have to take chances in life. If we don't, we get stale, become stationary, and end up being afraid of our own shadows. You've got the guts it takes to make it."

She opened her checkbook and said, "Okay, so six thousand for this one. Is nine thousand good for a deposit on the other three? Oh, by the way, minor detail — how long do you think it will take for the others to arrive?"

Ricky, a tad flustered, said, "I think they will take about five weeks. My supplier is in Tennessee. Once the base units are in my hands, it'll take me about two weeks' work to make them into what you've seen today." He paused and said, "Could be more like six weeks, to be safe."

She said, "Okay, so I'll make this check for fifteen thousand. But before I hand it over, let's take care of that contract."

They took their time with the details, and after only thirty minutes, they'd settled on the terms of their agreement. With the ink dry on the page and a firm handshake, Vivienne happily handed Ricky the rewards of his first sale. With check in hand, Ricky and Esme said goodbye to their new best friend, Vivienne Fontaine, who bid them "Au revoir, mes amis."

Ricky, elated and warm in the California sun, thought, *Oh yeah! Livin' the dream!*

Monday Afternoon, October 4, 1976

Back in the car and heading out of the alley, Esme and Ricky wanted to scream for joy. In their wildest dreams, they never would have believed that Ricky's first appointment would actually turn out to be his first sale. With an order for three more ponies, they were floating on clouds. Ricky managed to get them out of Beverly Hills. They were heading west on Santa Monica Boulevard to the U-Haul franchise on Sepulveda to be done and rid of the trailer that had followed them from Tennessee. After settling up and starting back toward Hollywood, they could only think about how and where they were going to find a place to live.

Esme pointed across the street to a Jack in the Box. "Let's go over there for lunch. We don't have to do drive-through. We can go inside and sit. I see a coin-operated newspaper box outside, and I've still got my quarters. I'll grab an *LA Times*. We can start in the classifieds. There've got to be ads for apartments for rent."

Inside the restaurant, Ricky ordered their cheeseburgers and fries. Esme returned from "powdering her nose" just in time to carry the drinks. They slipped into a booth and studied the apartments-for-rent section in between bites and sips. Esme wrote down several addresses. All of their choices turned out to be nearby and south of Sunset. She remembered passing many of the streets on their trips to and from Beverly Hills and Hollywood.

They spent the rest of the afternoon driving around, up and down, and back and forth. Esme circled ads for places they wanted to see in person. When they had run through their ad choices and were heading back to the motel, Esme said, "Let's drive up in these hills and look at the views."

At that moment, they were on Sunset crossing La Cienega. Ricky thought Laurel Canyon was closest and kept heading that way. As they approached the Chateau Marmont, Esme said, "Right before the Chateau, go up Marmont. Let's see what's up the hill."

Ricky cut left across traffic into the narrow little street. It turned out to be a steep, winding road. They were heading up into an older, established residential area of beautiful homes with lush landscaping that they couldn't hope to rent. A few blocks up the hill, they came to Hollywood Boulevard. They'd had no idea until now that it snaked along the hills like this. Hanging from a mailbox on the corner was a tiny sign that read "One-Bedroom Apartment for Rent." They pulled to the side of the road and parked on what was barely a shoulder — not a sidewalk in sight. They climbed the stairs to the front door of the house that seemed to belong to the mailbox and knocked.

A man in his late forties answered. "Checking on the apartment? Why else would you be on my doorstep? You don't look like robbers or ax murderers. My name's Sonny. And you two are?"

"I'm Ricky, and this is Esme. We'd love to have a look at the apartment. We've been driving around all day, checking out rentals from *LA Times* ads." Ricky didn't know what else to say at the moment.

"Well, the apartment is actually around the corner, if you'll follow me." They fell in line behind him as he carried on. "The unit was originally the second floor of my home." They followed him around the corner. "We sealed it off at the stairwell on both ends and by doing so, it gave the apartment a closet. It's completely private with an entrance right up here on Hollywood." To their left was a six-foot stuccoed wall covered in bougainvillea. They came to a locked wooden gate near the end of the thirty-foot wall. Nothing yet was visible on the other side of the wall. Sonny pulled a key from his pocket and unlocked the gate. "Well, here you are," he said.

Stepping through the gate, Ricky and Esme stood in a large kidney-shaped flagstone courtyard with flower beds on either side. The garden offered complete privacy. Ricky noticed a shed at the far end that could prove useful for ponies. Ahead of them was a blue Dutch door into the apartment. Sonny stepped up, unlocked and opened the door, and waved them in.

One step inside, Esme and Ricky fell in love with the place. There were windows everywhere. They were in a small entry area that could fit a dinette and desk. Through an open doorway to the left was a tiny workable kitchen with a single sink framed by cabinets above and below. The kitchen had a small, stand-alone four-burner stove with oven. Beside it stood an equally small refrigerator to match. Sonny explained that the appliances were intended for use in a mobile home. Esme thought they were perfect. The three stepped forward into a reasonably sized living room, maybe twelve by fifteen feet. It had two entire walls of windows. One wall faced south, the other east. They went to the windows and looked out. On a clear day like today, through one window they could see West Hollywood, Century City, and Catalina Island in the far distance. Sonny stepped over and pointed to an older, multistory brick apartment building below Sunset. "Bette Davis has the penthouse in that one. Keep an eye peeled, and you'll catch her out there smoking." The other window looked out over neighborhood rooftops and vegetation to the Chateau Marmont and downtown Los Angeles beyond.

A short hallway led to the bedroom on the right and the bath at the end. The floors throughout the apartment were covered in a tan carpet, except, of course, the kitchen, which was a gray, slate-type vinyl tile.

The bedroom had sheer-covered windows on two sides toward

the corner. The king-sized mattress and box spring sitting in the bedroom could stay if they wanted to use them. Esme, being a certifiable germaphobe, figured she could disinfect the mattress and purchase two mattress covers just to be sure.

The time had come to finally ask the big question: how much? They were ready for a shock after scanning the prices in the area during their afternoon runaround. Ricky steeled himself and faced Sonny. "So what is the rent, exactly?" They both held their breath.

Sonny sensed their trepidation and smiled. "Six hundred a month with a one-month security deposit on a twelve-month lease. Any other questions or concerns?"

They looked at each other and nodded in agreement, and with complete elation, Ricky declared, "Sold! Can we move in October 15? We feel obliged to give at least a little notice to the nice people at the motor court. We're also going to need to find some furniture. We pretty much have nothing." Ricky took a breath.

"No problem. That's only eleven days. I'll prorate the half month, and we'll start fresh November 1. Any objections?" Sonny seemed happy enough.

"Hope you don't mind cash. No checking account without a permanent address." Ricky pulled out his wallet and counted out $900 in hundred-dollar bills. With October's rent and the security deposit in Sonny's hand, Ricky explained their move and circumstances. He assured Sonny, "We are financially solvent," as if the cash hadn't been a hint. Ricky continued, "We need to establish residency in order to open a checking account, like I said, and get California driver's licenses. Then we need a telephone, utilities, all that stuff. With a proper lease, we can get started on all that."

Sonny understood completely. "Let's go downstairs, and we can take care of the paperwork. I'm not worried about you two. Everything will work out just fine. I'll look forward to having such pleasant tenants. And I know you'll be happy up here." The three of them went down to Sonny's home office. They filled out his forms and completed the leases with signatures.

"Would you mind awfully if we start to bring a few things over? Maybe have furniture delivered if we find any?" Ricky asked nervously.

"Oh goodness, that's no problem at all." Sonny reached back into his pocket and handed over a key to the apartment.

Esme promised, "We'll keep it spotless and be the quietest tenants you've ever had."

"Well, you know where to find me. I live down here with my partner. We have a small dog who today happens to be at fluff-and-fold. You two are welcome to have a small pet — as long as it doesn't bark its head off. The courtyard is perfect for a dog. And now, I need to run and pick up Bingo, our dog." Sonny started walking them to the door.

Outside, Ricky freaked. "I don't know our address or zip code!"

"It's on your lease agreement in black and white. No reason to panic. See you soon." Sonny waved as he headed to his car.

Esme looked at the lease, and there it was: 3779 ½ Marmont Avenue, Los Angeles, 90069. They drove back down the steep hill to Sunset. Chateau Marmont was on their left, and around to the right a few doors was the Comedy Store. They were suddenly starstruck.

They spent the rest of the day back at the motel. Their first stop was the lobby. The front desk clerk came out when he heard them enter.

Ricky said, "We've found an apartment! We'll be checking out the fifteenth. We have thoroughly enjoyed being here. And you know what? We never learned your name!"

"I'm George Vann. Sorry about that. I should probably have a name tag. I actually own the court and live here. I combined rooms 1 and 2 into my own apartment years ago. Should have introduced myself the first day. I could not be happier for you two. I'll hold any mail and keep phone messages until you've got all that settled."

Ricky replied, "George, thank you again for your kindnesses. By the way, our trailer's gone. We returned it today. We moved everything out of it and into our room this morning. We'll gradually move stuff over to the new apartment. We both can't thank you enough. We'd love to take you out for dinner before we go. We'll work that out. See you later, George."

Back in their room, Esme dug out the industry rags she had bought their first night in town. She had dog-eared a page in *Backstage.* On the lower left of page 11, there was an ad for an open casting call for a new daytime soap. The title of the new program was *Life at Thirty Thousand Feet*. It was described in the ad as a drama all about pilots and stewardesses: their dramatic romances, flight crises, medical emergencies, passengers' issues. The description piqued Esme's interest. She intended to go and try out for a part. The open casting was being held at CBS Studios on Beverly Boulevard tomorrow. The whole thing should be easy enough. All she had to do was show up and sign in for an audition. Tuesday, top priority: casting call.

They decided that if time allowed after her audition, they'd spend part of the day shopping for a few pieces of inexpensive furniture for the new apartment. They had brought only a pair of old club chairs, two end tables, a chest, a few lamps, and several boxes of orphan dishes, pots, and pans — what amounted to castoffs from both their parents' attics.

Esme went back to the motel office. "George," she asked, "where can we go and buy some furniture that's actually in stock and ready to go?"

Without hesitation, George answered her question. "Rapport Furniture. It's near here on La Brea. It's between Beverly and Melrose. The store is huge. I mean, it's cavernous. You can't miss it. They have great stuff. You have to check it out. They show and stock very modern and expensive Italian imports right alongside very reasonable American-made upholstered furniture and case goods. They run a decent-sized ad every Friday in the *LA Times*, page three. Hold on a sec. I may have last Friday's paper around here." He ducked through the door behind the desk and returned in a flash. "Here you go, Esme." He handed her the corner of a page he'd torn from the paper. The ad was for a sofa bed called the

Moonlighter. It looked nice — wicker frame with cushions in what looked like a nubby neutral fabric. The price was right at $449.

Esme stared at the photo. "You know what, George? This looks perfect! You're a lifesaver! Thanks again!" She couldn't wait to show Eddy what she'd just found for their new apartment. George was a good man to know.

Esme

Tuesday, October 5, 1976

Ricky was still asleep while Esme tiptoed around the motel room. It was early, 6:15 a.m. She had not slept well. She was riddled with anxiety about the open call. A new soap opera for CBS — what were her chances? Esme had never even been on a studio lot before, so there was that too. She kept telling herself, *Esme, you need to relax. This is what you have always wanted. This is your first shot at a real acting job. You know you won't get it. Just the same, this kind of experience is important. If you don't try, nothing will ever happen. So stop it! Stop worrying!* Esme began to mumble out loud while staring at the street map.

Her mumbling was loud enough to wake Ricky. He wasn't going back to sleep, so he opened his eyes and looked at her. "Esme, what are you doing? You've been pacing the floor for ten minutes."

She started spouting every thought that had gone through her brain in the last hour.

When she stopped to take a breath, Ricky broke in. "So you are nervous. Who wouldn't be? This open casting thing isn't the end-all. Remember to be happy! We are finally here. You have to remember, too, that we're financially secure for at least eighteen months. Next week, we buckle down and start looking for jobs that pay. What we need to do right now is establish a budget for furnishings and stick to the number."

Esme agreed and said, "Funny, I was thinking the same thing. I came up with $2,500 max for everything, including kitchen and bath items. Then I had second thoughts. I changed my mind and figured $3,000. We don't have to buy everything new anyway. I'm sure there's a Goodwill store around here somewhere. You'd be surprised what you can find in those stores. We might be able to pick up some of what we need there and save a little money."

"Yeah, that's fine, but I do want some new furniture." Ricky was determined. "I don't want to start out our lives with our parents' old discards. Remember, this is a fresh start just for us. If you get out of CBS early enough, we'll go check out that place George told you about, okay? And come tomorrow, I'll call in my order for the three new horses. If Dex wants to take a road trip to Los Angeles, I can pay his way. Realistically though, it'll be way less expensive to ship the horses here by a common carrier."

"I'm fine with whatever. Right now I'm gonna fix some breakfast. You want eggs and toast with your coffee and juice?"

He smiled. "Sure, after you get back in bed for a little while. It's still cozy in here."

Later That Same Morning

Tuesday, October 5, 1976

They were out of their room at 8:20 a.m. Esme and Ricky hopped in the car and headed for 7800 Beverly Boulevard, Television City, USA, today's location for an open casting call for *Life at Thirty Thousand Feet.* As they came up Beverly, their eyes were drawn like magnets to the giant black CBS sign with its iconic eye logo on the side of the lot's tallest building.

Ricky turned into the entrance and slowed to a stop at the gate. The uniformed guard stepped out of the booth, clipboard in hand, and asked for ID. Ricky pulled out his Tennessee driver's license. He started to speak but was interrupted by Esme reaching across him from the passenger's seat. They both knew they weren't on any list on that clipboard.

"Good morning, sir! I'm here for this casting call." She thrust the page from *Backstage* toward the guard. "It's my first audition. We just moved here from Tennessee. The ad didn't say anything about calling for an appointment. Oh, please, I've just got —"

Esme's pleas were cut off by the guard. "Not a problem, miss. I've seen a number of first-timers so far this morning. Just calm yourself. You're fine. Take it from me, you want to relax before you get over there." He stepped back into the booth, grabbed a sheet of paper and a parking pass, and handed them to Ricky. "Here's a map of the lot. Stick this guest pass on your dash." Placing his finger on the map, he directed Ricky to the guest parking lot. With a pen he pulled from his shirt pocket, he circled the soundstage where the open call was being held and outlined a path that would take them there from parking. Stepping back into his booth, the guard lifted the barrier arm and, as they inched past, yelled to Esme, "Break a leg!"

Ricky found guest parking. The lot was quite full already. He tried to reassure Esme by telling her that audiences for game show tapings could account for a lot of the cars. They got out and followed the path to the soundstage laid out by the guard. As Ricky and Esme approached their designated location, they found a good-sized group of men and women of all ages milling around outside the door. No one seemed to know any better than they did what the morning held.

Ten minutes later, a man in khakis and a crisp, long-sleeved plaid shirt came out the door and handed out a sheet explaining all the protocols for the morning. He nevertheless spoke to the crowd aloud as well.

"Doors will open at 9:00 a.m. Inside, you will find ten agents who will conduct initial interviews and collect any headshots and CV you may have brought with you. Agents are totally random. Lines will form arbitrarily. Just please, try to disperse yourselves as evenly as possible across the room. Assistants will walk the lines to answer any questions you may have. Welcome!" He ducked back through the door.

Minutes later, it was 9:00 a.m. The doors were opened and secured. Eager actors filed into the huge facility. To organize lines, stanchions connected by drooping red velvet ropes created lanes to the interviewers. The ten agents were seated on folding chairs behind folding tables serving as desks. A folding chair was provided for the actor across from the agent. The desks were spaced far enough apart to provide some privacy. Esme selected her lane based on what she considered to be a kind face on the woman sitting at the desk ahead. She was seventh in her line. All the actors patiently waited for an interview. Ricky had decided to do his patient waiting outside in the fresh air. This was not his party. This was all Esme.

Finally, her wait was over; it was Esme's turn at the desk. She approached and took a seat. In Esme's head, she figured she'd picked well. This woman did seem warm and welcoming, even after she'd asked what seemed to be fifty questions. The questions had come in a barrage. "Date of birth?" "What is your city of origin?" "Tell me about your acting experience, in detail." "Are you a member of the Screen Actors Guild?" "Would you have any issues with joining the union?" "Are you aware that for nearly all productions, Screen Actors Guild membership is required, with the exception of your first union acting job?" She continued asking even more questions until she said to Esme, "Well, tell me a little something about you."

Esme replied, "Me? I'm game for anything. I have always dreamed of this day! And now, today, my dreams are coming true. I know you covered it, but I want to stress, this is my very first interview or tryout for anything other than a school play. I am fairly clueless as to how any of this process works. From the little bit I read in the ad for today, I love the concept behind this soap. I would be thrilled for an opportunity to read lines for any of the parts!"

"In that case, I can help," said the woman. "Take this. It's a scene from a trial script for *Life*. You'll see it's only eight pages. You'll read the part of Jennifer. The first four pages of this are simply backstory for the role. It'll give you a feel for who this girl is and where she came from. Read through that and then study the script. If you can memorize any of it on this short notice, go for it. When you get to the read-through, keep in mind who you are — Jennifer — and react with the backstory in mind. You'll have thirty minutes to prep. When it's time, that man over there" — she pointed — "will come and escort you to a room for the reading. We'll see what you can do with this script. Don't be nervous. I'm quite serious. Do whatever you can to remain calm. Think of all these people as friends. We definitely do not expect perfection on this type of audition. In acting schools, this process is called cold reading. It is exactly what it sounds like. You're given very little time to prepare. Reactions and memory play a big part."

Esme gladly took the stapled pages the woman handed her. The woman directed her to another area, where she sat down, opened the pages, and began to read and study her lines.

Thirty minutes flew by. The man the interviewer had pointed out arrived and walked Esme around to a small stage in another area of the building. She was asked to go up and read the script as Jennifer with an actor reading the other role in the scene. She was pleased with the amount she'd been able to memorize and felt comfortable in Jennifer's skin. The three people observing took notes throughout the short reading. After the scene ended, one of them stood and asked, "Since you didn't bring any headshots or other pictures with you today, would you mind if we get a few stills and possibly film a very short clip of you reading? It would be a tremendous help."

Esme complied with enthusiasm. Then, soon enough, it was all over. She'd had her first interview, completed her first reading, and even been photographed. Her interviewer, standing with one of the gentlemen from the reading, thanked her and told her that she had done very well and they would be in touch. As Esme's interviewer walked her out, Esme reminded her a last time about her temporarily transient living situation and confirmed she would definitely get any messages left with George at the motel.

As the door to the outside was opened, they exchanged a final "thank you." Esme spotted Ricky and ran to him.

"So really, how'd it go?" Ricky was dying to know.

"They said I did very well. Oh gosh, I did it, Ricky! I did it!" Esme was high as a kite!

"I'm so proud of you. Does my starlet have time to go shopping for furniture?" In that moment, Ricky was as happy as Esme.

Even Later That Same Day

Tuesday, October 5, 1976

They left CBS Studios the same way they had entered earlier that morning. At the gate, Ricky asked the same guard for a good place for lunch in the area. The guard suggested, "Oh, for sure, go over to the Fiddler on Third Avenue. It's around the corner. Take a left onto Fairfax and a quick left on Third. You'll see it. It's more comfort food than anything else. Lunch is always good there. Hope it went well, miss, and that we see you again. Have a good day."

The guy was right — it was pretty much around the corner. When they entered the Fiddler, it was, again, just what he'd said: comfortable, relaxing, and with an easy menu.

As they looked over the menu, Esme said, "I think I did good back there. I am so excited!"

Ricky responded, "I know you did great! I hate saying the word 'impressed,' but I bet you wowed them." He continued, "You said they took an awful lot of notes. And two of them were smiling and whispering to each other? I can't wait to hear what they thought, if they ever tell you anything."

"Yeah, I know what you're saying. I hope so, too. At any rate, I did it! I am proud and glad it's over. You do realize that was my first audition or whatever you want to call it? I loved every minute of it. And I seriously think the little bit of acting I did in high school has paid off in spades."

Ricky said, "I agree. What do you want for lunch? I'm going to try a Reuben."

"I'll try the same thing. Sounds tasty." She smiled as the waitress came to the table.

Ever the gentleman, Ricky placed their order. "Two Reubens and two unsweetened teas, please." They got *that* look. "Right. Two iced teas with lemon, please. Don't need sweetener."

After lunch, they got back into the Tempest and found their way to 435 North La Brea Avenue and Rapport Furniture. George was right. The place was huge.

They walked in. Rapport looked like a stage set. Black carpet, raised platforms outlined by Tivoli lighting. Dramatic. The receptionist said, "If you would, please sign the register and fill out this card with your names and addresses. Then I'll call your designer to show you the store."

All that just to get inside? With a slight hesitation, Ricky asked, "Why are we doing this?"

Rosalyn, the receptionist, answered, "The owner, Mr. Rapport, just likes to know where people come from and how they have heard about us. We do not use these cards for mailing or any other reason. On the bottom of the card, you'll see a question, how did you hear about us?' Please be sure to fill that out. Honestly."

Esme smiled as she explained to Rosalyn, "We're in the middle of relocating from Nashville, Tennessee. We just rented an apartment but won't be moving in until the fifteenth. Is it okay if we list that as our address?"

She said, "Of course, dear. Welcome to Los Angeles. I thought I picked up a little southern drawl in your tone. I'm originally from New York City. Been here twenty years, and I've still got a little New York in me. But oh, I love it here. It takes some getting used to, but once you do, it's pretty easy. The people are great. I am so glad you found us." She paused and announced on the loudspeaker, "Stuart, front desk, please." Addressing them again, she said, "You will be working with a young man named Stuart."

"Thank you, Rosalyn," they both chimed.

Rosalyn pushed a button, and they were buzzed into the salesroom through a locked, black-paneled half door. Now out of reception, they saw that the showroom was overwhelming.

A young man approached them with a clipboard in hand and introduced himself. "Hi. I'm Stuart. I am the person assigned to help you." He smiled and added, "If you need help." He laughed a little at his own bad joke.

Esme smiled. "Hi, Stuart. I'm Esme, and this is Ricky. We just moved here from Nashville. Is it okay if we look around for a few minutes, and then, if you will, you can come find us? Oh, and can you give us a brief layout of the store? It looks huge!"

Stuart began talking and walking while Esme and Ricky followed. Pointing to the stairs in the distance to the right, he said, "The bedroom section is up that stairwell. You exit that and cross over there" — he pointed ahead — "and you'll find dinettes and various other pieces. Sofas, dining tables, and all sorts of everything are scattered throughout the entire store. Oh, you need to learn the pricing." He took them to a glass-topped table and pointed. They saw two price tags taped face up to the underside of the glass top. He began to explain, "Since we are a discount showroom, we list the retail price on the top of the tag and your price on the bottom. This particular tabletop comes in two sizes. Glass tops are always priced separately from the bases. The base is listed here." He pointed to the tag on the left. "And the pricing and sizes for the two tops are here," he continued as he pointed to the price tags to the right. "Just add the two together, and you'll have the complete price of the table. The pricing is fixed, but does not include the cost for delivery. We charge extra for delivery. If you want, you can pick it up yourself. The men in our warehouse will even load it for you, for free. But to continue ..."

Stuart aimed his pointing finger in another direction. "Sofa beds are in that area over there, and everything else is pretty much mixed. Oh, and we carry many fine imported pieces. Don't freak out when you see some of the pricing on those things. I'm pretty sure that's not what you're looking for right now, anyway. We have an abundance of furniture in our showroom that is very affordable and accessible."

Esme said, "Thank you, Stuart. We'll look around a little. Can you check back on us in about ten minutes?"

Esme and Ricky were still going back and forth with each other over how dramatic the store felt. Esme, especially impressed with the decor, said, "I know I have never seen black carpet anywhere in my entire lifetime. It shows off everything so beautifully. It really makes stuff pop. Let's go over to the sofa bed area first and find that Moonlighter."

As they walked across the showroom, they touched and ogled everything. When they eventually found themselves in the sofa bed area, they were once again in awe. There must have been at least twelve different styles, all in neutral colors. Ricky proceeded to sit on every sofa bed to test for comfort. "All of them are comfortable except that one," he said as he pointed to a white canvas-covered sofa bed with low arms. "That sucker's as hard as a rock."

Esme said, "Ooh, look over there. It's the one in the ad, the Moonlighter. I love it!"

They walked over, and Ricky gave it another sit test and gave Esme a thumbs-up.

Stuart appeared out of nowhere. "Do you have any questions?"

Esme, ever practical, said, "Yes, please. Would you show us how this works so we can feel the mattress?"

Stuart said, "Sure," and removed all of the cushions and pillows to open the bed of the Moonlighter. He explained, "This sofa bed comes standard with this foam mattress. It's great for the occasional guest. But for sixty dollars extra, it can come with an innerspring mattress which is heavier and more resilient. The arms here are wicker wrapped over steel. The entire frame is very sturdy. The fabric that you are looking at is Haitian cotton. Now, you need to know a little bit about this fabric. Haitian cotton is very durable. At the same time, liquid spills are not easily cleaned. I advise against eating or drinking while you're on the sofa. Here's the reason: the fabric is a natural raw cotton and still has seeds in it. When the seeds come in contact with water, or any kind of liquid for that matter, they can bleed and create a stain that is near impossible to remove. Other than that, this is a great piece of furniture. The fabric and frame of the Moonlighter are strong and durable. It has been one of the most popular products in the entire store. I happen to have one myself and love it. The other plus is the price. It's really a great value for your money."

Esme looked at Ricky and said with a questioning expression, "Sold? I love it. Let's add the innerspring mattress too. We might have to sleep on it sometime."

Ricky looked at Stuart and said, "She's decided. Now what else can you show us as far as a reasonable dinette table and chairs, bedroom, and coffee table? We're working within a limited budget right now."

After spending two hours sitting and testing, Stuart tallied up their wish list. Their total came to $2,679 for everything, excluding tax and delivery. They'd started, of course, with the Moonlighter, to which they'd added four neutral-colored porcelain lamps, two bedside tables, a matching double dresser and headboard in natural birch imported from Italy, a small glass-topped chrome-plated dinette table with four matching chrome chairs covered in camel-colored vinyl, and in the end, a small coffee table in a wicker that matched the sofa bed. They were thrilled.

With Stuart helping, they figured out the where and when for delivery. Ricky was still walking around with a wad of cash in his wallet and used some of it for their deposit. Stuart then surprised them by saying, "You'll need to pay the balance with a cashier's check on delivery."

Ricky asked about that. "Like we said, we are new to the area and have not set up any local bank accounts yet. We actually only got a permanent address on Monday. Any suggestions? Y'all have totally different banks from Nashville."

Stuart answered, "I used to bank at Security Pacific. I found it to be so impersonal, I switched to Home Savings. They are all over the city. Actually, there's one next door to our store. They are nice to deal with, and they pay great interest rates on savings accounts. I'm pretty sure their savings rates are at least a percentage point higher than most other banks."

Ricky looked at Stuart and said, "This is great! We can just go next door and open an account. I have my checkbook here from Nashville. I'm sure they'll be able to help us transfer our money here."

Esme agreed. "Well, Stuart? You have been so helpful in so many ways. We can't thank you enough! This store is wonderful!"

They'd been with Stuart for a couple of hours. Fortunately, when they went next door, the bank was still open. It took them some time at Home Savings to get everything settled. When they left the bank to go back to the motel, they were both completely satisfied with what they had accomplished during the day.

Ricky drove them back to the motel. When they reached their room, a note was attached to the door. It was from George and read, "Please come to the front desk." It had been a magnificent day, and they couldn't wait to tell George all about it.

George felt their excitement when they came through the door. "Can't wait to hear about your day. Esme, here you go." He handed her a message.

She took it from him and let out a squeal. "It's CBS! They want me to call them back to set up another meeting!"

Ricky pulled her into a tight hug and said, "I told you! You were good!"

Yvonna

June 1977

Today was a nice change for us. I was able to coax Frank away from the store long enough for the two of us to enjoy a lunch out together. He still puts in long days at the grocery, and it's rare for him to be able to leave for any reason, let alone for lunch with his wife. I drove him back and did the week's grocery shopping. I've been in a reflective mood lately. There's been plenty of time for introspection during the past year. It was exactly a year ago that our family's quiet, mundane existence took a number of drastic turns and changed us all forever. In the general scheme of things, most all of those changes have been for the better.

Now as I turn into our driveway, I remember how busy our house used to be. Our three girls were constantly coming and going, with each other, singularly, with and without friends. We were all happy. Frank and I are pretty much on our own now. I hate that "empty nester" phrase. We have a number of friends we see on a fairly regular basis. We keep busy around the house. Shell's still here in town, but she has her own life to lead, as do her sisters. I'll be honest — with the three of them gone, there have been, and are, a lot of days when I feel pretty empty and lonely.

After shuttling and putting up a week's load of groceries from the car, I've decided to walk to the park. Why not enjoy a nice, peaceful afternoon, sitting on my favorite bench, watching the ducks in the pond? I love the ducks in this pond. They're all Pekin ducks with their fluffy white feathers, orange bills, and orange webbed feet. If you look closely at each one of them, each has its own personality. Personally, I like listening to all of their quacking. They have an actual rhythm that I choose to enjoy rather than ignore. I wish I knew what they were saying to each other; actually, it's probably better that I don't. Pretty sure that'd be "crazy duck lady" stuff.

As I think of the ducks' little personalities, my mind once again wanders, and I think back to my girls. They are all fine. I am proud of that. If I had it all to do again, I don't think there'd be much I would change. Everything in their lives has fallen together pretty well, which makes me think about the little kaleidoscope my father gave me for my tenth birthday. Happily, I still have it and have carried it with me from that very day. These days, it's in my purse. It is one of very few things I still have from childhood. It's handmade from rosewood. At times, I find it inspiring. Here's the reason: When I look into the viewfinder and start turning the end, all of the teeny, tiny colored chips, brilliant in the light, shift and fall into myriad patterns until I stop, and the pieces fall together in consonance. I like to think that's how life turns out if we let it happen as it naturally unfolds. But just as fast as the little fragments all fall into harmony, the moment I once again turn the end, the little pieces are back in motion and rebuilding — just like life, just like living, birth and death, change. That brings to mind lines from a favorite poem by Lawrence Ferlinghetti: "I am awaiting perpetually and forever a renaissance of wonder." Do you find that arcane? I think it's lovely. Renaissance as in rebirth, a rebirth of wonder. I think life begins filled with wonder during childhood. It's hard to hold onto that wonder as we get older. That's a matter of change, again — acceptance, maybe, that life is a circle. Well, that's probably enough of my musings. You must want to hear about my girls. So I'll shake my head, wiggle my brains, and get on with this beautiful day.

Shell and Eddy are finally engaged. After a year of courtship, do we still use that word? Well, whatever. They are inseparable. Frank and I adore Eddy beyond words. Shell started working with him at The Dancing Flower. She has developed her own unique style of floral arranging, which continues to evolve. Her designs have helped sales at the shop and added a happy twist to their reputation. They have planned the wedding for next April. The venue has been chosen and booked. At this point, their guest list is still in the works, but they are close to finalizing their invitations. Weddings are work — lovely, but work. Shell has kept her weight off. And I swear, she is more attractive than ever, if I do say so myself.

Wally still lives downstairs from Shell and has become a close friend to all of us. He even helps Flanda and Minnie from time to time. And yes, he still makes his twig furniture and sells it at craft shows around Tennessee. I actually think he does quite well for himself.

Esme and Ricky are doing great. Esme ended up landing the very first part she auditioned for way back last October. The studio began shooting in December. Her soap airs, like most, Monday through Friday afternoons. It's quite a twisted drama. One of the writers has a knack for tongue-in-cheek lines. *Life at Thirty Thousand Feet* has become a rather popular show.

Ricky's business has skyrocketed. I think he has sold over fifty Waxing Ponies to different salons all over this country. As if the ponies weren't enough, he worked out a skin-care line with his business partner and very first client, Vivienne Fontaine. The two have branded a new line of facial creams and fillers that they developed with help from a chemist friend. The brand is becoming very popular. A few department store chains bought into the line and have it stocked on their shelves. Esme and Ricky, though they love their apartment, have started looking to buy a home in the West Hollywood area of Los Angeles. The prices there are high, but they calculate they can afford a two-bedroom, two-bath home in a nice area, maybe off Melrose Avenue.

That brings me to Sorina and Helena. Their careers have skyrocketed. With the help of an agent and a popular songwriter, they are close to recording their first album. One of their songs has already had good airplay across several media outlets. Sorina and Helena both have blossomed in their personal lives as well as their careers. When they perform together, it is hard for me to take my eyes off of either one of them.

Sorina is still carefree. She is more stunning than ever. Her voice has mellowed, and her speech fluency has improved so much that it's a rare occasion when she actually stutters. Her stature is so perfect that you could think she's walking with a book on her head. Sorina still wears her hair in that high ponytail most of the time. Her new wardrobe can only be described as chic, which I guess is a must for someone in her business.

Helena went through holy hell before she visited that rehab center. Now she has happily accepted "perfectly normal" as her axis. She is content in herself. Helena and Johnny are also engaged. It hit me the other day that her name will be Helena Montana. I hope for their sake that they never move to Montana. If they have a baby boy, certainly they'll have enough sense not to name him Butte. Johnny is a gem. As drop-dead handsome as that man is, you'd think he'd have a swelled head. His looks are only a veneer to be sure. When you know him, you discover he has one of the biggest, most loving, most generous hearts on this planet. I adore Johnny. He and Helena are a perfect pair.

Frank and I are content. We're still in love and happy. He gets three weeks' vacation time every year now. We went out to California for the first time to visit Esme and Ricky. We loved it. We even went to Disneyland. We drove up the coast highway and stopped in at Hearst Castle before driving that cliffhanger road into Carmel-by-the-Sea. We finished the trip in San Francisco, where I bought that book of Ferlinghetti poetry. We do our best to go wherever Sorina and Helena are performing when they're in town. One of our longer getaways was what I consider the dreaded camping trip. Frank loves to go fishing and camping. I got to gut and clean the fish, obviously not one of my life's greatest pleasures. I'm all for being out in nature — don't get me wrong. But let's face it, there are critters and snakes out there. I am terrified of snakes. When we are out in his boat, I keep an oar ready, just in case I have to smack one over the head. But I sincerely did have fun "roughing it" with my hubby.

I miss my mother every day. I still cannot believe she was struck by a bus the very day President Kennedy was assassinated. I continue to cry over the news coverage of that every year. It was just the saddest day all around. It was hard burying my mother when the entire country was burying the president. I don't think we were able to mourn Mother's death properly. I still get waves of guilt that I didn't do enough for her at that time. It took years for me to come to terms with that period. But we have to adapt, don't we?

So I smile and move on. A little bread for the ducks, and I'll head home. I think about the wonder of a child's world, the magic of looking up into a night sky scattered with stars. I remember the cotton-candy dreams I had growing up. Some of them came true. Our lives are what we make them — good choices, bad choices, our choices at the forks in the road. In 1969, Cass Elliot sang a song called "Make Your Own Kind of Music" by Barry Mann and Cynthia Weil. Two lines from that song say what I want you to know: "You gotta make your own kind of music / Sing your own special song."

So, I'll tell you this before I leave. I have found a comfort in believing everything will all be okay. Life is just a temporary situation.[2]

---

[2] *From this writer: Please listen to a recording of "Make Your Own Kind of Music" by Mama Cass.*

Afterword

Parts of The Lapone Sisters are small segments of my life. First and foremost, I want to acknowledge the stuttering issues experienced by approximately one percent of the U.S. population. I was a stutterer, and sometimes I still am. I want this story to bring awareness of the issues experienced by individuals living their lives with a stammer. Stuttering is real and can be disabling. Many learn to live with and even overcome a stammer with the direction and assistance of professional speech therapists and even help from their own family members. My intent is to bring attention to the issue of speech fluency. The experiences of my character Sorina are both real and pure fantasy. I lived through many of the same fears Sorina lived through. I was fortunate to have the aid of a speech therapist from the Bill Wilkerson Center in Nashville, Tennessee. I learned to live with my stammer and obtained tools to help myself wean and grow out of the condition. If you know someone with a speech issue, help is available. Many colleges and universities have speech departments that offer programs to help. I like to tout the Vanderbilt Bill Wilkerson Center, Department of Hearing and Speech, here in Nashville. They do brilliant work. I also want to acknowledge The Stuttering Foundation in Memphis, Tennessee. It is a place that offers free online resources to those who stutter and their families, as well as support for research into the causes of stuttering.

Many of the locations of The Lapone Sisters are and were real

— others are not and never were. Green Hills is indeed a suburb in Nashville. Some of the shops mentioned existed, some are memories and others are purely fictitious. The characters in my story are purely fictional and only creations of my imagination. Parts of the Los Angeles adventure were and still are very real. Our first apartment was the second floor of a house in the Hollywood Hills that had been sealed off at the stairwell. And yes, we could see Bette Davis's penthouse from our living room window. Rapport Furniture was and is still an authentic retail furniture store. I worked there from 1980-1987. Los Angeles locations like Lucy's El Adobe, The Fiddler, and many of the streets and stores mentioned existed and still may. Vivienne Fontaine et Associés along with The Waxing Pony were strictly my own design.

Certification in floral design does exist, but certainly not through the path created here for Shell. The acronym FTW, Free the Wedgie, was invented purely for my character Shell and Helena.

These characters and places have traveled with me for a very long time. I have enjoyed their company and stories. I hope you have enjoyed the ride as well.

Acknowledgments

I want to thank Lucy Sellers Lawrence for pushing me to complete this novel. Lucy has been my friend since high school. Now retired, Lucy was a paralegal who spent many of her working days editing and correcting legal briefs and papers. When I began writing this story in 2008 during down time in my professional career as an interior designer, I would send her short sections as I wrote. Lucy read those segments, laughed and told me she enjoyed the characters. What she was reading was a train wreck. I knew it and shelved the project. When Covid hit, Lucy encouraged me to pull what I already had written off the shelf and complete the story. She was the first person who read and re-read the initial version. Lucy graciously helped polish that manuscript by applying her experience in punctuation and editing. Without her help, I could not have shown this to my life partner, David Ellis. He is a stickler for details.

David had read the original and was reticent to re-read the newer version. He did not want to say it was horrible. When I began the self-publishing process, he took it from me and spent two months polishing the story. Of course, our dog had just died, and he needed the distraction. He connected the dots for continuity, omitted extraneous words and passages, insisted on dialog in lieu of description of conversation, and encouraged me to rework a good many portions. What you have read is a result of my imagination,

Lucy's punctuation and editing advice, and David's collaboration for the final polished narrative.

Since this book is my first experience with publishing, I have had a million questions. Many thanks to my friend Deborah Lovett who is familiar with the literary publishing industry. She guided me to websites that schooled me on self-publishing versus trying to woo a literary agent. I purchased and read the books she suggested. Writing this book was tediously fun. Little did I know getting a book published would be like climbing the stairs to the observation deck in the Empire State Building — long and slow.

Finally, I must thank Deena Capron who has been my concierge through part of this process. She made it fun, educational, and, above all else, gave me direct answers. We had a good time talking on the phone as she guided me, step by step, through the process of publishing this novel.

Thank you all.